JUSTICE
IS A
HALF-INCH BOLT

JUSTICE
IS A
HALF-INCH BOLT

D.Malisch

Justice is a Half-Inch Bolt

Published by D.Malisch
Copyright ©2021 by D.Malisch

ISBN   978-1-7373079-2-1

The characters and events portrayed in this book are fictitious.
Any similarity to real persons, living or dead, is coincidental and
not intended by the author.

Printed in the United States of America

To Mom,

Who Loved

All Her Kids

Contents

PROLOGUE

On a perfectly clear day, the lightning flashed through the dark clouds roiling over a small city in central Kansas. Below the heavy overcast, rain, hail and wind whipped the aged building of the Danson Bolt and Fastener manufacturing facility. As the mortar between the red bricks of the building eroded, the battering wind from the micro storm, ripped a sheet of corrugated steel from the roof where it had rested for the last fifty years. Spinning like a buzz-saw in the wind, the steel sheet sliced through the air until it crashed through the company fluorescent-sign, shattering it beyond recognition. The sudden darkness was surely an omen of things to come, for those who took advantage of others.

Most folks still living in the town are reluctant to talk about it, but the brave witnesses say there were strange forces at work that sent them scurrying for cover in that rat-infested factory. The accounts are probably inaccurate, because by the time the storm hit, all the smart rats – the four legged variety – were gone.

As the lights flickered inside, angry words squeezed from under the manager's office door. "You're too stinkin' weird to fit here Madrim; you're stirring up the other workers. You don't think the way the rest of us do, and its unnerving. If I'd had my way you'd never been hired. I'm tired of all this ab-ra-ka-dab-ra garbage! Now get your hocus-pocus trash and get out– you're fired!"

The excommunicated employee mixed a grimace with a smile before raising his fully extended arms over his head. "Curse this scourge of life! Damn this hole of suffering! Let the Angel of Justice be summoned to vent wrath on Earth. By the power of – " he screamed – and the name was covered by an instantaneous thunderclap.

"Stop this production and smite injustice!" A blinding flash of lightning ripped through the factory skylight, striking Madrim's old workstation. The automated machine making half-inch bolts released a loud, strange, high-pitched noise. Some workers say it was a hiss, others swear it was a scream. Whatever it was, the machine metal turned white hot, the paint vaporized, and the related electronic control system ceased to exist. From the sagging jaws of the thread cutter dropped a glowing, white-hot, half-inch bolt.

Within a week, the fastener plant closed its doors for good. Jobs be damned, the factory workers were certain strange and powerful forces inhabited the workplace. While no ghosts or evil things were ever sighted, those who had persecuted Madrim experienced some very unusual events, in their lives. The remaining workers couldn't cope. They quit their factory jobs en masse, forcing the factory to close its doors. The production equipment and available product was quietly sold to distant, unsuspecting wholesalers.

*   *   *

Chapter 1   The Would-be Pimp

Protagonist: Detective Brian Weeder
                         (San Francisco PD)
Guests:
Rookie   Detective Sue Cushing (SFPD)
Trevor Hogan   Stick up artist
James Nellis   Jimmy-the-Pimp
Nicholas   Jimmy's construction contractor
Viki Tompson   Wannabee prostitute
Sue Cushing   San Francisco Police Homicide Detective
Babi-cakes   Aging prostitute

Trevor Hogan, a small time burglar – turned robber, examined his empty wallet. His money was now in someone else's pocket, thanks to the local game last night. Disgusted with his own stupidity, he put away his wallet, and rubbed a sore spot, left by the cold park bench he slept on during the night. With a shiver, and a sneeze, Hogan pulled his thin wind-breaker tighter against the icy breeze coming off the Pacific Ocean. The strong chill badgered him, reminding him how reckless he had been to gamble away his car and cash in the same game.

As he trudged down the dirty sidewalk, now homeless and penniless he tried to ignore the fact he hadn't eaten during the past twenty-four hours. Thinking it was early morning, he glanced at the empty space on his left arm, where his watch had resided before the game. With a grimace, he paused to look upward, searching for the dim shape of the sun trying to burn its way through the thick, wet, fog covering the city of San Francisco. From the angle of the sun's dull glow, he gauged time to be just past noon, and time to eat again. Hoping he could appease his unsympathetic, empty stomach, he thought, *"Maybe I can stick up a fast foods place. Then I could get both cash and a burger at the same time."* Hogan looked down the busy street for familiar restaurant signs. Seeing one, he headed toward it. As he arrived, he held the door for three young women who were leaving. "Hey sweetheart," he flirted, stepping in front of the little, thirteen-year-old blond. "How 'bout you and me getting it on tonight?"

Startled as a doe in headlights, the teenager froze, looking into his eyes, her mouth open.

"Bet you never had a man," he swooned, helping himself to her bag of french fries, "I could make you real happy."

The second woman stepped around Trevor, grabbing her younger sister from him. "Buzz off dirtbag," she scolded. Snatching the sack of fries, she handed them back to her sister and sneered at Trevor, "Why don't you go crawl under a rock – Toad!"

Trevor ogled them, making faces and obscene gestures, until they disappeared around the corner.

Once inside, he walked through the lunch crowd until he located the restroom. A quick tug on the locked door convinced him that his luck hadn't changed; he remembered bathroom doors are often kept locked in large cities.

Mumbling an obscenity, he reversed course in the narrow hallway. Before he went far, the sound of a door opening behind him caused him to stop. Turning quickly, he changed direction again, moving fast to slip by the patron coming out of the men's room and grabbed the door before it could close.

The noise from the lunch crowd disappeared as the door clanked shut behind him. Quickly Trevor ducked into an open stall and reached for the silver .380 automatic in his coat pocket. The clip was empty, but there was one cartridge left in the chamber. He spit out another obscenity, which echoed around the small room. Trevor made a mental note to be very careful and not to get into a predicament that required a shoot out – having only one bullet for your gun is a distinct disadvantage. Grumbling something about remembering to purchase more ammunition, he left the bathroom.

Back in the busy, crowded dining room, Trevor took his place at the end of the ordering line. He examined the menu while waiting his turn at the order counter. Enticed by smell of fresh food, the five minute wait seemed like hours.

Trevor glanced around the busy place. He didn't like the size of the crowd. If something was to go wrong, he could be attacked by a dozen red-necked union workers and beaten to death. Maybe it would be some woman who attacked him? He imagined losing his gun and being held down while old ladies poked him with the sharp ends on their umbrellas. Having only one bullet for your gun is a distinct disadvantage.

"May I help you?" the order clerk asked.

"Uh – Yeah, I'd like a double cheeseburger with everything. . . large fries, chocolate shake, and small cherry pie – make that to go."

The attendant marked the order and replied, "Thank you, for your order sir. Your number is eighty-four. Please pay at the register when they call your number."

Trevor moved into the cluster of people waiting to pick up their food. Robbing people always made him edgy; he needed another line of business. Nervously, he slowly rotated round and round, trusting no one behind him. His only comfort was in the steel automatic in his coat pocket. He caressed it constantly, playing with the trigger.

"Excuse me," someone said, bumping into him with a tray of hot food.

The bandit recoiled instantly. He tried to slow his pounding heart and ignore the throbbing in his head. Hogan knew his order-number would be called soon. Looking at the clock on the wall, he estimated he would be eating lunch and counting money in another five minutes.

"Eighty-three!" the lady at the register called.

A heavyset lady, with three whining children, bellied up to the counter and opened her purse. Her children pulled and tugged at her clothing while she slowly counted out change. Her count was interrupted several times to scold them for taking food from the tray, before she could portion it out to them.

Hogan tensed even more, anticipating his number would be called next. He scanned his surroundings for potential problems. Except for the abundance of people, everything was fine, there were no red necks, or umbrella wielding old ladies. Best of all, there were no cops in the crowd. Trevor's confidence level rose.

The food attendant placed an order of fries in the bag with the cheeseburger, milkshake and pie. "Number eighty-four," she announced loudly.

Trevor's head pounded like a flat tire striking pavement at sixty miles per hour. He stepped forward to make his move.

"That will be nine-fifty" she said, looking first at the register then at Trevor.

Hogan's hand tightened on his firearm but froze as he attempted to remove it from his pocket. Two alert police officers, on lunch break, just entered the establishment and took their place in the order line.

He wasn't wanted in this city, yet, and he doubted they would recognize him, but he was unprepared for such contingencies. Having only one bullet for your gun is a distinct disadvantage.

"That will be nine-fifty," the girl at the cash register stated a second time to Trevor.

Today just wasn't his day: too many people, too few bullets and now – too many cops. He muttered another obscenity while, releasing his grip on the pistol. "Uh! I forgot my wallet," he lied. With a smile to the food attendant, he offered, "I'll just take this out to the car and bring back money from my wife." Trevor reached for the bag, but the woman pulled it back.

"Sorry," she explained, "Money first."

A glance back toward the lawmen confirmed he had just lost his lunch and his hold-up money.

"Be right back," he said, excusing himself.

The would-be robber quietly left the restaurant and trudged down the block. "Money. Damit, I need money," he muttered to himself.

* * *

A few blocks away, Nick, a frustrated, small-time contractor, raised his voice above the soft music emanating from the expensive stereo equipment in the new penthouse suite. "I'm sorry Jim, I won't have time to finish it today," he lamented. "My grandpa died and I gotta go to the funeral."

Pausing briefly to pluck a piece of lint from his tailored suit, James Nellis, alias "Jimmy-the-Pimp," argued with his friend, Nick. "Look! I've got people coming over later this afternoon and I need everything to be perfect – you understand!"

Nicholas envied this man of leisure, this man of pleasure, this man of women. Besides being a friend with connections, Jimmy always paid well, and his business was appreciated. It would be a mistake not to help him. "Yeah. Sure I understand, and I can finish the work tomorrow, but the funeral's today."

Oblivious to his expensive, lighted paintings and sculptures adorning the deeply carpeted room, Jimmy debated, "Can't you send your helper, uh, what's his name, in to finish up?"

"Naa – I had to let him go last week, he was rippin' me off. There ain't nobody but me now. You gotta wait."

"You want me to call another contractor?"

5

Nick looked into his friend's perturbed face. "Hey – Jimmy, I'm sorry, but I just can't do it. My grandpa almost raised me and I hafta be there."

The pimp chewed his toothpick in silence.

"He's family," Nick pleaded. He had known James Nellis most of his life and respected him. Except for his vocation, Jimmy was a nice guy who seemed to treat his friends and his girls well. He felt awful letting Jimmy down on such short notice, but there wasn't any alternative.

Straightening his lavish gold ring, Jimmy sighed. As a man of means, he was more than accustomed to having his way. Excuses annoyed him, but Nick had bailed him out of lots of scrapes and was a good, reliable friend. The pimp worked the wooden toothpick around his mouth as he reflected on the time he'd gotten high on drugs and beaten one of his best girls to death. Nick had put his own house up as collateral to get him free. At the trial, Nicholas told the jury what a nice guy Jimmy was – the jury voted for acquittal. Jimmy studied his friend, Nick, with respect. He'd never told Nick the truth, about the killing, but Nick never asked. In his line of work, as a pimp, Jimmy knew he'd never find a better friend than Nicholas.

"Okay, okay, you go to your gramp's funeral. . ."

Nick felt terribly guilty, "Don't I always help you when I can?"

"Yeah, yeah, yeah," Jimmy agreed. Shoving his right hand into his coat pocket, he removed a large roll of money. After smoothly stripping a fifty from the spool, he stuffed the bill into Nick's shirt pocket. In a sympathetic voice, the pimp relented, "Here, buy the old man some flowers."

"Look I'll be over early tomorrow morning with a bolt to hold the fixture to the mechanical arm," Nick apologized. "I'm sorry if it screws up your schedule but it's just gotta be that way."

"Tell you what," Jimmy said, "Maybe I can finish the job myself." The pimp strolled past the canopied waterbed, set off by gold-thread drapery. Stopping next to the sunken tub, he looked upward at the long, mechanical arm with a heater balanced on it. He squinted in the subdued room lighting at the heater mounting bracket. It was too dark to see. Nellis pressed a button on the waterproof console, next to the tub, to open the thick curtains. A panoramic view of the San Francisco Bay, and bustling city below, begged for appreciation, without response. "I used to do some mechanical work, years ago — before I could afford to pay someone to do it for me," Jimmy boasted. "Now I've got all this," he said, with an affluent wave of his hand around the posh room. "You say all I need to make this thing work — is to put a bolt in it?"

Stepping from the white, pile carpet onto the gold-edged, ceramic tile surrounding the oversized tub with whirlpool, the young contractor smiled enthusiastically, "Yeah, that's right." Pointing upward, he lectured, "The heat projector is just balanced on that arm right now, and if you buy a half-inch bolt," Nick gestured with his finger and thumb, "about three inches long. . . and if you put it in that hole and tighten it good. . ." Nick looked back at Nellis to emphasize his point, " 'Course you gotta have a nut and a lock washer on the other end to keep it from coming back out."

"Yeah, I could do that," Jimmy drawled.

"Okay, I gotta to go now." Nick slipped into the coat he had dropped on a dining chair earlier. Backing toward the elevator door he reiterated, "Don't forget to tighten the nut and test it before you turn the switch on."

"I won't forget — in fact, I'll go to the hardware store right now and get the bolt and a couple of wrenches. Wait and I'll ride down with you," he said, reaching for his Mercedes keys.

* * *

Fifteen minutes and numerous blocks later, Trevor found himself in front of a hardware store window. It was a prosperous

7

looking place, cluttered with merchandise and the register was not in clear view of the street. Maybe they had money? He entered the store and browsed near the register until a customer in the store purchased an item. As the register was opened, the robber-to-be eyed the cash supply. It would have to do, he judged.

Trevor waited until the transaction was complete, and the customer at the counter left, before approaching the clerk at the register. He scanned the store again for possible interference. Having only one bullet for your gun is a distinct disadvantage. He noted the remaining shopper in the back of the store seemed quite busy in the bolt section.

Placing an item on the counter as though he wished to purchase it, Hogan waited until the clerk picked up the piece, "This is a holdup!" he shouted, "Gimme all your money in a bag."

The middle aged man looked up quickly in a state of shock. "What?"

"You heard me. Give me all your money, and be quick about it."

The store clerk stepped back as Trevor produced his .380 automatic and released the safety. "Is this some kind of crazy joke?"

"It ain't no joke, Mac! Gimme all the money in the register." Trevor pointed toward the cash drawer with the pistol for a brief instant.

When the man froze, the robber leaned over the counter, grabbing a handful of clothing below the clerk's chin. Intending to intimidate his victim, the gunman pulled the store-clerk close enough for the clerk to smell his bad breath. Hogan placed the gun barrel against the clerk's chest, over the heart, leaving no doubt he meant business.

The terrified store attendant attempted to push Trevor's pistol hand away. The reflex action of Trevor Hogan's hand caused his finger to close on the trigger.

A muffled pop echoed through the store and the clerk shrieked before collapsing.

Hogan stood in shock. He had never killed a man before. It was far easier than he had imagined. Yet it was sheer horror! Now he was a murderer! Even worse, there was a witness. . . the other customer. He looked at his gun, the barrel remained extended from the housing indicating it was empty. Quickly he shoved the housing forward to conceal the weapon's state of un-readiness. Looking over his shoulder he locked eyes with the customer at the bolt station. The man began to move toward the door. "Wait! You there! Stop!" Trevor demanded. "Come over here," he ordered, leveling the empty gun at the man's well dressed body.

The man, who was better known as Jimmy-the-Pimp, complied, carrying with him, a half-inch bolt.

"Over there," the murderer pointed. Fear showed in the eyes of both men. What to do with him was Trevor's big problem. He was out of ammunition and couldn't leave a witness. Someone was likely to enter the store any second, although the gunshot wasn't loud and probably wasn't heard more than half a block. Perhaps he could lock the man in the back room and leave. What to do. . . ? What to do. . . ?

Jimmy froze. He had seen and used guns before but had never been a target. Perhaps he could knock the gun from the man's hand and escape. . . No. The guy looked too experienced and too confident.

Pointing toward the back room Trevor nodded. "Back there – Go!"

Jimmy stepped backward into the display shelf, knocking items to the floor. He caught his balance and turned toward the back room. As he walked, his mind raced. Knives – there was a display of knives coming up on his right, if he could distract the murderer so he could grab a big kitchen knife – With his left hand, Jimmy dropped the half-inch bolt to distract his guard. Quickly he grabbed a long,

9

slender knife, turning swiftly as he felt his fingers wrap around the heavy, black handle.

With his thoughts centering on disposal of his second victim, Trevor was caught off guard. He tried to step aside as the man suddenly lunged toward him with a huge, glinting knife. Instinctively Hogan deflected the knife with his gun hand. The knife, with a metallic sound, slipped smoothly across the steel pistol, narrowly missing his body. Dropping his empty gun, Trevor used both hands to grasp the shopper's arm in an effort to control the threatening knife.

The pimp struggled to point the knife into the murderer's chest, but the man was strong.

The strange waltz began without music, save the heavy breathing and grunting of the two participants. They circled round and round, each looking for the advantage. It appeared to be an even match, until Jimmy stepped on the loose bolt and slipped to the floor. As he fell, the pimp relaxed for the briefest of instants thinking to catch himself with his hands.

Trevor fell with his combatant, but gained the advantage as the knife turned toward his second victim. The force of the fall and the direction pushed the knife up under the pimp's rib-cage and into his heart, causing a quick death.

The sound of running feet on the sidewalk outside, proved to only be a jogger passing by, but it served as a stimulus to bring Trevor to his senses. He quickly surveyed the situation and found a possible answer to his predicament.

Trevor removed all identification from the deceased customer, being careful not to move him away from his fallen position. He dragged the clerk's body over and placed it on top of the customer, in a position that might convince authorities each killed the other. The handgun was wiped clean of fingerprints and placed carefully in the customer's hand. The final touch was to place the clerk's hands on the bloody knife, and to mop up any traces of blood that might hint the clerk was moved.

Before leaving the store, Trevor removed his bloody shirt and coat, replacing them with an industrial shirt that would attract less attention. Already in possession of the roll of money from the customer's coat, a quick glance into the man's wallet convinced Trevor he had all the money and credit cards he would need for a while.

A set of keys removed from the customer boasted a Mercedes emblem. Only one automobile matching that label rested curbside on the block. Trevor tried the key. It matched, and he was on his way. A quick check of the vehicle registration sent him to Jimmy's penthouse. Trevor mused, "Fancy new, red Mercedes, wallet full of cash, Rolex watch, penthouse key. . . must be my lucky day after all." He pulled the half-inch bolt from his pocket, kissed it and put it back, "Luckier than a rabbit's foot I believe."

Intending to burglarize the apartment, Trevor placed the key in the elevator lock and turned it to gain access to the penthouse. When the elevator stopped and the door opened, the decadent luxury amazed him. "Hello, anybody home?" he called. When no answer came, he smiled. "I knew the guy was a pimp. Shoot! This has to be the best day of my life. I got it all now. Hell! I bet I can run his shop too." The cocky man danced lightly around the carpeted room checking the layout. Reminded by his complaining stomach that he had skipped dinner, breakfast and lunch, the murderer looked for food. A search of the kitchen area produced snacks and an expensive bottle of champagne. Counting on the fact the victim would never interrupt him, and thinking it would be days before police identified the pimp's body, Trevor satisfied his hunger and thirst before falling back on the bed to relax.

* * *

At the scene of the murder, Brian Weeder, a tall, brown-haired San Francisco Police Detective, in his late twenties,

11

arrived with his subordinate, — rookie Detective Sue Cushing. Four police cruisers blocked access to the street in front of the hardware store. Weeder eased his unmarked car equipped with emergency red strobe-light past the uniformed officer to double park on the street.

Working homicide together, the detectives followed the yellow and black crime scene tape to the store's entrance. Inside, a uniformed officer escorted them to the bodies. "Here they are sir," the officer reported.

Cushing took out her note pad. "Any witnesses?"

"No Ma'am, just the R. P. who found them."

"Where is the reporting party?"

"The R. P.? Oh, he's waiting in my unit outside, Ma'am."

Sue glanced at her watch, it was after four and she had skipped breakfast this morning. "We've got some things to do here. Take a statement and get contact information, then let him go."

"I understand Mam."

Detective Cushing looked back at the bodies, "Has the coroner been notified?"

"We expect him any minute."

"Thank you officer," she said, before bending down to examine the scene more closely.

Weeder looked at Cushing, "Been dead maybe twenty minutes, I'd guess."

Sue clenched her lips tightly, repulsed by the violent deaths.

Weeder stood up. "Go ahead and work on it, Cushing. I'll be back in a minute."

"Yes sir," she acknowledged.

Detective Weeder roamed slowly around the store, careful not to touch things. He stopped near the cash register to draw a chalk circle around a spent cartridge casing. A few minutes later he paused to make a call on his cell phone. When he finished, he casually strolled back to question the other detective.

12

"Got anything Sue?"

Cushing stood up to better see her supervisor. "Yes sir, I think I figured it out."

"And?"

"Looks like a robber – the guy in the dark suit, tried to rob the store." She examined Weeder's blank face for expression," But the clerk picked up a knife from the display and got the bandit. Before the thief died, he shot the clerk."

Brian studied Sue for a moment then asked, "How did they get here?"

"What do you mean?"

Realizing his helper was not yet fully trained, Brian tried to help her form questions in her own mind. "In what part of the store do you think the robber was stabbed?"

Cushing scanned the floor for signs of blood. Seeing stains only where the bodies lay, she answered, "Right here sir."

"Where do you think the clerk got the knife?"

"That's easy," she smiled, pointing to the display of knives beyond the bodies, she answered, "Over there. The large knife is missing from the display."

"Good," Weeder praised. "Now where, in the store, was the clerk shot?"

Cushing assumed the shooting had taken place at the time and place of the stabbing, but she realized Weeder was hinting at something else. "I don't know sir."

"Come on Sue, you can do it," Brian coaxed.

"I don't know sir."

"What kind of gun is it?"

"It appears to be a small automatic."

"That's good, now what happens to a shell casing when the weapon is fired?"

Sue's face showed signs of enlightenment, "Ah yes, where is the casing?"

13

Weeder nodded.

Slowly, Cushing wandered around the store until she found the casing Brian had circled with his chalk. She looked back at the bodies. They were nearly seventy-five to eighty feet toward the rear of the store. Quickly, she returned to the corpses. Rolling the clerk slightly, she examined the bullet wound over the heart. "This doesn't add up sir," she said in a puzzled tone.

"What doesn't?" Brian asked, playing dumb.

"The clerk couldn't travel that far with that kind of wound."

"How many shots were fired?"

"I only found one casing"

"That's all I found too, Sue." Glancing down at the bodies, Brian asked, "How many rounds are left in the weapon?"

Putting on her gloves, Sue reached for the gun.

"Before you touch it, note which hand is holding it."

Sue made a quick note on her pad. Carefully she removed the silver weapon, taking care not to touch areas where the lab would look for fingerprints. She pushed her pencil into the barrel and released the clip. It was empty.

"Is one in the chamber?" Brian prodded.

"Can't tell without cocking it." She answered.

"Sure you can," Weeder said, "just check the empty space in the barrel."

Feeling like the rookie she was, Sue pushed the pencil, until it "bottomed-out." She marked the end of the barrel on the pencil with her thumbnail. After removing the pencil, she gauged the length along the side of the weapon. It was obviously empty. "It's dry."

"Thought so," Brian said, rubbing his chin. "Notice anything unusual about that?"

"Yeah," Cushing said with a smile, "someone closed it after it fired the last round."

"You'll make a fine detective yet, Cushing," he chuckled. "What did you find in the gunman's pockets?"

"They were empty."

"Did you check his right coat pocket?"

"Yeah, I did."

Brian walked around to stand behind Cushing, who was still crouched beside the bodies. "What do you suppose the gunman does for a living?"

Sue studied the clothing for a few seconds, "He's obviously a businessman."

"What's his business?"

She noticed his expensive shoes and manicured fingernails. "Oh my word! He's a pimp!" she said with great surprise. She stood up slowly, turning to face Brian. "But what's a pimp doing holding up hardware stores? And what happened to the bullets for his gun?"

"Explain?"

Sue looked at Brian and sighed, softly. "As far as I know, prostitution is still profitable. . . so – unless this guy forgot to buy ammunition, his gun should have had more than one bullet in it." She shook her head as she reached her own conclusion. "Someone is trying to fool us. . . this is a set-up."

Brian smiled, "That's right." Handing her the note pad that she dropped on a nearby shelf, he offered, "If you get permission from your husband, I'll buy you lunch."

"Deal," she agreed.

Weeder's cell phone interrupted by ringing.

"Weeder."

"Yeah."

"So what did you find?"

"Okay, hold on a second." Brian took Cushing's note pad from her and jotted down an address.

"I got it, thanks," he said, hanging up.

15

Returning the pad to Cushing, Brian confessed, "I didn't tell you I actually know the dead man holding the gun. It's a guy better known as 'Jimmy-the-Pimp'. I went to high school with him years ago." Looking down on the deceased man, he lamented, "It's ironic. . . Jimmy and I have been on opposite sides of the law for years. Now I have to use the law — which he despised — to find his murderer." Brian turned and walked slowly toward the entrance.

Cushing caught up to her supervisor. She nodded to the coroner, just arriving.

"I called the office a few minutes ago," Brian admitted, "I don't know where Jimmy lives these days, so I called Records for an address. Records didn't have a recent address for him either, but they gave me the street address where his girls were last picked up."

Prodded by her empty stomach, Sue looked at her watch again, "Thought you were buying me lunch?" She glanced back at her boss hoping they would have lunch first, "It's already after five."

Brian opened the driver's door of the car and slid in. Sue reluctantly climbed into the passenger side.

"I will," Weeder promised, "but we have to solve this case first."

Suddenly wishing she hadn't burned off all those extra calories at the gym last night, Cushing tried to ignore the painful messages sent by her empty stomach.

Detective Weeder navigated to the street where Jimmy's girls worked. Slowly, he made his way down the street cluttered with double-parked, delivery trucks and jaywalking pedestrians. The buildings were mostly old; some still had unsafe brick fronts or cornice overhangs. In front of an old second story hotel with peeling paint, Brian spotted several women in tight clothing with extensive leg exposure. He rolled up to the curb and stopped. Brian pressed the button to lower the window on Cushing's side of the car. One of the women came over to the passenger side of the vehicle and leaned down to speak with them.

"What'ja need?" When the hooker realized Cushing was female, she backed up a few inches, unsure of their intention. "Is this a bust?" she asked.

Weeder displayed his badge. "No, just looking for information." He looked up and down the block. "You work for Jimmy?"

"Maybe," she said, trying to avoid giving incriminating information to a police officer – yet, she knew lying would also bring trouble.

"You know where he lives?"

Without hesitation, she shook her head no.

"Where can I find Babi-cakes?"

"Oh she went upstairs to lay down." The hooker nodded her head in the direction of the stairway behind her.

"How long ago?"

"Maybe fifteen."

"We'll wait," Brian told her.

The hooker glanced at the car that pulled in behind the detectives. Recognizing the driver as a regular customer, she dismissed herself saying, "Gotta go, my ride's here."

Weeder rolled up the window as she walked away.

"Who's Babi-cakes?" Cushing asked.

Brian watched the people walking along the sidewalk as he answered. "She's like the crew chief for Jimmy's girls in this part of the city. She scouts new talent, and collects proceeds at the end of the shift."

"I see," Sue said thoughtfully, "And she'll have a key to his residence."

"I hope," Brian said, glancing back at the entrance to the cheap hotel.

A pair of long legs entered Brian's field of view on the stair case. As the woman owning them descended the stairs, her short blue skirt rhythmically flapped against her black thighs with each step. Reaching the bottom step, she tugged down on the overly tight garment, trying to make it more comfortable on her aging, somewhat overweight body.

Weeder lowered Sue's window again and called to the hooker, "Babi-cakes!"

The woman instantly heard Weeder's male voice and approached the car. She gave Cushing a quick visual inspection before looking past her at Brian. "Oh it's you," she said with a hint of disgust. "What do you want now?"

"I want to trade information," the male detective bargained.

"I don't want to do that, 'cause every time I do, it gets me in trouble with Jimmy." The hooker's voice and body language clearly showed she wanted nothing to do with the police or their investigation.

Brian tapped the button to unlatch the door, behind Cushing. "I know that." He motioned toward the back door, "Get in."

Babi-cakes paused to look for her girls on the street. Seeing no sign of trouble, she opened the rear door and slipped in behind officer Cushing.

"What's up?" she quizzed, as though her valuable time was being wasted by the detectives.

Both detectives rotated in their seats to better see the prostitute. Weeder took the lead role in the questioning. "Where's Jimmy live these days?"

The hooker shook her head, "I can't tell you that. Jimmy said he'd slap me around if I told anybody."

"Well, I got good news and I got bad news honey." Brian's gaze fell on the rapidly aging woman's face. "The good news is Jimmy won't be dealing out any punishment – anytime soon." Brian watched her face for any change of expression. "The bad news is that he just had heart surgery at a local hardware store this morning."

All the years of hard living had prepared her for this? Babi-cakes sat quietly staring straight ahead, while a tear slowly formed in the corner of her eye. When the tear was complete, it rolled over her lower eyelid, over the blue eyeliner, past thick-mascara lashes, down her wrinkling cheek and dripped onto her large, sagging bosom. Her painted expression never changed as she wrestled internally with the bad news.

"I'm sorry," Brian said softly.

The grieving woman sat silently thinking about the man who had been her lover, brother, father, husband, owner and banker. Now, months from the end of her career, he was gone along with the retirement he had promised her. She had nothing. Somehow, it didn't even matter who killed him, just that fact that he was dead, numbed her.

Though it seemed calloused, Weeder knew he needed to get on with police business. "Will you help us locate Jimmy's residence?"

The grieving woman cleared her throat. Though she had been arrested many times by the police, she considered jail a career hazard, not a vindictive tactic by law enforcement. Police were not her enemy, so she answered honestly, "I loaned my key to a new girl today, so I can't get in," she answered calmly.

"Can you give us an address?"

"Yeah – it's the new penthouse over on Geary."

Weeder studied her for a few seconds before simply saying, "Thanks."

Without response, the prostitute waited for Weeder to lower her window. When the window dropped, she reached outside to lift the door handle. Dazed, but never defeated, the black woman climbed out of the car. She stepped back onto the sidewalk to start her life over – one more time.

Detective Weeder started the car and drove away.

* * *

The soft bell tones interrupted Trevor's brief slumber. He scanned the darkening room, before remembering where he was and the events that brought him there. His first instinct was to not answer the phone. What if it was the police? That was silly – the police would never call first, he reasoned. What if it was a customer, wanting service? For a brief instant, Trevor considered what he would do. In the end, he realized he would be more than happy to take the man's money. Answering the phone he started, "Trev - Oh, I mean, James Nellis here. What can I do for you?"

A sweet voice on the other end tinkled, "Mr. Nellis? This is Viki – You know, the new girl – I'm in the lobby. You wanted to see me?"

"What?" he stumbled. His head still felt groggy from his interrupted, short nap. Trevor hadn't expected a woman's voice – but, she sounded exotically feminine. Following his own lecherous instincts, he pressed onward. "We have an appointment?"

"Yes, Babi-cakes said you would want to meet me."

Sensing the new girl probably hadn't seen Jimmy before, Trevor felt she wouldn't realize he was an imposter. "Oh yes, now I remember," he lied, "Should I come down to get you?"

"No, that won't be necessary. Babi-cakes gave me a key and said I should come up before I go to work for you."

"Yes, of course. Is this your first job?"

"Yes it is Mr. Nellis. I've never worked for anyone before. Is that all right?"

"Well. . . I like my girls to be experienced, but I'm sure we can work something out. Come on up and I'll see you shortly."

Moments later, the elevator door opened, revealing a well-proportioned woman, in her late teens, with a pretty face.

"Viki. Viki. Don't be shy. Come on in," he bid with a wave of his arm.

"Mr. Nellis, this is a wonderful place. I'm really impressed!"

"Why don't you call me James."

"Babi-cakes said everyone called you `Jimmy'. Would you rather I call you `James'?"

"Uh, no. . . that's all right. Jimmy will be just fine."

"Just look at this view," she sighed. "If my girl friends could see me now."

Trevor moved behind Viki and placed a hand on each shoulder before sliding his hands down to rest on her hips. He pulled her closer and planted a lustful kiss on the back of her neck near her shoulder. "Let's get you out of this and into something more comfortable," he whispered. He unzipped her dress, allowing it to fall carelessly to the floor. "Do you like me?" Trevor questioned.

She looked at his industrial clothing; he wasn't wearing the business suit she expected. She studied his unshaven face; he was just a man, not particularly attractive. She could find nothing to either like, or dislike, about him. In the end, her naivety ignored the complexity of Jimmy's profession, while her faulty logic ignored Jimmy's luxurious penthouse, allowing her to conclude Trevor might be a "very down to earth" person. Still – he seemed strange to her. "I hardly know you, Jimmy," she giggled.

"That won't be true for long," he laughed lewdly.

Viki turned to face him. "Want me to help you?" she offered, unbuttoning his shirt.

Trevor sighed deeply and erotically.

A short, startled, gasp came from Viki as she saw blood under Trevor's shirt. "What happened? Were you in an accident?"

"Huh?" he replied, looking for himself. "No, I just helped some accident victims on the way to the hospital. Nothing happened to me." He reached into his pocket and removed the black half-inch bolt, tossing it onto the coffee table.

"I'm glad."

"Look, why don't I take a bath?" he suggested as he walked toward the sunken tub. "Or, better yet, why don't we take one together? You'd like that. Wouldn't you?"

"Sounds like fun," she said, hoping to please her future boss.

"You draw the water and I'll get another glass for the champagne," Trevor directed.

Minutes later, the water sloshed, as Trevor stepped into the tub. "Come here, my little mermaid, we're going to make love," he teased. He wrapped his arms around the naked woman's waist to lift her into the water.

"No Jimmy! Wait. I can get in by myself."

"Oh, it's more fun this way."

"I'm afraid you might drop me." She begged.

Feeling that she would soon please him in other ways, Trevor relented, "Okay – you win." He pointed toward the kitchen area, "We need sponges anyway. Why don't you look in the cabinet under the kitchen sink. . . bring a couple."

Impatiently waiting for Viki's return, Trevor sat in the water, playing with the waterproof switches at the edge of the tub. The first one started the water-jet pump. The second one dimmed the room lights. The third one programmed the stereo to play the 1812 Overture, complete with booming cannons. The last switch caused the unanchored heater, which never got the half-inch bolt, to fall from the ceiling into the tub. The electrically charged water quickly and violently fried Trevor Hogan.

* * *

Detectives Weeder and Cushing arrived at the same time as the "911 Emergency Response" team. Cushing raced through the first floor of the structure, trying to locate the building manager.

Weeder questioned the paramedic team leader regarding the nature of the emergency. When Sue returned with the key, the detectives shared the elevator with the trained paramedics.

After a lengthy ride, the elevator stopped at the penthouse, leased by Jimmy-the-Pimp. As the door opened, the booming sound of cannon fire greeted them from the stereo system. Expecting an ambush, everyone crowded in the recess of the elevator car, away from the open door. With great caution, Weeder and Cushing checked for signs of an armed gunman, while the paramedics waited restlessly.

Followed by the others, Brian dashed out of the elevator across the soft carpet to a partial wall partition in the open living area. Peering into the bathing area, he saw Hogan's body, still lying in the tub, next to some electrical apparatus. The smells of several charred substances, permeated the air.

Sitting naked and cross legged, Brian saw a young woman sobbing helplessly beside the oversized bathing tub. The loud music completely masked her sounds.

Dashing past her, Weeder checked the only private enclosure in the room, the toilet stall. It was empty.

Behind the detective, the emergency response crew had already turned off the stereo and electrical power, allowing them to remove the body in a hopeless attempt to save the expired life.

Weeder walked up to the naked woman, now standing beside Detective Cushing.

"So what do you have here, Cushing?"

Sue handed a towel to the naked woman and stepped toward Weeder, out of hearing range of others. "According to the woman here, her name's Viki Tompson." Sue scribbled notes on her note pad as she spoke. "Says she called the emergency number that brought the paramedics." With a nod of her head toward the naked

23

man, Sue added, "Her boyfriend got the shock of his life when the heater fell from the ceiling into the tub."

Brian glanced over to the young woman wrapped in a large fluffy yellow towel. Showing no sign of emotion or movement, the woman's eyes were glazed over as if exhausted from a serious trauma. "I gather she wasn't in the water at the time of the accident?"

"Bet she wasn't," Cushing said, shaking her head, "No pun intended, but she acts like she's still in a state of shock." Cushing finished the line she was writing in her note pad and looked toward the woman. "As near as I can tell, she's the only witness."

Brian looked over at the corpse of Trevor Hogan. With a detached look on his face, he asked, "Did she give you a name for the guy?"

"The girl says it's Jimmy."

Brian shook his head negatively. "No way. We just saw Jimmy at the hardware store."

Cushing nodded. "I remember."

Brian adjusted his slacks before squatting in front of the small, black coffee table. He removed a pencil from his shirt pocket, under his grey suit-coat. With a short pushing motion, he poked at a half-inch, silver-colored bolt lying on the tabletop. Sensing a connection, Weeder looked up at the bare mechanical arm over the pool. He studied the arm for a few moments before his gaze dropped to the heater still resting in the water-filled tub, beneath the arm. Shaking his head, he stood up slowly, returning his pencil to his pocket.

Noticing her boss's interest, Cushing pointed to the mechanical arm, where the heat projector had balanced prior to the accident. "Looks like someone removed the bolt; I'll send it to the lab for prints."

Brian nodded.

Looking back at the body, Cushing watched the paramedics counting chest compressions and breaths for the victim as they administered CPR.

Detective Weeder wandered toward the "would-be hooker" to ask a few questions.

Viki didn't make any attempt to acknowledge Brian's approach, and she didn't respond immediately when he asked her, "Your boyfriend?"

After some delay, and continuing to stare straight ahead, she shook her head indicating a negative response.

Brian walked closer to the row of penthouse windows. Under the red glare of the setting sun, a ship slowly and silently made its way under the silhouette of the Golden Gate Bridge spanning the mouth of the bay. Across the scenic view, lights glistened everywhere, buildings, streets, ferries and freeways. The view was breathtaking. A twinge of romantic desire tingled inside Brian's head; he'd wished many times for an opportunity to share such a view with a beautiful woman of his choice.

Eventually, Weeder's eyes focused on the reflection of the occupants within the room where he stood. The long, exposed legs again caught his attention, almost making him wish it was another time, and another set of circumstances. Turning around to face her, the detective asked, "How long have you known him?"

Viki looked up slowly. Their eyes made visual contact, but she kept her mental distance, as if to say the detective and his desire for law and order were from an older, nonfunctional generation. When Brian continued to wait patiently for her answer, she finally said, "I came here about an hour ago to go to work for him."

For the briefest of moments, it seemed to Brian, he had seen her somewhere before, in his youth. . . perhaps in college. Ah yes, her oval-shaped face, honey-brown hair pulled into a bun on the top of her head, the towel complementing her female figure with a lovely

25

knee slightly pushed forward, it all reminded him of drawings and sculptures of Greek goddesses. Brian sighed softly; he realized his better judgment was clouded. Looking closer into her tear stained face, he reminded himself she was not a Greek goddess but rather a suspect in a murder investigation. "Why weren't you in the tub with him? You were obviously ready to take a bath."

"He sent me for the sponges."

"Sponges?"

"Yeah, under the sink," she said nodding toward the kitchen area of the large room.

"How long you been hooking?"

There was no reply from her. She bit her lip and looked away.

Brian stepped back as Cushing handed the young woman clothing discarded before the accident. In a firm, but gentle tone he said softly, "Better put your things on and come down to the station for a few questions."

* * *

The hours of questioning showed on the two detectives as they stopped for a deserved coffee break. Brian seated himself at the table in the break room, across from Cushing. Leaning back, he attempted to relieve tension in his tired neck.

Cushing sat quietly. . . apparently thinking.

Silence lingered for a minute or more. Finally, leaning forward, Brian tried to sum up the facts as he understood them. "We have a dead pimp, knifed in a nearby hardware store. The pimp was holding the gun that shot the hardware clerk. We have a fried john doe, in the pimp's penthouse. Is it coincidence that he just happened to have the pimp's keys and identification?" Brian shook his head negatively, "I don't think so."

"Me neither," Cushing agreed.

"According to the only witness, the John Doe tried to impersonate the pimp. Was this robbery or was he a guest?"

"I'll vote for robbery," Cushing said.

"Me too, especially since the witness was not a known hooker, has no criminal record, and since she had obviously never seen Jimmy before."

"Yeah, her story seems consistent," Cushing nodded, "It helps that she was the one who phoned for help and stayed around for questioning."

"I agree," Brian admitted, "but how did the bolt get out of the heater and on the table?"

Cushing shrugged. "I doubt the girl removed it."

Making a face after he swallowed the last of his coffee Brian added, "And I don't think she would know how to remove a bolt even if she had a wrench."

Sue wasn't pleased by the remark, since it sounded a bit like a stereotyped view on women, but she did agree with her boss in this instance.

The conversation was interrupted by a department clerk who silently dropped a short stack of FAX papers in front of Cushing and went on to make other deliveries. Sue studied the papers for a few silent moments then announced, "So. . . it seems our john has a long list of previous run-in's with the law." Looking up, she added, "His prints say his name is Trevor Hogan. And in his spare time, he likes to hold up gas stations, fast food places, and claims he does it all to pay gambling debts."

Brian smiled drily, "You mean he liked to – past tense."

"Uh yeah," Cushing agreed.

"He ever shoot anyone?"

"Not according to his rap sheet."

"Does he normally carry a gun?"

Cushing studied the pages for a few seconds. "Yes, he was in violation several times."

"Small automatic?"

"Was that a guess?"

"Just a calculated one," Brian said, tossing his wadded cup into the nearby trash can. "Have the forensics come back yet?"

"Due any time."

"I'll bet you a cup of coffee, paraffin tests will show burned powder on his hand and clothing." Brian rocked back in his chair again, "And I'll bet the pimp's hand will be clean – this time."

"What about the bolt?" Cushing shoved the stack of FAX papers toward Brian for his observations.

Brian took the stack of papers and asked, "So, who took the bolt out? And was it murder?"

"I donno," Cushing shrugged, "but I'll go back tomorrow and look for a few more answers."

* * *

The following afternoon, Cushing stopped by Brian's office. She had a funny smile on her face.

"You look like your husband finally said yes."

Cushing laughed lightly, "Almost as good."

"What do you have?"

"I bumped into the contractor who installed the equipment for Jimmy."

Brian, still sitting at his desk, made a rowing, coaxing motion with his right hand, "And. . . ?"

"This contractor sent Jimmy down to get a bolt from the hardware store to secure the heater the afternoon he was killed. The contractor said he warned the pimp about the danger of it falling. Jimmy swore he'd fix it right away."

The two detectives stared at each other, then shook their heads.

A clerk from the lab came into the room and dropped a baggie with the half-inch bolt on the desk along with the fingerprint analysis. Brian picked up the bolt; Cushing picked up the report. "So who did it?" Brian quizzed.

"The print matches Trevor Hogan, the victim in the tub."

With a sigh, Brian reached for the cardboard box on the floor behind his chair. "I guess that's justice, but I would never have expected the bolt — or its absence — to have served revenge on a murderer." Brian studied his initials engraved into the head of the bolt for identification. "That's one for the book," he muttered to himself, as he dropped the bolt into an evidence box destined for the police storeroom.

* * *

Chapter 2   The Local Gang

Protagonist: Detective Brian Weeder SFPD

Guests :
Timmy (Tim)   Young paperboy
Dad   Timmy's father
Nick   Local bully
Bobby   Timmy's classmate

A t the police auction, young Timmy waited impatiently for the bicycle, he saw earlier, to come to the block for bidding. He looked around the bleacher seats at the strange and interesting people in the crowd, wondering if they also wanted the same bicycle. Except for the quick explanation from his father, the teenage boy knew nothing about auctions, but was learning quickly. His father had explained the items sold here were nearly all a byproduct of a crime, but Timmy really didn't know, or care, about things he didn't understand. What he did know and understand, was that he desperately wanted and needed the bike.

"Will it cost much, Dad?"

Tim's father gave his pre-teenage son a squeeze, "Depends on who bids against us."

"Promise me we'll get it Dad. I really need it for my paper route."

Suddenly, the boy's father raised his card to register a bid on a small box of miscellaneous items, mostly bicycle parts.

"Why'd you buy that?" Timmy asked, "Are you sure you still have enough money for the bike?"

"It's okay Tim," he explained, "We might need the hardware to fix your bike — if we get it."

The dusty bike — with one flat tire, dangling wire basket, and torn seat, was rolled into view.

The auctioneer asked for a starting bid of ten dollars. Timmy tensed as his father sat silently — waiting.

The starting bid dropped. Still, the boy's father waited.

Not understanding why his father wasn't bidding, Timmy fidgeted nervously on the hard, metal, bleacher seat, "Aren't you going to buy it Dad?" he asked, impatiently.

"Just wait, son. We'll start soon."

The auctioneer lowered the starting bid again, asking for two dollars.

Timmy's father raised his biding card, along with several other bidders. The auctioneer picked the first card he saw, but it wasn't Tim's father. The boy worried.

The auctioneer sang his song, with many nonsense words, then asked for the next bid of five dollars; Timmy's father raised his card. A spotter saw the card for the auctioneer and relayed it; Tim and his father were in the bidding. Timmy felt his heart beat faster.

The auctioneer sang his song again, raising the bid to ten dollars, but there were no takers. The official dropped the bid, to seven, and a junk dealer in the front row raised his card. Timmy realized they were under the bid. "Dad, he's going to get it."

"We're not through yet, Tim," he said, trying to ease his son's fears.

The rhythmic song continued, as the auctioneer raised the bid again to ten dollars. Tim's father didn't bid. The song continued once — then twice. Timmy felt a knot form in his stomach as the auctioneer was ready to sell to the junk dealer.

"Do something Dad!" he pleaded.

31

D.Malisch

"Eight dollars!" Tim's dad shouted, raising his card. The auctioneer saw it this time. The race was on between the junk dealer and Timmy's father.

"I have eight dollars! Do I hear nine?" The auctioneer called. There were no takers. The official sang his song, then just as he was ready to close the bid, the junk dealer raised his card.

Timmy's heart raced faster, realizing they were below bid again. He squirmed and chewed his finger nails.

"I have nine," the auctioneer called, "Do I hear ten?" His eyes focused on Timmy's father, who raised his card.

The auctioneer sang his song, asking for eleven; the junk dealer obliged, by raising his card."

A wave of panic raced through Timmy, as he bit one of his fingers. Realizing he was chewing his nails, he quickly sat on his hands, lest they find their way back into his mouth. "Dad!" he protested.

"We're doing fine son," he said coolly, while keeping his eye on the official with the gavel.

The song continued, and as soon as the auctioneer asked for twelve, Tim's father raised his card.

The auctioneer sang his song once, then twice. He locked eyes on the junk dealer, who shook his head "No."

"Sold for twelve dollars to number eighty-nine!" the official announced with a rap of his gavel.

The bike was Timmy's. The boy exploded into celebration. At last, he possessed the independence of his own set of wheels and the added advantage of having a tool that could help him earn money on his paper route. At twelve, what more could a guy want?

Luckily, the following day was a weekend, allowing Timmy and his father to do a bit of repair on the newly claimed treasure. Unfortunately, there was a lot more to the repair and adjustment than Timmy had anticipated, even more than his father had estimated for that matter. But, by the end of the weekend, the vehicle was ready for service save one small problem. A bolt was needed to anchor the wire basket to the front fender. This was a trivial problem — left until the other, more important, items had been solved. Now it was Timmy's turn to fix this last problem by himself. The hole in the fender had rusted, probably as a result of the neglect suffered from the previous owner. Timmy dug around inside the box for a suitable fastener. His hand closed on a shiny half-inch bolt. The boy examined the bolt, curious about the engraved letters, B.W. on the head. He studied them for as long as his attention span would stretch. Anxious to complete the repair, he dipped into the box again, and stirred the contents until he came up with a mating nut and washer. With a little tongue chewing and a couple of grunts, he cinched the wire basket in place.

* * *

Timmy's new bike was like a dream come true; he no longer had to shoulder all the papers on his route. In the early morning, he could quickly finish his route and not have to run the last half mile to school.

Best of all, the bike allowed him to take a two-block detour, away from all the drug dealers who controlled several streets leading to the school. Lately, it seemed nearly all of his lunch money ended up in the pockets of the dealers, or young bullies, targeting sales to reluctant, young children. Timmy reflected on the morning he had been severely roughed-up by a larger boy. Nick, the older boy, told Timmy, "You only buy from me!" And as he pinched Timmy's bleeding face, he added, "And you buy, every day! I'll be here every day — Understand?" Timmy knew and understood. He knew Nick would take his lunch money, giving him addictive drugs he didn't want. But — Nick didn't know about the few dollars from the paper route that Timmy pinned to

33

the inside lining of his jacket sleeve. Several times, Timmy considered telling the authorities at school about the extortion, but Nick and his buddies made it obvious that such action would be met with deadly force. The adults always preached that telling on the thugs was the right thing to do, but these same adults were never there to support him, when he faced Nick. And, if he did tell – it was obvious to Timmy – he, or one of his classmates, would suffer. To avoid the situation, Timmy often tried to leave early for school, to take another route, but ironically his mother refused the schedule change. She told him she didn't want him to have enough time to loiter and possibly get into trouble. To the pre-teenager, the new bike was a godsend to avoid trouble.

Three weeks passed without incident for Timmy. He had nearly forgotten his previous status as a victim; when, on his way to school, he encountered Nick on a street where he had never seen him before. Nick jumped from the place, where he had hidden, grabbing the handlebar on Timmy's bike. The bike spilled. Timmy lost skin on his left knee, banging his helmet as he fell. As the two recognized each other, Nick growled, "So this is where you went. Thought you could get around me eh!"

"Uh no!" Timmy lied, "I moved and this is a shorter route to school."

Nick smacked Timmy's face with the back of his hand, "Don't lie to me, baby-face. I want the money you owe me."

"I don't owe you anything!" Timmy protested.

"Yes you do!" Nick boiled, "I want the money I missed since you started coming this way. . . all of it." Then throwing Timmy back against the building, he screamed, "And I want it now!"

"But I spent it on my lunch," Timmy pleaded.

"That's too bad," Nick sneered. Admiring the bike lying on the pavement, he grabbed the frame and brought it to its wheels. "Guess I just got a new bike, butt-head!"

Timmy winced. Reasoning that he could more easily explain a loss of money from his paper route, than the loss of his bike, he tried to deal with his personal bully. "Uh! – Tell you what," Timmy said, trying to show a serious, businesslike manner, as taught for collecting money, after his paper delivery. He pulled himself to his feet and approached Nick with a calm voice. "I'll get you some money tomorrow, and meet you on your old corner."

Nick shook his head negatively. "No chance dipstick. I'm keeping the bike 'till you cough up the cash."

"But I need my bike for my – " Timmy hesitated. The last thing he wanted, was for Nick to know he had a paper route that could be tapped as another source of cash. "Uh. . . for my homework," he lied, grasping for a believable excuse.

"Huh? What you talking about?" Nick sneered.

"I have to go to a friend's house tonight to help him with his homework."

Nick's eyes lit up. "How much is he payin' you?"

"I don't get paid. He's a friend," Timmy argued.

Using his extra bulk, Nick shoved his prey against the wall a second time. With his fist knotted in the clothing below Timmy's chin, Nick snarled sarcastically, "Then you don't get no bike – not until I get money in my hand, understand?" With a final slam, Nick released the boy and added, "Bring the money here – tomorrow morning, this is my new corner."

With a reluctant nod, Timmy acknowledged.

That evening, Timmy hid the absence of his bike carefully from his parents. In the morning, he got up early, shutting off his alarm clock before it rang and set out to deliver his papers on foot. Except for being chased by a couple of neighborhood dogs, delivery went pretty well. Before going to school, Timmy quickly added up how much money he would have lost to Nick, had he taken his old route to school. He took the money from his paper route cache – putting the money in his pant's pocket before appearing at the breakfast table. He gulped his cereal and left before his parent's conversation could delay him. Following his regular route, including the detour he had used for the past few weeks, he approached the corner where he expected to meet Nick. Sure enough, the short-tempered thug was waiting, as was his bike. But the bike had two flat tires, slashed by Nick's knife, no doubt. The paint and seat had something sticky all over it, probably a cola or other soft drink. Well, that was something that Tim half expected.

Nick leaned against the cement building, his arms folded across his chest, the bike behind him. "Got it?"

Timmy nodded.

The money was handed to Nick in a wad. Although this thug had never been an "A" student, he counted money pretty well.

Satisfied, Nick stepped away from the wall, allowing Timmy to push his damaged bike down the street toward the school. "And don't forget to stop by tomorrow – sir!" Nick mocked.

Later, that night, following repair of his bike, Timmy didn't sleep well. He lay awake forming a strategy. In the morning, he planned to find yet another route – one that did not have any blind corners or easy hiding places where Nick could catch him again. It's true Nick was bigger, but not necessarily faster or smarter for that matter.

The next few days, Timmy successfully evaded Nick. Pleased with his achievement, he discussed his experience with his classmates and made an interesting discovery. "So I've been riding down Charlotte, to Oak then Red street and following it into the School." Timmy said, with a smile.

Bobby grinned carefully, "You better watch out Tim. Nick can be really mean if he catches you."

"He can't catch me if I don't go down his street."

A second classmate added, "Yeah, but his street could change again."

"Huh?" Timmy questioned.

"Uh huh – he changed streets last time because the mob's moving in."

"What's that mean?" Timmy puzzled.

"The guys, who supply drugs to him are being forced out of the area by organiz'd crime." Bobby commented.

"Aw, how do you know that?"

"I heard my dad talking about it. He saw it in the paper."

So, even Nick had a bully he couldn't fight. Timmy marveled at the thought. That's why Nick did the same thing – moved to a quieter street. Maybe there is justice in the world. . . Timmy smiled, as he considered the thought.

The glee was to be short lived however. On the following morning, Timmy spotted Nick ahead of him on the street and quickly reversed direction to go down, yet another block. Timmy felt sure he could make it past the far intersection before Nick could run to the corner, make a right turn and run down to the intersection where Timmy crossed. For once Nick's bulk worked against him and Timmy escaped with plenty of room to spare.

On two other days, that week, Nick got closer, but not close enough to grab him. Timmy was getting worried. He was especially worried when one of his classmates was beaten and quizzed by Nick. Under pressure of the beating, the classmate told Nick that Timmy had a paper route, and named the streets where the papers were delivered. Nick now knew enough to wait in ambush. Timmy was worried.

Early in the morning, Timmy carefully made his rounds. He watched for any sign of Nick hiding in the bushes and listened for any dogs to bark down the street, indicating Nick's trap. As a paper boy, he would recognize the bark of most dogs, and he knew they kept an eye on the street by looking through the knot holes and cracks in their fences. Nick, with his heavy foot steps would never sneak past the four-footed sentries.

Near the end of his route, a lump formed in Timmy's throat as he caught a glimpse, across a neighbor's backyard of someone, about Nick's size walking down to the intersection ahead. Timmy quickly, and as quietly, as possible, stopped his bike and wheeled it into the yard of the corner house, behind the hedge. He crouched down and peered through the foliage at the pedestrian. Yes, it was Nick. Worse yet, he was carrying a big wooden club. This really meant trouble if Nick found him. The foot steps got louder and louder as Nick approached the corner house. Nick suddenly stopped, looked both ways down the street and started to run toward the hedge where Timmy was hiding.

Terribly afraid his hiding place had been discovered, Timmy was nearly ready to bolt and run.

But it wasn't Timmy who was in trouble this time. Just before Nick reached the hedge opposite Tim, a car screeched to a stop in the middle of the street and three husky, young adults jumped out. They ran toward Nick; he was trapped.

The first man pushed Nick into the thick hedge as he screamed, "Didn't I tell you this ain't your street no mo'?"

Nick's voice cracked from fear as he raised his stick like a baseball bat. "Get back — I ain't sellin'. I'm looking for someone."

"An' you jes found him," a second assailant answered. "Now, it's plain you gotta be taught a lesson."

"No wait!" Nick pleaded.

"Ain't no use beggin'. You done chose your punishmet!"

"Get back," Nick warned, "I'll use this."

From his hiding place a few feet away, Timmy saw the men step back a few feet and draw guns.

"Guess you just don't get it," the tallest man said, "You ain't goina come around here no mo!" Without further delay, the three of them opened fire, knocking Nick down to the ground, quickly. "Empty 'em, I don't want him comin' back."

What seemed like a million shots to Timmy, kept banging, like a blacksmith's hammer on a steel rail. The clanging continued on and on, drowning Nick's last, muffled cries. Even with his fingers in his ears, it made Timmy's ears hurt. Until, at last, there was silence.

"Let's get!" one of the men shouted and they ran toward the car.

Timmy was terrified. He was on his bike in a flash. His chest heaved, but it seemed he couldn't get his breath. All the hairs up and down his back stood straight up, like those he had seen on a frightened dog one time. Luckily, nearly all of his papers were delivered, making his bike lighter, but somehow it didn't seem to matter. He dashed through the opening in the hedge, where he had entered earlier, and raced down the sidewalk, away from the murder and the three men who committed it. No matter how fast he turned the crank and pedals, it seemed his feet were in a heavy mud. He couldn't make them go fast enough. He didn't look back, but from behind him, he heard a shout, "Hey! There's a kid. Get him!"

Timmy shifted gears twice and pried against the handle bars to force more pressure onto the pedals. He had never traveled so fast on a bike before. Off the curb onto the street he raced, the bike didn't seem to touch the pavement for the longest time.

Timmy dared a glance over his shoulder. What he saw wasn't good. The car, with three men in it, began to move. Worse yet, it moved toward him. He heard the screech of rubber and saw the headlights in the morning twilight swing around the corner and aim down the street behind him. The roar of the large engine increased rapidly, telling Timmy the distance was closing much too fast. With a sudden shift, Timmy made an unscheduled left turn down a side street. The car shot past the turn, screeched to a halt, the rear wheels burned rubber as it backed up. The engine raced as though it would fly apart while the driver jammed it into a forward gear. . . forcing a loud screech, it accelerated again.

As the car approached, Timmy leaned left again, riding up a driveway to gain access to the sidewalk. The car slid sideways as it careened up the driveway behind him. The boy heard the sound of small shrubs, trees and fences being obliterated behind him. The sound became louder and louder until he could no longer hear his own breathing or the sound of his basket rattling, as the bolt holding it worked its way loose.

The frightened cyclist dodged behind a big elm tree into the street, gaining scant seconds as the murderers screeched to a stop, to avoid wrapping their vehicle around the huge trunk. Less than a heartbeat later, the car bounced off the curb, sending a solid thud-sound from the undercarriage striking the pavement. The chase resumed.

Timmy chose a right turn at the next side street. His legs burned; his chest ached from his rapid breathing, but he kept moving as fast as his legs would allow. In the middle of the road, he failed to see a small pothole. The front wheel of the bike bounced into the hole, separating the nut from the bolt which fastened the basket to the fender. The bolt dropped into the street as Timmy's back wheel cleared the pothole. An instant later he again saw the headlights aim down the street behind him. He tried

40

desperately to catch his long, terrified animated shadow that raced in front of his bike.

The sound of burning rubber and horrible roar of the racing engine drowned the brief prayer he uttered. Timmy heard an explosion immediately behind him as the car almost touched him. Suddenly, the car leaped into the air and passed him on its side. Timmy had a clear view of the dive-shaft, and spinning wheels while it slid past him, showering him with thousands of sparks. Continuing its spin, the vehicle rolled onto its top, sending even more sparks from the roof grinding and ripping away on the pavement. The deafening sound reminded the boy of a bucket of gravel dumped down a metal slide. All of this abruptly ended in an ear-numbing bang and cloud of dust, as the car slid into the rear of a garbage truck, making its morning rounds.

Timmy put on the brakes to stop. He slowed carefully, uncertain if his pursuers would exit the car and take chase on foot. There was no sign of movement from the car, just a lot of smoke and dust along with the smell of hot fluids dripping onto the pavement. Timmy glided to the curb and tried to get off his bike. His legs shook so hard he couldn't stand. Releasing his bike, he sat down and cried.

Through the cloud of dust, back lighted by the disposal truck lights, the men from the garbage truck ran around and around the inverted car – dismayed by the sight. House lights went on, up and down the block. People came racing out of their houses in bed clothing to see what had happened. After some time, a woman approached Timmy, to ask if he was injured, then the police arrived. The officers raced up to the overturned car with their flashlights and looked inside. Seeing there was nothing they could do for the occupants, they fetched their note pads from their patrol car and talked with the driver of the damaged truck. During the conversation, one officer looked at Timmy when one of the

41

garbage men pointed toward him. Shortly afterwards, the policeman came to talk with him. Timmy's parents were called and they came to take him home.

Minutes later, Detective Brian Weeder arrived after dropping off another detective a few blocks away where Nick had been murdered. Brian talked with the officers on the scene; he talked with the garbage truck men and examined the overturned car. As one of the officers approached, Brian asked, "Have you determined what made the driver lose control?"

"Yes sir," the young female officer replied, "Seems they blew a tire in the front. This one," she said, pointing to a deflated tire.

Brian took his pencil and pushed against the tire to roll it around. He was surprised when he found a half-inch bolt protruding from the carcass. However, he was completely dumfounded to see the set of initials he recognized as his own, that marked the head of the bolt.

*   *   *

Chapter 3   A Leap of Faith

Protagonist: Detective Brian Weeder SFPD

Guests:
Raymond Martez: Father to Carlos
Carlos Martez :   Son of Raymond
Rachael Smith :   Classmate of Carlos
Mother Superior :   Supervisor of the convent and school
Sister Bonnie :   Tteacher for Carlos & Rachael
Richard Benedari :   Mastermind of Mercury armored car robbery
Chuck Black :   Partner to Richard Benedari in robbery

Nine-year-old Carlos Martez did his best to behave while waiting for his father to finish his visit with Detective Brian Weeder at the San Francisco precinct. Somehow he had expected to see policemen wrestling crooks into jail cells for a lengthy stay, but Carlos was disappointed. There were no jail cells here, nor was there any sign of the bad guys. There wasn't even a lot of guns laying about for him to look at and maybe touch if his father wasn't watching. Looking around the room, all he saw were a lot of people talking and writing things down on paper; it was all very disappointing and he was terribly bored.

Carlos studied the square floor tiles beneath his feet; he observed the patterns that ran first left then right. To occupy his time, he lined his right foot in the direction of one of the tiles then turned his left foot ninety degrees to conform with the adjacent tile. In an awkward shuffle, he tried to walk in a pigeon-toed manner, matching each foot with the appropriate tile pattern. Just as he was getting the hang of it, he bumped into a desk, knocking a phone handset loose from its cradle. The noise caught his father's attention.

"Carlos! Stop that! I told you this morning, you'd have to behave if you came with me." Pointing to the chair beside Detective Weeder's desk, he ordered, "Now, get over here and sit down quietly." Shaking his finger at the errant child, he questioned, "Do you hear me?"

The boy did hear his father and obeyed silently. The hard wooden chair proved to be a bit too large for Carlos – his legs dangled at the edge, cramping blood circulation. He swung his legs back and forth to minimize the effect, until his father gave him a stern look of disapproval.

Carlos watched passively, until his father looked back at Detective Weeder to resume the never-ending conversation. The detective's desk was cluttered with piles of paper; it was untidy along with all the other desks in the room. Carlos sighed, there were no toys or family pictures to occupy his time. Leaning forward for a better look around a stack of paper, something shiny attracted his attention. He strained for a better look. A silver object – a bolt rested near the center-edge of the desk. He glanced back at his father, to see if he was being watched. There was no response. Slowly, Carlos extended an arm out toward the metal object, pausing just before making contact. A glance back at his father was uneventful. Carlos grasped the object and pulled it toward him. Lifting it over the papers, he set it at the edge of the desk, by his elbow. His father wasn't paying attention. Carlos picked the object up; it felt slightly warm, and as he held it, a very strange thing happened. The color turned from silver to gold. This was the most interesting thing he'd seen, so far, on his trip to the San Francisco, police station.

Realizing the object didn't belong to him, Carlos set the bolt back on the desk and released it. Seconds later it resumed its silver color. Again, he picked it up and examined the gold object from every angle, looking for electronics or a battery compartment. There wasn't anything, except the metal, to be seen.

The boy's father and Detective Weeder moved toward another desk to visit with a detective that just entered the room. The nine-year-old was concerned he might be left behind; he followed, bolt in hand. The conversation was short. The men shook hands and exchanged greetings. His father obviously knew the man when he had worked in the office several years ago. The men continued on. . . around the room, shaking hands and talking briefly with various people at their work areas. Carlos made momentary eye contact with his father several times, but otherwise followed quietly.

It seemed the visiting would never end, but eventually the circuit was completed and Raymond Martez, father of Carlos, looked at his watch, "Well it's been great seeing all the old gang again, Brian. But we need to go."

Detective Weeder shook Raymond's hand, "I'm glad you stopped by Ray, and I'm glad the new job is working out for you."

Raymond smiled, "Yeah, but it's nice to see the old familiar faces again."

"Well, stop by – and see us again, when you get over this way."

"I will. I will, but my new job keeps me pretty busy." Raymond flashed a toothy grin, as he pulled Carlos forward to shake hands with Brian. "Say goodby to Detective Weeder, Carlos."

Carlos moved the bolt to his left hand, freeing his right hand for shaking. "Good bye sir." The boy looked up at the detective, "Thanks for inviting us."

45

Raymond caught sight of a gold object in his son's left hand. "What's that you have in your hand, Carlos?"

The boy, reluctant to lose his prize, was slow to respond. The strict look from his father hurried his decision to open his hand for inspection of the bolt. "It's something – " he hesitated, not knowing exactly what to call the object.

"Looks like a bolt," Raymond said, surveying the object without touching it. "Better put it back; it's time to leave, now."

The youth looked back, across the sea of disheveled desks. He had no idea which one belonged to Detective Weeder. "I don't know where it goes," he said meekly.

"Maybe Brian knows," Raymond said, with a promising note.

Brian looked at the bolt. "I've got one just like it, on my desk, except it's silver," he said, lifting the boy's hand up to get a better view of the head of the bolt. No initials meant, to Detective Weeder, it wasn't the bolt from his desk or one marked as evidence by anyone in the police department. "That's a very nice bolt, Carlos. Why don't you take it with you?"

The boy nodded agreement.

At church school on Monday, Carlos sat in the shabby, aging classroom with twenty-eight other children. He had heard Sister Bonnie give the lecture before. It seemed she was always giving advice on behavior and it bored him. Thinking about the last time he was bored, he removed the half-inch bolt from his pocket and set it on his desk. It was convenient that he sat behind "Fat Freddy," because, Sister Bonnie would never see him – or at least, that's what he believed. Carlos played with the bolt. As he placed it on his desk, it would turn silver, then as he picked it up, it would turn gold. Rachael Smith, who sat across the isle, on his left, watched curiously. Christopher Jorden watched across the isle on his right. The new kid, behind Rachael, showed interest too.

Carlos handled the object, carefully, making sure he never dropped it. Any "clunking sound" was sure to alert Sister Bonnie. After a time, Carlos realized Sister Bonnie had stopped talking. He peered carefully around Fatso toward the head of the classroom. Where was Sister Bonnie? Carlos leaned to the other side of Fatso, looking for his teacher. She was gone? Carlos was puzzled. Then Fatso turned around to look at him. It was then, Carlos realized every student in class was looking his way. Carlos smiled. Thinking Sister Bonnie had left the classroom for a few minutes, Carlos began to make faces. He licked his finger and wet his eyebrows. He puffed his cheeks and squeezed the air out by slapping his hands against them. He held the bolt up to his nose, like Pinocchio. It was all great fun and he made everyone laugh. Carlos was in his prime, until he caught the sight of Sister Bonnie's shoe on the floor, behind him. As he looked up, the classroom quieted, and he wished he could simply disappear.

Sister Bonnie was really very nice, but she had warned him about class disruption before. Perhaps she had forgotten? Carlos studied the Sister's young, pretty face, hoping for any sign of amusement by his antics. Seeing only her strict expression, he smiled broadly at the sister, showing his pretty teeth.

"Carlos! What are you doing?"

"Uh – I was just – "

"Didn't we have a talk, just last week, about your behavior?"

Carlos knew better than to lose eye contact, when he was being disciplined. He paused briefly to study the black pupils, in the sister's blue eyes, which crowded his personal space, before answering, "Yes, Sister Bonnie."

"And – what did I tell you would happen the next time?"

"Uh – I forgot," he lied.

The students all roared in laughter.

Another stern look by the sister cut the giddiness short. "Lying is a sin, Carlos. Would you like to reconsider?" her tone told Carlos, his only choice — was to reconsider.

"Yes Sister Bonnie."

"And — what did I tell you would happen the next time?"

"You said I would go with you to the office to talk with Mother Superior," he said regretfully.

"Let's go."

Carlos slowly got up from his seat and sluggishly headed for the door. He certainly didn't look forward to seeing the "Wrinkled Sister" or "Iron Penguin," as the other students called her.

Sister Bonnie, paused just long enough to issue "busywork" to the class before she marched Carlos to the office.

The errant boy, in no hurry for punishment, walked slowly. Sister Bonnie caught up with him easily, and with her hand on his shoulder, improved his pace through the dark, Spartan hallway, where paint peeled and lighting fixtures failed in the aging school. The office area of Mother Superior was no better. The high ceilings, with flaking, yellowed paint, echoed every sound, as if to mock the things said there. The School Administrator, wearing her black habit, sat at her wooden desk. Overhead, a dim fifty-year-old light, hung from the ceiling far above by a frayed, black cord.

The office area of Mother Superior, somehow reminded Carlos of the police station, but of course, this time he was the bad guy. Carlos waited uneasily with Sister Bonnie, in front of the splintering, wooden desk while the school administrator finished her phone conversation.

" — and what would that cost?" Mother Superior picked up her pencil to jot down a number. "That much? That will never do," she scolded. "How do you people sleep at night?" The nun fumbled through the stack of papers on her desk, pulling one from the center of the pile. "Of course, we need the job done, but our budget doesn't allow for such extravagances. We are trying to run a school for children here, not − " she paused. "Of course we want the best, but at your rate, we'd need thousands more to cover the costs." The supervising sister showed signs of anger. "Well Mr. O'malley, I'll let you think about it. I'm sure you'll do the right thing for the children." She placed the handset on hook, pausing to write down the estimate. Without looking up, she asked, "Mr. Martez, I see you are back in my office again." She tore off the page from the tablet and stapled it to another sheet, filing the pages in a nearby ledger on her desk. She briefly looked over her reading glasses, at the boy, before admonishing him in a strict tone, "I thought we had an understanding. Why did you break it?"

Carlos fidgeted, silently.

"Speak up young man. Why are you here?"

In a barely audible level, he answered, "Playin' in class."

Sister Bonnie nudged him, "Show Mother Superior your toy."

Slowly he lifted the bolt from below the edge of the desk so the nun could view it.

"Put it on the desk, Mr. Martez." With a nod of her head, she dismissed Sister Bonnie. The Iron Penguin pulled open her desk drawer, "Hold out your hands," she growled. Quickly she grabbed his hands and spanked them, until they turned red. With the ruler still in her hand, she pointed to a chair in the corner, "Sit there until I tell you to go back to class, young man."

Fighting back tears, Carlos did as he was told.

The wrinkled sister returned to her desk. Before sitting down, she looked at the silver bolt. Had it been gold before, or had she only imagined it? Perhaps the strain of managing the decaying school was getting to her. She reached over to pick up the bolt; it felt unusually cold to the touch, almost as though it had been in a

49

deep freeze. As she prepared to drop it in her desk drawer with other confiscated items, she noticed the color had turned coal-black. With a shrug, she dropped it into the drawer, before returning to her work.

Minutes later, after the red had faded from his hands, Carlos was sent back to class. As the boy left Mother Superior's office, she was reminded of the bolt. Standing by her desk, she opened her drawer to remove it. The color had reverted to silver. Puzzled, she picked it up. It became very cold, and very black as she handled it. Just as dry ice would, the cold burned her fingers until she was forced to release it. The bolt bounced on her desk several times before it came to rest. As she watched, ice quickly formed on its surface until the black color was nearly hidden by a white frost. She stepped back in shock, crossing herself. A cold chill raced along her spine as she spoke to it, "What are you?"

Of course there was no reply from the object, so the frightened administrator left the room for help. Going from classroom to classroom, she gathered the teachers; the children were excused early for recess. The parade of puzzled Sisters followed the Mother back to the office where the silver-bolt lay. The change of color stymied her. Looking at Sister Bonnie, she asked, "Do you know anything about this thing?"

"Isn't it the thing Carlos was playing with?"

"It is. . . but the color is different," the Mother corrected her.

Sister Bonnie looked more carefully, "Oh yes, wasn't it a gold color?"

The school administrator looked at the other nuns that had gathered in the room. "Do any of you know anything about this object?"

There was a murmur of questions and comments in soft, passive tones, but no one stepped forward with an explanation.

Before she could be warned, Sister Bonnie grasped the bolt for closer examination. "It looks like something from an automobile, except it doesn't seem to be greasy." To the horror of Mother Superior, the young nun handled it and passed it around the group with no sign of a problem. Finally Sister Bonnie handed it back to the mother.

Very cautiously the school administrator took the object, but immediately dropped it as it began to freeze and turn black again. The process stopped as soon as the bolt was no longer in her grasp. It was then, she realized the object had some kind of problem with her, not the others. Her first and prevailing instinct was to be rid of it. "It's a thing of the devil!" she screamed. She crossed herself a second time, saying a short prayer. "Take it out and bury it in the shadow of a cross!" she ordered. "I don't ever want to see it again."

The Sisters, unsure what the problem was with the Mother, did as they were told; they buried it.

Three days passed, and Carlos had almost forgotten his punishment among the list of similar offenses at the school. Still, in the back of his mind, he thought it unfair the Iron Penguin had taken his golden toy. Perhaps she thought it was too valuable for him to own; he didn't know? Whatever the reason, he had a different objective today. Carlos had never owned a dog, and a small basset hound, probably living nearby, had befriended him several days ago. He enjoyed sharing his lunch with the sad looking creature. In fact, it had become somewhat of a game. The hound would bring Carlos a stick and she'd be rewarded with a bite from his sandwich. Carlos glanced around the yard, it seemed there were no available sticks in sight. He wondered what his canine friend would bring him in return, for a bite of his sandwich. "Go get a stick!" he prompted.

The hound pushed her nose in the air and sniffed; she blinked her sad eyes then set her nose to the ground, and away she went. She crisscrossed the yard, finding no available sticks to buy her lunch. Suddenly as if she had caught scent of some fleeing varmint, she was off, through the small opening in the fence and out across the courtyard into the cemetery.

Rachael Smith, a classmate, watched Carlos. She was attracted to this rogue of the classroom, but was unsure what she could offer to gain his affection over a stray hound. Perhaps a little conversation might do the trick. "Bet she won't come back."

Carlos turned to see who spoke. "Oh it's you," he said with a sigh. Carlos resumed his watch on the small hole in the fence where the basset had disappeared. "He'll be back," he countered with an air of confidence.

"Bet she won't."

"He will too!"

"Uh-uh."

Carlos was becoming agitated by this "butt-in-ski". To win his point quickly, he became offensive, "You don't know anything about dogs, and it's my dog, and I know he'll come back."

Rachael, repelling his attack, fired back, "I do too know about dogs. I know more than you."

Carlos was incensed. "Ha! You don't even know what kind of dog he is."

"Do too."

"Do not."

"Do too."

"Okay. What kind of dog is it?"

Rachael paused. She really wasn't sure what breed the dog belonged to, but she was sure of one thing, "Uh — first of all, the dog's not a he."

"Is too."

"No it isn't"

"How do you know?"

Rachael drew a breath and was just about to give her classmate a lesson in animal husbandry, when the basset came back through the fence covered with dirt, carrying a shiny silver object.

"That's my thing!" Carlos beamed. He took the half-inch bolt and wiped the dirt from it, using his pants-leg. The stain showed on the trouser-leg of his school uniform, but the boy didn't care. He hugged his canine friend, rewarding her with the balance of his sandwich.

"What is that?" Rachael questioned.

"Uh – it's magic."

"No it isn't," Rachael rebutted.

"Is too."

"Okay. Make it do a trick."

Carlos knew of only one thing it could do. He set it on the ground and it turned silver. He picked it up and it turned gold color again. "There – see!"

"Let me try?"

The boy was unsure if it would change color for Rachael. He was equally unsure if she would take it from him. Feeling possessive, he denied her access, "Uh-uh."

Rachael was fascinated by the bolt's response. She wanted to touch it. "Why can't I try it?"

Carlos hesitated. "Because it doesn't work on girls."

"Will too."

"Will not."

"Hey look, it's turning black!"

The boy looked down. Rachael was correct, the bolt had turned black. He dropped it on the ground. . . it turned silver.

Rachael picked it up; it turned gold. "There!" she howled triumphantly, "It does too work on girls."

53

"Give it back."

"No."

"It's mine."

"No it isn't," she defended, "It's mine." As she argued, the bolt turned black. Afraid her classmate would see it turn black in her hands, she dropped it.

"Hey, you turned it black!"

"Did not!"

"Did too."

"Did not, Carlos."

"Okay," he said, picking up the bolt. The color restored to a gold pigment. "It doesn't like girls, and if you touch it, it'll turn black." The bolt shifted to a black pigment as Carlos held it.

Rachael was unsure, perhaps Carlos was right and it didn't like girls. Should she give him the chance to know for sure, by touching the object? As she saw the bolt turning black in his fingers, maybe the rule was the other way around; maybe it didn't like boys. "Look you're turning it black Carlos!" she jeered.

Surprised, Carlos quickly handed the object to Rachael, where it shifted to gold.

She held and admired the color. "See, it likes girls, best." The bolt turned black. Seeing the color change, Rachael tossed it to Carlos.

Carlos caught the bolt, which turned gold. "Hey, Rachael, I know what's going on."

"What?"

"It turns black each time you lie."

"Really?"

"Yeah! Watch this." Carlos held it up where Rachael could better view it. Looking around for an example, he saw the basset resting nearby. "Dogs are really cats," he lied. The bolt turned black. Carlos smiled broadly, showing a missing front tooth.

"Dogs are dogs and cats are cats," he corrected. The bolt turned gold.

Rachael was intrigued. She immediately seized on a golden opportunity. "Carlos, do you like me?"

The youth paused. He really hadn't thought much about it before, but she was sort of cute. Of course she got in his face a bit too much, but he actually liked the fact that she noticed him. If he told her yes, she might expect – well, he didn't know what she'd expect. Maybe she'd want to hold hands all the time, and that would get him in trouble with the Iron Penguin. Even worse, the other boys would tease him. No, he couldn't let her know he liked her. "No, of course not," he lied. Suddenly he realized it was not a question, but a trap as the bolt turned black.

Rachael smiled, "I like you too," she said sweetly. She glanced around the yard for watchful eyes of the nuns. Seeing they were occupied elsewhere, she moved closer to Carlos, preparing to plant a kiss on his lips.

Carlos backpedaled. He was interested, but suddenly felt shy. How could the class cutup feel shy? He wasn't sure, but everything was getting a bit too real for him. He didn't know how to kiss, and she was getting really close. Her face was closer than the new kid he fought with last week. Her lips were puckering, and he couldn't move.

Across the yard, a nun blew three blasts on her whistle. Lunch break was over. It was time to return to class. Carlos turned and ran, leaving a frustrated Rachael behind. Secretly, he wished he'd stayed, but it was just too risky.

* * *

A few days later, Sister Bonnie escorted Carlos and Rachael into the office of Mother Superior. The children were scheduled to attend a youth meeting in another town sixty miles to the north. When the Supervisor failed to acknowledge them, the Sister spoke softly, "Mother Superior, I brought the children for the monthly youth meeting."

Still, the Mother continued to make notes and shuffle papers, without looking up.

Sister Bonnie waited patiently, lest she incur one of the nasty reprimands the Mother had become famous for giving the other sisters who lived there. After a minute, of no response, the children were becoming restless, but they remained on their best behavior.

The Sister was about to renew her notice to the Mother when the older nun spoke, without looking up from her messy work-desk. "Sister Bonnie, I want you to drive the children to the youth meeting this evening."

"Isn't Sister Evelyn taking them?"

"Sister Evelyn has the flu."

"I see," Sister Bonnie said thoughtfully, "That is going to be a problem."

"Are you refusing my request?"

"Not exactly," she answered, trying to be as diplomatic as possible.

The Iron Penguin looked up, her dark eyes peering over her reading glasses. "Then do as I say."

Sister Bonnie fidgeted. "I can't."

A stern look from the Supervisor gave the young teacher a feeling of dismay.

"You're new here, aren't you, Sister Bonnie?"

"I've been here two years, Mother Superior." She took a deep breath, "I'm not trying to tell you I won't drive the children; I'm trying to tell you I can't, because I have other duties."

"Such as?"

"You assigned me the task of coaching the girl's basketball team while Sister Anne has gone to visit her dying brother."

A blank look, followed by a sigh of unrest, from the matriarch was not a good sign. The administrator drummed her fingers on her desk as she thought. Seconds later, she rolled a desk drawer open and located the duty roster. Light sounds of muttering came from the older woman as her fingers traced though the list of names for a substitute driver. When she reached the end of the list and everyone was found busy or not available, she tossed the list in the drawer and slammed it shut. "Pickle!" she exclaimed, "I suppose, I'll have to drive them myself." She tossed her reading glasses on the stack of papers and stood up, shaking the wrinkles out of her black habit. "Send the children to the car and have them wait until I can get my things."

"Yes Mother Superior." Sister Bonnie motioned for the children to step into the hallway. Squatting down to straighten the collar on the coat Carlos wore, she gave instructions, "Carlos, I want you to be on your best behavior. It is very important you set a good example for our school."

"Yes Sister."

Looking at Rachael, she smiled, while continuing with her instructions to Carlos, "I want you to treat Rachael as a young lady and stay beside her as a gentleman would. Do you understand?"

"Yes Sister."

"Now go to Sister Evelyn's car and open the door for Rachael, as a gentleman would." The teacher stood up, looking at both of the youngsters. "Wait in the car quietly until Mother Superior can drive you."

"Yes Sister," they both answered. Their footsteps echoed in the darkened, empty hallway as they walked side by side.

True to his word, Carlos opened the rear door on the passenger side for Rachael. She climbed in and promptly slid across the seat behind the driver, where the piercing eyes of the Iron Penguin wouldn't find her as easily.

Carlos recognized Rachael's strategy. "Some girlfriend," he thought. It was bad enough to be supervised all day in class and all evening by a nun, but this wasn't just any nun. While they had frequent conversations, he and the Iron Penguin certainly weren't fond of each other. Carlos was beginning to regret letting Rachael talk him into volunteering for the trip.

The young boy slid into the back seat beside Rachael. He thought for a few seconds, searching for any excuse to urge her to leave the coveted seat behind the driver. "Hey! Weren't you suppose to bring a Saint Christopher's medal?"

Rachael looked through her papers and purse she was carrying. Carlos was right; she had forgotten it. "Run back and get it Carlos. I think it's still hanging on the wall by the bulletin board in Sister Bonnie's room."

He had her where he wanted her, "No, you get it."

Rachael looked at Carlos, "Please?" she begged.

"It's your responsibility; you should get it."

The young girl agonized over the importance of the medal for the meeting. She knew the boy sitting next to her would not be enough of a gentleman to fetch it for her, and she too wanted the coveted seat. "Let's go together," she coaxed.

Silence was the reply.

Quickly, she opened the door and dashed back into the building and down the dark hallway to retrieve the medal. Moments later, medal in hand, she was not surprised to find her seat was now occupied by Carlos.

"That's my seat," she said, looking through the window at Carlos.

"No it isn't"

"Is too."

Silence.

"Show me the bolt," Rachael urged.

"What?"

"Show me the bolt, I want to see if you lied."

"I didn't lie."

"Then show me the bolt and we'll decide."

No response.

"You're afraid."

"Am not."

"Then show me the bolt."

Carlos reluctantly dug into his pocket, retrieving the bolt. Its color was gold. "See," he said, with relief in his voice that the bolt wasn't black.

"Now tell me you didn't get me to leave so you could take over my seat."

He knew the bolt would turn black. Maybe if she saw it turn black, she would just leave him alone. No, he reasoned, she wouldn't let it rest if it turned black; she'd hound him. Then he concluded, it was his bolt and he was in charge of it. Slipping the bolt back into his pocket, he announced, "I'm in charge and I don't care what you think."

Rachael fumed.

Carlos folded his arms and sat by the locked door, looking straight ahead.

Not knowing what else to do, she walked around the car and climbed in the rear seat, leaving a wide space between them.

"You didn't answer my question," she said, watching his face for signs of expression.

"What question?"

"Did you trick me to take my seat?"

"Of course not," he lied. He felt confident the black color would be impossible for her to see inside his pocket, so — it was as if lying, didn't count.

The bolt had other ideas about justice. Suddenly, the object got warm, very warm in his pocket. Carlos tried to get it out, but it was too hot to touch, he tried to stand up in the car, but the roof was too low. Carlos frantically fumbled to unlock the door and scramble outside. The bolt was getting warmer and warmer. He unlatched the belt on his pants and forced the fabric down and away from his leg. The cool air felt good on his skin, but Rachael's laughter did little for his male ego.

Carlos touched the object through the lining of the pant's pocket. It had been very hot, but not hot enough to burn skin; now it was cooling rapidly. Just as he was preparing to pull his trousers up, Mother Superior approached the car.

"Mr. Martez, what! What are you doing?"

Rachael giggled.

"Well – I – " Carlos was unable to come up with an answer. He realized he didn't have any answer that would be suitable. He didn't want the disciplinarian to know he recovered the bolt. So he couldn't tell her the truth. If he lied, the bolt might burn him a second time. It was bad enough to be caught pulling one's pants up by a nun, but if he lied again and had to take them down a second time – in front of her – well, it better not happen.

In a sympathetic gesture, Rachael motioned Carlos into the seat behind the driver. She reasoned, the nun's eyes would be on Carlos, no matter where he sat.

The boy took his seat and fastened his seat belt; he then closed the door carefully, to avoid another lecture.

The nun put a few things into the trunk of the car, including the children's coats.

Out of sight of their chaperon, Rachael kissed the palm of her hand and tapped it on the back of Carlos's hand. He folded his arms and looked straight ahead, his reddened face still flushed from embarrassment.

Minutes later, they were traveling through town.

* * *

In front of a bank, a few blocks away, Richard Benedari and Chuck Black descended on an armored car owned and operated by Mercury Armored Car Inc. On a signal from leader Benedari, they pulled guns and forced one of the two guards to surrender his weapon and his bag of cash going into the bank.

"And get over here! Now!" Benedari demanded.

The second robber, had jammed a large prybar into the crack of the door, preventing its closure. Black pried against the door, slowly gaining an opening against the guard inside, who tried in vain to close it. The struggle lasted less than thirty seconds, before the door swung open to the bandits. The guard inside grabbed for his shotgun, but Black shot him before he could touch it.

"Inside." Benedari motioned to the remaining guard, with his gun. The guard hesitated at the door. "Get inside! Now!" the leader ordered.

In a daring, covert move, the guard dragged the string for the ignition key across a sharp metal decoration on his empty holster, freeing it from the key ring. He let the key drop onto his shoe for a quiet landing. With a gentle side step, the key was pushed into the storm drain, where it would take time to retrieve it. He then climbed into the back of the armored truck as ordered.

Richard looked up and down the street for signs of police, but saw nothing. He climbed inside, behind the guard. "Where's the key to the ignition?"

The guard hesitated.

"The key?" Benedari asked again.

No response.

The barrel of Benedari's gun hit the guard in the face. The wounded man fell onto his deceased partner.

61

Richard stood over the guard, "I'm not telling you again. Where's the truck ignition key?"

Trying to buy time, the guard, fumbled with a key ring kept in a small leather pouch, next to his holster. Slowly, he handed the ring of keys to the leader.

The crook snatched the key ring and jumped down from the rear of the truck. In a flash, he was trying to open the driver's door on the armored truck. Precious seconds passed until he found the proper key to open the door. More seconds passed as he searched for the missing ignition key. When he discovered the key was not on the ring, the angered man climbed from the cab and ran to the rear of the truck. Pointing the pistol in the direction of the trembling guard, he discharged a round that embedded itself into the deceased guard. "Where's the key!" he screamed.

The guard made no attempt to move.

Hatred filled Benedari. He aimed at the guard's chest and pulled hard on the trigger. The bullet slammed into the guard's chest and the man died seconds later.

"Forget the coins, get the tens and twenties and let's go," the leader ordered.

Each of the two thieves grabbed as many bags as they could carry. They left the truck with the two dead guards behind.

Down the block, the two bandits saw a string of cars stopping for a red light. The blue sedan at the crossing had an old nun and two children inside. Richard temporarily dropped several bags of money to free a hand. Yanking up on the latch handle, the front-passenger door opened. "We're taking your car, Sister," the murderer ordered. "Tell the brat behind you to open the door and slide over."

Badly angered, Mother Superior resisted, "Get out of this car! You'll get no cooperation here!" she shouted.

Richard pointed the gun at Rachael. "Do as I say — or you'll be giving last rites."

She relented.

"Tell the brat behind you to open the door."

"Mr. Martez, please do as the man demanded."

Carlos didn't think it was a good idea, but he had no choice either. He unlocked the door for Black.

"Get over," Black ordered. When the boy didn't move fast enough to suit him, the thief rested his bags on the roof of the car and placed a foot on the boy's leg. He shoved. Carlos screamed in pain.

"Undo your seat belt, Carlos," Rachael screamed over the noise. Carlos was too busy holding onto the strap across his chest. Rachael leaned over, her arm barely reaching the release. She pressed it. The belt retracted, and assisted by the outlaw's foot, Carlos nearly flew across the seat into her.

The thief threw his bags into the back. Some landed on the laps of the children, and some landed on the crowded floor. Black slid into the vacant seat and slammed the door shut.

Up front, Benedari had already settled, with money bags strewn around the riding compartment. He looked both ways up and down the cross street and commanded, "Let's go Sister, we gotta get down the road."

"But the light's red?"

"Not as red as your blood's going to look on your habit, if you don't punch it," he said, waving his pistol at her.

She said a silent prayer and sped across the intersection against the red light.

"Here! Get on the freeway," Richard ordered.

The driver made an unsafe lane change and went up the ramp.

"Good! Now, keep it going south until I say otherwise."

"You have no right to do this!"

Richard waved the gun at the nun, "See this? This gives me the right."

"You'll be caught and you'll pay for your sins," she threatened, while changing lanes to navigate around a slower moving vehicle.

"I don't intend to be caught," Richard said, looking behind, for signs of the police. "And if you don't want to pay for my sins right now, you'll shut up and drive."

"You'll – "

"I said shut up!"

Richard turned the knob on the radio, hoping to hear news. The radio was quiet. "How do you make this thing work?"

"It's broken," the nun said.

"That's convenient. Why don't you have it fixed?"

"We can't afford to have it fixed."

"Ha! That's a hot one. You pass around the basket every week, don't get taxed, and still are broke." Richard made a cheeky sound, "Give me a break."

"I'd be happy to stop and let you out."

"Boy, you're a sassy old woman. Didn't I tell you to shut up and drive?"

A deafening silence filled the car as it careened through freeway traffic. Richard leaned over to view the speedometer. "Hey, slow down a bit, we don't want to attract attention."

"How much?"

"Just travel a little faster than the other cars."

"Just how much is that?" The mother relaxed pressure on the accelerator petal. "Cars are traveling at different speeds," she argued.

"Slow down a bit more."

The bandit checked the off-ramp signs. "Take the next off ramp, Sister."

The car slipped into the ramp and slowed as it approached the turn. "Now what?" she asked with a defiant tone.

"Go that way," Richard said, pointing to the west.

"Where are you taking us?"

The murderer said nothing. He simply scanned the area for any sign of police.

"Will you let us stop and get out? We'll give you the car."

He gave her no response.

Mother Superior slowed the car as she approached a wide spot.

"What are you doing?" Benedari yelled.

"I'm stopping the car."

"I didn't tell you to stop! Keep going."

"We'd like to get out."

"There are people in hell wanting ice water too," Benedari said mockingly.

"You may be one of them some day," the mother replied.

"Talk like that can get you killed, Sister. Now shut up and drive."

The murderers routed the car up into the hills. They watched for side roads, and had her turn onto one they selected at random. Finally they ordered her to stop in a wide spot.

Richard, the leader, opened his door, giving instructions to the nun, "Shut off the motor and give me the keys."

"What are you going to do?"

"Relax Sister. We're just going to make a little room up front." The thieves climbed out of the car. They put all of the money except for a loose twenty in the trunk.

65

"Okay, we're all shipshape," Benedari said. "Let's see where this road goes." He handed the keys back to the Sister, motioning for her to continue up the dirt trail.

Five, dusty minutes later, they discovered the road ended in a wide turnaround near a small power distribution substation.

Sitting in the front seat, Richard looked at his wrist watch. "We'll wait here for a while," he said, while holding his empty hand toward the nun. "Give me the keys and get out."

"Can we get out too?" Rachael asked.

"Yeah, you kids get out too," Richard ordered.

Taking charge, as always, and treating the children as objects, Mother Superior spoke strictly to them, "Come children, I want you over here." The nun and the two children moved away from the car, toward the edge of the clearing.

The clearing mainly consisted of the turning radius set up for a large truck to carry heavy equipment to and from the site. Above them, a set of high tension wires carried power to the large transformers that hummed safely inside an area circled by a tall chain-link fence. The small installation shared access to the flat turn-around-area for ease of moving equipment in or out of the station. On either side of the fenced area, a ditch, about a meter deep by two meters wide, sloped upward at a thirty-degree angle toward the thickets of brush and trees. At the closet point, the distance to the tree line would take the aging nun about two minutes to reach at her fastest run. The dry, knee-deep grass, between, would provide no protection from small arms fire and would likely prove slippery for street shoes.

"Let's make a run for it," Carlos whispered.

"It's too far to the trees," Rachael whispered.

Horrified they might make decisions on their own, the nun scolded, "Don't do anything unless I tell you to do it." She gave them a stern look, "Do you understand?"

66

Losing eye contact with Carlos, she singled him out, "Do you understand Mr. Martez?"

"Yes Mother Superior," he said meekly.

"Hey! Not too far," Richard shouted from the car, "Stay out of the woods."

Mother Superior surveyed the terrain around them. There wasn't much resource here for help. No telephone, no people, no real place to hide, unless they could make it into the woods. For that, she'd have to distract the outlaws long enough to cover an escape. *"It was such a pain,"* she thought, *"being in charge of children."*

The men got out of the car and leaned on it while smoking. They watched the nun and children across the clearing. In return, the children and their guardian seemed to be watching them.

Black carelessly tossed his lighted cigarette onto the dirt, next to the dry grass.

"Hey Chuck, don't do that."

"Do what?"

"Don't toss your cigs into the grass."

Black looked around at the dry grass and trees. "Yeah, like it would really hurt something for all of this to burn up."

"Maybe not, but we don't want the police and fire engines up here."

"Yeah, never thought of that." Chuck pushed his backside up on the trunk of the car, using it as a seat. "What are we going to do with 'em?" he asked, nodding toward the captives.

Benedari watched them for a few seconds then turned his back, as if they might read lips. "We'll whack 'em, when the time comes."

Black remained silent.

"Ever whack anybody, Chuck?"

"Just did."

D.Malisch

"No, I mean before that."

"Yeah, I fixed up my drug dealer back in Texas. He was sellin' me crap."

Silence.

"What are we going to do next, Rich?"

Benedari removed his gun, popped the clip and replaced the spent cartridges from spares in his coat pocket. "I figured we'd wait till early morning and head into town." He paused to spit. "Then we might buy a car and dump this one." Sunset was approaching and he looked up at the position of the sun in the western sky. "We could go to Texas or somethin'."

Chuck nodded agreement.

The crunch of footsteps in the decomposed granite alerted Benedari they were being approached. He turned to see the nun within speaking distance.

"Why don't you let us go?" she asked.

"Why don't you go take a flying leap?" Chuck responded in a nasty tone.

"We can't be of any use to you, now that you have the car," she said softly.

"We been considering that," Richard said, wiping the barrel of his gun on his sleeve.

"You wouldn't dare!"

Benedari pointed the handgun at her. "You have no idea what we'd dare, lady." He gave her a chilling smile – one where the mouth moves, but the eyes stare like a dangerous animal.

"But they're just children; they mean you no harm."

"Makes it more interesting."

She turned to look at the children, who seemed occupied with some sort of game. "Have you no conscience?"

"Why should you care? You treat them like strangers."

"I do not!" she protested.

68

"Sure you do," Richard jabbed back.

"How can you say that?"

"How can you call the kid mister?"

"Well I – "

"Well you better get it together Sister, because you're no better than I am."

They studied each other silently, before the nun turned and walked back toward the children. When she saw Black's cigarette butt next to the dry grass, she paused to look back at the two men. They seemed to be ignoring her, so she carefully nudged the butt into the dry grass with her shoe before continuing back to the children.

"Prepare yourselves to run when I tell you," the guardian told the children, "it won't be long now."

"To the trees?" Carlos asked.

"No, of course not, run down the road."

"When?"

"Soon – but wait until I tell you."

Together they watched the men, but only the nun knew the plan; she didn't trust the children. A minute or more passed then a thin whisper of white smoke began to wind its way up into the sky. The bandits, seemed preoccupied with their conversation. The fire spread quickly, gaining momentum, until flames could be seen. As the flames grew larger, a crackling sound caught the attention of one of the men. They ran around the car looking for a shovel, for something, for anything to put the fire out.

"Now children, run!" she whispered hoarsely.

They ran. Down the hill they went, the children in the lead. The Matriarch's black habit flapped in the wind, and her white stocking showed as she lifted her skirt for a longer step. They raced down the steep incline, around the corner, through the twisting section and back onto a straight section with steep canyon on one side and a sheer rock wall on the other.

They were out of breath but pressed onward, never looking back. Just when they thought they could run no more, they suddenly heard the sound of a vehicle behind them, its engine racing. Mother Superior's heart sank when she turned to see the vehicle mere steps behind them. There was no chance. They had been caught. The two shots over her head, pulled her up short. She called the children back, and together they stood and gasped for air.

As a punishment, they were forced to walk back up the hill. The car was parked as before. Again, the men stayed by the car, while the nun and children stayed across the clearing, but away from the trees. Perhaps the only things different were the newly acquired charcoal-smudges on the faces and hands of the men with matching smudges on their clothing. The disheveled-look included several new rips and footprints on their windbreakers, used to stomp out the fire. It was obvious the men were angry, and if they had suspected the mother had started the fire, her life would be terminated. Now, the beastly look of their clothing, matched their nasty dispositions. Perhaps the one benefit of the fire diversion, was that the men were too tired to antagonize anyone.

"I'm sorry children, I tried," the Mother apologized. She sat on a pie-sized rock, her dark skirt spread upon the pale dust around her.

"It's okay," Rachael smiled, "We have a plan."

The nun held up her hand, "No! No! No! You children are my responsibility and you'll not make any decisions here."

"That's okay, Mother Superior," Carlos grinned, "we've included you in our plan."

For the first time in years, the nun felt a binding with the children. While the youths showed no fear, she reasoned, it might be best if she treated their conversation as though it were a game. She wanted to keep the children occupied and doing something besides fearing the inevitable. Who knows, with God's help, she might even come up with a better plan as they played? "Easy, now," she said, checking over her shoulder to see if they were out of earshot of the two dangerous men, "Let's take it slow and talk this over." Looking back at the children she asked, "What's your plan?"

Carlos and Rachael looked at each other. They had expected a lot more resistance from Mother Superior. Perhaps she was their friend after all. They both began to speak at once.

"Wait! Slow down." The nun held up her hands in a push-back gesture. "You first Rachael."

The girl looked at her co-conspirator, then spoke slowly and as carefully as she could. "We have this plan, but it isn't finished yet. We're still working on it."

"Tell me what you have."

She took a small stick and wrote in the sandy granite soil. "COAT, BEND, KEY, TIRE, FLAT," she said as she finished.

Puzzled, the guardian questioned the words. "I thought you had a plan? These are only words."

Rachael nodded, "They are, but we must do these things to escape."

"How do you know this Rachael?"

"Uh – we had some help."

"Help?" She looked at Rachael, "Who helped you?"

"You're not going to like it," Carlos said with a tone of doubt in his voice.

"What is it – that I'm not going to like, Carlos?"

The boy paused, trying to decide if he'd be punished or not. "Are you going to punish me?"

D.Malisch

"For trying to escape? Certainly not, my child." She leaned forward and gave Carlos a gentle hug.

Carlos wet his lips and reached for the stick Rachael was holding. He pointed to the first word. "COAT," he said. "I think we ask for our coats." He pointed to the second word, "BEND." He looked back at the nun, "I think this goes with the word 'KEY', but I'm not sure." He looked for any sign of disapproval from his personal disciplinarian. Seeing none, he continued, "I don't know why, but I think we need to bend the key." He moved to the next word, "TIRE," he said. "I think this goes with 'FLAT'. We're supposed to make the tire go flat."

As an adult, the nun immediately saw the diversion. "We ask for our coats, get them from the trunk and bend the ignition key. That's pretty clever. But, when do we flatten the tire, and how do we do it without being seen?"

Rachael admitted, "We don't know yet? We haven't gotten that far."

"Far?"

"Yes, those are all the words we've found so far."

"Wait." The mother thought for a few seconds, "I still don't understand? Who is giving you these words?"

"Why – the thing that Carlos has."

"Huh?" The nun asked, with a puzzled look, "What are you talking about?"

From his kneeling position, Carlos leaned sideways to straighten his leg and allow his hand to reach deeply into his pocket. He pulled out the half-inch bolt and slowly opened his hand.

Mother Superior jumped back when she saw it, nearly falling off her rock. She crossed herself and said a prayer. Looking back at Carlos, she reprimanded him. "How did you get that back?"

"A dog gave it to me."

"Carlos, I thought we talked about lying."

"It's the truth," he protested.

"It's true," Rachael backed him. "I saw the dog bring it to him."

"Well – it's a thing of the devil," she scolded.

"No, Mother Superior, it prevents us from lying."

"What are you saying child?"

"Show her Carlos."

The boy held the bolt where it could be easily viewed. "Notice the color, Mother Superior – gold. Now watch if I say something false." He made eye contact with the woman and said, "Dogs are cats."

The bolt immediately turned black. Carlos paused for her to see the color, then he corrected his statement, "Dogs are dogs, and cats are cats." The bolt returned to its original gold color.

The nun was speechless. Her mouth gaped open.

"Would you like to try it, Mother Superior?" Rachael asked.

"Oh no," she said, waving her hand." It won't work for me." She remembered it freezing her fingers, and after having it buried, she wasn't sure what might happen to her if she touched it again.

"It won't hurt you," Carlos beamed, tossing the bolt to his guardian.

She caught it by reflex and nearly threw it away until she saw it remained a golden color. She tried the simple test used by the children several times until she too, was convinced it wouldn't harm her. At last, she repeated her question to Carlos. "So how did this give you the words?"

"That was Rachael's idea."

Rachael smiled, "Have you ever played 'Twenty Questions'?"

73

Feeling young again, the mother smiled, "Goodness yes. And I was pretty good at it too, if I say so myself." She looked at the bolt; it remained gold.

The look of relief on the nun's face made the youngsters laugh.

The children came closer to the Mother, each sitting at an elbow, while Rachael continued with her story. "First we asked this thing if it would help us by saying: 'Thing will help us.' Of course it didn't change to black. Then we tried different sentences to guess how it might help us."

"That's very clever, Rachael." The nun smiled. It had been so long since she had smiled, it almost hurt her face. "Let me try to fill in the pieces." She glanced toward the west, where the sun was kissing the Pacific ocean. "We should escape now." The bolt turned black. "I'll try again," she said with an air of confidence. "We should escape tonight, after dark." The bolt glowed gold.

For the next few minutes, the nun and children worked quickly to fine-tune the plan of escape.

When it became so dark they could barely see one another, and the temperature was beginning to drop, the matriarch walked back toward the men leaning against the car. "We'll need our jackets," she said flatly.

Except for a blank look, there was no response.

"It's getting cold, and the children and I need our coats from the trunk."

"So?" Richard asked mockingly.

"So, I need the keys to open the trunk."

"It's not cold enough to need coats."

In the fading twilight, she looked Richard in the eye and held out her open hand. She waited patiently for several seconds, until he complied.

She opened the trunk, and moved the key ring to the hand away from the bandits. As she dug beneath the sacks of money for the children's coats, she pretended to lean against the lip of the trunk. The pretense allowed her to bend the ignition key badly enough it would take them some time to make it work.

Gathering the coats, she closed the trunk and tossed the keys on the roof of the car, where the damage wouldn't be seen until later.

The warmer clothing helped the children and nun go on with their plan. They watched and watched for an opening, but when none came, they worried a bit.

Soon, it became cold enough the men wanted shelter. Unfortunately, they couldn't just get inside the car and allow their hostages to roam free. So they called them over to the car. "We're getting tired and we're going to get inside the car. We don't want you running off, so we decided to take the girl inside with us. If you run off, she dies. Get it?" Richard told her.

"I don't suppose you'd consider taking me instead?" the nun asked.

"Not a chance. It's a small car and you'd take up too much room."

"I thought so. . . "

Black took Rachael by the arm. "It's too bad that you aren't a few years older, sis. We'd get along just fine," he said with a lewd tone in his voice.

In the nearly pitch-black conditions, an expression of unhappiness glistened on Rachael's face. She extended her free arm back toward Carlos.

Carlos charged Chuck Black. When he caught Black, he hit him as hard as he could in the stomach. The man doubled over, but only for an instant. He grabbed the boy by the back of the neck and pushed him to the ground. There, the angry man kicked

75

him several times until he felt he had been avenged. Carlos, bleeding and in pain, curled into a ball and sobbed.

Rachael ran to Carlos and knelt over him. "I'll be all right Carlos, just keep watch," she cried.

The boy reached up and took her hand. He shoved the bolt into her palm and closed her fingers around it. "For luck," he whispered in a painful voice.

She put the bolt in her coat pocket as Black dragged her toward the car.

Mother Superior helped Carlos to his feet, and together, they reluctantly returned to the area they had occupied all afternoon.

In spite of the cold, San Francisco-fog creeping across the coastal range, Carlos and Mother Superior kept their spirits high by talking about many things. Instead of talking about their differences, they mainly talked about the things they had in common. Finally, they just sat and watched the car, in the starlight.

Perhaps as many as two hours had passed before Carlos, though sore, felt much better. The twilight was now gone, and the area was very nearly pitch black. Carlos noticed the nun was snoring lightly, meaning she wouldn't be watching so closely. He got onto his knees and very carefully, and very quietly, worked his way across the clearing to the left-front tire of the car. Earlier, he had observed Richard resting in the front of the car, with his back to the passenger-door. The boy was confident letting the air out of the tire on the other side of the car wouldn't disturb him. It took several minutes, but Carlos let the air escape slowly and quietly.

When the air was gone, the boy crawled around to the passenger side of the car. He softly, tapped twice on the window. Rachael, resting on the floor, tapped twice in return. From her response, he knew she wasn't sleeping. He listened for sounds of snoring. Both men appeared to be sleeping. Carlos grasped the door handle behind Richard. He stood up and yanked the door open. The sleeping crook fell out head first. The jolt jarred him awake, but impacting the ground knocked the wind out of him. The car light came on, and Rachael found the lock, releasing it. Carlos swung the door open for her and they left quickly.

The shouting awoke Mother Superior; she climbed to her feet as the children reached her. Together they raced down the pitch black road. Their exit wasn't fast, but this time they had the full advantage of good planning.

At the car, Richard finally caught his breath, but banged his head badly on the bottom of the passenger-door as he tried to sit up.

It took a minute or so for Chuck Black to realize there had been another escape. He grabbed his gun and began shooting in different directions. His voice screamed threats of death when he caught them.

Richard, rubbing the knot on his forehead, made his way around the car to the driver's side. He slid into the seat and fumbled quickly with the keys. The key wouldn't go into the lock. He tried a dozen times or more, before he held the key next to the courtesy light to see the problem. He cursed solidly for a minute or more as he realized he'd been duped. Carefully, he straightened the key and fit it into the lock. It started the car, then they discovered the flat tire.

The thieves searched the car for a light to see to change the flat tire. All they could find inside the car was a bolt, lying on the floor near the back seat. Under the courtesy light, it appeared to be very black and very cold.

In the morning first-light, the crooks found the jack and spare. They took their time changing the tire, since the hostages had been gone for hours. Upon starting the car, they received another surprise when the radio came to life, full volume. It played only long enough to hear there was an A.P.B. on the missing vehicle. They needed to get another set of wheels as soon as possible. On their drive back to a neighboring city, they watched for the nun and children but never saw them.

Richard pulled the car into the parking lot of a fast food restaurant. The drive-through had a sign blocking the path. The sign indicated the car service was temporary out of operation, but customers were welcome inside.

"Chuck, go inside and get us some food," Richard demanded.

"Aren't you coming?"

"No, the car might not start again, if I shut it off."

"Okay. What do you want?" Black asked.

"Get me a scrambled egg and juice and a muffin," Richard growled, unhappy with the way events had evolved.

Chuck nodded and closed the door. A minute later, he returned to the car empty handed, "Was that scrambled light or with bacon?"

"With bacon." Richard thought for a second, "No wait! If the bacon isn't crisp, don't get it."

"Okay." Chuck went back inside only to return empty-handed seconds later. "Did you want the eggs on a muffin or plain?"

"Plain!" Richard shouted with an irritated tone.

Chuck waved and returned to the restaurant. Seconds later, he came back, "What kind of muffin did you want?"

"What kind they got?" Richard said, with strong irritation in his voice.

"I donno?"

"Hell, just get a raisin muffin."

Chuck ducked back inside only to return seconds later, "What about the juice?"

"What about the juice?" Richard asked, his voice raised to nearly the level of a shout.

"What kind you want?"

"Orange," he yelled.

Chuck returned to the order counter only seconds before dashing back to the car.

Richard saw him coming and he had played this game long enough. He left the car running and ran across the driveway and into the restaurant behind Chuck. "Hey! Can't you make any decisions on your own?"

Chuck looked startled, "I didn't want to upset you or anything – I tried to get everything right."

A look of complete frustration crossed Benedari's face. He grabbed Chuck by the front of the shirt. In an intimidating but quiet voice he gritted his teeth while saying, "Look, we gotta get food and get out of this town before we get caught. Don't you understand?"

"Okay," Chuck said meekly.

The leader released him, with a little push, saying, "Okay, now go up to the counter and get the food."

Everything went fine. Richard watched from a few feet away. When Chuck got the bag and they turned to leave, they were totally unprepared to see the car driving away with teenagers in it.

Richard threw open the door and sprinted across the lot after the car. When it didn't stop by his shouting, he pulled his gun and fired a couple of shots. The vehicle accelerated and was gone in seconds.

At the door of the restaurant, Chuck Black was unsure if he should run away or bring Richard his breakfast. He knew Richard was not a "happy-camper." He chose to meet him half way.

The bandit leader, swore continuously as he walked toward Black. As the distance closed, Richard pointed his pistol at Black's chest. "Say anything stupid and you're dead."

Chuck dropped the bag of food and held his hands away from his body. He stood there silently, sweating in the frosty morning air.

The gun shook in Richard's hand. It shifted toward Chuck's head, paused, then went back to Chuck's chest. Finally, Richard put it away. He stepped forward and grabbed the bag of breakfast and walked on. Chuck breathed a sigh of relief. He watched his buddy walk away for a few seconds then followed behind, like a hungry dog.

* * *

The nun's car, complete with money and three very stupid teenagers raced along the highway. Within seconds, after passing a police car, the officer recognized it from the "hot sheet" and gave pursuit.

"Where'd he come from?" the driver asked. "I din' see no cops?"

"Well, he's there bro'."

"What we gon' do?"

"Not get caught," the front seat passenger quipped.

The youths had no idea the car was already on every "hot sheet" in the bay area. The car raced down the lightly populated freeway that was rapidly filling with morning commuters.

A second police car joined the pursuit.

"We got a nodder' one," the youth in the back seat said nervously.

At the next exit they got two more cars joining the chase.

"Better get off the freeway and find some ol' road," the front seat passenger said, hanging onto the seat and dashboard as the car rocked back and forth changing lanes.

"Next exit," said the voice from the back seat. "Then head straight up into the hills."

The driver complied, with eight police in hot pursuit.

The car swung left and right, climbing the narrow road to the top of the grade. In the back seat, the young passenger felt something bump repeatedly against his foot. Looking down, he saw it was a bolt. Annoyed with the thing, he rolled down his window and threw it out onto the highway. It bounced several times before coming to rest at the edge of the road. The police cars screamed past, indifferently.

Minutes passed and the driver nervously eyed the fuel gauge. "Hey! This thing's out of juice?"

"Say it ain't so."

"Wish I could bro', but I think we had it."

The car went another three miles along the skyline road connecting the coastal mountain peaks. Then it began to slow. It rounded a corner and rolled past a nun and two children walking along the road, before coasting to a stop. The police were on the joy-riders before they could make it down into the ditch and up the bank into the trees. Within minutes, all three were spread-eagle on the ground, waiting for another free ride back to the city juvenile detention center.

Mother Superior looked at the officer, writing his report. "You're not going to believe it. I know I certainly don't. But that's my car."

The young C.H.P. officer looked at the nun. "I'm sorry, did you say this is your car?"

"Yes, officer." She pulled the children closer to her. "This is Rachael and this is Carlos," she said with a smile. "We were kidnaped yesterday and have spent the night, walking back toward town."

The officer looked at the A. P. B., "You're right?" he said with a puzzled look, "I can't believe they led us right back up to you." He looked at the boys lying beside the pavement, near the sedan. "They look awfully young for armored car robbers."

"Oh no, officer, they aren't the robbers. They're just kids."

"Then – what are they doing with your car?"

"I don't know, officer. The last time we saw the car, two desperate men, with guns, had it."

"Where'd they go?"

"I don't know, we ran away from them up on the hill last night. We've been avoiding every car coming from that direction since we escaped." The nun looked at her two charges. "It's been a long night and we've been walking toward town for hours. Do you think you could give us a ride back to the school?"

"Of course, ma'am. I'll have an officer take you in a few minutes."

"Thank you officer."

The policeman looked back at the A.P.B. for several seconds. "What did they do with the money?"

"The money? Oh goodness yes. They hid it in the trunk," she said pointing to the back of the car.

"You don't suppose?"

"Please look, officer."

The highway patrolman removed the keys from the ignition and opened the trunk. Inside was nearly a million dollars in sacks and sacks of bills. The officer inspected the contents briefly then checked his paperwork. "You might want to know, Sister, the Mercury Armored Car folks have offered a big reward for return of this money."

The school administrator looked upward through the Yew trees and said a silent prayer. She now had the money to make the badly needed repair to the school.

* * *

Walking their way along the El Camino Real, Benedari finally relented, allowing his partner-in-crime to share breakfast. Richard still wasn't happy, but he slapped his friend on the back saying, "Come on, Chuckie, there's a lot more money out there, let's hijack another car and go find an armored truck. We still need cash to get out of town."

Chuck laughed.

Stepping just off the sidewalk into a small alley, they checked their weapons. Armed with a look of ambition, they stuffed their weapons back into their holsters, prepared for anything and everything. As they walked briskly back toward San Francisco, they started watching for a suitable car. On the road ahead, traffic backed up behind the red light at a major intersection. A right turn would take them onto the freeway and they'd be back in business.

"Ever drive a van?" Richard asked.

"Lotsa times — even in my sleep."

"What about the white one? Fourth from the front, closest to the sidewalk?"

"Why not?"

"Light's changing, let's hurry."

The bandits ran out into the street behind the van and up to the driver's door. The traffic was starting to move quite rapidly, but a small car ahead of them stalled at the light, temporarily holding the flow of traffic.

"Perfect," Richard said, with a smile, "I can't believe our luck."

Richard grabbed the handle on the driver's door and swung it open. A big dog inside bared its fangs and lunged across the lady's lap at them. Instinctively, the bandits jumped backward, right into the path of a fast moving Mercury armored truck. They had taken life yesterday, inside a Mercury armored truck; today a Mercury armored truck took their lives.

* * *

Chapter 4   Intellectual Property

Protagonist: Detective Brian Weeder SFPD

Guests:
Gris Williams   Stanford graduate / engineer
Edward Williams   Uncle to Gris and owner of Navitech Engineering
Darrel James   Navitech engineer
Turk Fawson   CEO of C.I. (Compass International)
Mr. Ladlow   Patent Attorney
Ben Hetter   Flight Mechanic for C.I.
Greg Walston   Flight Mechanic for C.I.
Silvia   Secretary for Gris and Ed Williams
Glide   C.I. attorney
Boonee   C.I. attorney
Detective Lopez   Palo Alto Burglary detective
James Magar   Brian Weeder's supervisor
Navitech   A small company of about 50 people that develops and manufactures global navigation systems

C.I.   Compass International, a world wide corporation that markets navigational equipment; serious competitor for Navitech.

Red faced from the heated discussion with his uncle and owner of Navitech, Gris Williams pounded the table as he emphasized, "If we don't think big and act big, we won't get the accounts we need to survive." Drawing a breath he added, "What's more, our competition will catch and overtake us in a few months."

"Gris, we just don't have the money to develop your Global Guardian on the scale you want. We'll have to build one or two, sell them – then build three or four when we get revenue," Ed Williams argued.

Weary from debating with his Uncle Ed for the last hour, Gris Williams leaned on the windowsill in his tiny office and stared at the fifty cars in the parking lot. He slowed his breathing to control his stress level as he considered his lack of options.

Money – it all boiled down to money. All his life he had needed money. His Uncle Ed always found cash in the amounts needed for school or to support him, but it was always a couple hundred here, or a thousand there – not the kind of funding needed to expand this small company for a global project. Gris was in the real world now. He was a Stanford graduate and full partner at Navitech, his uncle's company. The money, if they could get it, would allow development of the Global Guardian, a navigation project designed by Gris. Every day the project waited without funding, meant the potential loss of tens of thousands of dollars of revenue to Navitech.

His Uncle Ed, founder of Navitech, was equally weary from the arguing. Staring at his ceramic coffee mug sitting on the edge of his nephew's desk, Ed let his mind slip for a moment. Fifteen years ago, Gris, as a small boy, had given him the cup as a Father's Day present. Today, that same boy was a brilliant engineer with a state-of-the-art design for a global navigation system. The design would very likely revolutionize commercial navigation throughout the world. It was all a matter of money and timing.

A strong, prideful man, Ed knew what Gris wanted; he wanted the same thing, but the cash wasn't available. He'd hidden the fact from Gris that he'd hocked his house and small company of fifty people to pay for the boy's education. At times he wondered if he did the right thing to offer Gris a partnership in his struggling company instead of encouraging him to join a large corporation after graduation. Arguing was a waste of time. Ed knew this, but didn't know how to tell his young partner the development money was gone and there wasn't any more.

Gris lowered his voice and spoke toward the window while watching his uncle's reflection, "So tell me again how we develop the Global Guardian without development money?"

The uncle sipped his coffee, it was cold and disgusting, but he swallowed it anyway. "We'll take in some partners, who have the money to help us set it up."

"They'll want to control it."

"Maybe."

The thought of anyone outside of Navitech having control of his design was totally unacceptable. "Then there's no other alternative?" Gris asked with a sigh.

Ed shook his head negatively.

A terrible feeling of disappointment swept over Gris. He felt as though he'd just failed on the final, critical play at a college championship game. Gris struggled to cope. He was weary of the discussion and was careful not to step back into the argument just finished. "Got any good prospects?"

"Maybe."

"You'll let me read everything before you sign it?"

"You're my partner aren't you?"

They stared at each other silently, exchanging respect, family love and of course, friendship.

The moment was interrupted by Ed's secretary knocking on the closed door and peering through the glass panel beside it.

Ed leaned forward to reach the door of the small office. "What is it Silvia?"

"You have a two-o'clock meeting."

Ed glanced at his watch. If he left immediately, he'd barely have time to drive through the traffic and not be late. He dismissed Silvia with a nod and turned to speak to his nephew. "I'll keep you informed."

"Do that," Gris said in a business tone.

Ed gave him a nod and closed the door.

The following day, Gris sat at the computer console in the laboratory with the system technician. Gris played with commands sent to the prototype navigation system. At last, a smile of satisfaction crept onto his face. "Yes! I think we've got it." Gris shared a "high-five" with the technician. "Ed's got to see this – " He left the laboratory to search for his uncle. When he couldn't find him in any of the offices, he stopped by Silvia's desk. "Seen Ed?"

"He hasn't come in today," she said, looking up from her keyboard.

Gris checked his watch, it was nearly noon. His uncle was a morning person; it was unlike him to not be at Navitech this time of the day. "Perhaps he overslept?"

"Would you like me to call his house?"

"Good idea," Gris agreed, heading into his office, "Let me speak to him when you get him on the phone."

"Yes Mr. Williams."

Gris turned and gave her a reminding look.

"I forgot — " she said, apologizing for the formal salutation. She knew the young engineer preferred to be addressed on a first name basis. "I'll call you when I get him," she added.

Gris closed the door to his office. Inside, he updated the hardware changes to the master schematics for the prototype. After several minutes, he glanced at Silvia through the glass panel beside the door. She appeared busy with the phone. Gris pulled up the progress log on his computer to update development on the prototype. He smiled as he thought about the press release he'd write as soon as the revised patent was filed next week.

Silvia's knock at the door brought him back to earth. "Gris, I can't find your uncle anywhere. I've even paged him a half dozen times."

She had been Ed's secretary for nearly ten years. If Silvia couldn't find Uncle Ed, no one could. Concerned, Gris asked, "Has Ed said anything about any new health problems?"

"No, he hasn't."

"You checked with his old army buddies?"

"I did -- nothing."

"Did you call his neighbor, Mr. Wilson?"

She nodded, "Yes, he says your uncle's car isn't at the house."

Something was wrong. Gris grabbed his jacket and cell phone. On his way out of the building, he ordered Silvia, "Check the hospital. Call his doctor and car mechanic. Call me if you find him, I'm going to look for him myself."

Gris spent the entire afternoon searching. Everywhere he looked, old friends, medical clinic, hospital emergency rooms, police station, no one had seen him.

Hours later, Gris returned to his uncle's house and searched for notes or any clue to his uncle's disappearance. He checked closets for missing clothing and shoes. He checked the bathroom, for medicines or the absence of them. Had his uncle been living at the house during the past few days? Gris searched for clues. He checked for missing tooth brushes, he even checked expiration dates on the milk in the refrigerator. Everything seemed to be in place except his uncle.

A feeling of cold despair crept over him. There were a great many details about his uncle he suddenly realized he didn't know. Even though he spent an hour, in direct contact, yesterday with his uncle, he was unable to remember what the man had been wearing.

Gris phoned Sylvia. "Hello Sylvia? It's Gris here. – Find anything?"

"Nothing. How about you?"

"Nothing here either," Gris rubbed his head as he thought. "Who was his last appointment with?"

"C.I."

"Is that Compass International?"

"Yes, I believe so."

"Who'd he see there?"

"Let me check," she said, opening his calendar on her computer terminal. "Uh – says he was to meet with Mr. Fawson, yesterday afternoon at two."

"Turk Fawson!" he exclaimed. A bitter taste of bile, reached his throat, adding to his distress. Gris did meet Fawson once, but took an instant dislike to the man. Fawson had an ego that wouldn't quit and he reeked of power and money and arrogance. Perhaps Uncle Edward had gone there for financial backing. Gris shivered – he'd like to think his uncle wasn't that desperate for financial help. Pushing the phone handset closer to his mouth he asked, "Did you call C.I. ?"

"I did," Sylvia replied, "But Mr. Fawson's secretary said their meeting was brief yesterday and Ed hasn't called him back as promised."

Gris opened the electronic address book on his uncle's desk in the study. He punched in C.I.; the address and phone number appeared. "I'll give Fawson a call myself."

"You have the number?"

"Yes, it's here on Ed's desk." Gris put his finger on the receiver button of the phone, preparing to end the conversation with Silvia, "I'll let you know if I find anything."

"Okay," Silvia said, hanging up.

The nephew pressed the button to terminate the connection. He quickly dialed C.I. when the dial-tone sounded again.

"Compass International. How may I direct your call?"

It was one of those dammed automated answering systems. Gris tried several times to find a human voice at the other end, but finally gave up in frustration. He slammed the phone down in disgust.

With a sigh, Gris glanced at his watch. It was nearly five o'clock in the evening. He knew Missing Persons wouldn't take a report unless the person had been missing over twenty-four hours; Uncle Ed qualified. Gris grabbed a recent picture from the desk and headed for the Palo Alto police station.

The police accepted the missing persons report, but the investigation would take time.

Gris agonized through the second day without word of his uncle. On the third day, he decided to take his bike for a ride on the skyline highway connecting the hills along the San Francisco Peninsula. The nephew was sure the fresh air would do him good, and he desperately needed to do something with his pent-up energy.

The climb up the winding road to the top of the hill had been more than Gris remembered. He made a mental note to do this more often, lest his office job make him soft. At the top, he stopped for a brief rest to replenish his body with water.

Following the short break, the cyclist positioned his helmet and sun glasses. He pushed heavily on the pedals with his bike aimed north, toward San Francisco. His speed increased smoothly until he cruised along at a solid twenty miles per hour. Ten minutes down the road. His front tire went flat. The cyclist was unhappy, but he'd seen flat tires before; they were part of the biking experience, like rain and sun and traffic.

Coasting to a stop, Gris unsnapped his shoes from the pedals and pulled the bike to the shoulder of the road. He looked up and down the highway. It was pretty straight and he could be easily seen from either direction by passing motorists. If such a place existed, this was a good place to have a flat. He busied himself with the task of repairing his tire.

As he was gathering his tools to put them back into the small kit he carried in his back pack, he saw an interesting object lying within reach at the edge of the pavement. It puzzled him he hadn't noticed the half-inch, gold-colored bolt before. He picked it up and examined it. It felt slightly warm to the touch, though it was resting in the shadow of a tree beside the road. He shrugged. On a whim, he tossed in his back pack, taking it with him.

* * *

Detective Brian Weeder, examined the bludgeoned body found in the mud at the edge of the bay. He stood up to look at the surroundings, hoping to see any window where a neighbor might have seen the perpetrator or perpetrators of this heinous deed. There were no houses, only blind, old brick walls in the aging industrial area of the city. That's exactly why the body was dumped here. Brian wasn't surprised; he'd seen bodies here several times before.

Pulling on a pair of thin plastic gloves before reaching into the man's pockets for identification, Brian sighed. "Such a waste," he said, to himself. Carefully, he probed, being mindful to avoid any sharp objects such as syringes or razor blades often found in the pockets of the dead. The corpse had nothing in his pockets. Brian leaned forward, trying to see what was left of the man's face. Whatever object struck him, had left some very distinctive marks, but had destroyed the face enough to make him unrecognizable. Judging from the business suit, the man wasn't poor or homeless. His fingernails were clean. Brian looked at the man's legs. The shoes were gone, but it's a common practice among the homeless to scavenge bodies dumped in that area. Brian stepped back, and motioned for the coroner to take possession of the body.

Two days later, with the forensic evidence on his desk, Brian thumbed through the recent filings of missing persons, hoping to make a match. On a report from Palo Alto, the distinctive, dark-purple suit caught his attention. He pulled his magnifying glass from his desk and examined the snapshot. At times like these, he wished fuzzy photographs were illegal. The detective squinted and moved the picture into better lighting. The picture was quite blurry, but he felt fairly certain it matched the fabric weave of the suit worn by the john doe he was investigating. He checked the other "stats". Weight, race, age. . . well, the coroner's report set the man's age in his late fifties. Brian checked race and hair coloring. The match was close; he'd run the thumb print through the Department of Motor Vehicles. Ten minutes later, he had a match. The man was Edward Williams.

After attaching a copy of the missing persons report to his clipboard, Brian signed out of the office and drove down the peninsula. He wanted to personally inform the nephew, Gris

Williams, of his uncle's death. Notifying relatives and friends in person is good practice since the surviving person might have a medical condition that would result in mortal shock or injury, when informed.

Dutifully, Brian stood in Gris Williams' office after giving him the bad news about his uncle. "I'm sorry for your loss, Mr. Williams. It's always harsh when a loved one dies, but even worse when someone close dies in such a violent death."

"You say my uncle was mugged?"

"On the surface, it appears that way."

Gris slowly stood up to look out the small window behind him. The weather hadn't changed from the day he argued with Ed, but somehow, the sun didn't seem to shine as bright. As he looked onto the parking lot, his grief blinded him. Uncle Ed was like a father to him; it was a terrible loss. In silence he suppressed the tears.

Detective Weeder looked around the tiny office. A small bookshelf beside the window held engineering reference books. The wall to his left held several pictures of Gris Williams and his uncle from past years. Brian glanced back at the young man, still facing the window. He was young and he'd adjust – they nearly always do, he reasoned.

As Brian turned to leave, an object on the desk, beside the desk calendar, caught his eye. The detective looked a second time. It was a silver, half-inch bolt. Brian reached over the cluster of pencils held upright in a beer mug. He retrieved the bolt for a closer look. He knew what he was looking for, yet it shocked him to see his initials on the head of the bolt. How did it get from his desk at the police station to Mr. Williams' desk? He had no idea. Well, now that he knew where it was, he'd make the effort to reclaim it. His initials were proof. "Uh – Mr. Williams," he began, not wanting to add stress to the nephew's grief, "This is an interesting bolt you have."

Gris turned to face the detective, eyes reddened. He said nothing.

Brian tossed the bolt gently, playing with its mass. "Can you tell me where you got it?"

The young man sat down in his chair behind the desk. He plucked a tissue from the box on his desk and blew his nose. He wadded the tissue and tossed it into the trash can beside the desk before answering, "Found it."

"May I ask where?"

"On the Skyline."

"Skyline?"

"That's right. It was lying alongside the road when I stopped to fix a flat."

Brian made a face, "That's very interesting."

"Why is it interesting?"

"Because it belongs to me."

Gris looked up at the detective. He pondered the claim for a few seconds before answering, "What makes you say that?"

"Well, because it has my initials on the head."

"It does?"

Brian smiled lightly, as he turned the bolt to show the young man. "See the initials are right here." He pointed to the head of the bolt.

Gris stared through his blurry eyes, but could see no indication of the detective's claim. "Where? I don't see anything?"

Brian leaned over to locate them again for himself, but no matter how he looked, or turned the bolt in the light, the initials were gone. "Uh – that's strange, I saw them just a minute ago."

Gris shrugged. "I had a similar experience."

"You did?"

"Yeah, when I threw it in my back pack to take it home, I could have sworn it was gold. But when I took it out, it was silver."

Brian suddenly recalled the day it disappeared from his desk. He remembered a young boy, visiting at the police station with his father. The boy had a similar bolt – gold in color. He remembered checking the bolt for his initials; there were none.

The detective recalled each encounter with the bolt. On every occurrence, it had been at the scene of a crime. Something was very unsettling about all of this. Perhaps he should play his hunch and leave the bolt here, to see if it would cross his path again. He dropped the bolt on the desk, in front of Gris. "Maybe it has one of the prism-reflecting surfaces that change color depending on how the light shines on it."

Williams picked the bolt up and handled it. He turned it various angles, but it changed nothing.   "Perhaps," he agreed passively.

"Well, I – " Brian broke off.

The young engineer offered the bolt to the detective, "Want it back?"

Brian put his hands up in a push-back gesture, "Uh, no. I don't see my initials on it now. I was probably mistaken."

Gris insisted, "You're welcome to it, if you want it."

"No that's okay, you keep it, but let me know if my initials reappear."

The nephew shrugged and tossed it back on his desk, beside his calendar. "Okay, but you're welcome to it."

There was a knock on the door; Gris motioned for Silvia to enter.

"I'm sorry to interrupt you, Gris, but your attorney, Mr. Ladlow, would like you to drop by this morning, if possible."

Gris checked his watch. "Tell him I'll be there in about an hour."

The secretary nodded and left the office, returning to her desk.

Brian changed the subject, "I have to leave now, Mr. Williams. It's been nice meeting you. I'll be in contact when I find more information on your uncle's death."

The nephew leaned across his desk to shake hands. "Thank your Detective Weeder. Please let me know if you find the killer. I'd really like to see whoever took my Uncle Ed's life punished."

They shook hands and Brian took one last glance at the bolt before leaving. *"Strange! Very Strange!"* he thought to himself.

Before the door closed, Silvia stuck her head inside the nephew's office. "Was the officer here about Ed?"

Gris motioned for her to come in and sit down. "Ed's been killed," he said bluntly. He felt dragging it out was the wrong thing to do. "Detective Weeder said it looks as though he was mugged."

The secretary made a sound like someone just threw cold water on her. She drew a deep breath and cringed. "Do they know who did it?"

"Not yet."

"When was he killed?"

"Probably the day he was last here." Brian said, looking down at the top of his desk.

She reached for a tissue from the desk top.

"His car's still missing too," Brian said, before remaining silent for a time. Finally, he asked, "Can you help me with his final arrangements, Silvia?"

Still holding the tissue over her nose, she nodded silently.

Gris leaned forward on his desk, rubbing his forehead, as though it would help. After several seconds he added, "Oh yes, we'd better let the staff know what's happened. If you'll ask them to gather in the lunch room, I'll make the announcement in a few minutes."

Silvia sniffled.

After the announcement, Gris drove to Mr. Ladlow's office. The patent attorney was busy with another client but dismissed him quickly when notified that Gris had arrived. He immediately motioned for the young engineer to come into his office.

As soon as he closed the door behind Gris, Ladlow began speaking, "We've got a problem, Mr. Williams." He seated himself behind his desk and pulled open a drawer to remove a folder. He thumbed through the folder, stopping when he found a copy of a document. He checked it briefly to ensure it was the one he wanted to show Gris. Placing the paper in front of the younger man, he resumed his explanation, then suddenly interrupted himself, "It seems your uncle – " The lawyer paused. With a concerned expression he asked, "By the way, has your uncle been located yet?"

Before Gris could answer, the lawyer added, "Your secretary said he disappeared several days ago."

"He's been killed," Gris said with a sigh.

Ladlow was silent for a moment, unsure what to say.

Gris drew a deep breath, realizing this was just the third of many times he'd have to relate the story. "I just finished speaking with Detective Weeder, a San Francisco policeman. He said they located a body yesterday that has been positively identified as my Uncle Ed."

The lawyer sat back in his chair and removed his reading glasses. "What happened?"

"They say it looks like he was mugged."

"How awful – "

Gris tried to look passive, but his face took on the look of sadness, "Yes it is."

"I didn't know — "

Gris sat in silence.

Ladlow looked disturbed. "This changes everything," he said, with a note of panic in his voice. "It complicates everything even more than before."

"I don't understand?" Gris said, making eye contact with the lawyer.

Putting on his reading glasses, the patent attorney leaned across his large, wooden desk. He pointed to the document which was up-side-down to him as he spoke. "This is a copy of a sales agreement brought in here, late yesterday, by a lawyer for Compass International." He stopped to draw a breath, "It says your uncle sold the patent rights to the navigation system Navitech was developing for a relatively small amount of cash."

"What?"

"Yes, that's what it shows." Ladlow pointed to the signature at the bottom. "Is this your uncle's signature?"

Gris scrutinized the document. "It looks similar, but the loops look a bit larger."

"I thought that too, but I'm no expert. We checked it against his signatures we have on file, and the writing is close."

"Fawson!"

"I beg your pardon?"

"Fawson!" Gris fumed, "He's been trying to steal it, ever since he got wind of this project!"

"Who's Fawson?"

"He's CEO of Compass International. C.I. is a large, international company that produces navigational systems. Their budget is at least a hundred times the budget of Navitech." Gris made eye contact with the attorney, "And Fawson's afraid Navitech will put him out of business."

"I see," the lawyer said, "It's starting to make sense." He looked back at Gris over his reading glasses. "It sounds as though the man is unscrupulous."

Gris fumed, "Fawson and a couple of his body guards invited me for a ride in his limousine one Friday night, after I stepped out of a nightclub. They thought I'd be too drunk to say 'no' to them."

"What did they do?" Ladlow asked, as though he had never heard of such a thing.

"They wanted me to sign a paper to give them my patent rights." Gris tensed his shoulders as though he wanted to fight. "They offered me a hundred thousand at first. When I wouldn't take it, they went up to a half million."

"Obviously you didn't sign."

"Heck no! I didn't sign."

"Did they threaten you in any way?"

"Of course they threatened me, but I had no witnesses. There was nothing I could prove."

"What happened?"

"Well, two guys — big enough to eat hay — jumped out of the shadows in the parking lot. They grabbed me by the arms and dragged me into their boss's car for a business conversation at two in the morning. It was one of those deals I dared not refuse if I wanted to go home that night. I sure as heck wouldn't call it being sociable."

"Did they physically strike you?"

"I didn't give 'em the chance." Gris fidgeted as he remembered the incident.

"What did you do?"

Gris stood up from the chair in front of Ladlow's desk. He paced the deep carpet as he breathed heavily. "I told them I drank too much and needed to throw up."

"And?"

"They let me out of the car, so I wouldn't barf on them or the Fawson's nice upholstery. Soon as I got them to stand back, I ran like hell."

"Did you report it to the police?"

"I thought about it, but they had all the witnesses."

"Did you tell your uncle?"

The nephew paused, finally answering softly, "Yeah, I did. I warned him to watch out for them."

"What did he say?"

Gris laughed. "Uncle Ed? He was fearless. He said they'd have to kill him before he'd sign anything."

"You think he meant it?"

"If you knew my Uncle Ed, you wouldn't ask such a question."

"Explain?"

"Uncle Ed served in Vietnam. He was decorated twice for bravery. Ed was one of those guys who felt that people of power abused the loyalty of the soldiers. On the other side of the issue, he felt the people in the peace movement were cowards. He felt they didn't have any heart or loyalty toward their fellow countrymen serving as serviceman. But Uncle Ed always thought any man in his unit, deserved Ed Williams' life, if he needed it."

Ladlow looked impressed. He paused for a moment before asking, "Was the meeting outside the nightclub, your only contact with people at Compass International?"

"No, their attorneys came to the Navitech several times to negotiate a deal."

"What happened?"

"We threw 'em out."

Ladlow smiled. He slid the document back to his side of the desk and filed it inside the folder again. "Did you tell the detective any of this?"

Gris stopped his pacing and leaned on the desk. "No, I didn't." He looked tired for a moment. "It simply slipped my mind when I heard about Uncle Ed."

"I'd tell him as soon as possible, if I were you."

"I intend to."

* * *

The following day, everyone at Navitech was quietly trying to cope with the loss of Ed Williams. Many of the key people, including Gris and Silvia buried themselves in their work to forget. The funeral would be the next day, and there would be time to remember the personable man who founded the company.

Silvia saw them first, two cars, and a limo, followed by a luxury sedan. They blocked the driveway at Navitech. A woman and a man in expensive suits, carrying briefcases got out of the luxury sedan. Shortly afterwards, a short man wearing a three-piece business suit climbed out of the limo behind his two, bulky body guards.

"The short guy with the cigar is Turk Fawson," Gris said to Silvia, as they watched through his office window.

"Weren't they here before, about three months ago?"

"Yeah, they were," Gris acknowledged with a nod.

"What's he want?" she asked with a puzzled tone.

"Thinks he's got us on the run, I suspect."

"Because of the forged document, we talked about this morning?"

"Yeah, he knows we don't have money to fight him in court."

"So – what are you going to do?"

"Fight him. What else can I do?"

"Can't the police arrest him?"

Gris shook his head, "No, not without proof he killed Ed or forged Ed's signature on the bill of sale."

"What do you want me to do?" Silvia asked, frightened of the unwelcome guests.

"Go down the hallway first, then out into the lab and tell everyone to put away anything confidential. These guys aren't engineers and probably won't know the difference between a bolt and a hall-effect sensor, but I don't want to take any chances. Tell our guys to keep everything hidden until they leave."

"Okay!" she said, departing quickly.

Gris stepped outside of his office into the small lobby area in front of Silvia's desk. He glanced at the appointment calendar showing on her computer monitor. He closed it, allowing the screen saver to pop up. Crossing his arms, he turned and faced the entrance door, waiting.

Thirty seconds later, the woman and man with briefcases entered, chatting about their golfing game. Gris guessed they were attorneys. The two body guards entered next; each took a position on opposite sides of the door. Fawson strutted in last, smoking his cigar. He looked around as though he just bought the place. He took off his expensive sunglasses and brushed his way past the two attorneys to take the lead.

Pointing toward his chest with the cool end of his lighted cigar, the short man began, "I'm – "

"I know who you are," Gris interrupted. "What are you doing here?"

Turk pointed over his left shoulder with his lighted cigar, "This is Ms. Boonee," he said. Then pointing to the man on his right with the cigar he said, "and this is Mr. Glide. They're my attorneys."

"You'll have to take it outside," Gris interrupted.

A look of surprise hung on Fawson's face, "What?"

Gris planted his feet apart to form a comfortable stance. Crossing his arms, he looked the little man in the eye saying, "You'll have to take it outside," Gris repeated himself.

"You're a fearless son-of-a – " he said, before Mr. Glide cut him off.

"He means the cigar, sir."

"Huh?" Fawson said, looking back at the male attorney.

"It's illegal to smoke inside of the buildings in California." Gris warned.

"Really?" Fawson asked, raising an eyebrow in surprise.

"Yes sir," the lawyer replied, "You better get rid of it."

"Oh," he said. With a smile, he turned and handed the cigar to one of the body guards, "Take it outside and finish it. It's Cuban."

The guard left with the lighted stogie.

"You're not welcome here, Fawson," Gris informed him.

The little man ran his tongue around the inside of his cheeks. He surveyed the room. The focus of his dark eyes danced along the ceiling where the walls met it. Scanning down the wall to the business licenses, he paused as though he owned time and licensed its use to everyone else. "You may not like me, Williams, but we're going to do business together."

"You're right about at least one thing. . . I don't like you, Fawson."

Turk studied the young engineer, obviously looking for a chink in his armor.

Williams sternly locked eyes with his opponent, biding his time.

Fawson finally lost the eye contest. He nudged Mr. Glide saying, "Show him."

Silvia returned. She quietly pressed against the walls of the small room, trying to work her way back behind her desk, where she'd feel more comfortable.

"I'm not interested in your forgery, Fawson. Why are you here anyway?"

"Since C.I. owns the patent rights to your gadget, I'd like to make you an offer to buy this thing you call a company."

"That's enough!" Gris shouted, "Get out."

Mr. Glide, stepped between the two men, "Please wait, Mr. Williams. Mr. Fawson was only joking. He really does want to do business with you."

The nephew seethed, but did step back. Perhaps it was curiosity, perhaps it was to watch for them to do something incriminating that he could prove. He decided to wait.

The lawyer opened his briefcase, removing a list that he handed to Gris. "Here, Mr. Williams, is a list of items and personnel that Compass International believes it can use. If you are willing to part with these items, C.I. is prepared to pay you top dollar."

The engineer glanced down through the list. Most items were names of key development personnel, programmers, testing hardware, and of course any existing hardware and software prototypes. He flipped back to the cover page, noting the date. Making eye contact with Fawson he slowly wadded the list into a ball and dropped it into Silvia's trash can, beside her desk. "I see your spies have been very busy, Fawson. But I'd rather burn the place down than let you have any of it."

Turk Fawson opened his mouth, but was interrupted by his lawyer, Boonee.

"Mr. Williams, I have something I think you really should see, before making any decisions."

105

"I don't care about any of your offers. I just want you all to leave," Gris said, raising his voice.

"Mr. Williams, you're not being fair," Boonee said, raising the pitch of her voice in a teasing manner.

Gris counted to ten, as Uncle Ed had always taught him. He didn't like any of these people, but the lawyer was only trying to do her job. He could always say "No!" Gris stepped toward his office and glanced inside for anything confidential that might be open; it was clear. He turned back toward his secretary, "Silvia, watch them. If they try to go anywhere except outside, call me."

"Yes, Mr. Williams," she replied, intentionally using the formal protocol.

"No one can say I'm not a fair man," Gris said, as he faced Boonee. The owner and new CEO waved Ms. Boonee into his tiny office. "Just what is it you have, that so tempting that I can't resist it?"

"Well sir, Mr. Fawson mentioned he has approached you about doing business before and you have refused."

"Don't remind me."

"Well sir, Mr. Fawson would like you to look over these figures. He estimates you could make several millions more if Navitech and Compass International joined forces to build your guidance and navigation system."

Gris studied the figures. He wasn't interested, but the numbers were very educational. They gave a lot of detail regarding methods and procedures to be used in building and marketing the system.

Boonee sat quietly, looking around the office. Her eye fell on the half-inch bolt, beside the desk calendar. She picked it up and was preparing to examine it more closely when it gave her a sizable electric shock. She recoiled immediately, throwing the bolt into the air. The object bounced on the desk-top with a loud bang before coming to rest almost exactly where it had been found. The only difference was its color. It had turned coal-black.

Gris looked up briefly, but otherwise ignored the incident. He continued to memorize as much of the detail as he could, hoping it could be of use to him, in some way, at a later date. After finishing the last page, he looked again at Ms. Boonee, who sat quietly twiddling her thumbs, apparently afraid to touch anything in the office.

"Ms. Boonee," Gris began, sharing eye contact with the middle-aged woman, "I rather like your proposition."

Boonee smiled.

"In fact," the engineer admitted, "If Fawson had offered me this deal first, I might have taken it."

The attorney's lower lip puckered in distress, "You said 'might have'?"

"Right."

"I don't understand?"

"It's simple." Gris said, looking her in the eye.

"Please explain?"

Williams leaned back in his chair. The room was too small to prop his feet on his desk, so he pushed his chair sideways until his shoes barely gained purchase on the right corner of his desk. He closed his eyes and smiled.

"But Mr. Williams, we offered you a very handsome price for your company. We guaranteed positions and benefits for your employees at C.I. We even guaranteed your name would be associated with any and all success. Plus, we offered you stock options and millions in salary, regardless of success. What more could we possibly give you that we haven't?"

Opening his eyes, Gris put his feet down. He stood up and slowly walked to the open door of his office. He motioned for Boonee to leave, handing her the proposal.

Fawson held his hands as though he expected to catch a basketball. "Well?"

"It was a very enlightening proposal, Mr. Fawson. But I'm not interested."

"Why?" Fawson screamed in rage.

Gris turned to Boonee. "The one thing you can't give me in this deal that I really want — is my Uncle Ed." He turned back toward Fawson, "But the one thing you did — give me, was who killed him."

"What are you talking about, Williams?" Fawson said, with an icy stare.

With a smile of satisfaction, Gris said, "Check the details in your super proposal. You offered me everything, but nothing for Uncle Ed. Now check the date on your document, it was dated two days before my uncle's body was found."

"Huh," Fawson exclaimed, "Let me see that!" He grabbed the document from Boonee to see for himself. "It's a mistake — a typo!"

"It is and you made it," Williams said smugly, "See you in court."

"Burn it," the little emperor ordered. He pointed his finger at Williams, "It's your word against ours."

"It always was," Gris admitted. "And you're going to have a hard time getting my Uncle Ed to cash payment that never existed, for the forged sale of patent rights. Now get Bonnie and Clyde out of my building before I have you all arrested for trespassing."

The agitated group left only to have Mr. Glide rush back through the door. He raced directly to Sylvia's trash can where he dived into it for his discarded proposal. It would be terribly unwise to leave it behind as evidence.

* * *

Two days later, Uncle Ed's car was found not far from where his body had been found several days earlier. Detective Brian Weeder patiently waited while the crime lab technicians dusted the car for fingerprints. When the car was opened, he watched as the team collected samples of hair, and other debris from the interior. There were two, notable items collected that caught Brian's attention. The first was a phone number written on the inside of a matchbook cover. The outside of the cover advertised a local bar. It occurred to the detective that someone had been watching too many old, black-and-white movies.

Brian had a hunch about the car that would be very difficult to prove. He personally had checked this street shortly after finding Mr. Williams' body; the car had not been there. It meant, the car had been dumped later. The second item found inside was a small bag containing a bicycle spoke-wrench and a credit card slip for the purchase at a shop in the Silicon Valley. Not many muggers travel by bicycle. The purchase tag showed a date for the next day after Ed Williams' body was found. It reeked of planted evidence, but Brian decided to keep an open mind.

Armed with the matchbook, Detective Weeder searched for the bar advertized on the cover. He located it easily, parked his car and went inside.

The bar was dark and small with yellowed walls from years of smokers lighting up. A half dozen small, round, wooden tables lined the floor. They were old, and nicked, most of them soiled by years of patrons' hands rubbing their surfaces. The bar, likewise, was an old wooden counter, hand varnished, with signs of renovation to accommodate the newer conveniences of computerized cash registers, and liquor-dispensing equipment. Behind the bar, a large mirror reflected images back of the patrons, who chose to sit at the bar. The bartender, a man in his mid fifties, seemed to be the only one in the place except – for two regulars keeping him company at the end of the bar.

Brian knew something of the place. He knew bets could be placed here on games. Illegal, but nearly every bar had its covert gambling to a larger or smaller extent. On a hunch, he looked for the public phone, finding it near the rest rooms. In the dim light, he dropped the coins into the slots and dialed the number inside the matchbook cover. The bartender, glanced down at his feet. In the darkened room, a small lamp beneath the counter cast dim shadows of the man against the rows of bottles in front of the mirror. The bulky bartender went into the back room, pausing only to remove the key from the cash register as he left. Brian got an answer on the other end of the line.

"Jakes?" the deep voiced man gasped, nearly out of breath.

"A friend gave me this number," Brian lied.

"So what'a ya want?"

"What have you got?" the detective replied.

"I got 'em all. What's your pleasure?"

"Niner's?"

"Yeah, what game?" he puffed.

"Cowboys."

There was a long pause. Only the sound of labored breathing came to Brian's ear pressed to the pay phone.

"Say! Who is this?"

"Don't you have odds on the game?" Weeder asked.

"They already played that game. Who is this?"

"I'll meet you at the bar," Brian said, hanging up.

He strolled over to the bar and waited for the bartender to return to his post.

The burley man plugged the key back into the register as he rounded the corner from the back room. He spotted Brian immediately and came directly to him. "Yeah? So what was that all about?" The heavy man nearly wheezed with each breath.

"What's your name?" the detective asked.

"Who want's to know?"

The detective pulled his credentials and displayed his badge. "The SF PD wants to know."

The man leaned against the counter and shook his head in disgust. "Should'a known."

"Relax. I just need information today."

"Try the li-bury."

"I said, relax. I'm not here to bust you. I'm looking for information."

The bartender looked at the two regulars at the far end of the bar. One of them was getting empty. "Be with you in a sec.," he said, as he turned to take care of business. Another beer was taken from the refrigerator, opened and placed in front of the patron. A short conversation was exchanged between the bartender and the second customer, then the bartender came back to Brian. He took his pencil, kept next to the register and recorded the beer on the customer's tab.

"Have to keep 'em happy."

"Understand," Brian agreed.

"So what'a ya need?"

Brian handed him the matchbook. "Recognize this?"

Without bothering to pick it up, the man leaned on the counter, his palms equally spaced on either side of the object. "Yeah, I got a million of 'em. So what?"

"That your hand writing inside?"

Continuing to lean on his left arm, the man picked up the cover with his right hand, flipping it open with his forefinger. "Nope, never slash my seven's."

"Got any clients by the name of 'Williams'?"

111

D.Malisch

"Don't think so?"

"I want you to check," the detective insisted.

The bartender slapped the matchbook back onto the counter. Sighing deeply as though he was being driven against his will, he started toward the back room. He suddenly stopped, returned to the register where he retrieved the key. In the process, he gave the detective the evil eye – Brian struggled not to laugh. Seconds later, the bookie came back with a small ledger. He dropped the book in on the counter and ran his pudgy finger along the line of entries for the last month. "Yeah, here's one."

"Got an address?"

The man looked at Brian with an indignant look. "Don't use 'em."

"What do you have showing?"

He grumbled something unintelligible. Locating the name again, he added, "Owes me a lot of money."

"How much?"

" 'Bout forty grand."

"Ed Williams owes you forty thousand?"

"No."

"How's that?"

"Gris Williams owes me."

The eyebrows rose on Brian's forehead. He hadn't really expected the debt to belong to the nephew. "How long's he been in the rears?"

The bookie, thumbed through the pages, examining the entries for several seconds. "About a week."

"Can you be more precise?" Weeder asked.

"Nine days."

Making a mental calculation, Brian estimated that was about two days before the uncle was killed. That would give motive, if the nephew killed his uncle, but it didn't feel right.

Looking up at the bartender, Brian said, "Thanks, I'll let you know if I need more information."

"Oh sure! Anything to help a cop," the bartender answered sarcastically.

The investigation seemed to be going down a path Weeder hadn't expected. He needed to check a few things to make sure he wasn't experiencing a red herring.

After returning to the station, the detective placed a call to the credit card people. He confirmed the card number used on the purchase tag wasn't reported stolen and belonged to Mr. Gris Williams. It looked bad for the young engineer.

Weeder remembered the bolt, on the young graduate's desk at Navitech. Was it significant? He didn't know? Brian picked up the phone and called the father of the boy who had most likely carried the bolt out of the police station a couple of weeks ago. The conversation was very enlightening. Brian remembered the armored car robbery. In fact, he'd handled the investigation, but no one had mentioned a bolt in all of this. After hearing the story from the boy's father, Brian called Mother Superior at the boy's school. Again, he was fascinated by the story. She related the lessons the children taught her about the bolt and the way it changed color depending on truth. She was a believer, but had no idea where the bolt was today.

Given the fact the bolt was not black when Gris had handled it, Brian was further convinced the young man had done no wrong to his uncle. He'd need to search further to find the killer or killers.

Brian dialed the bookie's number again. It rang five or six times before being answered.

"Jakes?"

"Hello, this is Detective Brian Weeder, we talked earlier today, remember?"

"Wish I didn't."

"Tell me. . . did Gris Williams ever come in to see you personally?"

"Oh sure. Everyone has to come in to set it up. But once I know the guy, we can work out other arrangements."

"What did Gris look like?"

The bookie thought for a few seconds, "Oh, I'd say he was about six-three, maybe two-hundred-sixty pounds."

"I see," Brian said, encouraged, "About how old would you say he was?"

"About mid-thirties. . . yeah, that's about right."

"I understand. Thanks, I'll remember your help."

"Hey if you see him, tell him he owes me. Will ya?"

Brian laughed, "When I see someone matching your description, I'll be sure to let him know."

As far as Brian was concerned, that let Gris Williams off the hook. It was some kind of a frame up, unless there just happened to be someone else by the same name running around California. He logged onto the Department of Motor Vehicles' data base and confirmed there wasn't but one Gris Williams.

Weeder was thinking about the problem when the police captain walked into the room. He spotted Brian and came directly to him.

"Uh Weeder, we got a hot tip on that mugging you found last week."

"Oh?"

"Yeah, some guy called in and said the nephew killed him."

"That doesn't surprise me," Brian said, realizing it was the next step in framing the nephew.

"It doesn't?"

"No, I've been looking into it, and I've — "

"Good. Good," the captain said, "Now hustle on over to see Judge Wong and get a search warrant to search his house and car. We want to get this thing wrapped up as soon as possible."

"That's not what I meant – "

"That's okay, Weeder, we all need a little help now and then, so pick up the paperwork from Sharron and take to Judge Wong, before he leaves for the day."

"But!"

"End of conversation, Weeder. Now go!"

Detective Weeder did as ordered, he got the search warrant, contacted the police in Palo Alto, arranged for the search and joined them an hour later.

The sun had already slipped behind the coastal mountain range and the amber street lights were beginning to come on. Brian had a bad feeling about this search. He didn't know what, but he knew they'd find planted evidence somewhere.

As the key figure in Navitech, Brian knew Gris would not be home for at least another hour or more. The locksmith let them enter and they went from room to room in the house. Nothing seemed unusual until one of the searchers discovered a heavy oriental vase hidden in the bottom of his bedroom closet. Closer inspection showed damage to its surface and traces of blood, as though someone had tried to clean blood stains from the surface. It was logged as evidence.

Twenty minutes after the house search was finished, Gris drove up in his car. He was ordered out and it too was searched. Beneath the rear seat, they found a rather sizable check issued to Ed Williams. The memo line stated it was the first of several payments for purchase of patent rights on the Global Guardian system, designed by Gris for Navitech. Also under the seat was a copy of the document, with his uncle's forged signature, stating the terms of the sale.

"It's a C.I. trick!" Gris screamed. "It's a forgery and C.I. planted it."

Brian was sick. He knew the young man was innocent, but the evidence said otherwise. He was forced to arrest Gris for his uncle's murder.

Weeder left the questioning to other detectives. He had no heart to harass the innocent. After hours of interrogation, Brian asked the other detectives to leave the room, so he could speak with Mr. Williams alone.

He looked at the young man, exhausted by an eighteen-hour day, then arrested and questioned for another six hours. It was out of his hands for the moment. "Gris I'd like you to know I don't think you killed your uncle."

Gris didn't respond. He just hung his head and tried to sleep, leaning on his elbows.

Brian walked by him on the way out the door. He patted him gently on the shoulder as he passed. Outside, he ordered the detectives to have the prisoner put in a cell for the night. He scheduled himself to be the first to speak with him in the morning.

Shortly after dawn, Detective Brian Weeder signed into the jail, preparing to speak to Gris Williams while still in his cell. Weeder was heartened to see a few hours rest had improved the young man's responses.

"Good morning Gris. You're looking better this morning."

Gris continued tying his shoe after glancing up at the detective.

"Do you remember anything I said to you last night?"

He shook his head, "No, it's all one big blur."

Weeder motioned for the jailer to lock the door and leave them alone until he called. The detective sat down on the bunk beside Williams. "I told you I believe you're innocent."

The nephew stopped tying his shoe, listening.

"I think you're being framed, but I don't know who is behind it?"

He resumed tying his shoe. "C.I.," he said.

"Do you have a name?"

"Fawson. Turk Fawson killed my uncle." He said, not looking away from the shoestring.

"How do you know? Do you have proof?"

"Can't prove it, but he slipped up." Gris still didn't look up. He wasn't sure of Weeder's intentions, but wasn't convinced the detective hadn't lied about thinking he was being framed.

"What do you mean by 'he slipped up'?"

Gris pulled the shoelace tight and straightened the bow before looking at Brian. With a normal voice used for conversation, he said, "Fawson's been trying to cheat me out of my navigation system ever since I tried to patent it. He and two of his thugs tried to force me to sign papers several months ago in the parking lot of a local bar."

"What happened?"

"I got away." Gris looked into Weeder's eyes, "And I think my uncle didn't."

"Anything else?"

"Yeah, they faked his signature on that document they found under the seat on my car yesterday."

"I see."

"Yeah, and get this." Gris stood up, facing the detective, who also stood up. "They tried to force me to sell my company a few days ago, but their document had a date before you found my uncle's body, yet the document didn't include anything in it for him."

"Do you have a copy of the document?"

"No, didn't try to keep one; they'd claim it was a typo."

117

"I'm sure they would."

The room fell silent for a moment.

"You going to get me out?" Gris asked.

"I'm certainly going to work at it."

"By the way Gris, do you still have that bolt we talked about?"

"Yeah, it's on my desk. Why?"

"Has it changed color, by any chance?"

"Yeah it did."

"What color is it?"

"Black."

"Black?" A sign of worry crossed the lawman's face.

"Yeah, ever since that lady lawyer for Compass International touched it."

Brian's face brightened. "I don't know what's going to happen, Gris, but I've got a feeling, you've got justice on your side."

"When can I get out?"

"I don't know yet." Brian said, making a few notes to himself.

"I thought -?"

"I believe you, but you'll have to put up with incarceration a while longer. Just be sure you always tell the truth." Weeder stood up and walked toward the cell door. "You ready to go to the interrogation room for another round?"

Gris made a grimace, but nodded that he was ready.

Brian whistled for the jailer to open the door.

They walked together in silence to an interrogation room. Weeder, used the key to open it. Inside, the darkened room smelled of stale cigarette smoke (illegal inside the building) and empty soft drink containers. He motioned for Gris to take a seat. As he talked, Weeder emptied the ashtrays and collected the soft drink cans. "They give you breakfast this morning?"

"Yeah, oatmeal."

"No ham and eggs?"

"Prefer oatmeal."

"Oh." The detective picked up one of the napkins left on the table to wipe up a liquid spill. The coffee had already dried, leaving a scum of cream and dried crystals that resisted his best cleaning efforts. "The D. A. is going to want your hide, you know."

"Figured that."

"If it hadn't been for that vase with traces of dried blood, found in your closet, you'd probably be on the outside now."

Gris nodded, "They hammered on me pretty hard last night about it."

"What about the check issued to your uncle?"

"Never saw it before."

"Good, it probably won't have your fingerprints on it. They didn't find your uncle's fingerprints on it either, though his prints and several other prints were all over the agreement and envelope found with it."

"Forged."

"I know," Brian said, continuing to clean the room. He placed the over-loaded trash can in front of the door, so he wouldn't forget to put it outside a few minutes later. "Ever gamble?"

"A little."

Weeder stopped to look at him. "How much is 'a little'?"

"Oh – " Gris looked at the ceiling as he considered the question. "A buck or two on the Super Bowl. . . an occasional lotto ticket when the mood strikes me. . . maybe twenty bucks in Reno during a skiing trip."

"Doesn't sound like you're much of a gambler."

119

D.Malisch

Gris shook his head. "Uncle Ed didn't believe in spending any more on gambling that he'd normally spend on entertainment. And when he lost that, he'd consider his entertainment was over. Taught me to do the same."

Brian relaxed a bit. It was comforting to know his suspicions were probably correct and Jake's number on the match book was a plant. "You and your uncle get along pretty well?"

Gris laughed. "Yeah, pretty well."

Brian paused to look at the young engineer again. "What's so funny?"

"Nothing in particular. We just had our differences of opinion. Uncle was always fair, but it seems his vote always counted more than mine."

The napkin began to tear, forcing Weeder to pick another one from the stack of clean ones at the end of the table. He continued cleaning the table in silence.

"He often took me fishing over in the Delta when I was a kid, and we'd have a contest over who would catch the biggest fish." Gris smiled as his mind wandered through old memories. "Uncle always caught the largest fish, probably because I didn't have the patience to sit still long enough to let a fish catch my hook. I always lost the bets until one day. . . On that day, I saw him purposely drop a big fish so I'd win. After that, it wasn't much of a contest." Gris looked at the lawman, "I never told him I saw what he did, but we were a lot closer from then on. I knew he was on my side."

"What did you two argue about, the last time you saw him?"

"Development money."

"What's that?"

"Oh it's just money you use to develop a product."

"Like your invention?"

120

Gris nodded.

"Anything else you can tell me about Fawson's operation?"

"Don't know much except for the proposal he wanted me to sign."

"Anything you remember?"

The nephew thought for a moment before answering, "He had already contacted a purchasing agent in the Seattle area to sell it. Fawson wanted them to advertise the navigation system as a standard feature on all of their aircraft."

A knock on the door interrupted them. Weeder walked over to the door and let the man inside. It was Williams' lawyer.

Setting the heaping trash basket outside the door for the janitor, Brian dismissed himself, "I'll keep you posted, Mr. Williams; I've got a few things to check out."

* * *

Two days later, Ms. Boonee and Mr. Glide, lawyers for C.I. walked lockstep into the jail to visit Gris Williams. They brought Turk Fawson, without his body guards. (Perhaps his body guards had warrants for their arrest due to past deeds?) Fawson and his lawyers marched up to the bars and looked through them at Gris.

"Ready to do business yet?" Fawson asked, chewing on an unlighted cigar.

The nephew gave them a sneer. The lawyers were dressed in light grey suits and Fawson sported a flashy green three-piece suit. It didn't seem equitable or just to Gris. Why weren't they on the inside and he out there?

"Ya got no company, Williams. Ya can't make payroll. Your people are leaving to survive. Why don't you face facts and take a little cash to end all this?"

"There's an old quotation from an American general boxed in the desert by Rommel's forces that sums it up Fawson."

"What's that?"

121

"Nuts!"

"That's all?" Fawson removed the cigar from his mouth, "I don't get it?"

"You wouldn't," Gris said, as he reclined on his bed and closed his eyes to ignore them.

"Suit yourself," Fawson shrugged, turning to leave, "I got other ways to get what I want."

That evening, the Navitech building was burglarized by Ben Hetter and Greg Walston, two aircraft mechanics from Compass International. The thieves were very specific in their operation. Though they tried to cover their motives, by messing up the office, it was obvious they had come for the prototype and schematics.

"Hey Ben, I think I found them."

The second burglar got up from the computer at the secretary's desk where he had been attempting to guess the password to gain entry to Navitech files. "Let's see?"

The first man unrolled the large, hard copy schematic on Gris Williams' desk. When it wouldn't quite fit, he shoved items to the extreme edge of the desk. What he failed to see in his efforts was the half-inch bolt falling into his open briefcase on the floor. The black coloring of the bolt slowly faded into a light silver as it waited for the men to finish their work and take it back to their leader.

"Where's the printout date?" Walston, asked, as he scanned the border area of the document.

"In the lower right corner, next to the company logo."

"Got it."

"Is it recent?"

"Yeah, it's only a couple of days old. It must be the one."

Hetter tried to step back in the small office while his buddy rolled the schematic into a long tube and secured it with a rubber band. "You get the prototype?" Hetter asked.

"Yeah, found it in the lab."

"Did you tag the connections?"

"What do you think, Benny? I ain't no dummy."

"I was just checkin'. Fawson don't want no screw ups."

Walston handed the schematic to his sparing partner, Ben. As they left the room, Walston paused to grab the calendar from the desk.

"What do you need that for?" Hetter asked. "You already got a calendar."

"It might have names, dates, phone numbers of sources and clients."

"Yeah, never thought of that," Hetter admitted.

"That's the problem," Walston quipped.

"What?"

"You never think."

"Oh come off it Greg! I'm tired of you tryin' to insult me all the time."

Walston ignored him. He turned out the light and stumbled to the small window where he used a small flashlight, with a red lens, to find the push-pins used to hold the opaque blanket over the window. "Kill the lights in the lobby before I take this blanket down, Ben."

"Sure."

"You got everything?" Ben asked.

"Yeah, the prototype is in the cardboard box."

"Good, I guess we got about as much as we can carry. Let's get out of here before someone spots us," Hetter said, looking around nervously.

Together they carried their booty to the white van out front. Walston closed the front door to the Navitech building carefully, leaving his jumpers to bypass the alarm in place.

* * *

The newsboy threw the paper against the front door of Brian's apartment, causing him to lose count of the number of spoons of coffee metered into the pot. "Shasta!" he growled, "Gotta get that kid to stop banging the darn door." He put the pot together and plugged it in before going to the door to retrieve the morning news. After the coffee perked, he sat down with a Danish and coffee to read his paper. His eye hung on the burglary headline with Navitech's name. He stopped to read the story in its entirety.

A few minutes later, when he arrived at the station, he looked up the numbers for the detectives in Palo Alto, where the Navitech burglary occurred. He phoned them. "Detective Lopez? This is Detective Brian Weeder, with the San Francisco police. Are you working the Navitech burglary?"

"Good morning Detective Weeder. Yeah, I'm the guy on the hook for that."

"Any suspects?"

"Not yet."

"Say, Lopez, I might have some information you'd be interested in hearing. Can I meet with you this morning?"

"Hey! I can use all the professional help I can get, come on down."

"Are you going to Navitech anytime this morning?"

"Yeah, I gotta take a bunch of statements from the employees when they show up." He paused to add, "I understand a lot of them might not show up where they don't get paid."

"When are you going out there?" Brian asked, pausing between sips of his coffee.

"I was just fixin' to head that way now."

"Okay, I'll hop in the car and be right down, meet you at Navitech," Brian said, hanging up the phone.

On his way out of the building, Weeder stopped to check in with his supervisor. "Gotta minute?"

Jim Magar pointed briefly to the chair on the other side of his desk as he continued to work.

"I'm still investigating the Williams' case. Have a few loose ends to clear up," Brian offered.

Jim stopped working and looked up. "I thought we had that all wrapped up except for furnishing the D. A. with paper?"

"Not really?"

"What do you mean?"

"A few things don't add up."

"Such as?"

Brian hated being put in the hot seat, "Well, the bookie gave me a description completely different for Gris Williams."

"He's a busy man. See's lots of people. . . Probably forgot."

"Williams doesn't have a single print on the check or the document found in his car."

"So?"

"So I think it's a plant."

"Ever heard of gloves?"

Brian hated arguing with the chief, he always made you feel like a rookie. "I had the lab check for traces of latex and other fibers; they found nothing. Besides, why would a guy wear gloves to handle a check if he needed to endorse it anyway?"

Magar paused a second. "Look, our case load is getting out of hand, let's get this thing wrapped up as soon as possible."

"I will, but I wanted to let you know I'm going down to Navitech this morning to check up on a burglary that happened there last night."

D.Malisch

"Navitech?"

"Yeah, it's the business owned by Gris Williams and his uncle."

"Burglary?"

"Yeah. I think it's more than coincidence the company is burgled while we've got the owner in our jail."

Magar took several seconds to consider, before waving Weeder out of his office.

Nearly an hour passed before Brian could fight his way through the heavy rush-hour traffic to Navitech. When he finally arrived, Detective Lopez had set up shop in an empty office to interview the remaining staff at Navitech.

Weeder peeked into the office through the glass panel beside the door. He displayed his badge for Lopez to see.

Lopez motioned for Brian to open the door.

"Brian Weeder," he said, shaking hands with Detective Lopez. "I see you're busy, so why don't I let you continue. We'll talk when you get a break."

"Sounds good."

"Mind if I look around Gris Williams' office? I might notice something changed."

"Oh yeah, you were here last week, weren't you?"

"Yeah, when the uncle's body was found."

With a wave of his hand, Lopez dismissed him, "Sure have a look, just let me know if you notice anything."

Brian gave him a two-finger salute, before going to Williams' office. His real purpose for going to the engineer's office was to check for the half-inch bolt. He wasn't a bit surprised to find it missing. Just to make sure, he checked inside the desk and on the floor of the cramped office; it was gone. Brian smiled. His Trojan horse was inside the enemy's camp.

Weeder finished examining the tiny room. He stepped outside the office to speak with Silvia when Lopez walked up to him.

"Find anything?"

"A couple of items."

"What do you have?"

"Well, his desk calendar is missing."

"We got that listed. What else?"

"Mr. Williams had a half-inch bolt, about three inches long that was lying beside his calendar. It's gone."

"Half-inch bolt?"

"Yeah, said he found it while riding his bike up along the Skyline."

"Was it valuable?"

To Detective Weeder, it was priceless, but he couldn't tell that to Lopez. "Uh – it looked ordinary."

"What would a bolt like that cost?"

Brian made a gesture of puzzlement, "Oh I donno? Maybe a buck?"

Lopez put away his pencil and notepad. Looking up at Brian who was nearly a foot taller, he asked, "You said you had some information for me?"

"Yeah," Brian smiled. He put his hand on Lopez's back as they walked back to the office that the Palo Alto detective had been using for interviews. "Have you ever heard of a company called Compass International. . . ?"

* * *

Inside of an unmarked building, a few miles away, rented by his two burglars, Turk Fawson met with the men who took the Navitech prototype.

The empty building was dark except for the eerie yellow-green light coming through the skylights high overhead.

The shafts of light illuminated the dust floating on the nearly stagnant currents of air, giving one the illusion of being under the ocean, looking up. Within the empty building, the two vehicles, a white van and white limousine rested silently, parked next to each other at oblique angles under a shaft of light from one of the plastic skylights, overhead.

"Let's see it," Fawson ordered eagerly.

Mechanic Greg Walston slid open the side door of the van, the sound of its sudden stop echoed loudly throughout the open area. "There it is," he grinned, stepping aside for his boss to look.

Fawson picked up the package, about the size of a loaf of bread. He turned it this way and that, trying to absorb the genius of its technology.

"Careful with the wires sir; we don't want them to fall off, or we won't know how to hook it up again."

"Oh yeah," Turk said, not wanting to admit he really didn't know much about the technology of electronics. He held it for a few seconds more, then thrust it back to Walston, "Here you take it and don't break it."

"Yes sir," he said, taking the guidance system. "When do you want it set up?"

"As soon as possible. Start now," Fawson ordered as he reached for a cigar.

"Yes sir," Walston said with an acknowledging nod.

Fawson peeked back inside the van.

"Is that the test rack where they had it?"

"Yeah, complete with the computer and code to test it."

"What about the schematics?"

"Right here," Ben Hetter said, preparing to place his briefcase on the hood of Fawson's car.

"Hey! Not there – you idiot!" Fawson objected.

Hetter, hesitated, then placed the briefcase on the concrete floor before opening it.

The little man squatted to examine the prize. "What's this?" he questioned, as he touched the half-inch bolt. He drew back quickly from the small electrical discharge given him by the object. The bolt remained silver, apparently having further plans for Mr. Fawson. He picked it up a second time without shock. "This come out of the unit?"

The two mechanics looked at each other; each shrugged.

"We ain't never seen it before," Ben admitted.

Fawson handed it to him, "Well, take it with you, but keep track of it, just in case we find we need it."

Hetter nodded, placing the bolt in the pocket of his lab coat.

Turk Fawson stood up slowly, holding his back as though it pained him. Making a face of discomfort, he instructed, "I'll send over some engineers and technicians to get this thing going. But I want you to get a sign made for the building, so it'll look official and call it Pacific Engineering. Once we get this thing going, we'll transfer our own prototypes back to Compass International." Fawson paused to light his cigar. He was excited, but tried not to show it. He signaled for his body guards to bring him the cash to pay the mechanics.

Walston took the case, opened it, and began counting the bundled cash. Less than a minute later he complained, "Hey, where's the other half?"

The little man stepped back between his body guards. "You'll get the other half when I'm sure the thing works and you two clowns didn't damage it." He glanced around the empty space inside the building, "Now get some lights turned on and get some work benches set up to do some work."

* * *

Detective Weeder began to investigate Compass International and its Chief Executive Officer, Turk Fawson. While it was true that the corporation had been involved in lawsuits, none of them seemed to encompass the stealing of patent rights. Turk Fawson, on the other hand, did have a criminal record. Apparently he had been arrested a decade ago, trying to run a protection racket in the Los Angles area, but charges were dropped because the witnesses all mysteriously disappeared. A few years later, he joined Compass International and worked his way to the board of directors, where he was placed into his present position.

Armed with this information, Weeder was able to confirm several of the fingerprints found on the document hidden under the rear seat of Gris Williams' car. The fingerprints of at least two other people found on the envelope, were still a mystery.

The report from the crime lab on the vase found in the bottom of Williams' closet suggested the blood may have been painted on the object, because it had partly dried before application. The nephew's fingerprints were on the vase, but there was considerable dust over them, leading Brian to conclude the young man had not handled the vase in recent months. Forensics had established that the object which killed Ed Williams was not a rounded surface, such as a vase, but rather a box-shaped object that left considerable dents wherever it contacted him.

Brian was relieved. He felt he could go to the D. A. and have the charges dropped, but until he had the real culprit, he knew the media would beat this thing to death. As he saw it, Fawson and at least two accomplices were responsible, but he'd need proof.

Nearly a week passed while Detective Weeder argued his case with the D.A. to get permission to go before a judge and get a search warrant on Compass International. Brian hoped it would at last turn up signs of the missing prototype and implicate Turk Fawson in both the burglary and in the killing of Ed Williams. At last, armed with his warrant and accompanied by an engineer from Navitech to identify the prototype, Brian parked his car in front of Compass International. Within minutes two Palo Alto policemen and Detective Lopez arrived to aid in the search.

The receptionist phoned Turk Fawson. Without telling him about the police, she asked him to come to the lobby for a matter of urgency.

When he arrived, several minutes later with his body guards, Brian showed his credential and introduced himself, "Mr. Turk Fawson? I'm Detective Brian Weeder, San Francisco Police." He pointed to each of the others as he introduced them, "This is Detective Lopez of the Palo Alto police department and Darrel James, Navitech engineer and officers Rompenski and Chang of the Palo Alto Police."

The two bodyguards behind Fawson looked pale and stepped back. Fawson, on the other hand smiled broadly as he extended his welcome, "Good morning officers. It's not that often we have the honor of so many law enforcement people visit us. What can I do for you?"

"We have a warrant to search the premises for stolen property."

"Stolen property?"

"Yes," Brian said, "A Navitech prototype was stolen last week and we have reason to believe it may be here."

"Here?" Fawson said, with a look of surprise. He fumbled his unlighted cigar, dropping it purposely. "I assure you – "

Weeder interrupted, "Never mind the theatrics, Fawson, lead the way to your laboratory."

"Uh it's in another building," Fawson said, attempting to delay the search.

Weeder shook his head negatively, "No, it isn't. We checked. This building houses your development laboratory."

"You're very thorough, Detective Weeder."

Brian motioned for the C.E.O. to lead the way.

They searched the lab and all of the offices in the building, finding nothing. It was beginning to look as though the man was going to get away with his evil deed.

At the end of the search, the party left, except for Detective Weeder, who stayed behind, engaged in conversation with Turk Fawson.

"You look clean Fawson, but I know you are in this up to your neck."

"You can leave now Weeder, and don't come back, or else my lawyers will sue for harassment."

The two, exchanged looks of mutual animosity.

As Brian drove out of the lot, the little man waltzed back to his cavernous office. Passing his body guards, he gave each a "high five" salute. He crawled up in his chair behind his immense desk and propped his feet up while he lit his cigar. Puffing on the stogie, he ordered one of his body guards, "Call Hetter and Walston. Tell 'em I want to see 'em right away."

When the two mechanics arrived, they were sent into Fawson's office. "Close the door," Fawson ordered. He smiled between successive drags on his cigar. Finally he asked, "How's the progress on the system?"

Both mechanics remained standing, but Walston answered, "We've got it responding to most commands, but seem to be having a few problems yet. Why?"

The C.E.O. ran his tongue around the inside of his mouth before speaking. "We just had the cops search the place today for the prototype."

Both mechanics showed expression of alarm.

"No. It's okay," he said, waving his cigar as he talked, "They didn't find a thing, so they can't come back. Not likely the judge will sign a second warrant, when they couldn't find nothin' the first time. We can bring everything over here and get on with it." He stood up, walking across the room to his wall calendar. "Let's see — yeah, that would be about right," he said speaking to himself as he calculated dates. Suddenly he turned and addressed the mechanics again. "I want you guys to check out the Cessna. I want to fly it with one of the prototype systems installed. I gotta go to Seattle next week, so get it installed for me. Understand?"

Both nodded yes.

"Oh yeah, and check out that problem with the landing strut, it still acts weird when I take off or land."

"Yes sir," Hetter acknowledged.

"Yeah, and let me know when you finish checking out the new nav-system, I'd like to have a look."

* * *

Weeder was disappointed, but not discouraged. His instincts told him he had the right animal up the tree, but he just couldn't prove it. He couldn't be right all of the time, could he?

Short on time, the homicide detective set about searching for buildings that Compass International may have rented recently that weren't officially populated yet. He worked with Detective Lopez to search for building permits issued recently in the hope one would pop up with C.I.'s name on it. They weren't that lucky. After four days, they still had nothing.

Trying again, they used the computer to search all contractor permits issued by the city for new utilities in the last month, particularly those for Compass International. During the next three days they communicated with each contractor; all leads were dead ends. Seven permits were issued to C.I., each one for the building just searched. There were no unlisted buildings for C.I., as far as the Weeder and Lopez could discern.

133

Brian was paged numerous times by his supervisor, wanting to know where the paperwork on Gris Williams was, and when would it be on the D.A.'s desk? He ignored the calls, knowing he'd pay for it later.

Coffee seemed the best solution for the moment. Both detectives paused to take a break.

"This is maddening," Brian confessed, "Got any better ideas, Lopez?"

The detective just shook his head, as he stared into his coffee.

"Maybe we could talk to the boys who run the 'roach coaches' in the area? They'd certainly know if a new building opened."

"Probably not," Lopez sighed, "We'd have to talk with each and every driver."

"Yeah, the companies usually don't let the food guys inside the buildings either."

"No, they don't. Besides, what we want, has got to lead back to Fawson himself."

"Yeah," Brian said, in a regretting tone. He thought silently for a moment before saying, "Hey! Wait a minute. You might have it."

"What?"

"Let's check Fawson's list of phone calls."

"What will that prove?"

Weeder got a devilish grin on his face as he realized the nature of the beast he had been tracking. "Fawson is a little guy with big ego. Right?"

"Sounds right."

"Well – he'd never waste time on his cell phone to talk with anybody unimportant except – "

Simultaneously they both said, "The burglars!"

Lopez quickly found the information by checking the local cell providers until he found the one with Fawson's account.

Together, they checked the numbers called during the last week. One number was used numerous times during the day and also very late at night, on the night of the burglary. They traced the number to a Greg Walston. The detectives got his home address and decided to follow him to work the next morning.

Not aware he was being followed, Greg Walston led the detectives through the heavy traffic to the rented building. Armed with hard hats and clipboards, the detectives parked next to Greg and followed him into the building, as though they had official business of another kind. None of the employees for C.I. sent to work there, realized the equipment was stolen, because the building showed Pacific Engineering as the company name. They were told they were aiding one of C.I.'s subcontractors. Security was lax.

Except for a few workbenches along one wall, the building was empty, no receptionist, no offices set up, no manufacturing line, etc.

Weeder motioned Lopez to follow him. They walked slowly over to the electrical bus along the wall and pretended to write down circuit numbers for the outlet boxes. Brian would read them off while Lopez pretended to write them down. Together, they moved around the portable benches, looking for items matching the descriptions of the missing items from Navitech.

Brian walked to the junction box and opened it, pretending to be labeling the circuits.

"Did you see what I just saw?" Brian whispered.

"You mean the rack for the prototype?"

"Yeah, but I didn't see the actual box, did you?"

"No," Lopez whispered back, "He must have moved it."

Brian nodded toward the fabrication test area at the end of the row of benches. "Those units over there resemble the description of the prototype."

"I think you're right Brian. What do you want to do?"

"It's your game, Lopez, do you want to call in the troops?"

"Okay, you keep watch on things while I step outside and use my radio. It may take an hour or more to catch a judge to sign a warrant."

Brian nodded.

Fifteen minutes later, the whole area was surrounded by police units.

Weeder and Lopez immediately took Walston into custody. Within minutes he told them about Fawson's trip to Seattle.

Lopez gave instructions to the police Sargent how to handle things, and he left with Brian for the San Carlos Airport.

As they raced along the freeway, lights flashing, they tried to develop a plan of action.

"Walston said Fawson was flying out in the Cessna about eleven o'clock." Brian checked the clock on the dashboard of the car. "It looks like we have about ten minutes, if he's punctual."

"You realize he's going to make a run for it when he sees us?"

"Yeah, hate that," Brian admitted. "Too much like Hollywood for me."

"Yeah, for me too."

"Got your gun ready?"

"For what?"

"To shoot out his tires, so he can't take off."

"You serious, Weeder?"

"I hope not."

At the San Carlos Airport, Turk Fawson waited impatiently, while Ben Hetter scrutinized the color of the fuel, during the pre-flight check.

With a frown of disapproval, Ben looked over at his boss, "Wish you wouldn't smoke around the fuel area, Mr. Fawson."

"Ah – hasn't caught fire yet," he said puffing on his cigar. There wasn't much chance Fawson would pay attention to rules, especially ones he didn't invent.

Ben circled the aircraft, checking the hinges on the movable surfaces. "Since you got the new nav. gear installed, why'd you want the old Navitech prototype for this trip, anyway?"

Fawson grinned, "Hope you kissed it good bye, 'cause it's goin' for a swim."

"What do you mean?"

He knocked the ash from his cigar, using the heel of his boot. "I'll drop it in the ocean somewhere off the Oregon coast. Can't come back to haunt us from there, eh?"

Hetter nodded, while checking the propeller for cracks, "So that's why you were in such a hurry to get copies of the new prototype made?"

Restlessly wandering around to the left strut, Fawson kicked the tire, noting the lack of play in the assembly. "Looks like you fixed it."

Ben walked over to the strut and pointed to the new silver half-inch bolt anchoring the axle bracket. "Used that bolt you gave me to keep." He smiled, "That way you'll have it with you, wherever you go."

Fawson laughed. "Better be tight."

"It is."

The short man opened the door and climbed into the pilot's seat. Ignoring the pilot's checklist, he started the engine. He let it run while he patted the stolen prototype sitting loosely in the passenger seat beside him.

Looking through the partly open door at Ben, he shouted over the engine noise, "You'll get your money when I come back in a couple of days."

Ben doubted he'd ever see the balance of the money. He closed the door, waving as the plane taxied out to the start of the runway.

The smug pilot ignored ATIS weather information as he grabbed the microphone to talk to the tower. At the end of the taxi way, he paused to run-up the engines briefly.

Approaching the freeway off ramp, Weeder and Lopez sped toward the airport entrance. They reached the parking area just in time to see the yellow Cessna waiting for clearance to take off. Brian turned onto the airport perimeter road, hoping to position their car on the runway to thwart Fawson's takeoff.

In the aircraft, the little man saw the flashing emergency lights approaching. He obviously knew it meant big trouble if he was caught with the prototype in his possession. He decided not to wait for clearance. Setting the throttle, he released the brakes, letting the loaded aircraft charge down the runway.

The accelerating plane picked up speed, ten. . . twenty. . . forty. . . sixty knots per hour. . . Just ten knots short of lift off, a violent shaking signaled that something came loose. The loud clank of the object impacting the under-side of the craft startled Fawson. He erred by relaxing pressure to the steering pedals. The plane veered slightly to the left as he looked back to see the source of the noise. The left wheel slipped off the edge of the asphalt into a gopher hole, shearing the two remaining bolts holding the axle bracket. With the wheel gone, the strut plunged into the soft earth and swung the aircraft violently to the left. The plane ground looped, catching the right wingtip on the ground. Brutal kinetic forces ripped the wing and heavy fuel-tanks from the aircraft. The fuselage, now sideways to the runway, vaulted into the air over its right strut only to impact the asphalt time and time again as it sheared off the horizontal stabilizer, propeller, and rudder. With a grating sound it slowly slid to a smoldering stop in front of the detective's car on the runway.

Brian left Lopez near the wreckage; he knew what he was looking for as he followed the asphalt apron toward the launch point. He found it about half way down the runway. The half inch bolt rested there, glowing a bright red. As he watched it, the color changed back to silver, and the threads slowly reappeared on the surface. Brian reached into his pocket for his chalk and drew a circle around it.

When Weeder returned to the tangled remains of the aircraft, he realized the degree of justice the bolt had dealt. Inside, Turk Fawson was unrecognizable. Just as he had beat Ed Williams with a heavy metal box, the Navitech prototype, left untethered, had ricocheted around the cabin, beating the man to a pulp.

It was a simple matter to get confessions from Hetter and Walston. The mechanics admitted helping Fawson move Ed's body and planting evidence against Gris. Now, with the bolt coming loose, it made things appear as if they not done their jobs as certified flight mechanics. It probably wouldn't matter though; their pending convictions would bar them from future work throughout the aircraft industry.

The new C.E.O. of Compass International was appalled by the actions of his predecessor. He immediately returned all properties belonging to Navitech. In addition, he denounced Fawson's actions and promised marketing assistance and complete funding to Navitech, while developing its Global Guardian navigation system.

Of course, all charges were dropped against Gris Williams.

D.Malisch

*   *   *

Chapter 5   Missing Sister

Protagonist: Detective Brian Weeder SFPD

Guests:

Madelin Springer	Daughter of the murdered woman
Sherry Nicolas Gentre	Kidnaped little girl (now a woman)
Carol Nicolas	Murdered woman (Sherry and Madelin's mother)
Evelyn Jamison	Mother of the murderer
Bret Gentre	Son of Sherry Nicolas
Rick Weston	Treasure hunter
Anthony Spats	Chicago detective
Elana Yates	Biased Chicago judge
Bernice Gear	Chicago adoption agency administrator
Robert Wellin	Killer & kidnapper
Edgar Kirzwad	Chicago jailer (stepfather of adopted girl)

Canceling his weekend plans because of his heavy workload, Homicide Detective, Brian Weeder submerged himself in the backlog of cases on his desk. By his own choice, he had added to the burden when he agreed to cover for a fellow detective on a badly needed vacation from missing persons. It wasn't that Brian Weeder was a glutton for punishment, but rather that he felt it was his duty to support his friends. Yet, he knew his decision would cost him more than the weekend, since he'd miss the companionship of a very sexy young woman, who was now going to the festival with another man.

Brian stared at the report, reading and re-reading the same sentence at least seven times. It said something about a "missing sister. . . twenty years", but beyond that, he couldn't think straight. Inside him, his soul screamed to be elsewhere. Finally, in frustration, he slammed the report to the desk-top, to take a short break. Across the cluttered work-surface of the desk, the half-inch bolt teetered, then fell onto its side with a thud. For a moment, he studied the bolt silently, substituting curiosity for his desire to be elsewhere.

Weeder picked up the bolt. He surveyed it for a minute or more, while his mind wandered.

In all the cases up to now, the bolt had always selected the case for him. Would it be possible for him to choose a case and have the bolt help him solve it? He didn't know? His analytical mind shelved his tragic love-life for a few seconds, while he considered what type of case would make a good test. Perhaps something long considered unsolvable?

The detective ignored his heavy case load, to dig through the bottom of his desk drawer for something old – something unsolved. Stacking folders from his horizontal filing system into his lap, it seemed nothing was suitable. He wanted something that had remained an unsolved mystery for longer than the decade he had been with the police department. Twenty years or more, would do nicely. Suddenly he remembered reading that number, just minutes ago. He picked up the missing person's case he'd slammed to the desk. With a heightened sense of interest and importance, he scanned quickly through the details. . . A woman, now in her thirties, wanted the police to help her find her sister. Twenty years ago, her eight-year-old sister disappeared with their mother's boyfriend, following her mother's murder. The murderer was never identified or caught for the crime – it all sounded impossible and just what Weeder wanted. Best of all, solving this puzzle would shorten the stack of paper on his desk.

Now that he had the case to solve, how would he get the bolt to follow the scent? Brian didn't know? Perhaps he should leave the bolt with someone involved? Who was available? The missing person's report was submitted by the sister of the little girl; she could be the key? Weeder wrote down a few notes before driving to the woman's home in Daily City.

He knocked on the varnished, wooden door to her white stucco house and introduced himself. The woman, slightly older than Brian, greeted him, inviting him inside. Dressed in a violet, pastel dress, she appeared to be a pleasant, well fed, but not overweight, woman. The room was light and cheerful, with pictures of her family cluttering the walls of the modest house. They walked into the next room where Brian was shown a seat at the hand-finished, wooden table near the window. Through the thin, gauzy curtain, colored fuzzy shapes of cars whizzed along the residential street.

The detective asked the standard list of questions, but as the short interview neared its end, Brian reviewed certain answers with the woman, "So, your younger sister was approximately eight, when she disappeared?"

"That's right," she said, while sitting upright with her hands crossed upon her lap.

"And you were about ten?"

"Yes – that's correct."

"Tell me Ms. Springer, if your sister was taken by the man who killed your mother, why weren't you taken too?"

"Please call me Madelin," she insisted.

"Madelin," he corrected himself. "Why was Sherry taken and not you?"

143

She looked down at her hands in her lap, her face showing regret, as though she felt guilty for being away during the murder and kidnapping. "I probably would have been taken too, except I was at a slumber party for a classmate," she said softly.

"Classmate?"

"Yes, that's right," she agreed, looking up at the detective again.

Brian struggled to squeeze the balance of the interview on the page of his notebook. Sensing he had taken too much time with the interview, he asked questions as he scribbled answers, "Did your mother fight often with this boyfriend?"

"Oh goodness, yes – they fought like cats and dogs."

"Did he ever threaten to kill her?"

"Many times – it seemed like once or twice a day for months."

Silence fell on the conversation while Brian recorded the note. "And you don't remember the man's name?"

She gave him a sad look as she apologized, "No, I'm sorry, all I remember is that mom called him 'Stormy'. I don't think I ever heard his last name."

"Is there anything distinctive about the man that you remember, like tatoos or scars?"

Madelin shook her head, "No, he was a very big – mean – man. He looked huge to my sister, Sherry, and me."

"Have a temper?"

"Goodness yes! My sister and I were scared spitless of him." She ran her fingers through the reddish-brown curls of her shoulder length hair as she watched the detective.

"Did he ever try to harm you or your sister?"

She nodded. "Mom usually intervened," she said, lamenting the loss of her parent. "He beat her senseless numerous times." Madelin fell silent for a time, watching Brian write in his notebook.

"Anything else?" Weeder asked, without looking up from his writing.

"I just remember he was always insanely jealous of mom. He didn't even like her paying attention to Sherry and me."

"Possessive type eh?"

"Very much so. . ."

The mariner's clock chimed on the mantle: Weeder glanced at his watch. "Well, Ms. Springer – Madelin, I have another appointment in a few minutes, so I've got to leave now. I'll keep you informed on my progress solving the case."

"Thank you, Detective."

The bolt tumbled into Brian's empty hand when he pushed it into his coat pocket to find his car keys. "Oh yes, I nearly forgot," he said, pulling the object from his pocket. He handed the bolt to the woman. "Would you keep this for me until I drop by next time?"

She rightfully looked puzzled. "What is it?" Her small, rounded nose wriggled in a peculiar way as she pursed her lips.

"Oh – it's just a bolt," Brian lied.

"I don't understand? Why are you leaving it with me?"

"I'd rather not explain, if you don't mind. Just put it in your purse and take it with you everywhere you go, if you would."

With a thoughtful look, she exclaimed, "Oh it must have a hidden microphone in it."

Shaking his head, Brian laughed, "No, it's nothing like that, but that gives me an idea. Maybe I'll make one with a microphone in it." He winked at the woman as he stepped through the front door onto the stoop. "Just humor me and I promise to take it back next time I see you."

145

D.Malisch

The orange sun glowed dimly through the San Francisco summer fog. It never seemed like summer to tourists, and today was no exception. Brian hurriedly climbed into his car to avoid the wet chill. Inside the car, he let the engine idle a few seconds as he wondered what was about to happen.

The following day, Madelin Springer had her purse taken while riding the Muni-train. The purse snatchers, looking for drug money, deposited everything that wouldn't spend, into a nearby dumpster. Among the items left in the trash-bin was the half-inch bolt. (The bolt obviously came in contact with these unpleasant fellows, but their resulting punishment is unknown.)

Later that evening, a local homeless man, part-time dumpster diver, searched for discarded items he might sell for a little pocket change. Among the items he found was a silver, half-inch bolt. The man admired the flawless silver finish devoid of rust. He shrugged. "What the heck − it might fetch a nickel or more − " he said, taking it with him.

After numerous unsuccessful attempts to sell the bolt, the homeless man finally discarded it in the back of a pickup truck parked on the street. This truck belonged to a vacationing couple, from Chicago, visiting the city for a day or so. Since their vacation time had nearly elapsed, they chose to haul their trailer back home, across the Rocky Mountains. The bolt rode uneventfully, for several days, until the vehicle neared the outskirts of the "Windy City." When the truck struck a rather large pothole, the bolt fell through an opening in the bed of the pickup, striking the asphalt beneath.

The fastener rolled into a storm drain, falling through the grating into a pile of mud below. It would have rested there for a lengthy time except for the numerous complaints regarding slow drainage along the highway. The next day, a scheduled work crew came to clean it. Priding themselves on their efficiency, the crew

146

removed the glop and deposited it in a city-owned field for drying and later processing.

A self-styled treasure hunter made his usual rounds on Saturday, when he would not be harassed by city workers that worked only week days. Searching the field, with his metal detector, for lost coins, rings, and other valuable items, the man received a precious metal indication on his detector. With a screwdriver, he pried and dug through the hardening muck until he freed a silver, half-inch bolt. Not wanting to encounter the item a second time, he tossed it into his sack of treasure.

* * *

Inside a Chicago neighborhood bar, an aging man, in unfamiliar territory, nursed his beer while attempting to interest a much younger female patron in his virility. The woman, endured the man's ego, coarse comments, and frequent touching for nearly an hour, to drink his beer.

"Come home with me tonight," he ordered. His demanding tone was neither flirtatious nor passive.

She tipped her bottle upward, drinking the liquid slowly, while inventing an excuse. She stared past the bottle at the brown, plastered ceiling – thinking. Gently setting the bottle back onto the bar, she looked into the mirror at the man beside her. "Can't," she said, calmly.

"Why not?"

"My ol' man wouldn't like it," she lied.

"Hell with him. He don't own you."

She liked his beer, but knew he was serious trouble; she'd seen his kind before – or so she thought. She didn't answer, knowing it would only start an argument – solving nothing.

"He jealous?" the man asked, looking for an edge to make her change her mind, though he'd abduct her from the parking lot later, if necessary.

"Sometimes," she lied, while looking wistfully at the door, wishing the usual cast of friends would arrive soon.

"How come he didn't come with you?"

She estimated the amount of liquid remaining in her bottle. The man made her feel more than uncomfortable, and she'd be looking for an escape route soon. "He had other things to do," she said flatly, without making eye contact.

The wrinkled man touched her again, this time further up her arm. "Your ol' man probably has another skirt, on the side," he said in a disparaging tone, "He's probably pokin' her now."

Attempting to hide her repulsion for the man, she held steady for a few seconds. She disliked his huge-fingers wrapped around her arm, especially since they also rubbed against her breasts. Slowly she rotated the barstool away from the man. "Gotta go to the ladies – " she said. Looking at him in the mirror, she waited patently for him to release his grip. Smoothly she slipped down off the stool, pausing only to drain the last of the beer from the bottle.

The man watched as she sauntered into the bathroom. He surveyed the room for better prospects. None of the remaining four women in the bar appealed to him, and each had an escort.

The multitude of small, round tables scattered around the darkened room resembled mushrooms that sprout following a good rain. In the center of the cluster, stood one, group-sized, rectangular table. It was large enough to seat eight or ten patrons. A thin layer of tobacco smoke drifted over tables and people, flagrantly violating health issues. It was early in the evening, most of the "regulars" hadn't come to drink and laugh and maybe cry, depending on their need.

The predator waited.

The door to the street opened and a series of young men and one woman came in. Conversation was lively, but not distinguishable above the music selection playing. The woman with them, made a list of drinks before approaching the bar, to hand it to the barkeeper.

Out of sight of the woman in the bathroom, the older man, sitting at the bar, leaned toward the woman with the list. "Hey sis," he nodded back toward the group of men settled at a table near the center of the room. "Why don't you ditch those guys and have a drink with me?"

The woman sized him up quickly, but otherwise ignored him. She waited patiently for the drinks.

The predator eyed her silently for a time before asking, "Is one of them your ol' man?"

She turned her back, preferring to watch the industrious bartender.

The bartender snatched a tray from under the counter, setting the glasses on it.

She handed him two bills and he gave her change. She returned to the table with her friends.

At the table, Rick Weston, treasure hunter, laughed. "Yeah it was one of my better hauls. I found two rings, eight dollars in coins and this," he said, dropping the silver half-inch bolt onto the table.

His friends at the table laughed. One of them heckled him saying, "Hey Rick, where's the rest of the car, to go with the bolt?" They laughed again.

Rick tasted his drink. Finding it satisfactory, he smacked his lips before setting it down. "I'm sure it's out there; I just have to get it piece by piece."

The door to the lady's room opened, allowing the reluctant target of the old man to reappear. She headed slowly back toward the bar, but abruptly changed direction and speed when she recognized the group of regulars who just came in. "Hey guys! It's about time you showed up." She smiled and gave hugs before standing at the end of the table to chat.

The predator at the bar seethed.

"What ya got there, Rick?" she asked. She picked up one of the rings and slipped it on her finger. It was pretty, but much too large to fit her small finger.

"This is my latest treasure find, Liz. What do you think?"

Liz laughed, "I think you need to find more jewelry my size."

"Sit down gal; Wanda will get you a drink. Want your regular?"

She selected an empty chair at the end or the table. "Yeah, that would be fine," Liz said, glancing back at the big man she left at the bar. She knew he wouldn't be happy, but that was life, and he'd better get use to it.

"Hey!" The man at the bar yelled. Everyone looked up except Liz.

Liz continued the conversation as though nothing had happened. "So where did you find these?" she asked, playing with the coins.

"Oh, I can't tell you that," Rick teased, "you'd get a finder and put me out of business."

"No, I wouldn't," she countered, "I'd just pick up the jewelry that fit me."

"And if it had diamonds, you'd just throw it back?"

"Well. . . I might see. . . if I could get it adjusted. . ." she admitted. She held out a hand pretending to have a sloppy ring with a huge diamond.

Everyone at the table laughed.

The man at the counter yelled again, "Hey Liz!"

Conversation stopped; everyone looked, except Liz.

"New boyfriend?" Rick questioned, a hint of concern in his voice.

"Wants to own me 'cause he bought me a beer," Liz said quietly, so only those at the table could hear.

Rick nodded toward the husky youth sitting at the table, on his left, "Want Jimmy to tell him to shove off?"

Since she had not been entirely innocent in creating the problem, she felt responsible for solving it. She preferred the safety of numbers, but was reluctant to involve her friends otherwise. "No. Let me handle it if he comes over."

"Hey Liz! I ain't finished talkin' with you," the large man thundered.

Sensing an impending fight, the bartender came over to the group. Leaning on the table, he ignored the man sitting at the bar. "Want me to call the cops?"

Liz never looked at her antagonist, as she shook her head. "No, don't call anyone. I can handle it," Liz said, fearing she had lied.

The bartender shook his head, uncertain that the large man would take the rejection. "I'll give you the benefit of a doubt, but my instincts are to protect my regular customers and my bar." He made eye contact with each of them at the table before walking back to his station.

The wrinkled man wadded up his napkin and threw it at the table, but it fell far short, bouncing on the carpet.

Discreetly, the bartender walked over and exchanged some quiet words with the troublemaker.

The man threw his half-filled bottle against the line of decanters behind the bar, hitting just below the large mirror. Glass and liquid showered a small area.

Liz looked over to see the source of the noise. She trembled when she saw him hop down off the stool and tromp toward her.

The man stopped behind her. "Hey woman! I'm talking to you!" he bellowed.

Unsure of herself, she stood up only to look chest-high at the beast. "I'm sorry if I mislead you mister, but I'm not interested."

He reached out to touch her and everyone at the table came to their feet.

"You drink my beer and lead me on," he thundered, "What kind of whore are you?"

Rick caught Jimmy's arm as he started to move toward the intruder. Jimmy was about the same height and build, but much younger. About the only advantage the older man had – was just raw meanness.

"Look," Liz pleaded, "I'm sorry if I mislead you. I'll even pay for the beers – just go away."

The man sneered at her, then suddenly and without warning, he backhanded her.

Liz flew backward from the blow. Her body knocked over chairs at a neighboring table, before coming to rest on the thinly carpeted floor. Though hurting badly from the experience, she realized she was lucky not to have more damage than blood running from her bleeding lip and throbbing in her head. Before she could get to her feet, Jimmy ripped himself loose from Rick's grip and directly challenged the man physically.

The man fought back against the youth. But his pounding fists did little except to anger Jimmy even more. The man kicked and gouged, but his younger opponent kept coming. They fell to the floor with a "Whump" sound. The older man bit and growled; Jimmy pushed that much harder, striking the man over and over again until bones and teeth began to snap in the older frame. The predator suddenly produced a knife, hidden away in some covert area of his clothing.

Jimmy grabbed the wrist, smashing it again and again into the floor until the knife slipped away. Someone from the table kicked the deadly object beyond reach. Finally the man quit fighting and lay still. Jimmy sensed the change and stopped; he lacked the killer instinct. The bloodied man lay still until Jimmy released him. When the youth crawled off him and turned his back to get up, he was attacked again, struck with a kick aimed at the knees. The blow upset Jimmy's balance; he fell back onto his opponent, knocking the wind out of him and fracturing the man's ribs. Jimmy rolled over to fight, but it was all over, the man was through; he'd passed out.

The bartender ran over to the table. "Is he dead?"

Liz crawled over to check his pulse. "No, he's just out cold!"

Rick scooped his rings and coins, putting them back in the bag with the silver bolt. "Hey guys, let's scat out of here before the cops show up. I don't know about you, but I personally don't want to be asked any questions about this." Everyone agreed and started toward the door except Jimmy. He and the bartender stood calmly, looking down on the comatose troublemaker. Rick doubled back, grabbing his friend by the arm. "Come on Jimmy let's get out of here before trouble catches us."

The Bartender tagged along to the entrance, "Hey guys, come back tomorrow, and don't worry. If the cops ask me who the other guy was, I'll say I don't know."

At the hospital emergency-ward, the man was given medical attention and assigned a room. Since he had signed no papers and given no personal information, the hospital staff looked for next of kin. The man's wallet identified him as: Robert Wellin,

Chicago resident. They found a picture of a much younger man, posing with a lady, judged to be his mother. The picture was taken, in front of a cable car. Behind the car, the rails went up a steep hill. There was no address or name of the woman, just a date twenty-two years ago. The staff decided it could be only one place – San Francisco.

Detective Brian Weeder received the call from the hospital in Chicago. The admissions clerk, looking for relatives and someone to pay for the patient's care, had phoned the San Francisco police for help locating family. Weeder had them enlarge and send the picture over the Internet. A check of old phone records gave him an address for several Wellin residences. He compared them against current records, finding two that matched. A quick call told him neither were the party he was seeking. Brian guessed the woman must have remarried. He searched the marriage records. The woman could be Evelyn Jamison. Brian called her.

"Yes, I have a son named Robert Wellin, by my first husband," the woman answered, "but I haven't seen him in years and years."

Leaning back in his chair, Weeder relaxed. "Are you alone Ms. Jamison?"

"No, my neighbor and I were just watching the soaps. We do that every day, you know."

"Good, if someone is there with you, I can tell you over the phone, Ms. Jamison. A hospital in Chicago just contacted me to say your son has been injured and they'd like to speak with you right away."

"My!" she exclaimed. "Isn't that strange? Why I haven't see or heard from Stormy since his girlfriend died and he moved to Chicago with her daughters?"

A red flag went up! Brian immediately became suspicious. "Uh – Ms. Jamison, do you happen to remember the name of your son's girlfriend?"

"Gee, it's been so long ago, it's hard to remember – " she grunted as she searched her memory. "It seems to me it was something like – Sherry Nicolas. No! That's the name of one of the daughters." The old lady apologized, "I'm sorry Mr. Weeder; I just can't remember; it's been so long ago."

"You did just fine Ms. Jamison," Brian said with a tone of excitement in his voice. "I wonder, if I might come over some time today to discuss a few details about your son, with you."

"Oh sure, any time would be fine. Just don't come during my soaps."

"I understand," Brian laughed. "I'll come over about three." He marked his calendar accordingly.

The interview went fine, Detective Weeder was convinced Robert Wellin was the murderer of Carol Nicolas, mother to Sherry and Madelin. He did need to positively identify Wellin before making an arrest. To that end, he paid money out of his own pocket to have Ms. Jamison fly back to Chicago to help with the identification.

Inside the cab on the way to the Chicago hospital, Brian chatted with the likable old lady, "So how is it you didn't know your son only took one of the daughters?"

"That's an easy one, Mr. Weeder. My husband – Er, I mean my first husband and I were doing a lot of traveling at the time. We were in France that year, and the weather was so nice. Have you ever been to France?"

Flashing a smile, Brian answered, "No, except for military service I never got to go anywhere."

"Oh you would have loved it," she flirted, "A nice man like you and all those beautiful girls."

155

"I'm sure I would have, Ms. Jamison." Reverting back to the original question, he asked, "You didn't get word, because you were out of town?"

"Oh yes," she chattered, delighted to have a handsome young man to listen to her, "Stormy left a note in our mail box." She repeated herself, "We were touring France you know."

The ride ended, Brian paid the fare and escorted the elderly, teetering woman through the maze to the son's recovery room.

"I think that's him." Brian pointed to the large man, with a covering on his forehead and one ear.

"Are you sure?"

"Ms. Jamison, that is for you to determine, if you will."

She went closer, her eyesight not being what it once was.

The man's face was swollen badly from the beating. One eye was also swollen shut; the other one was blackened. His nose showed signs of treatment, having been broken along with numerous teeth.

"He's a mess," she whispered.

Weeder nodded.

"Stormy?" she asked, touching his arm lightly.

The man opened his only available eye. He studied the fragile woman, silently, like a snake studies a mouse before having dinner.

"It's me – your mom," she coaxed.

"Go away," he said in a muffled tone.

She paused while a nurse's cart clattered past in the hallway. "I've come to visit for a while," she persisted.

Her son eyed her in silence.

"Why haven't you come to see me?" she asked.

Before answering, he eyed the detective suspiciously, "Who's that?"

"Oh that's – "

"Your mother's escort," Brian cut her off. "Your mother is too old to make the trip here by herself." Pretending to be friendly, he looked at the I.V. in the man's arm. "I'd shake hands, but it looks like I might knock something loose." Weeder smiled with a fake smile.

"Why haven't you written, Stormy?" her voice wavered.

"You – changed your name," he growled.

Delighted with his response, she patted his shoulder lightly. "Oh I remarried about twelve years ago." She paused to lick her lips, "He's a really nice man – you'll like him."

The patient eyed Brian nervously.

Looking around for a chair to sit in, she asked, "Do you have any family?"

Brian pulled a visitor's chair over for Ms. Jamison. He seated her and stepped back, far enough to hear, but not be intrusive.

"No – no one," the man responded.

"What happened to little Sherry?"

He eyed Brian again, finally answering, "She ran away after I moved here."

"I'm sorry to hear that. And you never found her?"

"No."

"Why didn't you go to the police and ask them to help you find her?"

The man started to move, setting off a number of beeps from monitoring devices. A nurse passing by the doorway heard them and entered the room.

"Mr. Wellin, you need to not move around until things heal," she scolded. "Do you understand?"

He shifted his attention from Brian to the nurse, then back to Brian. He didn't answer.

157

As the nurse left the room, Brian followed.   He was convinced the man was Robert Wellin, the boyfriend to the murdered woman. As far as the detective was concerned, he just needed to be guarded until he was well enough to be transported back to San Francisco. The first step was to arrest him, but Brian lacked authority.   He moved away from the door, where he wouldn't be heard and dialed the Chicago police on his cell phone.

When the homicide detective arrived with a uniformed officer, Brian intercepted them before they came in visual range of the suspect. He explained the facts of the case and asked that Wellin be arrested and guarded, until papers to expedite him could be arranged. Wellin was arrested.

Not fully aware of the serious charges her son faced, Mrs. Jamison rested safely in the comfort of her motel room, watching her favorite soaps during his interrogation.

Discouraged with Wellin's lack of cooperation during the questioning, Weeder grabbed a sandwich from the food machine to satisfy the knot in his stomach. Several bites into the soggy bread, cured his weak appetite. He discarded the sandwich, choosing to finish his coffee. Wellin failed to give much information regarding the fate of Sherry Nicolas. He continued to deny harming her, choosing instead to say she simply ran away. Brian wasn't sure, but since Wellin's story was consistent, he might be telling the truth.

Armed with information where the beating had taken place, Brian took a taxi to the bar early in the afternoon. He strongly suspected Wellin received his beating as a bit of justice for the frequent beating of the woman he killed. If his suspicions were correct, the bolt might be found there. Gaining possession of the bolt would greatly aid him in locating the missing little girl – if still alive; she would now be a woman. He wanted the bolt.

Blinded by exposure to the strong sunlight outside, Brian strained to see inside the dark, empty bar.   When he got his bearings, he went over to the counter and climbed up on one of the swivel stools.

"Club soda please," he said, dropping a five on the wet counter.

The bartender made the drink and gave him change. "You a cop?"

With a laugh, Brian confessed, "Yeah, from San Francisco."

"Suit and non-alcoholic drink gave you away."

Brian nodded.

The bartender found his rag and wiped down the counter. "Be in town long?"

"Hope not."

"Aw, Chicago's a nice place, just gotta like the weather."

"I suppose." Weeder said, playing with his glass for a few seconds. "You guys did me a big favor the other night."

The heavyset bartender stopped wiping for a second to look at his customer. "Oh?"

"Yeah, you nailed a suspect on a twenty-year-old murder back home."

"Oh really!" he said with interest. Walking back opposite Brian, he stopped to give him his full attention.

"Yeah, whoever flattened him did a first rate job."

A reflection of suspicion crossed the bartender's face. He didn't intend to give away any secrets. "Well, I don't know the guy, but if I ever see him again, I'll tell him you liked what he did."

"Did the guy happen to have any hardware with him?"

"Guns?"

"No. No, nothing like that." The detective made a rowing gesture with his hand, "You know, like nuts and bolts."

The bartender looked at him as though the guy had just fallen off the truck going to the funny farm. "That's gotta be the screwiest question I've heard this week."

"I guess it does sound strange," Brian smirked. "I just lost a bolt, and was looking for it."

The rotund man thought for few seconds, "Say, if you lost a bolt, I know a regular that finds stuff like that. He's a real whiz at it."

"I'd be interested in talking with him," Brian sipped his drink. "How do I find him?"

Checking his watch, the bartender estimated, "He'll be in here tonight, I'm sure, in about – four hours."

The ice clanked in the glass as the last of the drink slid down Brian's throat. Setting the glass down, he told the bartender, "Okay, I'll drop by later to see if he can help me."

* * *

Weeder drove to the police station to visit the person in charge of the missing person's records.

"I'm not sure the records go back that far," the young man said with doubt. "Hold on for a second," the clerk said, returning to his desk to work at the computer terminal.

Brian nodded. He leaned on the old, wooden counter, for the first minute, watching the clerk at the computer terminal on the opposite side. After a while, the detective became bored. To pass the time, he visually surveyed the old building while glancing back toward the clerk periodically.

The bespectacled clerk eventually returned to the counter with a computer printout. "Yes, we do seem to show records back that far, but it took a bit longer to access them." The young man leaned sideways on the counter to point to a particular area of the printout Brian requested. "See here, it shows a young runaway picked up about ten days after the date you said her mother died.

160

She would only give her first name for several hours, but the officer finally determined it was Sherry Nicolas." He glanced over his glasses at Brian, "Never did say she was from out of town though. Only said her mother was dead, killed by the boyfriend."

"Of course you'd have no way of knowing where the murder took place, if it wasn't fairly local," Weeder added.

"That's true," the clerk said, looking up at Weeder. "And from what you told me, by the time her sister told her story, Sherry had already been placed in a foster home."

With a sigh, Brian nodded. "Did she ever say how he killed the mother?"

"Let's see – " he mumbled, scanning the page. Flipping to the following page, he caught a note. "Yes, it shows here," he said, pointing again to the printout. "She claimed the man wrapped an electrical cord around her mother's neck. Hair dryer, I believe – Yes, that's it – and threw the mother into the bathtub filled with water."

Brian winced.

"Let's see where the girl was sent – " The clerk mumbled to himself, as he scanned the pages. "Ah yes, here it is. She was placed in Mrs. Cook's home for girls. At this address," he said scribbling down the information.

Brian took the note, "Who was the case worker there?"

"Looks like Mrs. Bell."

"Okay, thank you very much for your help. I'll try to fill in the missing pieces myself."

The young man took off his glasses, "You're very welcome Detective Weeder, glad to be of service."

Brian smiled, "Perhaps someday, I can even answer some of your questions."

The clerk gave him a puzzled expression, "As a matter of fact, you might."

Brian hesitated, "You have a question?"

"Well yes," he began rather sheepishly, "Could you tell me what it's like to be in an earthquake?"

* * *

Mrs. Jamison was delighted to have Brian take her out for an early supper. However her glee was short lived when the detective deposited her back at the motel, after dinner, saying he had to return to a bar alone.

Since Brian had given the bolt to the sister that lived in San Francisco, and since Wellin suddenly surfaced after two decades of hiding, he was sure the bolt was responsible. Of course Wellin was beat up in the bar and the bolt was likely responsible for his punishment. Dressed more casually for his second visit, Weeder approached the populated table occupied by the treasure hunter and other members of that group. "They tell me you find things for folks," Brian began, speaking to Rick Weston

Looking up from his beer, Rick looked puzzled. "Uh – Yeah, I guess I do that – sometimes." He stuck out his hand for a hand shake.

Brian took his hand, "I'm Brian Weeder, from San Francisco."

"Pleased to meet you."

"May I sit down?" Brian asked, pointing to a chair.

"Sure, sure. Help yourself," he said pointing to various chairs available.

Weeder pulled a chair out and flipped it around, choosing to sit in it backwards as he leaned toward the table to look at Weston across the table.

"What did you lose?" Weston asked, looking at Brian.

"Just a bolt."

The din of fast pounding music clogged the air, making it extremely hard to hear.

Rick strained to hear the conversation. After several attempts shouting back and forth, he dispatched one of the group to turn down the volume a bit. "That's better," he sighed. "What is it you said you lost?"

Holding his thumb and finger about three inches apart, Brian repeated himself, "Just a bolt."

Amused, Rick rubbed his sandy hair. "What kind of bolt?"

"Common ol' half-inch bolt about that long," he said, gesturing again.

"Where'd you lose it?"

"Don't know."

A look of surprise formed on the man's face. "How do you expect me to find it, if you don't have any idea where you lost it?"

"Actually, I think you already found it."

Rick glanced around the table at his friends, wondering which one talked.

"No, don't blame them. I have my own sources."

"You what?"

Attempting to short-circuit the discussion, Brian made him a proposal. "Tell you what, Rick. If you check the bolts you found, and if one of them is a half-inch bolt with my initials, 'BW' on it, I'll give you ten dollars for it." He looked him in the eye, "No questions asked."

The treasure hunter probed his pocket until he found the car keys. He sorted out the trunk latch key and handed it to Jimmy. "Fetch my bag of treasure, will you boy?"

After dispatching Jimmy, Rick studied the thin, brown-haired man opposite him at the table. Aside from the feeling he was playing a game with the stranger, when he knew nothing about the rules or the stakes, of the game, Rick was at ease.

163

"You got me curious, Mister — what the heck's so important about this bolt of yours?"

"Let's just say I'm sentimental about it."

"Hell, for ten dollars, I'll drink to that," he toasted, raising his beer mug.

Everyone clicked glasses before drinking.

Jimmy's large frame came back through the outside door. As he handed the bag to Rick, Brian noticed the bandaged and swollen knuckles on the young man.

The contents clanked against the table top as Rick dumped them. He stopped when the bolt fell out. Picking the bolt up, he dropped the bag on the other contents piled on the table. "Let's see here," he said, straining to see in the dim light. "Anybody got a flashlight?"

Everyone fumbled and muttered for a few seconds, until Brian produced his own pen light.

"Thanks," Rick said, taking the light. He shined it on the head of the bolt, turning it round and round until he saw them. "Well, I'll be damned!" He said, looking up at Weeder, "It is your bolt!"

With a toothy grin and a ten-dollar bill, Brian took possession of the bolt.

"Now how did you know -?" Rick puzzled.

Brian dropped the bolt in his pocket. He raised his beer mug, "No questions asked, eh?"

Everyone at the table toasted.

His business nearly completed, Brian had just one more thing to do. He left the table to walk to the bar. He handed the bartender a twenty, telling him, "The big guy at the table — the one called, Jimmy. . . " Without pointing, or looking back, Weeder released the twenty saying, "I want you to give him drinks until this runs out. "Brian tossed down the remainder of his drink adding, "Tell him, there's a battered angel in heaven singing his song."

The following morning, the trip to the foster-home was uneventful. Mrs. Bell had died two years earlier. The detective was frustrated, but not stymied. He decided to check adoption records.

The walls of the old building were made almost entirely of brick, an omen of the people inside.

Weeder stepped through the door. The interior of the large, three-story building was broken up by numerous office cubicles. The detective introduced himself to the clerk of records, Bernice Gear. She was a short, badly-overweight woman in her late fifties, with dyed, jet-black hair.

"So I'm trying to locate the missing girl for her sister back in San Francisco."

Bernice adjusted the black-rim glasses that frequently slid down her ski-sloped nose. "I'm sorry, but you'll need a judge's permission to open any of our records, Mr. Weeder."

"Well, Bernice," he tried to personalize his contact with the woman, hoping she'd be more cooperative, "I just need her adopted name. I don't need to see the whole file."

"Mr. Weeder, we don't give out 'tidbits' here. You'll need a judge's order before we can tell you anything." She gave him a stern-faced bureaucratic answer, instead of telling him the records had been destroyed in a fire eleven years ago.

"Perhaps you could just look up the woman's name and call her to ask if she'd want to speak with me. You don't have to actually disclose the information to me."

"Sorry," she said, with an inflection that indicated no sorrow on her bureaucratic part.

Weeder studied his opponent. It didn't matter that he was a police officer or that the subject was now an adult. It didn't matter how he explained his need for the information. It didn't

165

matter if he didn't directly receive the information. The record's clerk wouldn't budge. She perched herself on her padded swivel chair, like a spoiled cat on its favorite pillow. She had all the unbending rules on her side and would share none of the risks.

"Would you at least call the adopted parents to see if they would speak with me?"

"You'll need a judge's order," she repeated herself.

The ringing phone interrupted the confrontation. Bernice picked it up. "Bernice, Records – " She reached for her pencil. She scribbled a note on a small writing pad. "The name?" She wrote it on the pad. "Yes – I'll get for you right away." Putting the phone back on hook, she jumped down from her perch. Without so much as excusing herself, she grabbed her notepad and waddled at a leisurely pace into the records room.

Brian was furious. He searched his mind for anything he could use to convince her to give him the information. He could think of nothing. . . Nothing except the bolt. *"Why not?"* he thought, perhaps she'd have a change of heart after touching the bolt. He dropped his business card on her desk and carefully set the silver bolt on top of it. He'd leave now, only to return tomorrow, to see if she'd make the information available.

The taxi pulled up in front of the hospital. Brian paid the driver and worked his way to Robert Wellin's room. He saluted the police officer guarding the door, before entering the room to join Mrs. Jamison.

"Oh, hello Brian," Evelyn Jamison greeted him politely, with her usual smile.

"About ready for your soaps?" he teased.

"What time is it?"

Brian glanced at his watch, "They'll start in about an hour. We've got enough time to catch a bite of lunch first though."

"Oh good. Do you think we can stop at that pink restaurant we saw yesterday?"

Movement from the bed caught Brian's eye. He glanced over to see her son, Robert Wellin tensing severely. "We'll talk about it in a moment, Ms. Jamison. Right now, I'd like you to go to the waiting room – you know, where they keep all of the magazines – and wait for me, please."

Following a brief moment of disappointment, the lady smiled again, "Then we'll have lunch together?"

"I'd be delighted, Ms. Jamison. I'll be with you in a minute."

Both men watched as she slowly made her way out of the room. They listened as she paused briefly to exchange idle conversation with the police guard at the door. Brian stepped back toward the entry to gauge her progress. She was slow, but doing fine on her own.

The prisoner had refused legal council, was not talkative and was not social at any level. His attitude disturbed Brian. He was unsure how to proceed. Being in the man's presence felt like being locked in a cage with an angry bear. Yet there were answers the detective needed about Sherry and her disappearance.

Weeder strolled to the prisoner's bedside and watched him silently for a few seconds. He hoped his silence would be taken as a sign of strength, not cowardice. It was terribly hard to read this man who lived by intimidating others. Weeder decided it might be best to start conversation on an aggressive note – a bear will always respect another bear, especially one strong enough to fight. "You should be ashamed, Wellin! You have such a sweet, innocent mother, and you give her such grief."

The beast muttered an obscenity.

"Just what kind of animal are you to bring this trouble into her life?"

"Get lost!" Wellin sneered.

"Ever have nightmares, Wellin?"

The man looked out the small window of the third story. He could see nothing but blue sky and a few treetops. He remained silent.

The detective knew the softer approach would be discarded instantly. Like the bear, the man needed to respect the power and aggression of his enemy. Only then would he be inclined to cooperate at all. Weeder moved closer, crowding the man's personal space. "You're dangling over a cliff, Wellin. You got there by your own doing. But I swear, if you don't tell the truth about little Sherry, I'll assume you killed her and I'll personally see you face the death penalty for your deeds."

The heart monitor, removed by the nurse earlier, left the detective with little to monitor his effect on the savage. He suspected the man's pulse rate was up, if his own pulse was any indication.

Wellin's face showed stress and his teeth popped from his jaw being severely clamped, but the killer remained silent.

Weeder pushed on, "Come clean, Wellin. You know more about little Sherry than you've told me."

Wellin turned and glowered at the detective in silence. His large jowls glowed a light pink, indicating he wasn't ignoring Weeder's irritation.

"You'd let your own mother go to her grave – thinking her only son wouldn't protect that little girl. Isn't that right?"

A massive fist knotted on Wellin's right arm.

"You're not a man – not a real man," Brian said, goading the aging murderer. Brian knew Wellin was nearly twice his weight and probably nearly twice as strong. Mindful of the danger, Brian watched Wellin's knotted fist as he feigned a move to turn his back on the beast while insulting him, "You're just a stupid jerk."

As if on cue, the strained arm, started to move.

Quick as a mongoose, Weeder turned back and grabbed the offending arm, mashing it into the hospital mattress. "Don't even think about it!" he shouted.

The police guard at the door, entered the room quickly. "Everything okay here?"

"How about it Stormy? Is everything okay?" Brian mocked. "Is the little girl okay?" he paused, "Or did you kill her to show your manhood?"

Slowly, Weeder released Wellin's arm, his eyes locked on the barbarian. He stepped backward, toward the guard behind him. "Yes, everything's okay. He's going to pay for his sins," Brian taunted, "He's going to pay for all of them."

Turning his back on Wellin again, the detective moved quickly away from the hospital bed.

"Hey!" the man yelled.

Weeder stopped at the door, by the guard, but didn't turn around.

"I didn't kill little Sherry."

That's all he said, but it was enough. Brian walked out of the room then smiled.

Before leaving with Brian for lunch, Mrs. Jamison wanted a quick word with her son. Entering Wellin's room, she found him in a highly agitated state. Her friendly smile was met with a tooth grinding grimace. She ignored his body language to approach his bed wearing a big smile of her own. "Stormy?" she called. "Oh, you'll be pleased to hear the news," she said bubbling with excitement, "I just talked with the nurse and she said they will probably release you tomorrow."

He eyed her nervously.

"You'll be able to come back to San Francisco with us, the day after that." Her enthusiasm didn't carry over to her errant son, but she went on, "Detective Weeder says he should have located little Sherry by then too. Isn't that good news?"

Wellin's fist tensed again. Sherry was the only eye witness and the only one to link him to the murder decades ago.

"Oh I'm so happy. It will be so nice for us all to be together again." She approached her son to give him a kiss on the cheek.

Wellin's upper body tensed, forcing his mending, broken rib to complain loudly. He obviously disliked his mother's constant upbeat form of prattle and hated her association with the San Francisco detective even more. The jowls on Wellin's wrinkled face hung like red curtains on a Punch & Judy puppet show.

Evelyn pecked him on the cheek. "Now be a good boy, Robert, and heal quickly," she chirped. With a school girl expression, the elderly lady confessed as she moved toward the door, "I've got a luncheon date with a handsome young detective and I don't want to be late." She picked up her step as she left the room.

When the clock crossed the boundary into the new day, Robert Wellin chose to make his move. He was a jealous man, guarding every woman in his life from all outsiders, male or female. It was truly sad that he failed to guard them from the worst danger – himself. His mother's fantasy with the California detective served to push her son over the top. Wellin was accustomed to being a wanted man, but up until now, he had never been identified as a murder suspect. Since Brian Weeder had linked him to Carol Nicolas, and with the improvements in DNA testing, Wellin knew it would only be a matter of time before he'd be linked to her murder. His only choice for survival was to destroy the link to Carol Nicolas by killing Brian Weeder, then lose himself, and his DNA, in society a second time.

Most of the monitoring equipment had been removed from his hospital room, its presence required elsewhere. There would be no telltale beeps at the nurses' station when Wellin disconnected. Wellin ripped the I.V. needle from his arm, throwing it aside in disgust. His huge fingers felt for a loose end to the bandage covering his forehead and left ear. Finding no end, he dug until he ripped into the sterile dressing, then with a growl, he quickly shredded it.

Wellin stuffed everything loose that he could find, in the room such as pillows, bedpans, tissue dispensers, and towels from the bathroom under the top blanket to make it appear that someone was sleeping there. He did reserve one hand-towel and a roll of bandaging tape he pilfered earlier for his plan.

In the corridor, the female police guard heard gagging sounds coming from inside the room. She jumped to her feet and stepped through the door to see what was happening. The room lighting was turned off, since it was shortly after midnight, but she was able to see a form, lying on the bed. She tried the light switch, but the bulbs had been removed – the room remained dark. From behind the door – in the shadows – the predator waited for his victim to move into position. His movement was unusually silent as he slipped up behind her, covering her mouth and nose with the towel in his hand.

The officer instinctively reached for her weapon, but a burley arm clamped her arm against her body. She tried to drop, in an effort to throw him over her shoulder, but as she lifted her legs, he simply held her aloft. She wriggled, and screamed and bit at the towel over her mouth; nothing worked. He held her tightly until she lost consciousness.

Wellin needed clothing, but the female guard was far too small for her uniform to fit him. He carried her to the bed, choosing to sit on the edge with the unconscious form resting on one thigh. He wrapped his other leg over the lower half of her body, in case she faked unconsciousness. Quickly he removed her weapon and radio, tossing them quietly on the bed. He stood up and laid her on her back. Hastily he taped over her mouth to keep her silent. The bed shook as he rolled her over and grabbed both hands to tape them behind her back. He bound her feet together, then bound them to the bed frame. The final touch was to pull the blanket over her, so that she became the substitute body.

The escapee grabbed the officer's weapon and radio. The two nurses on duty were occupied in a patient's room at the far end of the hallway; Wellin went the opposite direction. He watched for a linen closet to better clothe his half naked body. Failing to locate one, he reversed direction, heading toward the nurses' station. Inside of the circular counter, he searched for anything he could wear on the street. Nothing was available.

The phone rang. An unsuspecting nurse ran back to cover her abandoned station. Reaching across the counter, the petite nurse operated the phone from an inverted position.

"Third floor, Bagley speaking."

Wellin waited patiently, inside the nurses' circular counter, below her line of sight, below the phone.

"No. I'm sorry, but he's resting at the moment. We gave him a sedative about two hours ago. Can you call his room after seven? Yes – that would be fine. Thank you."

The phone rattled as she fumbled to place the handset on the hook. The sound of her squeaking shoes became fainter and fainter as she returned to help the other nurse in the patient's room.

Wellin resumed his search for clothing. He found nothing. A set of keys, resting on the work surface under the overhanging counter, caught the man's eye. He took them. A few steps away, Wellin pushed the down button to call the elevator. Coolly he waited for it to arrive. It bounced to a stop, the door retracted. Wellin stepped inside where he selected the second floor.

When the elevator stopped, he positioned himself in front of the floor-selection panel and waited. With a piece of tape, he'd clamped the button that told the computer in the elevator to keep the door open. He waited patiently.

The nurse on duty became curious. It was very unusual to have the elevator stop, door open, and have no one exit. The male nurse approached the elevator. It appeared empty until he stuck his head inside. By then it was too late.

The fugitive grabbed the man by the neck. Two well-placed punches, rendered him unconscious. Wellin abandoned him temporarily to search for clothing. He saw signs pointing to the scrub room. Inside, he finally located clothing large enough to wear. It fit much too tight, but it did cover him. He backtracked to the elevator. The nurse remained unconscious. Wellin chose the stairwell. At the bottom, he walked across the lobby and out the main entrance into the parking lot. There he searched the nearly vacant parking-lot for a car with the same brand stamped on a key attached to the ring he had taken. The key worked, he left.

* * *

Convinced the bolt would do it all for him, Brian entered the brick building where the state adoption records could be accessed. He found his way to Bernice Gear's work station.

"Good morning Bernice," he said, hoping the bolt had somehow changed her attitude.

Unfamiliar with Weeder's voice, she looked up briefly to see who was there. "Oh it's you," she said, with an unenthusiastic whine.

"Yes – I'm back to see if you can help me."

She continued to fill out forms, ignoring him.

Brian waited patently, expectantly.

173

"Where is it?" she asked without looking up at him.

"Is what?" he questioned.

"Where's the paper from the judge?" she asked looking only at the papers in front of her on her desk.

"I didn't bring one."

Bernice stopped her writing to look up at the detective. "I told you yesterday that you'd need a judge's permission to view the records." The woman obviously loved the ultimate power of her job. It was equally obvious that she had played this part many, many times, stretching the fabric of stress to the breaking point. She had a knack and enjoyed using it.

"I understand, but – "

The clerk tossed her pen on her desk; it bounced twice before rolling to a stop nearly out of her reach. She pushed back in her padded-swivel chair. "What's the matter with your hearing, mister?" She did her best to appear intimidating, "I've told you over and over, you'll get nothing here without a judge's permission."

"But I – thought the bolt – "

"Oh – well, you thought wrong, didn't you?" She pointed to the entry door of the building. Knowing the records were destroyed and unavailable in any case, she banished him saying, "You can go now – and don't come back without a signed, judge's order."

The detective was dismayed. It wasn't supposed to work this way. The bolt had failed him. With a sad expression pasted on his face, he slowly turned to leave.

"Wait," Bernice called.

Brian turned, hoping against odds she'd changed her mind.

She opened her desk drawer removing something. Holding out her hand she commanded him, "Take these with you.

You left them here yesterday." She dropped the business card and half-inch bolt into Brian's hand.

The bolt was black. Brian was startled. He knew it had a problem with her, but he had no way of knowing her intent to deceive him regarding availability of records had blackened it.

Weeder looked at the woman; he shook his head, giving her this advice, "I don't think you've been honest with me. This is not a threat, but a serious warning. Don't walk in front of any moving trucks, and don't allow yourself to be found in dangerous places." It was likely she'd be punished, but Brian also had no way of knowing the details of her penalty – the bolt had other plans for him.

Back at the motel, the grim-faced detective made a few phone calls to locate a judge capable of signing access papers to Sherry's adoption records. He made an appointment and left immediately. He decided to work off some of his frustration by walking the twenty blocks to the court house and judge's chambers. When he arrived, he signed in and took a chair, waiting patiently for the slow wheels of progress to turn. Two hours after his appointment was scheduled, he was granted access to Judge Elana Yates, in her chambers.

Judge Yates was in her late-forties, and had been a sitting judge for about ten years. She had seen her share of trouble and dealt with it quite fairly at first. In the past few years, her attitude had changed a bit, leading her to "bend the law" just a bit to suit her own whims.

Finally in front of the judge, Brian summed up his argument, "And so you see, Your Honor, that's why I need your permission to view the adoption records." The detective had made his best case, but would it help?

The Judge examined her notes, taken while Brian pleaded his need for her help. "Detective Weeder, I see no compelling

D.Malisch

reason such as life and death to give you access to such information." She looked over her reading glasses at the detective standing in front of her desk.

"But Your Honor," Brian pleaded, "A great wrong was committed when this girl's mother was murdered by the man who abducted her. She rightfully should be allowed to contact her remaining relative in San Francisco."

"I understand that, Mr. Weeder, but it isn't life threatening, and I'll not give permission."

"It's also important to the prosecution of the murderer, since the child likely saw her mother being killed. She could be a key witness in this matter."

"I understand that too, Mr. Weeder. But you haven't shown me proof she even witnessed the murder."

"How can I, when you won't give me access to records to find her?"

"Are you accusing me of being unfair, Mr. Weeder?"

"Yes I am, Your Honor."

The Judge seethed. She didn't like being pressured by anyone, especially from those she considered beneath her. "Mr. Weeder! I'll have you know, I've always been extremely fair and impartial in my judgments," she lied, "And I greatly resent any inference, by you, to the contrary."

"But Your Honor – "

"And if you continue to assault me verbally, I'll have you incarcerated." Her brow lowered as she threatened him. "I don't give a damn whether or not you're a police officer or not, I'll have you thrown in jail."

It wasn't going well for Brian. He'd met dead ends everywhere he searched for Sherry Nicolas. The bolt had gotten him here. It had located the killer. However, it had failed him in his search for the missing little girl. Would it work on the judge?

176

Did he dare try it? He knew if he didn't try – he'd never be able to look at himself in the mirror again. He desperately needed to explore every chance to find the missing girl.

"Think about your unfairness judge." Brian removed the silver bolt from his pocket. He dropped it in front of the judge, on her work desk.

She looked at the silver object, thinking it was something that belonged in a mechanic's garage. Puzzled by the detective's action, she asked, "What's this?"

"It's to help you render a fair and impartial decision, Your Honor."

"You must be some kind of kook, Mr. Weeder. I told you, all of my decisions are fair and unbiased." Having said that, she reached for the metal object, intending to hand it back to him. The bolt judged her impartiality otherwise. A bolt of blue lightning leaped nearly an inch to her thumb and finger as she attempted to pick it up. The jolt severely stunned her, causing her to fall from her swivel chair to the floor.

Surprised, Brian cried, "Your Honor, are you all right?" He rounded her desk to help her to her feet.

She reclined on the floor near her desk for several seconds, gathering her strength and thoughts.

Weeder wisely returned the bolt to his pocket, before assisting her to her feet. He breathed a sigh of relief the bolt hadn't killed her.

As she sat in her chair, trying to remember what had happened, the memory slowly restored itself. She shook her head, trying to clear it.

Wary of his action, Brian stepped backward, to return to his position in front of her desk. A crunching sound from under his shoe, told him it was going to be a very bad day for Mr. Brian

Weeder. He glanced down to see the remains of the judge's reading glasses under his shoe. "Some days you just can't win," he thought.

The cracking sound caught the Judge's attention. She made eye contact with the detective, watching him as he moved to the front of her desk. Nonchalantly, she moved her fingers below the edge of her desk, where she pressed a silent alarm button.

The court bailiff appeared immediately at the door.

Judge Yates looked at the black spots on her finger and thumb, "Lock this man up. The charge is: attempting to intimidate an officer of the court."

"But – But – " Brian protested.

"For how long?" the bailiff asked.

"Three days," she answered, "Now get him out of here before I give him more."

Brian Weeder knew the process. It was much the same back in San Francisco. He surrendered his clothing and possessions in exchange for a uniform declaring him a prisoner. He took it all in stride, though it wasn't anything he'd planned or even imagined.

The first few hours, Brian couldn't get his mind off the injustice the bolt had caused him. He hadn't done anything to the Judge to justify being locked up. Well, he had stepped on her glasses, but that was an accident, and it wouldn't have happened if the bolt hadn't tried to electrocute her. He sat on his bunk, feeling sorry for himself. Why had this happened to him? Suddenly it stuck him. He was in jail for a reason. The bolt had planned it. A big toothy-grin returned to his face. Now, he needed to know what the bolt expected him to see, hear, or discover.

Kicking off his shoes, he crawled up on his bunk to relax as he considered his objective. Finding Sherry Nicolas was the objective; how could it be anything else? He looked around him at the four-by-eight cell. Whom would he ask? He put on his shoes, before walking to the steel door. He looked up and down the hallway.

The jail consisted of many, small, cement-block cells. Each cell was sealed from the main hallway by its individual hardened steel door. Each door consisted of a series of steel rods extending vertically through flat metal ribs. It was just a basic jail.

Brian looked at each cell across the aisle. Each one seemed to have one or two people in them. He needed to talk with each person, because someone here knew about Sherry. Was one of them her adopted parent, or was one of them a husband or brother? He had no way of knowing. He needed to investigate. *"How ironic,"* he thought, *"Investigating from the inside out, instead of from the outside in."*

Rubbing his wrist, now absent from his timepiece, he tried to gauge the hour. Was it time for lunch? He was slightly hungry, but he wasn't sure. "Hey! When do they serve lunch around here?" he shouted.

"Anytime you want! All you have to do is order!" some smart aleck shouted back.

Well, he asked for that. If he wanted answers, he'd need to compose his questions differently. "What was that stuff they served for lunch today?" Brian thundered.

"Today?" a deep voice questioned.

"Hey I didn't get no lunch yet," a young guy across the aisle complained.

"How'd you get lunch?" his neighbor wanted to know.

"Is the new guy the one askin' those stupid questions?" a fellow down at the end of the block bellowed.

Feeling proud of himself, Brian smiled. They told him it was nearly lunchtime. He kicked off his shoes and fell back onto his bunk to wait.

A bell sounded and some mechanical mechanism opened the locks on all the cell doors. Clusters of prisoners started down the hallway toward the cafeteria. Brian joined them. Selecting an older looking man, who seemed quiet and well groomed, Brian introduced himself, "Hi, name's Brian."

The man shook his hand, "Fred. How you doin'?"

"Be doing better if I wasn't here," Brian boasted.

"I hear that. How long you get?" Fred asked.

They passed through a large set of iron gates into an enclosed walkway outside the building. Brian looked beyond Fred into a green field, guessing it was the exercise yard. "Judge Yates gave me three days, 'cause she didn't like me."

"Yates did the same to me — " the guy behind Fred quipped, "But I got six months."

"She didn't like me neither," the guy walking with Fred agreed. "I don't think them judges like anybody, 'ceptin' them-selves."

Brian laughed. The group walked through a second set of iron gates into an area with paper napkins, plastic food trays and plastic eating utensils. Except for a scene at one of the tables on the far end of the lunchroom, the comradery continued through the line and through most of the meal. Finally Brian gulped down his meager dessert and asked, "Know anybody who's adopted?"

Fred shook his head, "No, why?"

"Aw, I'm just trying to locate a little girl — adopted about nineteen or twenty years ago."

Fred nodded. He broke a plastic tang from his fork to pry at his teeth in place of a tooth pick. "What's her name?"

"Well it was Sherry Nicolas, before she was adopted."

Pausing only to shake his head negatively, Fred continued to pick his teeth.

"How about the rest of you guys? Know anybody adopted by the name of Sherry?" Brian figured in this small group, he'd probably get relatively honest answers.

No one knew her.

Weeder looked around the lunch room. There appeared to be more than five hundred men in the dining area. He had no idea if this was all of the prisoners or if the inmate population ate in shifts? One thing he did know, there were a lot more men than he could question in three days, but he'd keep trying.

At every opportunity, Weeder continued to search for anyone who might know someone named Sherry, who had been adopted. No one knew her.

On the afternoon he was due to be released, a guard came to escort him through the exit procedure. He was to be checked for identity, and given a quick inspection for injury acquired during his prison experience.

Brian had mixed emotions about his release. On one hand, he couldn't get out of there fast enough. On the other hand, he hadn't located his target, which meant his three-day stay would be meaningless if he left now. It was a terrible internal conflict, one that seemed to have no resolution.

The guard checked his paperwork. "Let's see – Weeder, Brian B." He paused to scan through the details, "Mmm says here Judge Yates sent you here."

Brian pulled on his street trousers, tucking the shirt tail into them before connecting the snap. "I'd be surprised if I was the only one."

The guard looked up, "You might be the last one though?"

"Oh?" Brian paused to listen closely.

"Yeah, newspaper headlines say there's a big recall on to unseat her."

"Oh really?" He resumed dressing, "Did the paper say why she was being recalled?"

"Didn't give many details except to say the recall leaders claimed she had a lot of innocent folks locked up to suit herself."

Brian smiled – he knew the bolt had served justice.

"Just never can tell," the guard reminisced, "back when I got my job here twenty years ago, you'd never hear of anything like this."

Twenty years ago? Brian snapped to attention mentally. "I guess you know my name already sir." He extended his hand to shake, "I didn't catch your name."

"Edgar Kirzwad," the guard said with a smile. "I retire next month, you know."

"No, I didn't know," Brian said, shaking his hand. "Bet you're looking forward to retirement."

"Gawsh yes," he chattered. "We raised our girl; now it's time to do a little fishing."

"Know how you feel," Weeder worked hard to sneak his next comment into the innocent conversation. "You adopted Sherry about twenty years ago, right?"

Looking down, Edgar stepped right in Brian's snare. "Yep, I guess it was the same time I got my job here that we got her." Suddenly the look on his face changed to a more somber expression. "Say. How did you know my daughter's name and how did you know we adopted her?"

Flipping open his badge Brian identified himself formally, "I'm Brian Weeder, San Francisco police. I've been looking for your daughter and I need to know your daughter's married name."

Edgar stepped back from Brian. "You're one of them, there, stalker types, aren't you?"

"No Mr. Kirzwad, I'm no stalker. I'm from the west coast, with the San Francisco police." Brian displayed his badge a second time.

Shaking his head negatively, Edgar backed up. "That's fake. You bought it at some costume store or hock shop. Fellers' in here get them fake badges all the time."

"No, Mr. Kirzwad, I assure it's genuine."

"Just get yourself dressed, young man, I gotta do my job, but don't bother askin' me any more questions 'bout my family."

The silver, half-inch bolt rested under the detective's hand. He toyed with it, wondering if he could make use of it. Finally he put it in his coat pocket and finished dressing. He signed for his personal items and called a taxi to deliver him to his motel room.

A sign on the door of his motel room asked him to contact the manager immediately.

"I'm sorry, Mr. Weeder, but there is a convention coming to town, and I'm afraid the convention booked your room more than two months ago. You'll have to move," the manager informed him.

"Don't you have anything else for a couple more days?"

"No, I don't. You'll have to find another place."

"I see," Brian sighed.

He spent the next hour calling around the city, looking for a pair of available rooms. Everything was committed except for a motel currently under a partial renovation. Management there hadn't booked its rooms that far in advance because the surging construction progress left the number of rentable rooms unpredictable from day-to-day.

"Then you have two rooms available?" Weeder asked.

"Yes, we have three available," the registration clerk on the phone emphasized.

"Are two of them adjoining?"

183

"Yes, all three are adjoining, if you need them."

"Great, just hold two adjoining rooms for me, and we'll be there in about an hour, or sooner. Name is Weeder — Brian Weeder."

"Yes sir, we'll hold them for you sir."

For three days, life seemed to be on hold for Brian. Now, within an hour of regaining his freedom, he was rushing around trying to stay on top of things. Life was crazy.

Brian knocked on Mrs. Jamison's door to warn her they were moving within the hour, then he returned to his room to pack his own things.

The move went quickly, but otherwise was uneventful.

Settled in the new motel, Brian escorted Mrs. Jamison to a small, family restaurant, across the parking lot.

"I'm sorry I wasn't available to take you to dinner during the last three days, Ms. Jamison. I was busy with a case I'm working on."

Seated at the table after ordering, Evelyn Jamison unfolded her napkin, spreading it onto her lap. While afraid of dropping messy things into her own lap, she innocently dropped a terrifying worry on Brian's shoulders.

"Oh that's no problem Brian. I had dinner with my Stormy."

Brian laughed, "I hope you didn't have to eat one of those soggy sandwiches out of the food machines at the hospital."

"Goodness no. Stormy brought me a nice steak sandwich, just like the old days."

"Didn't know the hospital cafeteria had such things."

"Oh we didn't eat in the cafeteria, Brian."

Brian's confused silence charged the air.

"Just where did you eat, Ms. Jamison?" he asked, with a sound of alarm in his voice.

184

"Oh. We ate at my old motel room," she said with motherly pride, delighted that her son had finally come to see her after decades of absence.

Weeder tried to grasp what he was being told, but he truly hoped the elderly woman was delusional. Because, if what he heard was true, he'd just lost his appetite.

Mrs. Jamison smoothed the wrinkles from the napkin in her lap. "You look pale, Brian. Is something wrong?"

Ignoring the question, Brian quizzed her, "Stormy is out of the hospital and he brought dinner to your room?"

"Yes, that's right," she said with a smile.

Alarm spread rapidly over Brian's self assurance. Robert Wellin's aging mother didn't have a mean bone in her body; her son must have gotten them all. However, she had a knack for innocently doing the wrong thing. Brian reasoned if Wellin had escaped, the Chicago police would be looking for him. He further reasoned Wellin wouldn't harm his mother unless she got in his way, but why had he not fled the area? Why was he making contact with his mother? Worse yet, How did he know where to find her?

"Ms. Jamison, how did your son know where you were staying?"

Evelyn gave the detective a big, prideful smile. She opened her purse and extracted a stack of business cards for the motel, where they stayed last week. She had taken the time to write her room number on each of them. "I gave him one of these when we visited in the hospital."

Brian slapped his forehead. How could he have been so stupid? Worse yet, what had Stormy done to escape?

The waiter brought the steak and salads.

Brian pushed his chair back from the table and stood up. "Don't wait for me, Ms. Jamison, go ahead and eat your dinner. I have some business to attend to."

"Are you sure, Brian?" she said looking up at him with concern on her face.

"Yes, I'm very, very sure," he sighed.

Weeder rushed outside and turned on his cell phone. A quick conversation with the Chicago police confirmed his worse fears; Wellin had escaped. There was an A.P.B. circulating on him, but he was still on the loose.

Brian considered their recent room change. Had the half-inch bolt somehow forced the change for their personal safety? A chilling thought came over Weeder as he realized Wellin might harm the new tenants staying in Evelyn's old room. He would call back to warn the Chicago police, so they would watch.

The problem Brian faced had suddenly sprouted another head. The escaped murderer was somehow interested in the mother left abandoned twenty years ago, and Weeder was sure Wellin had not converted to a kind, loving son – the fugitive was up to something. The second problem – finding the missing girl – couldn't be handled by anyone except himself. Priorities seemed backwards, but Brian decided he'd look for the girl – the local police could watch for Wellin. After finding Sherry, with the bolt's help, he'd see that the murderer was recaptured.

Anxious to complete the next step in his plan, Brian escorted Mrs. Jamison back to her motel room, after dinner. He needed to do a little gift-shopping before the stores closed for the evening.

Returning to his motel room, an hour later, Brian seated himself at the small, round, writing-table, beneath the hanging lamp. It made an excellent place to wrap a present. Placing several layers of tissue to cushion the shiny fishing lures, Brian squeezed the half-inch bolt in the box too. He taped the box shut before wrapping it in gift paper. After attaching a bow, he set the small package aside. Taking out his pen, he signed the retirement card and dropped one of his own business cards in the envelope before sealing it. He went to bed.

In the morning, Brian skipped breakfast to journey back to the jail, where he had spent three days, as guest of the county. He located the guard, Edgar Kirzwad.

"Edgar, I'm sorry we got off on the wrong foot yesterday. Please accept my apology for making you feel uncomfortable."

"That's alright, young man, so long as you don't ask me any more family questions."

"I won't," Brian, promised, looking him in the eye. He pretended to turn and walk away, but stopped. Acting as though he had forgotten something, Brian came back to Kirzwad. "Oh yes, I nearly forgot," he lied. "I meant to give you this for your retirement." Brian handed him the card and package from the bag he was carrying.

Without saying another word, the scheming detective turned and left.

Kirzwad was speechless. Apparently he had misjudged the young man. He opened the present. The fishing lures delighted him, but the presence of a silver, half-inch bolt puzzled him.

In the afternoon, Kirzwad took the present home. He showed his wife the fishing lures and the half-inch bolt. Then in typical fashion, he left them lying on the coffee table for the wife to deal with later.

As the sun sank into the west, Kirzwad's adopted daughter, Sherry and her eight-year-old son, Bret Gentre dropped by for a brief visit. They admired Grandpa's new retirement gift. Edgar wanted to tell his wife and daughter about the strange conversation with Brian Weeder, so they left the grandson alone in the living room while they gathered in the kitchen to talk.

Alone in the living room, the grandson played with the fishing lures – his grandpa had promised to take him fishing soon, and he was excited. Bret's attention finally centered on the half-inch bolt. As the boy picked it up, the color changed from silver to gold, and the object radiated a strange warmth. Something about it intrigued him. As grandsons often do, he dropped it in his pocket. . . borrowing it for a few days from his Grandpa.

The following morning, Sherry – the dedicated mother and longtime missing person – prodded her tardy son to keep him on time for summer school. Looking up the stairs, she admonished him saying, "Hurry up Bret! It's time to go!"

The young boy brushed his teeth – though some teeth got extra cleaning while others were almost entirely missed. Still, not in a hurry, despite his mother's warning, Bret dropped his soapy brush on the counter to better concentrate on his rinsing. After wiping toothpaste on the towel from his face, he paused to look at his reflection in the bathroom mirror. Intrigued by his own appearance, Bret then chose to do more important things – such as making faces at himself in the mirror.

The boy's mother checked the clock in the hallway. She went to the stairway again and looked upward for her tardy son, "Bret, I've got to go to work. If you don't want to walk, you'd better get down here right now!"

"Be right there, Mom," he said, abandoning his foaming, toothbrush on the counter. Bret raced into his room to gather a few items to show his classmates at school. Stuffing the items into his day pack, he paused to finger the half inch bolt. He liked it.

Sherry waited impatiently for him to descend the stairs. When he reached the bottom, she pushed her son into the garage and up to the car door. She quickly circled the car, crawling into the driver's seat while Bret, climbed in the passenger side and fastened his own seatbelt. Sherry hurried to make up for lost time by starting the car, opening the garage door and glancing at the clock on the dash at nearly the same instant. She knew she would be late for a meeting with the manager of a motel under reconstruction. As she backed the car from the garage, she glanced into the seat behind her to ensure the fabric samples were there to show her customer. Looking back at Bret, she passed his lunch bag to him. As she turned to reach her own seat belt, a glitter of something gold reflected in her door window. It was something in Bret's hand. She looked back quickly to see him putting the object into the lunch bag.

"What's that?" she asked, with the authoritative tone of a concerned parent.

"What's what?" Bret asked, afraid his mother would confiscate the object.

"What did you just put in your lunch bag?"

"Nothing."

"It didn't look like nothing," she said, holding out her hand, "Give me the bag."

He reluctantly surrendered the bag.

She dug around until she located the object. Pulling it out, she demanded, "Where did you get this?"

"Oh that – " he said, trying to play innocent, "Grandpa gave it to me."

The – "Don't lie to me!" – mother's look pressed him for a better answer.

He raised his eyebrows. "Actually it's on loan," he said, modifying his story in hopes she'd believe him, though he knew better.

She examined the shiny, gold object. It looked too expensive to lend to an eight-years-old. "I'll take it back to Grandpa today, after I stop at the motel," she said, shoving it down into her purse.

* * *

189

Weeder sat alone in his room, hoping he could aid the local police in locating Wellin with some little clue written into his notebook. He knew the half-inch bolt was now in the process of helping him find Sherry Nicolas, or whatever her name was today.

Suddenly and without warning, the lights and air conditioner stopped. The detective pulled aside the drapes over the window looking out on the walkway in front of his room. A glance at his travel alarm told him it was nearly nine o'clock in the morning. Using the light coming through the window, he resumed a search of his notes. Within five minutes the air in his room felt hot and stale. He reached for the phone to call the desk to complain, but decided to walk to the office. A personal appearance is often better, he judged – besides, he wanted to buy a newspaper.

The office lights were also off. Apparently, the power was out throughout the building. Approaching the manager he identified himself, "Hi, I'm Brian Weeder, room 156. My air conditioner stopped a few minutes ago."

The clerk, a man in his mid-thirties, fanned himself with several sign-in cards stapled together to resemble a Chinese fan. "Sorry about that, Mr. Weeder." Looking up at the un-lighted fixtures in his office he added, "As you can see, everyone is affected."

Brian glanced around, the small, uncomfortably-warm, stuffy office.

The clerk stared wistfully at the blank computer terminal, on the counter beside them. "The workmen are pulling some new wiring for the rooms into the power distribution box. They told me that it might take a couple of hours to hook everything back up." He gave Brian a quick grimace. "I hope it doesn't take that long. Lots of folks complain."

Sheepishly, Weeder realized he was one of them. "Yeah, I suppose it can get very uncomfortable in the rooms without air conditioning."

The man pointed, "You might try a table out by the pool."

Brian looked in the direction the man indicated.

"A breeze from the lake would be better than nothing," the clerk promised.

Weeder watched the string of workmen passing by the pool for a few seconds. "Maybe I'll see if Ms. Jamison would like to join me at one of the tables. I think one of those large umbrellas would give good shade."

"Oh they would, Mr. Weeder." The clerk said, rubbing his chin, "But if you were planning on taking a dip in the pool, you might want to reconsider."

"Why's that?"

"The water softener guy, accidentally dropped a bag of salt into the pool this morning."

"Don't think salt would hurt us, but we weren't planning on a swim anyway."

The man nodded in silence.

Changing the subject, Weeder said, "I need a couple of soft drinks and a newspaper."

The clerk motioned with his arms as he gave directions, "The newspaper dispensers and soft-drink machines are around the corner to your left, inside the alcove."

"Thank you," Brian said, leaving.

Moments later, Weeder returned to the office to complain again. "It seems the soft drink machines took my money but didn't give me any product."

The clerk nodded, "I'm sorry. I should have remembered. The power is off and they won't dispense, though your money should have returned."

Brian shrugged.

"Let me get my key and I'll open it for you." The clerk fished through his desk drawer until he found a small ring of keys. He left the office with Brian in tow.

"Watch your step over this cord," the motel clerk advised.

Brian stepped carefully over the bright orange cord plastered down with an abundance of silver duct-tape.

Talking over his shoulder as he led the way, the motel clerk said, "The workmen tell me, that's the only circuit they left hooked up for us, while they rewire. If you need power, you can borrow the cord for a few minutes, just leave it plugged in right here."

"That's handy," Brian laughed.

The man disappeared into the alcove, Brian followed closely behind him.

Turning the key around and around, the clerk smiled. "Good, it works." The door to the dispensing machine opened, showing the stash of soft drink cans. "What type did you select?"

"Cola"

"How many?"

"Two."

The man handed Brian three, "Here's a spare for your inconvenience."

"Thanks," Brian replied, "Now if I could only get a discount on my room for the inconvenience."

The clerk studied him for a few seconds, "Yes. Well, I suppose I could do that for you." He closed the soft drink machine and started back toward the office. "Tell you what, I'll give you a ten-percent discount. Would that be enough?" The thin man, in his mid thirties, turned to look at Brian.

"Better than nothing," the detective smiled. As the man started to leave, Brian pressed him, "Think you could give Ms. Jamison a break on her room too?"

The man stopped again. He turned to face Weeder, "She traveling with you?"

"Yes."

With a short pause, followed by a sigh, the man relented, "Well, I suppose it's only fair. I'll do it." Without further comment, he returned to his office.

After purchasing his newspaper, Brian knocked on Mrs. Jamison's motel door. A few seconds later, she opened it.

Dressed lightly, the older woman greeted him, "Good morning Brian," she made a face, "Have you noticed how terribly hot it's getting?"

"Air conditioning's off," he smiled.

"Oh? Is that the thing that makes noise in my room?"

"Yeah, let's go out by the pool for a while."

"Where's the pool?" she asked, looking up and down the walk way in front of her room.

"Follow me. I'll show you."

"I didn't bring my suit," she apologized.

"We could always skinny dip," he teased.

She giggled, "My husband would be jealous."

Brian held up the ice bucket with soft drinks, "I'll bring the refreshment."

Mrs. Jamison turned to go back into her room. "I'll fetch my room key and postcards for my friends back home. Perhaps I can finish them out by the pool."

Weeder waited patiently for a few seconds, then escorted her to a table near the deep end of the pool. They sat facing the pool with the construction to their right.

The rectangular shaped pool was ringed by concrete finished in small decorative stones. Between the concrete walkway and chain-link, perimeter fence, a host of plants capable of withstanding the cold winters gave the pool-side folks a touch of privacy and a hint of non-urban living.

Along the deep end of the pool, construction scaffolding reached up the side of the building to the second-story balcony of the motel. Sections of wrought iron railing and eight foot iron anchoring-poles, waited on the scaffolding for workmen to install them. The anchor-poles closely resembled heavy, black spears with pointed tips. Once welded in place, they would add a certain class to the motel's appearance. Meanwhile, the balcony walkway, was closed for construction.

Mrs. Jamison admired the pool setting, then studied the construction mess by the end of the pool to her right. She glanced at Brian, busy with his newspaper. Not wanting to disturb the young man, she decided to work on her postcards. She searched the items on the table for her address list. Assuming she left it back in her room, she excused herself to recover it. "I'll be back in a minute, Brian, I forgot my addresses."

Brian nodded as he changed pages.

Mrs. Jamison toddled along the walkway toward her room, watching the numbers. As she neared her room, she was startled by the door opening in the room next to her own. "Excuse me," she said automatically, as she came to a stop. An expression of surprise crossed her face when she recognized the huge man she called son. "Stormy! What a nice surprise."

Wellin was equally astonished to see his mother. "What are you doing here?" his voice boomed.

"We moved here yesterday," she beamed.

He quickly glanced up and down the walkway in front of his door. "Where's Weeder?"

"Oh he's down by the pool, waiting for me." She tilted her head from side to side as she talked sweetly about the young man

194

who had escorted her from San Francisco. "It was too hot in my room, so he invited me to sit by the pool with him."

"At the pool?" Tension showed in Wellin's voice.

"Yes," she smiled. Tilting her head back to better see the man towering over her, she lifted her bifocals to bring him into focus. "My goodness, Stormy, you're soaking wet."

"It's hot," he complained.

"Why don't you join us down by the pool? There's a nice breeze there."

Wellin grumbled something unintelligible.

"Brian would be delighted to see you again; I'm sure."

Irritated by her chatter, Stormy raised his hand as though he would strike her, but his mother, in her innocence, didn't flinch.

"I'll go tell Brian I found you. I think he's looking for you, you know."

Wellin lowered his hand. "I'd like to see him too."

"Good," she twittered, "I'll go tell him as soon as I get my address book."

"Wait!" her son commanded, his deep voice booming. "I'd really like to surprise him, so don't tell him I'm here."

"Oh, I love surprises," she confessed, her face beaming with enthusiasm.

"I've got to get something for him first," Stormy promised, "Now don't say anything when you see me out by the pool. I want this to be a total surprise."

"That's wonderful Stormy. I'm so glad you and Brian like each other."

Wellin gritted his teeth. Reaching behind, he closed the door to his motel room, while he planned his next move. He left his mother behind, to stroll down the walkway toward the pool.

The newly acquired work-pants taken from a hardware store pressed the stolen revolver into Wellin's sweaty flesh at the waist band. As he walked, the revolver's knurled surfaces ate into his skin until he stopped to reseat it in a slightly different position. He pulled the stolen work-shirt over the weapon to conceal it.

Nearing the pool and office area, the fugitive spotted the orange extension cord, taped to the walkway. It gave him an idea. He looked around for construction materials or boxes. A large cardboard box containing some kind of fixture rested on the walkway near the office. He crossed through the row of plants to get it. Holding the box up to conceal his face, he slipped by the detective, into the parking lot, unnoticed.

In the parking lot, Wellin pawed through the open bed of a construction truck, where he took a hard hat, drill, and clipboard and sun glasses.

A sedan pulled into the parking area, forcing Wellin to move his bulky body out of the space next to the construction truck. Sherry Gentre, (the missing girl) parked her car and grabbed her samples of fabric to show the motel manager. She glanced at the workman in the hard hat, but failed to recognize him.

Wellin, not wanting to have witnesses recognize him, hid his face. He didn't recognize Sherry, the only eye witness to the murder of her mother.

Sherry walked briskly into the office of the motel. "Hello. I'm Sherry Gentre, Interior Decorator. I have an appointment to see Mr. Welm, regarding decoration of the renovated rooms."

"Ah yes," the clerk said, taking her business card. "I'm sorry, but he hasn't arrived today." The clerk glanced at the clock on the wall, made a face. He then looked at the time piece on his arm. "Our power is off and it is terribly inconvenient that clocks, computers and air-conditioning won't run."

Sherry looked around the room. Wrinkling her nose she said, "I noticed it seems darker in here than the last time I was here."

196

"The owner should be in within the next twenty minutes," the clerk said, looking at Sherry. "Would you care to wait?"

"Sure. I'll wait." She wandered around the office briefly before saying, "Seems to be awfully stuffy in here."

"I know — and it's getting worse." The clerk walked smoothly to the entrance door and propped it open. "That should help."

"Not enough," Sherry admitted nervously, wishing she'd used more deodorant.

The clerk noticed her restlessness. Pointing toward the pool, he offered, "You can wait by the pool, if you wish. There's a nice breeze outside. I'll call you when Mr. Welm comes in."

Looking relieved, Sherry picked up her samples, "That would be great. I really appreciate it." She moved briskly into the fresh air, toward the pool.

Wellin emptied the appliance from the box he'd appropriated. He tossed the clipboard and electric drill, with bit, into the box. Shouldering the box, though it wasn't heavy, he headed back toward the pool. As he approached the motel side of the pool, opposite Detective Weeder, he passed the attractive, young lady he'd seen in the parking lot. She looked familiar. He couldn't place her, but pictured her with him — naked. Maybe he'd take her with him after he killed the detective.

Brian heard the rhythmic click of high heels on the sidewalk. He glanced over the top of his paper to see a young woman in a pink business skirt, with matching pullover, walking quickly in his direction. As a bachelor, he checked her ring finger; she was attached. Still — she was nice to watch.

Sherry slowed as she approached the table next to Brian. "Is this table taken?" she asked. Her small, rounded nose wriggled in a peculiar way as she pursed her lips.

197

D.Malisch

Immediately, Brian saw the resemblance. He suspected she might be the missing sister, but it seemed too easy to accept her without a few simple questions. "Do you have a sister named Madelin?"

Halted in her tracks by the stranger's question, Sherry switched paradigms. She had come to the motel to conduct business. Her thoughts were all centered around her objective. Suddenly she was forced to think about family and a nearly forgotten past. "Who are you?"

"That's a fair question," Brian answered. He found his badge, displaying it. "I'm Homicide Detective, Brian Weeder from the San Francisco police." He examined her face very carefully, "Is your name Sherry Nicolas, and you were abducted at the age of eight?"

The look of surprise on Sherry's face answered his question.

Putting his badge away, Brian said, "Your sister, in San Francisco is searching for you."

"Oh my word!" She trembled.

"Have a chair," Brian offered, pulling a chair out with his left hand. "Sit at our table."

Confused, Sherry hesitated. She rested her fabric samples and purse on the table, while looking at Brian's face. As her mind filled with questions, she finally sat down. The purse fell on its side and the half-inch bolt rolled out.

"I wondered when that would show up," Brian laughed, picking up the golden object to watch it turn silver in his hand. "Got my initials on it, you know – "

The woman sat down, terribly glad, confused, and inquisitive at the same time. "I don't understand?"

"I know," Brian chuckled, "It's not simple, either. "He handed her the extra cola from the ice bucket. "Have a drink and we'll talk about it."

The wind from behind Brian tugged on his newspaper. He wrestled against the strong breeze to fold it properly and set it aside on the glass table. To hold the paper down, he dropped the half-inch bolt on top of it as a paper weight.

On the opposite side of the pool, Wellin considered methods to work his way up behind the detective for a close shot. It wasn't likely anyone would pay much attention when the gun was discharged; several workmen were firing nail guns on the new construction. Wellin surveyed the situation. He needed to abandon the cardboard box and find another method to disguise himself. Glancing around, he saw the orange extension cord between the pool and office. He moved toward the cord, where he connected the electric drill.

Glancing back at his prey across the pool, Wellin moved steadily around the pool, stalking Weeder. With a clipboard in left hand, drill in his right, the murderer worked his way toward the end of the pool on Brian's right. Keeping his back toward the detective, Wellin paused to drill holes in the old wooden flower box along the way. At each stop, he'd pretend to consult a diagram on the clipboard. Everything went smoothly until he reached the corner and started along the deep end of the pool, under the scaffolding. The orange cord was beginning to drag into the pool.

Seeing the electrical danger, Weeder interrupted his conversation with Sherry to shout at the workman, "Hey Fella!" he yelled, pointing at the danger. "Your electric cord is getting into the water."

Wellin didn't turn around, or answer. He simply waved his clipboard as a sign of acknowledgment. The disguised workman pulled all available slack out of the cord before tying it to the metal perimeter fence at the end of the pool. Convinced the detective was again distracted, Wellin continued his movement along the end of the pool to Brian's right.

Drill and look at the clipboard – Wellin made steady progress. As he reached the corner of the pool nearest Brian, he knew the cord would begin to dangle across the water again. The hazard might catch the detective's attention a second time. Wellin chose to knot the cord around several of the pointed wrought iron posts resting on the scaffolding. He estimated after drilling two or three more holes and he'd be able to touch the detective.

Mrs. Jamison, who was not the speediest walker, approached Weeder and the lady in pink, sitting at his table.

Brian stood up to make the introduction. "Ms. Gentre, this is Ms. Jamison, and Ms. Jamison, this is Ms. Gentre – " Brian paused to touch Sherry on the shoulder while looking at the older lady who had met Sherry in her youth. "You'd know her better as Sherry Nicolas."

"Little Sherry?" Evelyn bubbled, "Why, you're so big and so pretty!"

Wellin heard the introduction and flinched. The only, living eyewitness who had escaped from him twenty years ago? He could fix that – and would.

Weeder waited until Mrs. Jamison took the chair across the table from him, before seating himself.

Sherry looked at Mrs. Jamison, "I remember you. You're the nice lady who always had chocolate chip cookies for us when we'd come visit."

"Oh yes," Evelyn blushed, "I'd nearly forgotten. Those were such wonderful times."

Remembering her mother and visualizing her horrible death, Sherry's smile disappeared. "Some things were not so wonderful, Mrs. Jamison."

Attempting to prevent conflict, between the two women, Brian turned to face Sherry, on his left.

From behind, Wellin discarded the electric drill on the concrete path around the pool. He pulled the gun from under his shirt. Using the clipboard as a shield, he took two steps, stopping immediately behind the detective. He tossed the clipboard aside and aimed the pistol at the back of the detective's head.

On the opposite side of the table, Mrs. Jamison suddenly discovered her son was behind her friend, Brian. What was the surprise he talked about? Suddenly she saw the gun! In disbelief, her mouth opened in horror, but no sound came out. . .

A gust of wind from the lake caught the newspaper on the table. The bolt rolled to one side, allowing the paper to take flight.

The distraction, caused Wellin to look, for a split second.

Brian jumped to his feet, attempting to catch the paper before it blew into the pool. As he rose, his shoulder knocked the gunman's hand upward. The revolver discharged into the air, harmlessly. Brian turned to his right to see the large, battered face of the murderer with a very angry, disappointed grimace. "What the —?" Brian uttered.

Wellin tried to level the gun at Brian a second time, but the detective caught his arm, holding it upward. The fugitive applied weight and strength to force the arm downward. Brian countered by planting his feet and shoving upward. Locked in a life and death struggle, the two men slowly rotated to the rhythm of grunts and heavy breathing.

Holding the gun in his right hand, the large man attempted to pull the gun downward by adding the strength of his left arm. Fortunately for Weeder, Wellin's bulk, prevented his left arm from reaching his gun arm. Blocked — Wellin decided to bash Brian's head with the massive left fist.

With the brutal blows to his head nearly knocking him senseless, Brian held on desperately, but knew he'd better think up something fast. Wellin out weighed him more than two to one, and had a killer instinct.

Growling like a bear, the large man tried to lift his gun arm upward, to pull Weeder off his feet, but the tall detective only shoved the gun higher. Wellin stepped backwards to pull the detective off balance.

Brian was jerked forward as though he were a rag doll in the grip of a large dog. He knew he would lose his footing, but there was nothing he could do about it. Lessons learned in the police training academy played in his mind. He remembered being told to use the opponent's weight to his own advantage. Weeder belted out a battle cry and charged toward the bulky man. The detective's feet moved quickly, looking for any purchase to thrush himself forward. Wellin was large, but too slow to react against the charge; he failed to reposition his right foot before the detective pinned it to the cement walkway.

Unable to lift his foot, the giant fell backwards onto the chain-link fence. His gun hand stuck the steel railing, knocking the revolver from his grip; the firearm fell harmlessly over the fence. Wellin's head grated down the inside links of the fence, leaving bits of flesh and blood on the wire links. Weeder fell on top of him. The giant roared as he used both arms to grab the detective's throat.

Reaching for his own gun, Brian found a layer of clothing in the way. He fumbled, grabbed and dug desperately for access to his firearm, but couldn't reach it. Wellin was crushing his larynx, making it impossible to breathe. Suddenly, Brian began to black out.

The brute, felt his opponent go limp. Wellin tossed the body to one side while he rolled over to his knees. From a kneeling position, he grabbed his opponent with intent of permanently disfiguring his face. Wellin positioned Brian to better strike him with a huge fist.

Sherry, both surprised to see her old nemesis and appalled by his brutality again, retained her composure. She jumped to her feet to avoid contact with Wellin. As she watched the struggle and saw that the detective was clearly on the losing end of the battle, she made a decision. Driven by countless nightmares to fight back against the monster, she tried to find a means to repel him. Without combat training and abhorring violence, it seemed she was helpless – yet she refused to give up as she did as a child. From the back of her mind, visions of Wellin wrapping the cord of a hair-dryer around her mother's neck came to Sherry. Looking down, she saw the orange extension cord lying on the concrete, beyond the combatants. Pressing against, the chain-link fence, she quickly slipped past the large man. With great haste, she came up behind Wellin, and as rapidly as she could, she wrapped turn after turn of the orange cord over his head and around his neck.

On his knees, bent over his unconscious foe, the angry beast followed his immediate desire. He smacked Brian's face, once, then twice, with great satisfaction. He was so intent on destroying his opponent that he failed to notice the turns of electrical cord being slipped over his head. It was only as the cord began to tighten that he knew he had a second opponent.

Unsure what to do next, Sherry pulled tightly on the turns of electrical cord around Wellin's neck. When he failed to respond, she placed a spiked heel in the middle of his back and pulled hard on both ends of cord around his neck.

At first, nothing happened – then slowly, Wellin turned to look at her. Shaking and too frightened to scream, she forced him back around by digging the heel deeper into his back while pulling more tightly on the cord around his neck.

Wellin clawed toward her, but Sherry remained just out of his reach. His huge body wasn't agile enough to reach behind. The spiked heel was beginning to seriously hurt him. He grabbed at the cord between his neck and her hand. He caught a portion of her left hand.

Sherry felt Wellin's massive fingers beginning to tighten on her hand. She panicked and pulled her hand back, hanging onto the cord from the other side of his neck. To keep her balance, she removed her heel from his back. Gripping the cord firmly with both hands, she pulled tightly, on the remaining end. The three turns rolled around Wellin's sweaty neck until all of the slack in the cord was again removed between his neck and the wrought iron spiked post lying on the scaffolding.

Consciousness began to creep back into Brian's head. He opened his eyes to see Wellin looming over him, but the man was busy, looking backward. Brian looked beyond Wellin. The murderer was trying to reach the woman – Sherry. Weeder struggled to move his arms, but they were pinned under Wellin's knees. Brian couldn't free them. With his arms pinned, he also couldn't reach his pistol, not that he could use his Glock, anyway. Sherry would be in his line of fire. Rolling up on his back, Brian wrapped his legs around Wellin's neck and tightened.

Too late, Wellin realized the detective had regained consciousness. He'd deal with the woman later. He turned back to finish his business with the detective. From behind, he felt the woman's heel against his back once more. Angered, even more, Wellin shifted his weight to deal with the lawman, the detective rolled with him. Sherry's push from behind somersaulted the beast into the pool.

Hanging on as tightly as she could, to the cord, Sherry watched in horror as a shower of iron poles were pulled from the scaffolding above her into the pool. She let go of the cord as she saw several of the tipped spears pierce Wellin's body.

The huge man, thrashed wildly at the embedded spears, and electrical cord around his neck. As he pulled on the cord, the electric drill fell into the pool. The exposed electrical wiring aided by the highly salted pool quickly exterminated the beast. Wellin screamed as he met his death.

* * *

After the coroner had taken Wellin's body, and Weeder had talked with the Chicago homicide detectives, he sat quietly speaking with Sherry. "You say Wellin wrapped a cord around your mother's neck before throwing her into the bathtub with the hair-dryer?"

Sherry nodded. "Yes, that's right."

"It must have been a terrible thing for an eight-year-old to see."

"It was," she admitted. Looking at the pool, still pink from Wellin's blood, she added, "I must have wished him dead thousands of times, but I was still unprepared to witness the actual event."

Brian gave her a sympathetic smile.

Sherry added, "I can understand Stormy drowning or being electrocuted, but being speared seems unjust, somehow."

Touching the bolt as they talked, Brian said thoughtfully, "I wondered about that too. But given the fact Wellin was a bully and a known murderer, I suspect he may have killed more than once." Weeder paused to adjust the bandages on his face. "I told the Chicago homicide detective to review all unsolved knifings or cases where the victim died of impalement during the last twenty years. It's likely that Wellin was involved in at least one of them. He had to pay for his deeds."

Sherry picked up the half-inch bolt. "Strange – it was gold, now it's just silver."

"Silver is its neutral color," Brian said calmly. "It has other colors too."

"I'd like to hear more about them some time," Sherry said. Glancing toward the motel office, she saw the police were leaving. "I've got to go now, Detective Weeder. Thanks for your help, but It's time for me to go back to work."

Brian stood up with her. He extended his hand, "Thanks again for helping me against Wellin."

Admiring the bruises and bandages on the detective's face, Sherry gave him a warm smile. "My pleasure Detective. . . When you get back to San Francisco, tell my sister I'll contact her in a few days so we can catch up on events." She shook his hand before turning to leave.

Brian turned to look at the door to Mrs. Jamison's room. He worried that the old lady would still be in a state of shock. He walked to her door and knocked. Seconds later the door opened and she ushered him inside. Once inside, he saw that the electrical power was on and she was watching her daily soaps. Apparently, she found the daily episodes to be more of a normal activity than seeing the violent death of her estranged son. Brian was sure she would continue her life based on her daily habit. She would be just fine.

*   *   *

Chapter 6   Birds of a Feather

Protagonist: Detective Brian Weeder SFPD

Guests:
Derrick Mills   Ranger in Pacific Northwest
Sky Feather   Native American
Ox   Poacher and leader
Sniffer   Subordinate to Ox
Loo   Broker for rare and endangered species
Pogrom   Gun totin' broker with a nervous habit
Brad   Helicopter Pilot for Loo

With his long day at the police station finished, Brian Weeder stopped at the mailbox to pick up his bills before going to his apartment. The handful of envelopes was mostly junk-mail from companies wanting him to spend beyond his means, but the hand written return-address on one envelope caught his eye. "Derrick Mills," Brian said aloud, as though the very name was an escape from his dedicated life as a policeman. Actually, the name was Ranger Mills, from the Pacific Eagle Wilderness, located – as the name would imply, in the northwest portion of the state of Washington. Derrick, who was an old college classmate of Brian's, had chosen to police the green wilderness instead of the concrete city.

Brian quickly ripped open the envelope in an untidy manner, which was rather uncharacteristic of the homicide detective. At least a decade had passed since he had seen his old college friend, and Brian's curiosity was begging to be satisfied.

D.Malisch

Clasping the bills and advertisements in the same hand that carried his briefcase, he walked slowly down the meandering walkway to the flight of stairs leading up to his apartment. Brian carefully read the contents of his letter, while dodging the children playing tag on the walkway. Though his mind was fixed on the letter and he didn't look up, he nodded at his landlady and bid her a pleasant afternoon as he passed. At the foot of the stairs, he set his briefcase on the first step just long enough to change pages. His concentration was so intense he blindly fumbled for the handle of the valise before climbing the flight of stairs. Using his peripheral vision, he navigated to his apartment where he paused in front of the door to finish the last page. The detective neatly folded the letter, slipping it safely into his shirt pocket. Still considering the invitation within the letter, Brian searched his right trouser pocket for his door key. If there was any doubt he would go, the stale air of his dark and gloomy apartment convinced him he had no choice.

Yes, it had been a long time since he had seen his friend, Derrick, and it had been a long time since he had taken a real vacation. Perhaps this would be as good a time as any, to combine a little camping with a chance to help out a friend. Brian reached for the phone to call the office and schedule a couple of weeks for a trip to the Northwest.

* * *

The late afternoon sun slid silently behind the multitude of Douglas Fir branches in the nearby forest. Brian, leaned back in his lawn chair and searched the horizon for signs of encroaching civilization. Except for a few small clouds, near the western horizon, all was clear; it would be a beautiful sunset. Waiting for Derrick to bring a pitcher of ice tea, Brian mused. . . perhaps, he had missed the mark by taking a city job instead of becoming a fellow ranger with Derrick. The sweet, strawberry scent of the pines wafted on the warm afternoon air, making Brian feel relaxed.

He was at peace with the world, and was truly glad for the absence of big-city noises — the traffic, the trash dumpsters being filled or emptied, sirens, jack-hammers, screeching tires, low flying aircraft, automobile horns and the like.

The "muffled thump" of a closing screen door on the back of the house, announced the return of the host, carrying a tray covered with snacks and beverages. The tall man wore a ranger's uniform and a big smile for his city friend, Brian. Switching expressions, Derrick looked serious as he placed the tray on the table beside his guest and sat down in the empty chair facing the detective. "I'm really glad you were able to come up here to give me a hand on this problem." Handing a tall ice tea to Brian, the ranger leaned back, loosened his collar then took a long swig from his own drink. After swallowing, the ranger looked across the table at his old classmate and said, "This poaching mystery has degraded into a serious problem. Last week a park guest told me about seeing a climber stealing chicks from an eagle's nest in the east end of the park. I went out to investigate with him, but didn't find anything. Two days later, the same guest apparently stumbled onto an operation in progress and was pushed over a precipice for his effort."

"Are you sure he didn't fall of his own accord?"

"I'm sure," Derrick nodded. "There were signs of a scuffle topside, and traces of his murderer's flesh under the victim's fingernails. I sent samples off to the FBI for DNA analysis."

"Any suspects?"

"No. There are plenty of strange people around the park, but that's normal. A lot of folks get along better with nature than with the city element."

Brian nodded in agreement. "So, have you gotten any help from the State authorities?"

209

"They're so backlogged and over budget, they won't help unless I have a clear-cut case."

Brian adjusted his sunglasses. Crunching down on a potato chip, he savored the flavor. "Got any idea how long you've had poachers?"

The ranger thought for a few seconds, "We've noticed a drop in the adult bird population for about two years now." Derrick sipped his ice tea before setting the glass back on the table between them. "But I thought it might be some type of chemical that got introduced into the environment. It wasn't until several people reported seeing helicopters and climbers raiding nests that I considered otherwise."

Brian set his drink down, "So why is it, you think I might be able to help?"

"Help?" Derrick looked away for a moment while a big grin crossed his face. "Who said I invited you up here to help? I just thought you'd been in the city for so long that you needed a chance to get back to nature."

Brian wadded his napkin and threw it at him. "Still full of it, I see."

Laughter erupted from both men.

When sanity returned, Brian and Derrick took a good look at each other. There was a strong bond between the two men, one of competition, understanding and camaraderie, the kind of bond usually developed by humans raised together or who shared the stress of war.

"I get the news from the city," Derrick began, "and I've read that you seem to solve a lot of the unsolvable mysteries." Derrick gestured toward the plate of sandwiches, inviting Brian to help himself. "I don't have much of a staff for this type of investigation, and what staff I do have, is usually occupied by helping tourists or keeping the wildlife and guests separated."

Taking a sandwich for himself, the ranger went on, "If we do encounter some armed, nasty guys, I'm not sure my staff is really trained for that kind of confrontation."

Brian looked stressed, "I'm not sure I'm prepared for that kind of situation either. Just because I see it often, doesn't mean I like it."

"Of course not," Derrick shook his head, "besides I expect this will only be an investigative operation, combined with a bit of fishing, horseback riding and camping in this wonderful wilderness."

Raising his glass in salute, Brian said, "I'll drink to that."

Derrick returned the salute, and sipped his drink before asking, "So what's the secret of your success? Do you have a magic amulet or psychic reader?"

Brian winced a bit at the thought, but then his ranger friend wasn't too far off the truth. "Something like that," he replied in a noncommital tone.

The ranger held out his hand in an inviting or coaxing mode, wanting more information.

Reluctantly, Brian offered, "If I told you, you'd think I went off the deep end."

With a laugh, Derrick said in jest, "I've always thought that of you anyway Brian!"

The conversation became quiet and it was apparent Brian was under a bit of pressure from his close friend for some kind of explanation. Brian reached into his pocket and located the half-inch bolt. He pulled it out, checked for his initials on the head then dropped it on the table in front of his host. Waiting patiently, Brian wasn't surprised by the ranger's puzzled expression.

"That's it?" Picking up the bolt, Derrick looked back at Brian for an explanation. It was obvious from his expression, he thought Brian was throwing him some kind of crazy bait to coax

211

him into a sucker position for a good laugh. "Come on Brian, you can do better than this."

The serious look on Brian's face stayed. Drawing in a deep breath, the detective added, "I know you think I'm making this up, but there is something unique about this object."

The man-in-green examined more closely every aspect of the metallic fastener. "Looks like an ordinary half inch bolt to me, except it has your initials on the head of it. So. . . what is it that makes you think it's unique?"

Brian reached for the pitcher to pour another glass of ice tea. Setting the pitcher down, he spoke slowly and quietly about the object he really didn't understand. "You've heard of Pandora's box? And you've heard of other objects from Greek mythology that do special things? Well, first – let me say that I don't believe in any of that stuff. I didn't even believe in this bolt – until it popped up in a half dozen of my investigations. Those are my initials on the top. They might disappear, but they never change. Sometimes, the bolt is pointed on the end; sometimes it isn't. Sometimes it seizes itself in a hole; sometimes it works its way loose. I've been told that on occasion, it can turn white hot or freezing cold. It can cross thread or not. It can give electric shocks. I've had the lab examine it for anything special and they tell me it's just a common half-inch bolt." Brian drew a breath, "Do you see any place where the bolt was shaved by the test lab for a metal test? No, you won't. The thing seems to heal itself. I don't even pretend to understand it. What I do know is – that whenever a criminal comes in contact with it, justice is done. . . And, the punishment seems to always fit the crime. Don't ask me how it works. . . I just know that it does."

"And it always comes back to you?"

"Well – yes, it seems to. Not always right away, but eventually it will find its way back to me."

Derrick laughed, "Brian, you've pulled some good ones in the past, but this is more than I can swallow. I can't believe this inanimate object can meter out justice. Period!" With that said, he tossed the bolt carelessly onto the table.

"I said you wouldn't believe me."

From high in a snag at the edge of the forest, a bald eagle, set flight into a nearly silent glide. Its flight path took it directly to the table, where the two startled men witnessed it snatch the bolt and flap powerfully off toward the sunset.

The expression of each man was first, one of shock, then the ranger laughed loudly, while Brian jumped to his feet, speechless.

"Well, so much for your game, Brian. Out here, nature has a way of dealing with the truth." With a laugh the ranger added, "I guess that's also justice for you trying to put one over on me."

* * *

At breakfast, the following morning, it was apparent to Ranger Mills that his friend Brian was taking the loss pretty hard. "Well Brian, we'll take a couple of horses and pack into the high country today. Maybe do a bit of fishing along the way."

When Brian just sipped his coffee without replying, the ranger added, "We might even see an eagle or two carrying around a bolt." With a strong laugh he added, "Maybe we should wear hard-hats, just in case."

Brian wasn't amused. The bolt had always returned to him in the past, but that was in the city with humans. He couldn't imagine how it would work with animals. Perhaps this was some kind of justice that the bolt was inflicting on him? He pondered his effectiveness against crime when he returned to the city without the bolt to help him solve cases. Still. . . he had to trust his knowledge of the object, try to locate it, and understand what kind of justice it was administering and to whom.

213

The scenery was breathtaking, with white, snow capped peaks resting on a blanket of forest-green slopes. The weather proffered deep, blue skies dotted with an occasional puffy-white cloud. The setting was beautiful – even the insects were elsewhere. In the cool breeze, it seemed the horses enjoyed the trek as much as their riders, plodding along the narrow dirt trail, through the creeks and up the ever-higher slopes of the coastal mountains. The lunch break found the party a thousand feet or so below the receding snow-line, along a small stream of fresh snow melt. Brian had been quiet all morning, but in otherwise good spirits. The ranger, checked in, on his radio, for word of poachers. Since there were no new reports, Derrick decided to allow the horses to follow the trail to the high country.

Between taking bites from his sandwich, Brian scanned the area below with binoculars. The valley, deeply wooded, was sprinkled with crystal clear lakes and no sign of humanity.

"We'll cross the pass just ahead and drop down into the valley on the other side," Derrick promised, "from there, we should be in the area where most of the poaching has taken place."

Brian nodded silently.

Several hours later, they set up camp alongside a small lake. A search of the shoreline with binoculars showed no other people camped on the oversized pool. Derrick handed a spare radio to Brian before taking a hike around the lake to make his rounds. Brian broke out the fishing gear and proceeded to try to catch dinner.

The enveloping darkness found the two men eating a freeze-dried tuna casserole, cooked on a grill over an open fire.

"I thought you were a better fisherman," Derrick heckled.

"I thought I was too," Brian agreed. "Guess the fish don't know it." With a slight smile he added, "Didn't see you trying to catch any."

214

"Gotta leave 'em for the guests," the ranger smiled.

"Sure – " Brian gibed.

The two men lay on their respective bedrolls near the fire, but far enough away to prevent sparks from burning holes in the outer layers of the fabric. They kept their voices low, as they traded stories and caught up on their separate lives for the last few years. Suddenly the crickets stopped calling for mates. Disturbed by sudden silence, Derrick put down his coffee mug and stared into the darkness. Smoothly, the ranger reached for his flashlight. "Probably a cougar on the prowl," he said quietly. As the bright beam flashed through the multitude of small oaks and fir trees surrounding the lake, it could find no eyes or bodies to reflect the light, giving no clue to who or what was out there. Derrick put away the light. They sat in silence for several minutes before the crickets began their song again.

In the morning, Brian woke to find the ranger gone from camp. His gear was still there, meaning he'd be back. Brian started the fire and made coffee. Remembering the radio, he picked it up and called.

"I'll be in shortly," the ranger replied, "Did you make us some fresh coffee?"

"I'm working on it," Brian replied.

They had breakfast and on their way up the trail, they took a detour so Derrick could show Brian what he'd found. "This is the camp where our intruder stayed last night," Derrick explained. "See the grass. . . how it's still bent, but is just now beginning to straighten? It's a sign of being slept on."

"Coulda been a deer," Brian offered.

"Not likely – no sign of droppings or fresh hoof impressions."

"Cougar?"

"Not likely, they don't sleep much outside of a den, besides, they're nocturnal."

"Who then?"

"Don't know, but I think it's probably that crazy Indian."

"Indian?"

"Native American. You know. . . This guy was educated at Harvard, but couldn't or wouldn't make it in the business world. Rumor has it that he decided to return to his tribal ways. Some of the guests have seen him, and one or two have actually spoken to him."

"Think he's into poaching?"

"Might be. . . the trouble started about the same time he started being seen in the park."

Brian scratched a mosquito bite, "I thought Native Americans had rights to some birds and fish not available to the general population."

Derrick nodded, "They do – there are special tribal permissions, but even they can't take birds and sell them to the outside world. It's against Federal law and tribal rules."

"So what are you saying here Mr. Ranger?"

Derrick returned to his horse and prepared to mount it. Looking across the saddle, he speculated, "I think we had a visitor last night. I think he was checking us out. And. . . I think we are currently being watched."

Brian mounted his horse and looked around. The smell of oiled leather and squeaking of the comfortable saddle bothered him just a bit as he turned to stare off into the woods. He could see nothing through the thick foliage and trunks of trees. The thought of being watched gave him the same feeling he got in the city, when he entered a bad neighborhood. He couldn't decide whether it bothered him more to have the sensation here in the wilderness or in the city – either way, he knew he didn't like it. He wondered if anyone was ever really safe from predators? There is one thing he did know: the most dangerous predator is the one you're not prepared to meet. . . and it's nearly always human.

* * *

The detective and ranger spent the day moving onto higher country and searching for signs of poachers. During the day, they encountered two parties; both were populated with guests Derrick had met and chatted with several times before, in past years. Nether party had seen anyone else.

Tired from their day's travel, they settled beside another lake. The lake was small, more like an oversized pond, but it was crystal clear and had some nice campsites. They made camp then walked the perimeter in fifteen minutes. There were no signs of other campers, but when they returned to camp, they noticed someone or something had fooled around with their camp gear. Since the horses hadn't spooked, it was unlikely the intruder had been a bear or cougar. Everything seemed to be there, except for two of their day's rations. Brian was relieved he had remembered to take his Glock 23 rather than leave it at camp, where the thief might have gotten it. A quick check showed no one had tampered with his spare ammo clips, kept in his pack either.

"I guess we need to do a little fishing, if we want to stretch our food supply," Brian kidded.

The ranger had a faraway look on his face as he unpacked his fishing equipment. "Well, at least we can find out who's the better fisherman."

"Hey!" Brian shouted, "You'll need all the inside info you can get just to keep up with me."

With banter coming and going, the two men headed for the water.

Sitting on the bank, both men kept a careful watch on their camp for additional intruders. Both were aware – it would do little good to lock the barn door after the horse had gotten out.

The fish weren't biting well, but it was relaxing to sit next to the water and look at the surrounding beautiful snow-topped mountains, nearby forested slopes, and watch the chilly, afternoon breeze push ripples across the water. Occasionally a fish would rise to take an insect on the surface of the lake. Just as the sun kissed the horizon, both men hooked and landed a couple of nice trout for the dinner meal.

After dinner, conversation went much as the night before, then Derrick let it slip that he probably knew where Brian's bolt might be. "So – I think Black Toe probably has it."

Showing a slight sign of surprise, Weeder eyed the ranger, "You mean you know the bird that snatched my bolt?"

Derrick nodded. "This bird was injured a couple of years ago, and spent some time up by the house recovering. It often swings by – to see if I have an offering of a fish or two for it." The man raised his eyebrows, "I must admit I was pretty shocked when she took your bolt, but shiny objects have been found in nests of birds for centuries."

Brian poured more coffee into the ranger's cup, while waiting for him to finish his explanation.

Derrick pointed toward a neighboring peak. "Black Toe has been the object of study for several years and her nest is on that ledge about fifty feet below the top of that crag."

The valley was in deep evening shadow, but the snow-capped peaks jutting up from the forested floor, still had fading sunlight on them.

Brian quickly looked in the direction the ranger pointed. Realizing they were still too far away to see the nest well, Weeder grabbed his binoculars. "She got little ones?"

Derrick nodded, "Yes she does. She's got two of the prettiest, little chicks you ever saw." He stirred his coffee then set the spoon on a rock next to the small campfire. "The problem is — we can't just drop in and poke around her nest until after the chicks are flight worthy."

"Why not? Don't the wildlife teams do it all the time?"

The government man smiled a little wryly. "They do, but it's in the best interest of the chicks not to disturb the nest until they are old enough to band anyway."

"How long will that take?"

"Several weeks, at least — "

Brian began a protest, but the ranger held up a hand and offered, "I know it will be longer than you will be up here, but what we can do is — confirm the presence of the bolt in the nest by binoculars, then leave it there until the banding crew can retrieve it for us. If it's there, it'll be safe enough."

Brian wasn't happy, but he realized his friend was right. Lifting his binoculars to look again at the eagle's nest, he hoped to see a glimpse of light reflecting from the bolt, assuming it was in the nest. What he saw, startled him. "Hey Mr. Ranger, grab your binoc's and take a look at the outcrop of rock to the left of the nest."

As he positioned the binoculars, Derrick questioned, Brian, "What did you see?"

"Looks like someone is up there."

"Oh yes. . . I see movement. It looks like. . . someone in buckskins sliding across the rock."

"Is he moving away?" Weeder asked, as he adjusted the focus on his binoculars.

"That's the way it looks." Derrick replied, without emphasis.

The men studied the climber for several minutes before the light faded on the face of the rock and darkness claimed everything as its domain.

The campfire crackled, and sparks flew a few inches before dying. "Do you normally have climbers up on the face this late in the afternoon?"

"Only the over brave or the inexperienced," Derrick sighed. The Ranger realized he could still receive a call from dispatch on his radio telling him of a stranded hiker, but he hoped it wouldn't happen. One thing about a ranger's job — it rarely consists of a nine-to-five routine.

* * *

In the morning, Derrick and Brian staked the horses in an area that had enough grass to allow them to graze without overtaxing the available ground-cover. Then the two men set out on foot to scale the ridge from the sloping back side. Climbing gear wouldn't be necessary, but it would be imperative to watch one's footing and be especially wary of stepping on loose rock. As they neared the fast running stream of snow-melt, the noise level went up and conversation ceased. Two minutes later, while climbing up the rock channel next to the stream, they saw movement and stopped. Looking across the wide gush of ice-water, a lone figure, dressed in tan buckskins, quickly and deftly made his way down through a pile of boulders toward a forested area. From the look on Derrick's face, it was obvious the ranger wanted to interrogate the hiker, but there was no way to cross the fast-moving stream safely. The man seemingly unaware of Brian and Derrick watching, carried a short bow and quiver of arrows. His long black hair and moccasins told his observers of his ethnic background. In his other hand, he carried a medium sized bag of some kind. It seemed to have feathers sticking out of it. Just before disappearing into the trees, the man stopped, turned toward his observers and stared. Then as quickly as a wild animal, he slipped into the forest and disappeared from sight.

When Brian and Derrick got away from the noise of the stream, they talked. "I think that was Sky Feather," Derrick said, as he puffed heavily to catch his breath at the high altitude. "At least he matches the description from those who have talked with him."

Brian was too winded to talk, and at this point he really didn't care. He just wanted oxygen in his lungs, lots of it. He stood and looked around at the view across the valley, then up at the ridge yet to climb. His mouth hung open and his chest heaved, but it seemed he would never get enough air. Finally the burning in his legs and back subsided and his breaths slackened enough to speak. "That's the Indian you talked about a couple of days ago?"

Nodding, Derrick added, "He's not as big as I expected, though I'm sure he's in good shape. I wish we'd been closer. I think he had a bird in the bag he was carrying. At any rate, I'd like to have had the chance to question him about it."

The noonday air had a chill about it. Like the breath from a deep freeze, it was terribly refreshing, but reminded you to keep moving to stay warm. Brian began to wish he'd thought to bring an extra layer of clothing.

Now above the tree-line, the narrow footpath worked its way around the base of a vertical column of rock jutting into the sky. The huge size of the boulders and towering rock face covered with bird droppings, made the men feel dwarfed – like ants crawling around a domestic garden. They stopped at the base to catch their breath, again.

Derrick pointed upward. "The nest is up there."

To Brian, it may as well have been on the moon, because there was no way he could scale the rock from the bottom. Fortunately, Ranger Mills knew about the path up the sloping backside.

The dirt footpath now free from the trees, was defined with sun bleached, school-bus-sized rocks scattered left and right as they rounded the rock face. Further up, the trail became a mixture of mud and granite as it continued upward again, at a fairly steep angle. On the back-slope, each side of the trail broke into a thin sheet of snow, with bare granite poking through in places. After catching their breath again, they continued upward on the switchback-path where icy snow-melt raced down the trail in places. Completing the first turn up the sawtooth, they suddenly heard the sound of machinery.

"What the heck is that?" Weeder asked, between heavy breaths.

"Sounds like a helicopter," Mills, replied – also between breaths.

Almost immediately, the sound of the backwash, coming from the rotor blade, echoed through the various rock faces around them. Looking up, they saw a high performance commercial helicopter brake and land on the top of the rock face above them and above the eagle's nest. There was a short pause, before it took off again.

"I think it left!" Brian said with a puzzled look.

"I think so too – but it must have left someone behind."

In the quiet, they heard the multitude of echos from a metal object being hammered topside.

Derrick tilted his head to listen carefully to the hammering sound, "They must be installing a piton for belaying down the rock face."

"Don't they use wedging types that don't destroy the rock these days?" Brian asked, still trying to catch his breath.

"If they intend to come back often, they might put in a permanent one, though the park doesn't approve of them." The ranger looked back at the detective, "We try to check climbers and advise them to use newer devices, but these guys apparently don't care, since it's also illegal to land aircraft in the park except in the case of emergency."

"I see what you mean." Brian looked upward at the steep, graveled slope. "I suppose we should go up and catch him in the act."

"It might be better if we split up," Mills thought aloud, "Don't know how many pitches he has with him, but he might have enough to rappel down the face. If you go back to the bottom of the face and I go up, we might trap him between us."

Brian nodded agreement. Drawing a breath he asked the ranger, "Do you have a weapon?"

"I'm armed, though normally I don't pack," Mills answered between breaths.

"Okay. I'll head back down and wait for your radio signal," Brian said, turning on his radio.

Derrick held up a hand, indicating he had more to say. "Watch out for falling rocks, and remember he may be armed."

Weeder nodded.

Still holding his hand up, Derrick advised, "Oh yes — probably better maintain radio silence unless something happens. We don't want him to hear our radios when I get close."

"Of course!" Weeder whispered loudly as he turned and jogged down the path.

Near the trail, beneath the rock face, Weeder waited patently. He remained just out of sight, while carefully scanning the rock column towering above him with binoculars, for any sign of activity. An hour passed — then two — without incident.

The first sign of activity came when Black Toe left her nest. Apparently the poacher was waiting for this to happen before descending from above, to the nest. Within minutes, Brian heard the tinkle of climbing hardware against the rock face. Above the

223

nest, the poacher climbed over the edge and descended down his rope. Small pebbles of sharp stone began to sprinkle around the detective, making him wish that he had a hard hat. Crouching behind a large rock, Brian watched as the climber reached the nest. From the binoculars, he saw him try to find footing on the ledge, but it was too small to support anything but the most uncomfortable grip. Nearly a minute later, the climber descended just below the nest and his rope dangled freely below him.

"Brian, are you there?" his radio crackled.

"Yeah, I just saw him reach into the nest."

"Good, then I can arrest him when he comes back up with the evidence," Mills replied.

"Ten-four," Weeder agreed, "Is there only the one?"

"Yes. I've had him under observation for the past ninety minutes. He can't be too smart climbing alone."

Watching the movement through the binoculars, Brian said, "I think he's got one of the chicks now." A glint of metal told Brian what the climber had extracted was not a bird, but was probably the half-inch bolt. Suddenly there was a loud scream and extreme thrashing by the man below the nest. Within two seconds, the man began a fall, end-over-end to the ground below.

"He's fallen!!!" Brian screamed over the radio.

"What? How?"

"Just get down here! We'll talk about it when you get here."

Brian rushed to the area where he saw the man land after striking a boulder head first. It wasn't pretty, but there was nothing to be done. The climber had removed the bolt from the nest, and it had, somehow, caused him to fall. Careful not to touch anything, Brian tried to preserve the crime scene as best he could, once he established the climber did not survive the fall. Brian sat back, leaned against a rock while he waited for Ranger Mills.

When the ranger arrived, he radioed for a rescue crew to pick up the body, then they tried to piece together what had gone wrong.

"Looks like he broke a number of bones in his fall," Derrick observed.

"Yeah and his stupid head too," Weeder sighed.

Derrick leaned closer to look at the climber's hand, "What's that shiny thing in his hand?"

"That's my bolt!" Brian said calmly.

"Your bolt?"

"Yeah – my bolt!"

Derrick looked at Brian with disbelief, "It was in the nest?"

"Looks that way," Brian said, as he opened his canteen to quench his thirst.

The ranger studied the body again for a few seconds. Then looking up, he asked, "How did it make him fall?"

Brian finished his drink and screwed the cap back on the container. After swallowing, he shrugged, "I don't really know, but it probably got hot and stuck to him."

"Stuck to him? How?" Mills dropped to a knee for a closer inspection of the bolt.

"Don't ask me," Brian shrugged again, "it looks like the thing welded itself to his skin."

"How?" The ranger asked, clearly puzzled.

Brian touched the bolt carefully. "The bolt's still a bit warm," he said, without emotion.

Derrick touched it lightly, jerking back from the warmth. He looked back at Brian with a look of disbelief.

The two men pried the fingers loose around the bolt, noting the imprint of the threads left on the skin.

"Musta been one-hot-potato," Brian quipped.

225

They extracted the bolt and Brian inspected it for his initials. The initials were right there, on the head of the bolt as before. The ranger took the bolt and marveled over what he had just happened. "How do I file this in my report?"

Brian just shook his head for several seconds. "Have this problem all the time." He took the bolt back from his friend. "I suggest you don't tell anyone what actually happened, or they'll throw you in the nuthouse."

"Well I can't just lie!"

The detective smiled, "I wouldn't, but I wouldn't mention the bolt either. If you were to lie, the bolt might do something to you when you touched it next, depending on what kind of justice it deemed necessary. If you just don't mention it, everything will be okay. If someone asks you specifically about it, tell them then, but not before." Brian unsnapped a pocket flap to put the bolt inside while adding, "He must have been the one who killed the hiker a couple of weeks back. The bolt generally seems to match the punishment to the crime."

Derrick stood there, just shaking his head in disbelief until he heard a voice behind him. Turning quickly, he found himself face to face with the man in buckskins they had seen earlier. The ranger reached for his weapon, but the man grabbed his wrist, pulling him up short.

"No need! I won't harm you."

"Are you Sky Feather?" Ranger Mills asked.

"Some call me that. Some call me other names." He turned and walked over to the body on the ground. Kneeling beside the deceased, he gently touched the body. "His spirit will never rest." Getting up, he walked toward Brian, "May I see it?" he asked, his hand extended – palm up.

At first Brian stepped back, standing his ground. When he saw the man was not aggressive, he reached into his pocket and found the bolt, handing it to the Native American.

As the bolt sat on Sky Feather's open palm, he closed his eyes, apparently having a vision. The bolt changed color, then changed thread-pitch. The end became pointed then flat and stubby. It glowed white-hot; then frost formed on it; finally it returned to its silver color and rested quietly.

Handing the bolt back to Brian, Sky Feather asked, "How did this object come into your possession?"

"What do you mean?"

"How did you first encounter it?"

Unsure of himself, Brian hesitated then answered, "I'm a police detective and I found it at a homicide investigation." Looking closely into the dark eyes of the man before him, Brian questioned, "What do you know about it?"

"You do not know?"

"Know what?" Weeder asked defensively.

"I see," the black-haired man said, "You have been chosen as most worthy."

"Most worthy what?" Brian asked, looking the man in the eyes.

Sky Feather explained, "This object is an icon. It is not real in the sense that you know real, yet here it is – in our world. It is a symbol from another reality. It is your guide. It is your protector. It is your guarantee of justice. You, on the other hand, are its vehicle – its servant – its benefactor. As long as you serve justice, it will serve you."

Sky Feather turned to go down the path. He looked back at the ranger. "Aren't you coming?" Without waiting for further discussion, he turned to trot down the path toward the valley.

227

Derrick looked at Brian. "Where are we going?" Watching Brian gather his day pack and canteen, the ranger showed his distrust of this strange, black-haired man, by asking, "And why are we going with him?"

With his equipment in place, Brian looked down the path after Sky Feather, but said to Derrick, "You want to catch the poachers, don't you?"

Brian and Derrick looked at each other, shrugged then hurried down the path to follow their new leader.

Minutes later, as Brian and Derrick became tired from the pace, they lagged back and eventually stopped for a rest period. Brian, terribly winded, realized a thought he must share with the ranger. "I think Sky Feather had a vision when he held the bolt." He puffed several breaths before continuing, "And I think he now knows information about the poachers."

"That's nonsense Brian, I think he's probably a partner with the poachers."

"No! Not true!" Brian wheezed. "If he was guilty of anything serious, the bolt would have probably done something to him by now."

"How long does it take?"

"For what?"

Mills made a hand gesture, "How long does it take for the bolt to do something?"

Brian shook his head, "Seconds, minutes — sometimes it takes days or weeks, but events always come to pass."

"I still think he's hiding something." The ranger added, "And didn't you notice he wasn't carrying that bag with feathers when we just saw him?"

"I still think he's okay," Brian puffed.

"Well, let's go before he gets so far away we can't find him," Derrick gasped.

They followed the path for another twenty minutes to the canyon floor. A clearing made specifically for helicopters to land during rescue operations came into view. Sky Feather, whom they had not seen for the last half hour, was nowhere in sight.

Derrick pointed to the other side of the clearing, "The trail continues over there; I come this way twice a week."

The men crossed the clearing and started down the footpath hurrying, to see if they could catch Sky Feather. A few steps beyond the clearing, they heard a sharp whistle. Turning behind, to locate the source, they saw Sky Feather waiting patiently beside a tree. He had his bag with him. From the short distance, Brian noted the feathers at the top of the bag were attached as decoration, and were not sticking out as originally thought. Sky Feather said nothing, just motioned for the two men to leave the path and follow him into the forest. Brian was amazed how silently and quickly the man slipped through the underbrush. Every now and then he'd step on a small twig, making it snap, but the noise was nothing compared to the two white men who sounded like a herd of buffalo clearing the woods for a new freeway.

Several minutes later, the Native American stopped, pointing to a small clearing. As the three men stepped into the clearing, they saw a camouflaged tent and inside the tent, row after row of wire cages were stacked. Most of the cages were empty, but more than a dozen of the wire containers held birds, mostly eagles. After a quick count, they determined nearly two dozen birds were captive.

"This is it, Derrick. Here's 'bird-station', the staging headquarters for your poachers."

The ranger removed his hat and scratched his sweaty head. "It's a bigger operation than even I imagined." Turning to the American Indian, he asked, "Sky Feather. . . what's your part in this?"

Looking the ranger directly in the face, he answered, "I've come to protect my brothers – the feathered ones – from exploitation."

"Let me ask you another way," Derrick grimaced, "Did you have anything to do with putting these birds here?"

"No," Sky Feather answered flatly.

"Do you know who did?"

"Not exactly," he answered, not blinking from the ranger's stern glare.

Derrick felt the answer was vague, "I need a better answer than that."

Sky Feather walked to the edge of the clearing and laid his bow, supply of arrows and feathered bag next to a tree. Turning back to his interrogator, he said, "I don't know names – just faces. And I know they will be back."

"And how do you know that?" the ranger asked, while feeling the suspect's answers were evasive.

Brian burst out laughing.

"What's so funny?" Derrick asked, looking over his shoulder to the detective.

"I see you know a lot more about 'rangering' and about the wilderness than I'll probably ever know, but you are missing the obvious."

"Like what?" he said, offended that Weeder was interfering in the questioning of the suspect.

With a sweep of his arm toward the caged birds, Brian pointed out the obvious, "Give Mr. Sky Feather a break. Any fool can see if there are caged birds here, and poachers are operating in the area, they will be back to pick up their cache." Playing on the friendly rivalry between himself and the ranger, Brian mused, "I guess the city kid knows more about evidence and questioning than the country boy."

Derrick didn't like Brian's tone; he especially didn't like being belittled in front of someone he considered to be a suspect. "Alright, city boy! Let's see you take over the questioning, if you think you can do better."

Brian almost wished he hadn't put Derrick on the spot, but he knew his skills as an interrogator were probably more polished than his friend's.

Reaching into his pocket to retrieve the bolt, he held it out to Sky Feather saying, "I need to know if you are telling the truth. Do you understand?"

The man in buckskins nodded yes as he took the bolt, holding it in his hand. Both men recognized any lie would be flagged by the bolt changing color.

Pointing to Derrick, Brian continued, "Our friend, the ranger, has a responsibility to uphold the laws governing this area he protects." Brian looked back at the native, "Do you understand?"

With a nod and a light smile came the answer, "As a graduate from the Harvard school of law, I can buy that. . . "

Brian and Derrick looked at each other briefly. . . each a little puzzled. The detective continued with the general questioning, "Are you involved with this poaching operation in the park?"

"I'm not working with the poachers, if that is what you mean."

"Good. Both Derrick and I know you're not a registered guest in this wilderness. We'd like to know what is your purpose in the park?"

A short hesitation took place while eye contact was made, first – with the ranger, then – with the detective. "My feathered brothers need my help. I come often to ensure their safety and health."

231

"What do you mean by health?"

"I know the old ways and the ways of modern medicine"

Derrick countered with, "No one is allowed to touch these birds without first holding at least a veterinarian degree."

Without hesitation, Sky Feather raised an eyebrow saying, "I have several, mostly from schools in other states."

Brian smiled when a glance at the bolt showed no indication of lies being told. "I don't know about you Derrick, but it looks like we have a fellow crusader in our quest to rid the park of poachers."

Derrick grumbled, "Well, I suppose so, but I still don't like the idea of him carrying a bow and arrow in my park."

"It's not your park," Sky Feather reminded him, "It belongs to everyone through the Federal Government."

"Hey! You two!" Brian interrupted, "Knock it off! We've got a common enemy to fight. We can argue the finer points later!"

Taking the bolt back from Sky Feather, Brian dropped it into his pocket and snapped the flap shut. "What do you want to do with these chicks, Derrick?"

"They probably need food and water. Maybe I can get a chopper in here to pick 'em up and take them back to the animal center." Derrick turned to speak to Sky Feather, but found he had already retrieved his feathered bag and was feeding something to the birds from it.

"I guess we now know what was in the bag, eh Derrick?" Brian joked.

The ranger smiled, but shook his head in disbelief.

Too busy to look up, Sky Feather said, "You fellows go ahead and do what you have to do. I'll look after my feathered brothers."

Derrick nodded, "We'll go up on the ridge and call for a helicopter to fly into helipad twelve. That's the asphalt circle in the clearing we just passed."

Shouldering their day-packs, the detective and ranger started through the woods toward high-ground. Derrick knew their approximate position and knew the general direction to the closest ridge where the two-way radio would work best. So he used his compass to guide them as they cut cross-country, through the small timber, to the rocky slope. Several times they took portions of a deer trail, but most trails lead down to water, so they weren't much help. After battling the brush for fifteen minutes, they broke out onto a grassy slope below some big boulders.

"I don't know which is worse," Brian complained, "fighting the brush or climbing over this rough granite."

"Must be a city kid problem," Derrick jibbed, "I'm not having any problem." With his next step, he slipped and banged his right knee.

"Now it's not nice to swear," Brian rebutted with a smile.

The old competition surfaced again and each tried to "outdo" the other to reach the top first. Brian lost by three seconds, when he tripped over his shoelace which came untied. "I'd have beat you if the lace hadn't come loose on my boot," Brian bellowed

"Oh stop crying in your beer and recognize you're just a wimp!" Derrick took his radio from his pack and set it for the correct channel to summon the helicopter.

"Eagle-one to Airbase," the ranger called.

"This is Airbase. Go ahead Eagle-one."

"Yes, my 'twenty' is up here by 'helipad twelve' and I have a need for one of your birds to ferry out some merchandise today."

"Ten-four, Eagle-one, but it will have to be tomorrow morning, because our bird is down for a quick repair, and the second bird was loaned out yesterday."

The ranger grimaced, "Well, if that's the best you can do, I guess we'll have to live with it."

"Ten-four. We're sorry about that, but the repair caught us off guard too."

"Understand, Airbase. We'll see you in the morning. Eagle-one out."

"Airbase out."

The ranger looked at the detective, "I'm thirsty."

"Me too," Brian admitted.

The men sat down and toasted their comradery with swigs of water from their canteens.

"How long does it take to get a chopper in here, Derrick?"

"About an hour, I'd guess, depends on who's available to fly it in for us." Ranger Mills attached his canteen back on the ring on his day-pack.

"Let me borrow your binoculars again," Weeder said, with a serious tone.

The ranger handed them to Brian who looked out to the west near the coast. "Looks like they're already on their way."

"Huh? What do you see?"

"Looks like a chopper headed this way. It's right over that saddle there. . ." he said, pointing with one hand and passing the binoculars back to his sweaty friend with the other hand.

"Can't be. . . They said tomorrow morning. . ." A puzzled look showed on Derrick's face, as he squinted at the small dot in the sky, near the afternoon sun. "Besides, the airport is east of here." Sure enough, as he looked through the lenses, he saw the silhouette of an airship headed their way.

"Shoot! We should have left a radio with Sky Feather. It's the poacher helicopter on the way back to pick up the birds."

"Think we can make it back to the stash of birds before they do?"

"No chance, Brian. The chopper pad is a lot closer to the bird-station than we are." The ranger agonized, "How are we going to warn him he's got bad company."

"I think he'll know and hear them before they ever reach the clearing where the birds are."

"Yeah, but how will he know it's not the chopper we just ordered?"

"Oh?" the detective said, as he realized the ranger had a point he hadn't considered. "Only one thing to do – we've got to warn him." Brian pulled out his hand gun, aimed it into the air and pulled the trigger three times.

The ranger nearly had a fit. "Hey! You can't shoot here."

"What do you mean? I just did!" he said, as the echos reached his ears.

"I know, but as a ranger I have an obligation to prevent accidents, so hand over the gun."

"Derrick, you've been in the woods too long. Isn't this the wilderness?"

"Yes, but you can't use firearms here."

"What did you want me to use, a squirt-gun? What are you expecting? – the bullets to fall to the earth and hit someone out here?"

"It could happen!"

"Get real!" Brian shouted, "The only way it could happen is if some guy already killed someone and was standing there holding the bolt."

"The bolt?"

"Yes the bolt. It could administer justice, but otherwise nothing could happen. The odds are too high."

Ranger Mills thought for a moment. "Do you think he knows three quick shots means danger?"

The detective rolled his eyes in disbelief, "Good grief Derrick, just because he's an Indian, you think he's never seen a cowboy movie before?"

"I donno?"

"Well, given the fact that he knows the direction we went and direction the sound came from, he should be able to deduce what it meant."

"You're forgetting the echos that will ricochet around the hills."

"Oh, never thought of that," Brian said quietly. "Well, let's get, or we'll never reach him before the poachers are there and gone."

The pair of lawmen scrambled down off the granite face and hurried back into the woods. Their path toward the bird-station took them along the same line they used on the way up to the ridge. Except for being downhill, the trip back was no easier than coming up the grade. Thick brush, steep ravines, and fast-moving streams forced them to retrace their steps several times. At least the elevation was high enough there wasn't much danger from snakes or poison oak.

All was quiet as they approached the clearing. Instinctively, Weeder hung back while Derrick plunged onward, intent on catching and capturing the poachers. The ranger stepped into the bird-station area and surveyed the emptiness. Even the tent was gone. "Hey, nobody's here," he said with surprise.

Brian stayed near the edge of the circle of trees, suspicious of the inactivity. With his eyes, he quietly searched the bushes and circle of trees for any sign of people hiding. He saw nothing.

Derrick turned and mocked his friend, "Hey Brian. Looks like your Indian buddy took the birds and left with his poacher friends."

A soft breeze rustled the tops of the trees, but Brian said nothing. He knew Sky Feather hadn't joined the poachers, but the emptiness didn't feel right. He patted the down jacket and flannel shirt covering his chest, wishing he'd not left his bulletproof vest back home in San Francisco.

The ranger squatted to look for footprints to prove his point. Unfortunately, the rocky ground had been trampled too often in the recent weeks to show sign. "I don't see their tracks yet, but I'll bet they took the birds to the copter." Derrick stepped toward the edge of the clearing nearest the landing pad. "Come on Brian, let's go get them before they can get away."

Not at all convinced his friend was correct, Brian agonized over leaving the small amount of cover offered by the trees to follow Derrick. Still, having dealt with more criminals than his old classmate, Brian felt obligated to keep the ranger from stumbling into serious trouble. The detective quickly abandoned his hiding spot in the trees to dash through the bird-station clearing, after his friend. They ran down a small deer trail, out of the woods, to the meadow. From the edge of the wooded area, they studied the poacher's helicopter with their binoculars; it appeared to be empty.

"Where'd everyone go?" Derrick asked, dismayed by the lack of people. The ranger scanned the knee-high grass in the meadow, looking for signs of human activity. As if to answer his own question, he mumbled, "Maybe they're taking the birds out by truck?"

Weeder felt the hair along his spine suddenly stand up. He had no idea what had happened, but he didn't like it. Feeling terribly exposed, since leaving his position at the edge of the clearing at bird-station, he stared back into the shadows of the

237

woods. The feeling of danger was as obvious to Brian as it was oblivious to his friend, Derrick. "We've got to find cover quickly," he whispered to the ranger.

"What are you talking about, City-boy? They're all gone."

"No – they're stalking us."

"You're crazy, Brian. They're probably out loading the birds in some four by four right now."

"No," the detective emphasized, "We've exposed our position and they know where we are, who we are, and how many there are of us. Now we better find cover in a hurry."

The argument was interrupted by the light snapping of a twig behind them in the woods. Brian lunged at Derrick, knocking him to the ground. "Shhh," he urged, "Someone's behind us on the deer path." The detective slid off the ranger saying, "Stay here, I'm going to look around."

Brian crawled on his belly for twenty meters or more before re-entering the woods. It was his hope to circle around and come up on the enemy from behind. He felt out of his element beneath the canopy of small pines. No matter how he tried, he couldn't seem to walk quietly past the trees without snapping twigs. He had nearly worked his way back to the deer path, when he heard the ranger call.

"Brian!"

Weeder didn't answer. He followed the deer path quietly toward the place he had left Derrick. Looking through the trees as he neared the edge of the meadow, he saw two men standing in the open. One of them was Derrick. The other wore a ski mask and held a rifle.

Brian tried to formulate a plan, but was interrupted by a deep voice behind him saying, "Don't move, mister."

He turned his head slowly to see the degree of his threat. A large, hooded man, wielding a shotgun, watched him from about

238

ten meters away. As the man spoke, a hint of a curly, black beard jiggled below the edge of the hood. Having a healthy respect for shotguns, Brian had no choice but surrender.

Derrick and Brian were marched back to bird-station and tied with their backs to small pines that encircled the wooded clearing.

The big man, with the shotgun, seemed to be the leader of the two men. He ambled up to Derrick and bent down to dig through the ranger's day-pack. After not finding whatever he was looking for, he stood up. Tugging on the strings to adjust the camouflaged cloth bag used as a mask, he positioned it to better see through the holes cut for his eyes. His heavy voice took on an angry tone as he looked Ranger Mills in the eye, "Where'd you put our birds?"

"I don't know what you're talking about," the ranger answered truthfully.

The large man pushed the sleeves on his beefy arms up toward his elbows. Stepping back, he studied the park official for a few seconds. When a worry began to show on the ranger's face, the poacher stepped forward to gently remove the ranger's baseball-style cap, placing it safely on the day-pack, a short distance away. The hooded poacher returned to study the park ranger again. For a moment, it seemed the poacher was concerned with a loose knot on Derrick's bindings, but it was only to catch Ranger Mills off guard. Suddenly the man drew a breath and punched Derrick hard in the stomach. Derrick bent forward from the blow as far as his bindings would allow. Within seconds, a shower of pine needles sprinkled down from the small tree that held him in place. The poacher grabbed a knot of the ranger's hair, yanking his head up, to better view his face. "Where are my birds?" he shouted!

"Don't know what you're talking about," Mills wheezed.

The big man hit the ranger in the face, causing Derrick's lip to bleed. "Let me know, when you know what I'm talking about, Mr. Ranger," he said, striking the park official again.

Derrick remained silent except for air being expelled by the heavy blows to his stomach.

Brian, who had been struggling against the rope binding his hands to the tree behind him, shouted, "Leave him alone! He doesn't know where the birds are."

The poacher held his punch, while he turned to see who dared to speak to him in such a manner. Slowly the large man stepped backward then walked over to stare Brian in the face. "I suppose you know where they are?" the green-shirted poacher boomed.

"Neither of us do," Brian volunteered.

"We'll see about that," the man said, drawing back to plant his fist in the detective's mid section.

Weeder instinctively drew a breath and hardened his stomach muscles, knowing it was going to hurt.

The punch nailed him against the tree, while the tree's small stubs of broken branches, pierced his clothing and skin from behind. Pain was not – in short supply. With his mouth open, Weeder gasped for the next breath, before the large man could administer a second blow. He lost the race. Breathless and hurting everywhere, his eyes and nose watered in sympathy.

"Where's my birds?" the man's voice thundered.

Even if he knew, he would be unable to speak until his breath returned. Brian tried to swallow and breath at the same time; he choked.

The large man stepped back from Weeder's sudden coughing spell. The poacher shook his head, "Wimp!" he muttered, ambling off to the far edge of the clearing to consult with the other poacher.

The lawbreakers talked for a few minutes, apparently trying to decide what to do next. The conference was interrupted by the poacher's two-way radio. The big guy pulled the radio from his belt and talked into it. His large hand wrapped around the small plastic case, nearly concealing it from view.

"Ox here," he answered.

"Are you at the site?"

"Yeah, we're here," the big poacher named Ox, said with a disgusted wave of his arm. His expression was hidden by his mask.

"We're ten minutes out."

"Ten-four," Ox said, "You're clear to land."

Struggling to put the small radio back on his belt, beneath his large overhang, he issued orders to his subordinate, "Hey Sniffer, take the ranger and his buddy back in the woods and tie 'em up, out of sight." Changing his orders, he yelled, "Wait! I'll go with you. I want a gun on them all the time – I don't want nobody gettin' loose."

As Sniffer began to untie Brian, Ox yelled again, "Hey! Take the ranger first. If they show up before we get back here, I don't want the brokers to know any park officials know about our operation."

Obediently, Sniffer removed the ranger first.

After both men were moved, and re-tied, Ox explained, "Don't say nothin' about the ranger or the other guy when the brokers come. If they learn authorities know about our operation, they might back out of the deal and start getting their birds elsewhere."

"What about the birds?" Sniffer asked.

"I don't think the ranger had time to move them far. The chicks were here this morning when we dropped our climber. They're probably stashed around here somewhere." Waving his arms he shouted, "Go get 'em before the brokers show up!"

241

D.Malisch

As the sound of the incoming helicopter whizzed by overhead, Ox removed his mask and followed the deer path toward the meadow. He arrived just in time to see the group of brokers for rare and exotic species climb out of their chopper. The bulky man sauntered toward the group of four men that had just left the second helicopter. Ox met them half way.

Looking at his own reflection in the man's designer sunglasses, Ox greeted the broker saying, "You're early."

"It was on the way," Loo said curtly. Looking as though he had escaped a mortician's lab, Loo's caulk-white complexion was speckled with brown, warty-looking growths on his cheeks and forehead.

"I don't have much to show you yet," the poacher admitted, "We left a man up on a peak this morning, and he hasn't come back this afternoon."

"We'll look at what you have then," the warty faced man said. Loo's voice had a cool, threatening aspect that made friends and enemies alike give him space.

The poacher bit his lip, knowing he had no specimens to show.

There were three men with Loo. Besides the pilot, two men of average build, wearing polyester black blazers, stood behind their leader. Bulges on their pockets, boasted a surplus of ammo clips, waiting to be spent, should the opportunity arise. The man in dark slacks carried a rifle, but was calm. Pogrom, the gunman wearing white slacks, constantly fingered the safety on his weapon. The frequent clicking sound bothered Ox – as it would bother the majority of people.

With little or no appreciation for the scenic beauty of the green valley ringed by snow capped peaks, Loo surveyed the area in the late afternoon sun. To him, it wasn't a home for eagles and other wildlife; it was simply a cash cow, as he quipped, "So this is

242

where the symbol on our money lives." Plodding behind the heavier poacher, the broker pushed his wraparound sunglasses back up on the bridge of his nose, with his index finger.

Trying not to march to the repetitive clicking of the safety on Pogrom's weapon, Ox trudged slowly up the deer path as he led the brokers to the empty clearing. He was painfully aware the eagle chicks would not be available to show the brokers when they arrived. He hoped to stall Loo until Sniffer found the feathered booty.

The late afternoon sun illuminated the tree tops as the group of lawbreakers finally entered the small clearing where the birds had been kept in days gone by. Without announcement, Ox stopped.

Unable to see well in the shaded, wooded area, the broker bumped into the large man leading them. Loo ignored the embarrassing, small collision, probably not wanting to appear as a klutz in front of his men. To prevent a second occurrence, he removed his glasses, stuffing them into the inside pocket of his expensive sports jacket. Casting glances around the empty clearing he asked, "So. . . where are they?"

"They aren't here yet," Ox defended.

Loo stared up at the poacher, nearly twice his size. Anger set in his warty-face as he scolded, "What is this? You invite us to come here to show us nothing?"

Pogrom, the man in the white slacks, continued to snap the safety on his weapon; the sound had gone beyond a simple irritation for Ox. Avoiding a direct confrontation, he tried desperately to ignore the click. . . click. . . click. . . sound.

"They'll be here soon," Ox said nervously.

"Soon?" Loo shouted, "What happened to the birds you said you had last week?"

The poacher had no answer – he remained silent, while trying to block out the click. . . click. . . click. . . sound.

"Gone?" the broker, questioned, staring at Ox with a deadly glare, "You sold them to another customer, after we made our deal?"

With his eye on Pogrom, Ox made a "push-back gesture," toward the smaller man. "No. No, it's nothing like that. A deal is a deal – and I have over a dozen birds to choose from."

"So where are they?" Loo demanded, his bloodshot, dark eyes dancing back and forth across his pale, speckled face.

"They'll be here; I tell you."

The dispute was interrupted by the sound of footsteps entering the clearing. All weapons were trained in the direction of the sound.

Sky Feather walked slowly into the clearing with his hands held up, just above his shoulders – Sniffer walked behind, with a weapon trained on the native American. "Hey Ox, look what I found," Sniffer said, obviously proud of his great accomplishment.

"Where'd you find him?" Ox asked. The bearded man looked Sky Feather over and laughed. "Looks like a damned 'Injun' with beaded buckskins." The big man shook his head, "I thought they was only in the movies."

Sky Feather studied the men, but remained cool.

Ox repeated his question to Sniffer, "Where'd you find him?"

"Out that way, by the meadow," he replied, pointing toward the general direction.

"Were the birds there?"

"I don't know; I had to bring him here first."

"Hey!" Loo interrupted "What's this got to do with my birds?"

Ox stroked his beard as he thought. The poacher knew he needed someone to blame for the missing birds other than himself; finding the Indian seemed to offer a workable solution. Turning toward Loo, the big man spun his lie, "I think this 'Injun' probably stole your birds, Loo. We been findin' moccasin prints around our camp for weeks." Ox watched Loo's face carefully for signs of disbelief. Seeing none, he continued, "And now our birds disappeared – "

"And you think he took them?" Loo finished the sentence for the poacher.

"Yeah!"

The pale-faced broker looked down at the ground as he thought for several seconds. His gaze lifted and settled on Sky Feather while he contemplated his next action. "Okay Ox, let's say you're right and this guy stole your – uh, my birds." Loo gave Ox a piercing look, "Just what are you going to do about it?"

Ox didn't know? He hadn't thought that far ahead. "Uh, I suppose I'd shoot the thief."

Loo shook his head negatively. In a business gesture, the warted man put his hand behind the bearded man's back and urged him forward where they could speak in private. After several minutes discussion, they returned to the area in front of Sky Feather.

"Tie him up," Ox ordered Sniffer.

"With the others?" the smaller poacher asked, uncertain exactly what Ox wanted.

"There are no others," Ox said with a wink to his subordinate. Ox truly hoped Loo missed Sniffer's reference to the other two prisoners tied out in the woods.

Standing within earshot, Loo heard, but remained motionless.

245

"Oh yeah, I forgot," Sniffer admitted, quickly tying Sky Feather's hands behind his back.

Ox shoved Sniffer aside, causing the smaller man to trip and fall to the ground. Turning to look at Sniffer, Ox set his jaw and doubled his large fist. Without warning, the large man swivelled on his feet and planted a punch on Sky Feather's face, knocking him backwards, to the ground. Immediately Ox rushed over and pulled Sky Feather to his feet where he hit him again in the stomach.

Sky Feather curled into a ball, but remained silent. He never looked at the man dealing him physical violence.

The bulky poacher grabbed Sky Feather's hair and pulled him to his feet. Tilting the Indian's head back, he yelled, "Where are my birds?"

The Native American said nothing; he simply took the beating and abuse. After several minutes, Ox was so tired he was ready to fall down. "Go shoot him, Sniffer."

Amused by the one-sided fight, Loo countered the order, saying, "Wait. We don't want him dead; we might want to question him further."

"Yeah," Ox puffed, still trying to regain his breath, "Just take him out and tie him up somewhere."

Looking a bit disappointed because he didn't get to shoot anyone, Sniffer led Sky Feather to the hidden place where Weeder and Ranger Mills were tied.

As he was being tied, Sky Feather glanced over toward the detective and ranger asking, "Is this an exclusive club, or can anyone join?"

Shaking his head, Brian tried to laugh, but his ribs hurt as he attempted levity. "Looks as though you already paid the price of admission."

Licking his lip and spitting out the blood, Sky Feather nodded, "Yeah, it was a lot of fun too."

Sniffer finished tying the knot. The small man circled Sky Feather and punched him in the stomach. Enjoying the feeling of power, Sniffer gave a punch to Brian and a punch to Derrick before leaving.

"Guess he showed us," Brian said, straining his sense of humor.

"I could have done without that," Derrick moaned.

Weeder looked at his friend Derrick, "You okay, ol' man?"

"Oh yeah. I'm havin' a ball," the ranger shot back.

"Anything broken?"

"Don't think so, unless my pride counts."

Turning his head to speak with the native on his left, Brian asked, "So how did you get caught, Sky Feather?"

The dark-haired man in buckskins smiled drolly before saying, "I surrendered."

"You what?" Brian exclaimed, nearly choking. "Why'd you do that?"

"I've been watching these poachers for a couple of months now, and I wanted to get a better look at them and the people they were selling to, in case they tried to hide behind the legal system."

Brian nodded, "How'd they find you?"

"Well, that was the problem; they couldn't find me for a long time, so I finally had to go out in the meadow and put up my hands and walk toward the guy."

"What the blazes did you do that for?"

Sky Feather looked at Brian and shrugged, "Guess I was getting lonely out there all by myself."

Weeder just shook his head.

Sky Feather looked at his two injured comrades. He offered an apology saying, "I would have been here sooner, if they had been able to see better." Making eye contact with Brian again, he asked, "What are you guys planning to do about the buyers who just flew in this evening?"

"Arrest 'em," the ranger grunted.

"Yeah, that sounds about right," Brian laughed against the pain his ribs gave him. "What other options do we have?"

"I have a plan up my sleeve," Sky Feather said with confidence. Glancing at the fading sunlight on the tops of the trees, the Indian suddenly cocked his head to listen.

"What's the matter?" Brian asked.

"Think they're making an organized search for the birds."

"Where'd you hide them?"

Sky Feather looked at Brian saying, "I left them with friends." He looked back at the darkening forest around them, "They're in very good hands."

"We thought you were alone out here?"

"Oh no," the black-haired man said, with a twinkle in his eye. "I never said that."

* * *

As the sun slipped behind the mountains to the west, a gunshot and a scream echoed through the valley, before dying out.

"What the heck was that?" Sniffer questioned, clutching his rifle tighter.

"Sounded like Loo," Ox said with an air of uncertainty.

Sniffer paused for a moment, "Yeah, it did," he agreed.

"We better go see," Ox looked around, "which way did the sound come?"

The sniffer looked helplessly at Ox, "I donno?"

"Well – he's the buyer and if you don't want to starve next week, we better find him."

Both poachers immediately set out to locate the source of the sounds. As usual, Ox took the lead.

After climbing through a creek bed, Ox and Sniffer moved constantly in the direction they believed the sounds originated. Several minutes later, Sniffer tripped over a body.

"What the heck?" the smaller poacher cried.

Ox bent down to examine the body. "Looks pretty dead to me."

"Is it Loo?"

"No, it isn't." Ox stared at the face in the rapidly fading light. "It's one of Loo's men though." Looking at the dark colored pants, Ox lamented, "Too bad it wasn't the guy who clicks his safety all the time – he makes me nervous."

Large crashing sounds in the brush nearby sent both poachers into a defensive stance.

"Who's there?" Ox demanded, his husky voice booming.

"It's me, Brad – Loo's pilot."

"Oh," Ox said, putting his shotgun down.

"I heard this noise," Brad began –

The sound of running feet trampling the brush came from behind them. All three aimed their guns up the small deer path only to see Loo and the nervous man in the white slacks approach them.

"He's one of your's," Ox offered.

Loo stopped short. He pointed toward the two poachers with the borrowed Uzi, "Move back away from him."

"You don't think we had anything to do with this, do you?" Ox asked, with a strong nervous sound to his voice.

"Just shut-up and step back," Loo ordered. Bending over the body, the wart-faced man strained to see in the dim light. Seeing there was nothing he could do for the gunman, Loo looked around for the expensive rifle. Without light, there was little hope of finding it.

"We found him just like that," Ox apologized. "But there's no sign of blood."

Loo stood up and stepped back, his silhouette barely visible in the twilight. Using his weapon to point, he ordered, "You carry him back to the clearing, Ox."

Not accustomed to taking orders, the bulky man was slow to respond.

"Do it now!" Loo ordered, firing off a short burst from the Uzi into the bush beside the poacher.

Ox jumped, then quickly handed his shotgun to Sniffer before shouldering the body for the trip back to the wooded clearing. Sniffer took the lead.

About fifty yards down the darkened, deer path, Sniffer banged his head on something projecting out from a tree. The impact nearly knocked him flat. As he felt the object in the nearly pitch-black conditions, he screamed.

"What the hell is the matter with you Sniffer?" Ox hollered, "You lost your stupid mind?"

"It's – It's –" he stuttered, failing to get the words out.

Ox set the body down gently and approached his subordinate. His chest bumped into something solid sticking out from the tree. It had no foliage. He felt it. It appeared to be a rifle stock. As the large man felt it, he suddenly began to swear.

"What is it?" Loo asked, confused by all the activity in the dark.

"It's a rifle and it's been wrapped around this tree like it was a toy."

"Move ahead and let me check," Loo ordered. He approached the rifle.

The wind shifted and a wave of unspeakable stench wafted on the night air.

"What the hell is that awful stink?" Sniffer demanded.

Suddenly the others smelled it too. Everyone had a repulsive reaction to the heavy musk odor.

A very deep throated rumble, like the call of an African elephant seemed to come from the left.

Loo pointed his Uzi in the direction and emptied the clip, spraying the trees and bushes with jacketed-lead.

Another deep throated rumble came from behind them, followed by a chorus of similar sounds. The sounds came from every direction except the direction of the bird-station clearing. The men broke ranks and ran for their lives, leaving the body of their comrade behind.

With night established, the moon, in all its splendor, set sail from the eastern ridge of mountains to glide silently across the night sky. As it rose, the pale shadows seen in the forest of Jack Pine seemed to grow unfriendly arms and legs and bodies and faces everywhere the law breakers looked. Their confidence waned.

* * *

For a time, the three prisoners discussed the noises in the distant woods made by the lawbreakers. Since there was little they could do about the situation, they went silent, as they leaned against their respective trees. Though he could barely see him, Brian turned to watch Derrick, concerned with the ranger's labored breathing. Satisfied Derrick's breathing wasn't life threatening, Brian looked toward Sky Feather again and was surprised to find the American native had moved to a tree further to his left. "Sky Feather?" Brian called.

"I'm here," the native admitted calmly.

Unsure if his imagination was playing tricks, or if the man had actually moved, Brian studied the silhouette of the buck-skinned figure for several seconds before saying, "Say – Weren't you tied to this tree closer to me?"

251

The dark-haired man looked at the tree next to Brian for a few seconds then shook his head, "Dang," he said, "Ever since I turned thirty, about a month ago, I keep forgetting things." Without another word, he simply lifted his arms from behind the tree and moved over to the tree next to Brian. Putting his hands back into the tied position, he leaned against the bark of the Jack Pine and pretended he had been tied there for hours.

"How'd you get loose?" Weeder asked.

"Got a knife up my sleeve,"

"Oh." Brian looked at the man, "They didn't check?"

"Heck no," Sky Feather said, raising an eyebrow, which went unseen in the darkness, "They're only poachers."

"Oh." Brian said, pausing to think. "You going to cut us loose?"

"Later," he promised.

"Where'd you go?" Brian asked.

"Feeding time for the birds," Sky Feather said, as he reached up to scratch his nose. He quickly put his hand back behind the tree as he heard a noise. "Shhh – I think someone's coming."

Slowly, the "Clomp, clomp, clomp" of the heavy-footed Ox got louder until the large man thundered back into the very dark clearing. The smaller poacher followed ten or twelve steps behind. Neither poacher wore their hooded disguise seen earlier in the day. Perhaps, they expected the moonlit darkness would hide their identities.

Brian worried. Perhaps it meant the poachers planned to terminate them soon?

Even in the shafts of pale moon light, it was apparent Ox wasn't happy. His expression said it all. He was under pressure to provide birds to his impatient, and well-armed brokers, and he had no birds to offer them for payment he'd already taken. The big man stomped up to the ranger's slack body and stopped.

"You going to tell me where you put the birds? Or am I going to have to use my shotgun on you?" he bellowed.

Ranger Mills gritted his teeth, "Go to Hades," he mumbled.

"I've had it with you," Ox growled. He raised his shotgun and pointed it at the ranger's chest.

Sky Feather kicked off one of his moccasins; it landed behind Ox, making a noticeable sound.

The large man turned rapidly to point the weapon in the direction where the shoe landed. Sky Feather bounded silently to Ox's right arm, waiting for the exact moment when the man realized there was nothing to shoot in front of his gun. At that exact moment, Sky Feather ripped Ox's hand away from the trigger and shoved the butt of the gun up into the big man's temple. The unexpected blow dazed him long enough for the native to swing the shotgun back the other direction, striking the large poacher hard across the bridge of the nose with the barrel. Ox dropped with the limpness of a load of washed clothing, waiting for the spin cycle.

Sky Feather positioned the gun on Sniffer, the smaller poacher, who immediately surrendered. "Drop your weapon and move away from it," Sky Feather ordered. The man complied.

The Native American slipped behind Brian and magically produced a knife to cut his bonds. He handed Brian the knife to do the same for the ranger.

Using a piece of the poacher's rope, Sky Feather bound the arms and legs of the big guy, before he could wake up. As he tied the hands of the remaining poacher, the American Native spoke to Weeder. "Now we've got a secondary problem."

"How so?" Brian asked, rubbing the circulation back into his wrists.

"I stopped by the bird-station clearing to listen in on the conversation, after feeding the birds," the native admitted, "and it seems these two groups don't like or trust each other very much." Sky Feather paused to make eye contact with Weeder, his dark eyes glistening in the spray of moonlight. "The buyers suspect they've been invited to a sting operation. And they think the poachers are working with us."

Weeder grinned, though it hurt his face, "I'll bet the half-inch bolt set that up."

"That could be," Sky Feather agreed, "But they are very angry and very dangerous."

"Enough to kill?" Brian asked.

"Yeah, enough to kill." Releasing the ranger, the American Indian watched Derrick stumble around in the darkness under his own power. "Worse yet, they have fully automatic weapons."

Watching the native heft his bow and quiver of arrows, Brian asked, "Are you any good with that thing?"

A look of frustration fell upon the Indian's moonlighted face. "Not too well," he admitted. Whispering back he said, "My mother made me stay in school all day and study most of the night. I never got a real good chance to practice."

"So much for another American legend," Derrick said painfully, as he tried to laugh.

Brian bent down and searched Ox for the weapons confiscated earlier. Finding Derrick's revolver first, he passed it to the ranger. After locating his Glock and holstering it, Brian offered the shotgun to Sky Feather, who refused it. Enjoying his freedom again, Brian suggested, "Maybe we ought to hide these guys from the brokers, so they'll be around to stand trial."

"I was thinking the same thing," the native agreed.

It took the power and cooperation of all three men to move Ox into a dry spot in the nearby creek bed. Stripping shoe laces from the poacher's boots, Sky Feather bound one man's head to the other man's feet before covering them with brush.

"I don't think they will be stupid enough to call the brokers for a rescue," Derrick said, as he groped in the darkness for his day-pack. The ranger removed his flashlight from the bag and tested it. Finding it broken, he tossed it back inside.

As the men moved away from the creek where the poachers were hidden, Sky Feather heard a sound and disappeared into the shadows. Unaware of the noise, Ranger Mills carelessly stood in the bright moonlight, brushing away the bark and dirt, from his uniform.

"I thought so," the angry voice of Loo broke the silence. The warty-faced man stepped out of the shadows with Pogrom, the gunman wearing white slacks – both carried Uzis.

Weeder reached for the shotgun, but before he could pick it up, a burst of gunfire from Loo's automatic hit it, sending it flying.

"Don't touch," Loo warned, as the echos of gunfire drifted back to their ears.

Brian raised his hands and waited.

Stepping carefully through the huckleberry, the two brokers moved closer to Weeder and Ranger Mills. Loo's pasty white face took on a ghoul-like appearance in the pale moonlight as he spoke. "So – it really is a sting operation after all."

"And if I denied it?" Brian asked.

"Deny it all you want. The ranger uniform says it all," the warty-faced man said smugly. "Now, I'd like to have my birds, please."

Brian watched the shadows for signs of Sky Feather, but could see nothing of him. "And if I told you there were no birds?"

255

"Well – I suppose our business would be concluded," Loo said smoothly. In an icy tone he added, "But that would also mean I'd be obliged to kill you."

"Well we wouldn't want that," Weeder admitted.

"No, we wouldn't."

"Look at it from my perspective," Weeder said. "You'll probably just kill us, right after we give you the chicks anyway."

"You do have a point," Loo admitted, "But maybe we could work something out." Loo's thin lips looked nonexistent as he stood quietly bargaining in a shaft of moonlight.

"Well I suppose if I do show you where the birds are, I will live longer," Brian conceded, "So I'll do it." Brian had no idea where the birds were hidden, but he knew Sky Feather was somewhere in the shadows. He also knew it would be extremely difficult for the native to take on two or more heavily armed men at once, though he saw him do it just minutes before. Brian turned to Derrick, "You stay here, I'll take them."

Before the ranger could protest, Loo objected, "No, we'll take him along. I wouldn't want him to get lonely and radio for help, or anything like that."

"Then I won't take you," Brian countered.

"Oh you will – and you'll savor every second of life doing it," the ghoul said, with signs of delight in his power of life and death.

Cautiously, Brian and Derrick stumbled through the very dark area, leading their heavily armed guards. Neither the detective or ranger was intimately familiar with the wooded area, but they pushed forward, trying to find their way down the well-worn deer path.

While his feet felt the way along the dark trail, Brian's mind raced through things he might do, to turn the tables or at least, escape. He remembered Loo had not bothered to disarm them.

The detective wasn't sure if it was oversight, or if the man just waited for any quick movement as an opportunity to end his and the ranger's life in a burst of lead.

For several lengthy minutes they plodded along, feeling their way through the darkness. At times they passed into full moonlight then back into heavy darkness. Weeder watched for Sky Feather in the shadows, and wondered when he would make his move.

The gentle babbling sounds of a small stream a few steps away fell upon the detective's ears. He expected the deer path to end at the stream, and most did. Brian led the group out into full moonlight and turned to look beyond Derrick at Loo. Suddenly he realized, that the gunman behind Loo was gone, taken out by Sky Feather, no doubt.

Loo turned to look back also. Startled to find no one behind him, he stared into the darkness, apparently thinking Pogrom had hung back to check for anyone following them. When Loo realized his mistake, it was too late.

As soon as their armed guard turned, Brian yanked on Derrick's coat and broke into a run. The sound of the small stream masked their foot steps on the thick mat of grass, grazed often by the hungry deer. As the lawmen neared cover, Loo discovered the escape. A rain of angry bullets sang through the night air, embedding themselves in small pines on either side of the fugitives. Luck, timing and distance were with the detective and ranger; they were not hit by the partial clip Loo fired at them.

Loo was now alone and exposed in the moonlight. He cursed the night; he cursed the men who escaped him; he cursed the luck he thought he had. He fumbled through his pockets for another ammo clip. Snapping it in place, he tried to find his way back through the wooded area on his own, without light.

257

Thinking the poachers were part of the sting operation, Loo was more than angry. He had given Ox a lot of money for birds he didn't receive. Now nearly everyone had disappeared.

As the wart-faced man stumbled along the dark trail, he felt he had been treated as a fool, which made his anger vent each time he banged his knee or each time a limb struck him in the face. Concentrating on reaching the clearing where he told the pilot to wait, Loo knew the night wasn't over. . . and he'd get his revenge using technology. His years of smuggling drugs, people and animals, prepared him an event such as this. He had the equipment. His helicopter was equipped with starlight and infrared imaging systems, frequently used to navigate unlighted air fields at night. He was certain his technology would swing control of the situation back into his favor. He would show them.

* * *

After dashing along the moonlit path to hide in the dark forest again, Brian and Derrick finally realized they were safe for the moment and stopped to catch their breaths. As they gasped for air, Sky Feather silently and magically appeared beside them.

"You guys alright?" the Native American asked.

"Yeah, thanks for the help," Derrick gasped.

Trying to see Sky Feather better in the shadows, Brian stared at him. "Did you get hurt?"

"No, I'm fine — guess that's where the training comes in handy."

Weeder was surprised, "Training? What training?"

"Special Forces."

"You were in 'Special Forces'?"

Returning Brian's look, Sky Feather nodded, "For a while — Didn't like it though — too many people sniping at you."

"Well welcome back," Brian chuckled.

Shaking his head in puzzlement, Derrick finally seemed impressed, "And now all you want to do is work with wildlife?"

"Well, yeah." The native paused for a moment to compose his thoughts, "I can identify with them. The birds are hunters, nearly pushed out of existence by ignorant or greedy land-grabbing people. Of course, I realize not all folks are that way – but there has to be balance."

"Amen to that," Derrick agreed, between breaths. Squinting at Sky Feather in the darkness, he asked, "What's the score so far?"

"Let's see, we tied up two of the poachers and left them in the creek bed. Then I took out the guy with the Uzi and he's tied up in the brush over there. One of the buyers died from fright when he got too close to the birds – that leaves Loo and his pilot."

Brian was surprised. "One of the guys died from fright?"

"Yeah, it sometimes happens. I'm sure the tribe watching the birds didn't harm him; they are a very gentle people."

The ranger sat down, next to a tree to rest. Leaning forward to remove a pointed rock from his backside, he said, "I'm surprised the brokers hung around after they discovered the birds were gone."

"I'm surprised they hung around to shoot," Sky Feather whispered, "Poachers must get a lot of money for my bird friends."

"Yeah too much," the ranger said, pressing the button on his watch to see the time. "It's about midnight. We better get some rest before our helicopter arrives in the morning. At first light, I'll go up on the ridge and warn them to bring help." The ranger fooled with his day pack, trying to arrange it for a pillow. Removing his lumpy canteen from the attaching ring, he offered, "Water anyone?"

* * *

For hours, Loo stumbled through the dark woods, trying to find the clearing where he had last seen the helicopter pilot. Cursing the darkness for making him walk in circles; he saw the outline of a fallen log illuminated by scattered moonlight. Thirsty and out of breath, he decided to rest for a minute or two. The warty man shuffled over to the old log, before turning to sit down. His first attempt to sit on the log failed when the sharp end of a broken limb poked his bottom as he lowered himself. He swore loudly. After seating himself a second time, a low moan caught his attention. Remembering the experience just after dusk, he flipped the safety off his firearm and waited to hear it again. As he listened, a small cloud of passing mosquitoes saw his infrared signature – each stopped for a drop of blood to enhance their breeding production.

Loo slapped wildly at the buzzing, biting insects. He cursed wildly, trying to keep them out of his ears and eyes. Leaning back as he fought against the aggressive cloud, the pale-faced man fell off the log onto something soft. "What the -?" he said, in terror. But the body beneath him only moaned. Still swatting mosquitoes, Loo felt around, discovering the body was bound and gagged. He removed the gag and spoke to it, "Pogrom? Is that you?"

Slowly, the bound man answered, "Loo?"

"Yeah, it's me." Loo fumbled for the knife in his pocket, "Let me cut you loose."

* * *

Weeder's three-hour slumber was interrupted by the sound of a helicopter orbiting overhead. Though he didn't know it yet, Loo had found his pilot and they were busy searching for infrared sources near the place where he and Derrick had escaped. It would soon be obvious that Loo no longer needed them and intended to track them down and kill them – then find the birds with the aid of technology.

Loo stared at the small, red display in the cockpit then tried to judge exactly where his targets were under the moon lighted canopy of trees below them.

A volley of shots snapped limbs and ricocheted off the rocks a short distance away from Brian and his friends. Scrambling for better cover, Weeder and Sky Feather instantly recognized Loo was using technology to track them.

"Down into the big boulders in the creek!" Sky Feather yelled.

"Which way to the creek?" Brian shouted back above the roar of gunfire.

"City kid!" Derrick shouted to Brian, "It's downhill from here."

The three men hurried through the brush and pines downhill to the creek. A hail of gunfire seemed to be all around them; each step could be their last. At the edge of the creek, they dashed across a small clearing into the icy, snow-melt water of the creek.

The gunfire from overhead followed them. It seemed Loo knew in advance where they were going.

The creek offered even less cover more than the forest. The large boulders, were not large enough to crawl beneath, and the few trees, creek-side, wouldn't hide them from the infrared camera.

Slipping and sliding over the icy-wet rocks, the three men moved from bank to bank, in search of cover that didn't exist. A bullet burned through Derrick's left arm as he zigged when he should have zagged.

The ranger's cry from pain infuriated Brian. The detective remembered lessons from playing chess. If you play defensively, you can't win. Rolling onto his back in the icy water, he removed his Glock and emptied the clip into the belly of the moonlighted chopper. The pilot wisely veered away to assess damage.

Brian replaced the clip from his day-pack as he strained to see his companions in the darkness. "Sky Feather, what are you doing?"

The Native American had found a clay area in the rocky bank of the creek. He was quickly rolling in the damp material and patting it on his head. "Insulation!" he shouted. "Wet clothing helps, but clay is better at blocking infrared."

Instantly Brian realized he was correct. Grabbing Derrick's torso, the detective forced him into the gooey clay. "Roll in it!" he ordered. Removing the baseball caps, Brian slapped a layer of icy mud on them. "Here!" he said, handing the cap back to the ranger.

Derrick had finished his wallow. With teeth chattering from his cold, wet clothing, Brian took his turn, rolling in the heavy, wet material.

"We need backup!" the detective shouted.

"It probably won't be available for several more hours," Derrick said, with his teeth chattering uncontrollably.

"Try your radio now!" Brian urged, "We can't wait. Call the military if necessary; we need help now."

Derrick tried several calls, but to no avail. The hand-held unit needed more height to make the contact with the base.

A short distance away, they heard the helicopter land. They even heard voices as the crew reorganized.

Bent over, the three men hurried further down the creek, slipping and sliding over the wet rocks. Moments later, they heard the sound of the helicopter starting, followed shortly after by the popping sound of the rotor blades as it lifted from the ground.

"This doesn't look good," Brian said, wiping the mud from his eyes with the back of his hand.

"Keep moving," Sky Feather prodded.

The helicopter buzzed overhead before descending on the streambed below. The pop of its rotor became louder and louder as it searched the tributary for humans. A short burst of gunfire behind them, upstream, meant they were being followed. The muddy fugitives were being squeezed between whoever was behind them and the helicopter coming upstream.

The machine passed over them, unable to see their profiles clearly on the infrared viewer. Only the solitary man they had dropped off upstream, showed on the viewer. The airship swung back downstream – searching.

Taking flight, like a herd of wild pigs, Brian, Derrick and Sky Feather crawled as fast as they could through the rocks, brush and debris in the creek-bed. The icy water splashed on their soaked bodies, washing away their body heat and worse, washing away their protective coating of mud.

Near deafening noise and a stiff vertical wind meant the helicopter was immediately overhead. Sky Feather dived into the leafy-brush, beneath the overhanging trees shading the stream. Shots rang out from above. A red-hot bullet grazed his buckskins above his left hip.

With his white slacks glowing in the moonlight, Pogrom suddenly appeared, in the creek-bed, sloshing toward them. Pointing his Uzi downstream, he released a spray of automatic weapon fire that ripped through the creek channel, ricocheting from boulders at various angles.

The chopper seemed to lose track of the three men for a few seconds as it continued downstream in its search.

A huge, bleached-log wedged crossway from a past winter storm, blocked the path. The three fugitives would have to exit the creek channel to continue onward. "Keep close to the log on your stomach and make it quick!" Sky Feather whispered. "I hear large rocks rolling and clanking in the creek-bed behind us, so whoever is back there, is getting close — really close."

Following the two lawmen, Sky Feather slipped over the log and quickly grabbed one of the stalks of a bush on the other side. Under the bright moonlight, the native made an estimate before thrusting his knife through the stalk and twisting to open it. He passed the nock of one of his arrows into the opening, and quickly lashed it with a piece of string from his pocket. Instead of cutting the string, he knotted it and set the wad in a notch at the end of piece of driftwood found in the creek. Carefully pulling the bush back, to arm it, he propped the driftwood so it would likely be kicked by the next person to come over the log. The steel broadhead of the arrow was razor-sharp and would presumably make more than a small impression on the hunter following them. Hearing sloshing on the other side of the log, Sky Feather knew the enemy was just upstream and it was time to leave.

His wet, muddy moccasins slipped on the smooth rock, causing Sky Feather to plunge into a small pool of water. The protective coating of mud flushed from his buckskins, making him visible to the infrared viewer on board the helicopter.

Loo immediately saw the image and ordered the pilot into a position for a fatal shot.

Return fire from the handguns of Brian and Derrick punctuated the bottom of the helicopter, a second time, buying a few more seconds of precious time.

Alarmed by the close gunfire, Pogrom peered over the log that crossed the creek and listened for sounds of his prey. Rapid movement of brush along the sides of the creek gave him a target to spray his bullets.

Sky Feather dashed toward deeper cover, where his friends waited. As he moved, clusters of shots rang out from upstream, cutting the brush around him. He reached for an arrow, but his hiding place area was too small to make use of the bow, and it would be suicide to stand up to take aim anyway.

Seconds later, they heard a scream of agony from upstream. "The trap must have gotten him," Sky Feather smiled. "That will either slow him down or make him mad as hell."

Suddenly, the helicopter noise increased again. Automatic weapon fire sliced into the foliage around them; they hugged the creek bank for protection. The firing stopped while the air ship crossed over the creek and positioned itself to fire again.

"Quick! Move to the other bank," Brian shouted.

The move was followed by even more gunfire. Except for rocks in the bottom of the creek chipping and striking them, the men were protected by the mud and steep rocky creek banks.

Looking at the detective, "It's time," Sky Feather shouted, "Please give me the avenger."

Huddled tightly against the bank and barely able to hear over the sound of gunfire and helicopter noise, Brian could only give a confused, "Huh?"

"Quickly, I need the bolt, for justice."

Brian shrugged and fished it from his pocket. "Guess it won't do us any good if we're dead."

Sky Feather cut a rawhide thong from the seam of his trouser leg. With his back to the wall of the creek, he quickly bound the bolt to the shaft of the arrow he held in his hand. His hands shook from the cold and pressure to hurry. He cut the excess length of the thong with the sharp broadhead tip on the arrow and kissed it for luck.

As if on cue, the thundering chopper swung around upstream and nearly overhead.

Sky Feather nocked his arrow, aimed through a small opening in the canopy of leaves, overhead. He held the bow string near his right ear, waiting patently for the helicopter to get into a better position to release the arrow. The leaves on the trees blew and danced around as though a tornado had attacked them. Limbs swayed and some of the smaller ones broke, raining down on his upturned face. Finally the open door of the machine came into view. Sky Feather took a deep breath and allowed the string to slide from his fingers. The arrow took flight, was deflected by the wind from the rotor and glanced off the windshield of the ship. Although the target wasn't the one he wanted, the bolt crashed into the rotor, shearing off a big section of the spinning blade.

The helicopter engine began to race wildly. Tipped at an awkward angle, and shaking violently, the spinning aircraft quickly lost altitude. The pilot tried to compensate, but a crash was imminent. In a dizzy spin, the craft spiraled down until it struck the ground, digging up and throwing a huge cloud of rocks dirt and vegetation.

For a few seconds, Brian couldn't believe it was all over, then he listened for sounds of activity. All was quiet save the cooling-popping sound of the crashed craft nearby. "Cover me, while I go check!" the detective ordered. He crossed the creek and scrambled up the bank to see the justice metered out by the half inch bolt. The helicopter crashed from a low altitude and had not disintegrated or caught fire, though it might shortly.

Loo and his pilot were stunned and not much of a threat, but Brian wasn't taking any chances as he approached the aircraft lying on its side. He found Loo and the pilot on board, both were injured, but would survive for trial. Brian reasoned they would remain caged for a very long time. . . a suitable punishment for caging and selling wild birds.

Above the creek, pinned to the log, by Sky Feather's trap, Derrick found an angry Pogrom in a lot of pain. His automatic weapon rested out of reach, on the bottom of the creek, under the log.

During later interrogation of the poachers, Ox admitted the climber had been the one who killed the park guest. The climber's death was an immediate punishment by the bolt.

Authorities combed the crime scene thoroughly for evidence. However – they did not find the half-inch bolt.

Sky Feather took Derrick and Brian to retrieve the birds. As they approached the area, the native picked up a rock and pounded a rhythmic beat against the side of a sun-bleached old snag. "My friends are kind of shy," he told the ranger and detective, "I want them to know it's okay to leave now."

The three men climbed up the hillside to a small trail. They followed the trail back into the woods, where the trees were a bit larger. Suddenly Sky Feather stopped and said, "Here we are."

Scanning the area and seeing no sign of birds, Derrick asked the obvious question, "So – where are the birds?"

Sky Feather smiled widely, showing his teeth for the first time. Pointing up, he simply said, "Where all birds belong – in the trees."

The two men looked where Sky Feather pointed. Nearly the height of three tall men above them, hung the cages, shrouded in pieces of the old camouflaged tent. Each cage was individually tied to a separate limb in the grove of trees.

"How the heck did you ever get them up there without a ladder?" Brian asked, "And how did you ever do it, in such a short time?"

"As I said," Sky Feather grinned, "I had help from my friends."

"Why did you send them away?" Derrick asked. "We could use their help to take the cages down. Besides, I'd like to meet them."

"Maybe someday you will," Sky Feather said, looking at the ranger's feet, "But today you'll have to just be satisfied standing in their foot print."

"Huh?" The ranger said, looking down at the giant footprint under his boots.

In shock and surprise, Brian and Derrick simultaneously shouted, "SASQUATCH?"

Derrick and Sky Feather became good friends. In fact, Sky Feather, with a little coaching from the ranger, became the local Conservation Specialist, a position that bestowed a full time, paid position on him, while watching over his feathered friends.

*   *   *

Chapter 7   The New Truck

Guests:
Buff Lansom   Current gang leader
Mako   2nd in command (past gang leader)
Paul & Wiky   Subordinates
Derrick Mills   Ranger

Buff Lanscom skipped school with three of his classmates to take his new 4X4 pickup out where he could test it. Although he was proud of the shiny new toy his father gave him, taking care of it properly was not his current objective. In his immature mind, if the television advertisements showed the truck bouncing twice its height while climbing boulders, it must be made to withstand that kind of punishment and more. The three buddies hanging onto the bucking vehicle were not so sure.

At the top of the ridge in the Pacific Eagle Wilderness, Buff cranked the wheel sharply to one side and slammed on the brakes, causing the truck to slide sideways in an unsafe manner. After the dust cleared, he looked through the rear window at Paul and Wiky riding in the back. They were covered with dust to the point only their eyes and mouth showed, and neither looked as though they were enjoying the ride much.

"Hey you wimps, back there, how come you're so friggen' dirty?" Buff heckled, then laughed. Inside, he looked over at his navigator, in the passenger seat, and demanded, "So where in the heck are we, Mako?"

"Heck! I don't know Buff. This map don't have no roads on it."

Buff grabbed the map, tearing it in the process. "Now see what you done!" He said blaming Mako. The young driver looked at the map for several seconds, but couldn't make any sense out of the paper projection. With a show of disgust, Buff wadded the map into a ball and threw it at his navigator.

"So where are we – Buff?" Mako asked, unfolding the map and pressing against the wrinkles.

Buff lit a cigarette and hit the power window button to lower the glass. He carelessly threw the poorly extinguished match onto the dirt next to the dry grass. He'd never admit being lost, because it wasn't the sort of thing a good leader would ever do; he'd learned that from his father. Buff leaned back and blew smoke at Mako. "You're sure a stupid donkey – Mako. Didn't you learn nothin' at school?"

Mako postured himself, setting an arrogant look on his tattooed face. After all, he had been leader of the group up until a week ago, when Buff showed up with this new, shiny white truck. "Don't give me no garbage, Buff. You don't know where we are neither."

While that certainly was true, Buff smirked. "Bet you a hundred I do, butt-head."

Mako was certain he had Buff this time. "You're on, meathead. Now where are we?"

After cutting the chain across the road, the drive along the dusty access road, down into the creek-bed and up onto the meadow, had taken at least forty minutes. The second half of the expedition, through the wooded area and out onto the steep slope of the ridge, consumed another half hour. None of the youngsters, especially Buff, remembered the actual details arriving at this point. There were no sign posts, or fast-food businesses the youths might remember along the way. They had simply let Buff's random selections guide them to their current destination. . . wherever that was. . . ?

As far as the bet was concerned, Buff had no desire to allow Mako a chance to win. He leaned forward and smacked a small plastic cover on an overhead-compartment, above the rear-view mirror. A fancy tray dropped several inches to allow viewing of a compass and global positioning system. Buff thrust a pudgy finger at the instrument and said, "There! That's where we are. Now where's my hundred?"

"What the heck is that?"

"Mako – don't you know nothin?" Buff threw his lighted cigarette out the window, which fortunately landed on a slab of bare rock, away from the grass. Pointing his pudgy finger, again, at the sophisticated device he lectured to the navigator, "That there – is a 'Gee Pee S' and it says exactly where we are on earth anytime."

Mako wasn't convinced, but he was impressed. "Okay, so how's it work?"

Buff wasn't expecting to give a technical explanation; in fact, about the only thing technical he knew about – was how to suck air in and belch it out, while farting at the same time. He'd won a few beers with that trick. "Look Mako, it's too complicated for you to understand!"

"Well you ain't getting no hundred from me until you say how it works."

"It works just fine," Buff hissed, "It's got gears or somethin' that go down to the wheels or somethin'. It never gets lost or nothin'." Buff looked at Mako, realizing the acquaintance wasn't convinced. In fact, for an instant, he wasn't sure if Mako was going to hit him. Grabbing the rifle, from behind the seat, the nervous driver jumped out of the truck. Peering through the telescopic sight, Buff looked around for things to shoot. He looked for birds, but didn't see any. He looked for small mammals but

271

didn't see any. He swung the gun around toward the back of the truck, causing Wiky and Paul to panic and jump out. They ducked behind the metal bed, on the far side. Buff laughed and fired a shot over their heads at the rocks behind. A singing sound of a ricocheting bullet whined through the air. Buff laughed again, before aiming the gun away. He walked around to the front of the truck and looked through the telescope at the valley below.

Mako, tired of waiting, honked the horn which startled Buff and embarrassed him. Mako laughed and shouted, "Come-on, let's go somewhere."

Buff turned and pointed the gun at Mako, who refused to duck.

"You better kill me with that, or I'll bust it over your head, you jerk."

Buff pointed the gun down and smiled. "I wouldn't waste the ammo." With his insult delivered, Buff put the rifle away on the rack behind the seat before climbing into the truck and starting it. He recklessly turned the truck around and watched as Wiky and Paul raced to climb aboard. Just as they almost reached the tailgate, Buff accelerated the vehicle just beyond their reach. He repeated the process for a minute or so, before tiring of the game and stopping to let the tired boys climb in.

Moments down the dusty road, they spotted a deer leaving a creek nearby. Apparently the animal had not heard the approaching vehicle because of the noises of the stream. The doe did see them soon enough to bolt up the bank and disappear into the brush, before the boys could stop and exit the vehicle.

Buff, with the rifle in his hand, waved in a casting motion to Paul and Wiky, "Fan out and herd him back this way so I can get a shot at 'em." The boys looked at each other and looked at Buff holding the rifle. Neither trusted him and neither had completely forgotten the shot fired over their heads a few minutes earlier.

"No way!" Paul objected. "You want him, he's all yours. You go get him yourself."

Buff looked at Mako, who said nothing, but shook his head negatively. "Well then," Buff searched for words to get his way, "you don't get no venison steaks."

"You can't shoot it anyway," Wiky argued, "You don't have no license or tag or nothin'."

What Wiky said was true, but it didn't bother Buff. He had been with his dad several times on poaching expeditions and he knew ways to improve his chances of getting away with it.

Buff looked at the three guys with him and quickly walked back to the truck and pulled the keys from the ignition. After dropping them in his pocket, he started down toward the creek, to cross it.

Mako waved at the other two and said, "You guys better follow him to make sure he doesn't hurt himself or get lost or nothin'. Could be a long walk out of here if he don't come back."

Buff and the two dusty boys walked around the bed of the creek until they spotted the tracks left by the doe. Their attempt at tracking failed a few feet away from the wet mud where the ground became so hard there were no impressions. Buff looked in the general direction the tracks led and continued in a straight line. "Come on! He's up here somewhere." Minutes passed with the boys thrashing around the woods, breaking limbs on trees and generally making enough noise that all except the most stupid of animals vanished from sight.

Meanwhile, at the truck, Mako carefully unfolded the torn map, then stepped outside to have a smoke and look around with the binoculars. He hoped to chart a path to find the shortest route home.

After a while, it became apparent to Buff that he wasn't going to find any animals to shoot at today. It never occurred to him that he and his buddies were the source of the problem. . . well, maybe he did suspect the others, but never himself. "Hey you idiots! Keep the noise down. You're scaring everything!"

Paul and Wiky shrugged it off. They knew Buff complained about everything they did; it was part of the pecking order and they were on the bottom.

Fifteen minutes later, out of sight of the truck, Buff decided to turn back. The problem was – you guessed it – he wasn't sure which way was back. He remembered walking by that big tree over there, but the big rock wasn't next to it. Five minutes later, he was sure a short cut through the grove of tiny pine would cut several minutes off the return leg of their walk, so he took it, with Paul and Wiky tagging along behind, completely oblivious to their predicament and its dangers. Buff was getting tired and in need of a cigarette. "Hey you guys! Gimme a smoke."

Paul found one first, handing it to Buff.

Buff put it in his mouth and waited for Paul to hand him the lighter too. When Paul didn't respond, Buff snapped his fingers and pointed to the end of the cigarette, hanging from his lip.

"Oh." Paul said, digging through his pockets, unable to find a lighter.

Buff looked at Wiky, who shrugged back. Buff began to anger.

"I always borrow Paul's, when I need it," Wiky confessed.

Buff didn't bother checking his own pockets; he knew he didn't have a lighter; it was with his cigarettes back in the truck. In a fit of anger, he threw the cigarette down and stomped it. He then kicked a small log, stubbing his toe, which made him curse loudly. Paul and Wiky started to laugh at the sight of their leader dancing around on one foot, swinging the rifle wildly. They stopped abruptly, when Buff yanked the trigger and a bullet crashed into a log at their feet. Finally, Buff slowed down and limped away; his subordinates followed.

"What's that?" Wiky screamed, pointing to the home for the local packrat.

Buff stopped and stared, "Donno? Let's look." The three boys walked over and looked. They walked around the five-foot high pile of sticks and leaves and dirt. They walked around it again and again, mystified at the structure. They kicked at it.

"Well, what is it?" Wiky asked again.

Buff didn't know. He didn't have the faintest idea, but he had to show leadership. "Heck, it's a hut."

"Hut?" Wiky wasn't sure.

"Yeah, it's a hut," Buff emphasized, to show he was a knowledgeable leader.

Wiky poked at the pile of sticks with a branch found nearby, "For what?"

Buff wasn't sure about that either. He looked up and both Wiky and Paul were standing there, waiting for an answer. "Uh – it's like a small cave for a bear."

Gullible as they were, neither boy was buying Buff's story. "Ah – that ain't no bear house," Wiky said, shaking his head.

"Don't look like no cave to me neither," Paul agreed.

As usual, Buff was on the spot. "Okay, open it up and I'll show ya."

Paul and Wiky looked at each other. They looked at the huge pile of debris and back at each other, shaking their heads negatively. "I don't want to get no bear mad at me," Wiky objected.

"What a bunch of wimps! Here! I'll kill it for ya, then you can tear it apart." Buff fired ten or eleven shots into the pile at point blank range. Wiky and Paul jumped back after sticks flew out from the first shot.

D.Malisch

"I didn't hear nothin' die," Wiky admitted when Buff stopped shooting.

"It's dead," Buff said confidently, "Now open 'er up!"

When Wiky and Paul held back, Buff threw his rifle aside and tugged on the pile of sticks. "Come on idiots, start pulling it apart." Shortly, all three boys were ripping apart the home of the local packrat. Ten minutes later, their hands and clothing dirty, they had gotten to the core area, only to find no one home – no bear and no packrat. Just a lining of dry, brown leaves and grass.

Buff picked up his gun and probed the wad of leaves for any sign of life – none was found. He was surprised to find a silver chewing-gum wrapper, a bottle cap, and of all things. . . a shiny half-inch bolt among the treasures. "Hey, look at this!" Buff laughed as he held it up. It was the plunder of a great and fanciful battle. "I gotta show my dad this," he said, shoving it into his trouser pocket.

Just then, a doe trotted across the edge of the clearing on the way to the creek for her evening's drink.

"Hey! Did ya see that?" Buff shouted. He raised his rifle and took aim at the deer's posterior. He yanked the trigger several times before realizing he had expended all the rounds into the packrat's nest. The doe kept them in her sight as she quickened her pace but never turned to look back.

Digging through his shirt pocket, Buff found three extra rounds. He quickly jammed them into the gun's magazine and ran helter-skelter through the woods after the doe. Wiky and Paul followed.

Far better at navigation in the woods, the doe quickly outdistanced the mighty hunters and had her drink in peace. As she looked up, she was surprised to see her antagonists arrive, and completely startled to hear the three loud noises they made. She had finished her drink and knew it was time to leave, which she did quickly.

"Damn!" Buff swore. "I know I hit him." Waving his arms in a casting motion he commanded, "look around for signs of blood."

They looked and looked, but could find no blood. They couldn't even find the tracks she made in the pea gravel.

A slight evening breeze drifted down from the snow capped peaks to settle in the valley, now that the sun was over the horizon. Buff shivered, remembering he had left his coat in the truck. Wiky and Paul, both had coats, but he was bigger than either of them; it would do no good to take either of their coats. Looking around, it seemed much darker than up on the ridge a few minutes before. As he shivered, Buff felt the first pangs of hunger.

"Let's go back to the truck," Wiky suggested.

"Yeah, Wiky's right," Paul agreed.

Buff was in agreement, but didn't know which way to go. He suddenly realized they had no food, no shelter, no ammunition, no idea which way to go to the truck and soon would have no light to see to get there. "Let's go this way," he commanded, heading up out of the creek onto the tall grass.

"I think we should follow the creek," Paul objected.

Buff was incensed that his leadership should be challenged. "No butt-head, it's this way." He pointed downhill, away from the general flow of the creek.

"But we crossed the creek, just after we got out of the truck."

Paul had a point. Buff did remember looking for tracks in the soft mud. "Okay Butt-head it was by the creek, but which way? Upstream or downstream?"

None of them knew. Finally, Paul suggested, "Lets go downstream."

That settled it. Buff was sure it must be upstream. "We're going upstream. Now let's go before it gets dark."

The light was fading quickly. In another ten minutes it would be so dark you couldn't see your hand in front of your face. They had walked only a few yards upstream when they heard a horn honking. The echo was terrible. It seemed to come from everywhere.

"That's Mako at my truck. I know the horn," Buff said confidently.

They turned around and around trying to get a bearing. Suddenly, a set of lights came on a quarter-mile downstream. Now they knew which way to go.

Fifteen minutes later, they stumbled their way up the bank of the creek to Mako and the truck. "Where the blazes you guys been?" Mako chided. "I thought I was going to have to hot-wire this truck to get home tonight."

"Just shut up and get in!" Buff snapped. He fished the key from his pocket and plugged it into the ignition slot. As the engine sprang to life, it gave him a wonderful thrill to again be in control.

After climbing into the passenger seat, Mako turned on the map light, "While you guys were gone, I think I figured how to get out of here."

Pointing at the fuel gauge, Buff argued, "It better be good 'cause, we're about out of gas."

Hoping he hadn't made any mistakes, Mako gulped, then gave Buff the first set of directions.

The path out wasn't easy. Going cross country on an old, unkept, logging road is a lot easier in the daylight. They bounced along the nearly invisible road for several minutes, weaving in and out of the woods. The headlights danced along the knee-high grass as they dodged rocks and small logs strewn across the rutted old path. In places, the scrub-oak had nearly reclaimed the road. Buff squeezed through anyway. The sound of the brush scratching both sides of the truck was of no consequence to the youths. It was dark now, but it was difficult to see the stars through the tall Douglas Fir and Bull-Pine, that lined the road. The truck swung around a sharp bend only to find the road dead-end at an old logging site.

"Dang you Mako. You told us wrong!"

Mako wished he'd stayed in scouts long enough to learn the finer art of map reading before he'd elected to drop out and join his first gang. "We gotta go back the other way."

Buff was caustic, "What if it dead-ends too?"

"Look fat-face, it can't be a dead end on both ends, it has to go someplace – else you can't get no log trucks on it."

Buff reasoned Mako's logic did make some sense, so they bounced back down the road, dodging the huge rocks dotting the narrow passage. After leaving the woods, the road was flanked by a dirt bank ten feet high on the left and a drop off, who knows how deep, on the right. The fact the headlights didn't shine down into the depths made it all the more spooky.

The good news was, the road did continue back to civilization; the bad news was it had a three-foot gap where heavy rains had washed away a big chunk of the road bed.

With the truck stopped and the headlights shining across the crevasse, the boys squinted into the darkness, trying to determine the depth. "It must be about four feet or more," Mako estimated.

"May as well be a million," Buff growled. He went back to the truck and got his coat. With the sun gone, it was quite chilly at this altitude. A hunger pang pried at Buff's stomach, causing him to probe his coat-pockets for a candy bar. By feel, he determined he still had three left – the candy would last him about two hours, providing he didn't have to share.

Buff looked behind the seat for a shovel. It was his hope he could get the others to fill the hole, so he could drive across it. Of course, it still galled him that Mako hadn't taken them back the same way they had come up. Finding no shovel or similar tool, he decided to show leadership by commanding, "You guys start throwing all the big rocks you can find into that hole. We gotta get it filled so we can get home tonight."

Wiky and Paul grumbled, but started to move their half-frozen bodies to search the darkness for rocks. Mako, felt some responsibility for taking them on this road, so he joined the project. After several minutes, Paul noticed Buff was the only one not contributing, "Hey! Buff! How come you ain't doin' nothin'?"

Buff shoved the last of his candy bar into his half full mouth. "I am!" he shouted with a muffled voice. "I'm the contractor."

Mako carried a big rock over and dropped it into the hole, before turning to look at Buff who was leaning on the hood of the truck between the headlights. "What's that got to do with anything?"

"Don't you know nothin' Mako?" Buff said – his mouth clogged with candy. "Don't you know nothin'?"

"I know you ain't helpin' – that's what I know."

"Well Mako, for your in-fermation, a contractor supervises." Buff paused to swallow the chewy load in his mouth. "I know this stuff, 'cause it's what my dad does."

"Well you ain't your dad – and you don't know poop. Now give us a hand."

"Look!" Buff countered, "It's my truck and if you don't want to walk back, just shut your yap and keep fillin' the hole."

Mako gave Buff a seething look before turning to walk around the truck into the darkness to find another rock.

Buff held his watch in front of the headlight to see the time. "Hey you guys need to speed up!"

"It's gettin' hard to find rocks, Buff," Wiky whined. "Maybe you can back the truck up the road and we can pick up rocks along the road?" The others agreed.

Buff climbed into the cab. His first act was to lock the passenger door, so Mako couldn't get in. "You open the tailgate and ride in the back with the other's," Buff demanded.

If Mako would have had a large boulder in his hands, it would have gone into the side of the new truck. Instead, he just stood and glared through the window at Buff until the driver looked away. Then Mako did as he was ordered.

The unyielding bulge in his pocket caused Buff to dig out the half-inch bolt. He inspected his prize before dropping it into the soft-drink holder on the console, between the two seats.

Even in the daylight, in the best of conditions, Buff was not really a good driver, and tonight, in the extreme darkness, he was awful. Back up lights are wonderful, but they really don't make good headlights for any serious driving. Buff managed to lose control of the vehicle several times, smacking the tailgate and rear fenders into small fir trees and mud banks. Fortunately, after driving in reverse for a quarter mile, the boys had collected enough rocks and small logs to fill the gap so they could attempt a crossing.

"I'll guide you across," Mako offered as he crossed over the new road-patch.

Buff shook his head, "I ain't gonna take it slow, so those rocks can settle under my truck." He motioned Mako to step back, "You better get back a-ways, 'cause I'm making a run for it."

Mako looked at the roadway under the glare of the headlights. It looked passable, but it was narrow. There was a drop-off on the passenger side of the truck and a steep bank on the other side. Unfortunately, the road bent slightly to the left, which could be dangerous if Buff got too much speed for the crossing.

Buff backed the truck up about a hundred feet. He pushed the button to select the four-wheel-drive low-range. Wiky and Paul were ordered to move away from the filled crevasse. He got their complete cooperation; they had learned Buff was no precise driver. Buff floored the accelerator petal. The truck engine roared; the transfer case whined loudly as the wheels bit into the dirt, propelling the vehicle faster and faster toward the crude patch. As the front wheels rolled off the dirt onto the first of the rocks, the front-end began to sink, then climb, then sink on one side and climb on the other side, causing the truck to pitch wildly. The kinetic energy of the truck rising then falling on the loosely packed stones and logs compressed the patch even more than a gentle crossing. The front-end dipped low enough to catch the front bumper and winch below the level of the roadbed on the far side. The speed and power of the rear wheels forced to truck to erupt into a spectacular burst of dirt and small gravel, as it cleared the patch. Fortunately, the plowing action of the front of the vehicle provided an easier path for the rear wheels to gain purchase. They had crossed.

All four boys walked around the truck inspecting the damage. The driver's side had massive dents in the rear quarter panels, the tailgate wouldn't close, the front bumper was bent badly, the winch had been forced up into the grill work, shattering the plastic. The transfer case was dripping oil, but otherwise the vehicle was in great shape.

They all climbed aboard and were on their way. Wiky and Paul chose to sit up near the cab, to avoid falling out of the bed. Mako took his place in the navigator's chair up front.

"I got you through that one," Buff bragged, though he was a bit unhappy about the damage.

They followed the road for several minutes until they recognized an intersection they had passed earlier on the way up. Buff turned onto the road and continued his way back toward the gate where they had entered. The road was rough and rutted, with large rocks projecting up in places. Buff was anxious to get home, since his supply of candy bars was exhausted – he speeded up. The truck bounced wildly back and forth across the road as he tried to maintain control.

As they descended a steep grade, a wheel dropped into a large hole causing the vehicle to pitch wildly again, much as it had earlier during the crossing. The half-inch bolt, already dislodged from the ravine crossing, now rolled from under the seat and up under the brake. The pointed end pierced the deep carpet and foam pad as Buff jammed the brake pedal to slow the truck. Since the brake pedal couldn't move, the truck didn't slow down noticeably. It rocked violently, dropping the rear wheel into the hole just vacated by the front wheel. The vehicle bounced off the road and rolled over the embankment. Wiky and Paul, thrown clear, were fine, except for a few bruises. Of course neither passenger in the front wore seat belts, and they mixed it up pretty much, as the truck rolled several times before coming to a rest at the bottom of the grade.

Ranger Derrick Mills was making his final check in the evening, when he discovered the severed chain that normally blocked access to some of the high country in the park. He had just gotten out his flashlight to look for fresh tire tracks and other clues, when he heard a disastrous sound coming from the road up the canyon. Then he heard the sound of an automobile horn running constantly. The ranger had a bad feeling about what might have happened, so he alerted dispatch before they could close for the day. Climbing back into his truck, he headed up the road toward the canyon.

D.Malisch

Arriving at the scene, he found, as he suspected, an unauthorized vehicle had been rolled about fifty feet down an embankment. Through the cloud of dust, he saw one headlight still shining. The horn was blaring, and two boys were running around and around the overturned vehicle. Derrick stopped with his truck lights illuminating the scene, then grabbing his flashlight, he quickly ran toward the vehicle.

Looking inside, he saw two dazed teenagers. Except for superficial scrapes and bruises, they appeared to be uninjured. Derrick helped them exit the vehicle and move away from the accident scene, lest the vehicle catch fire. The next order of business was to get a large bar from the back of his truck and silence the squawking horn, so he could talk with the boys.

People began to arrive on the scene while Derrick interviewed the teenagers. "So tell me what happened here?" Derrick asked the pudgy driver.

"I donno man. We was just comin' down this road and things started happenin' really fast – then I hit the brakes, but there weren't none and next thing I know, we're goin' round and round."

Derrick took information and wrote notes as fast as he could, while constantly being interrupted by calls on the radio and constantly being interrupted by the multitude of emergency people at the accident. Finally, the tow trucks pulled the vehicle over into the upright position and dragged it back up onto the access road.

Ranger Mills inspected the inside for signs of intoxicants. While he didn't find any, he did discover the half-inch bolt lodged under the brake pedal. He used a big pair of pliers to extract it. He examined it carefully. The silver bolt really looked like the one he remembered seeing several weeks before, except this one was pointed on the threaded end. Derrick turned the bolt around to examine the head – and though half expecting it, he nearly fainted when he saw detective Brian Weeder's initials on it.

Derrick spent the next forty minutes questioning the boys about their association with the bolt. Of course they denied almost everything regarding entering the park without a pass, cutting the chain, driving on the restricted roads, shooting a firearm within the park, hunting without a license and harassing the wildlife.

Derrick laid the bolt on the hood of his state vehicle while assisting the tow truck driver during the hookup.

With the ranger distracted, Buff looked around for witnesses and grabbed the bolt, stuffing it into his pocket. The ranger returned minutes later and wrote Buff a citation for the park violations. It was only after the tow truck driver had driven off with the boys that he remembered the bolt. He looked, but was unable to locate it, on or around his vehicle.

The boys had no knowledge of the bolt, or of its charter. It was never recognized by the teenagers that the bolt also renders justice for − even small animals such as the packrat, who lost his home and valuables to the boys who vandalized it.

The destruction of Buff's pickup would cause him to incur his father's wrath as well as cause him to lose status as the new leader of his gang. The loss would also deprive him of pride of ownership, the pleasure of its use, comfort of its protection during foul weather. Did the innocent packrat lose as much?

* * *

The question begs: Is justice really rendered, if the perpetrator or the victim has no knowledge of the equalization? We are told that true justice is blind; perhaps this means justice, like the speed of light, is a constant that does not depend on a human mind to record it or measure it.

* * *

285

Chapter 8   Real Estate Swindle

Guests:

Buff Lanscom	Leonard's son
Leonard Lanscom	Escrow owner (secret partner to Jess)
Jess Samuels	Realtor (Leonard's secret partner)
Klazzi Korner	Leonard's sexy girlfriend
Wolf	Everit Bondano, schemer
Bert Johnston	Prospective property buyer
Prosecutor Keys	Friend to Bert Johnston
Sheriff	County law-man
Mrs. Waverley	Escrow accountant

Leonard Lanscom had expected his son to be home from school at the usual time that day. Now it was well after ten in the evening, and the grumbling sound of a large truck, navigating the driveway after dark, startled him. Glancing out the third-story window of his sprawling mansion next to the heavily wooded lake, he was even more surprised to see the badly wrinkled remains of his son's new pickup-truck, in tow. In disgust, Leonard threw the papers he was reading onto his desk and jammed his cigar in the brass spittoon before charging downstairs.

Buff, who was Leonard's son, clambered down from the tow truck and hurried to open the assigned garage door for his terribly damaged, new truck. Positioning himself inside the garage, he made his best attempt to direct the tow truck driver.

Confused by the boy's strange arm waving, the driver, used his own judgement to ease Buff's trashed pickup truck backward into the empty garage stall.

The main door on the house beside the ten-car-garage flew open, allowing a large man with greying hair to rush out toward the tow truck. "Hey! Hey!" Leonard shouted. Swinging his arms, the tall man bounded across the yard yelling, "Hey! Don't put that junk in my garage. What the heck do you think you're doing?"

Masked by the noise of the truck, the driver failed to hear Leonard until he began pounding on the hood of the tow vehicle.

"What the -?" the driver said, startled by the sudden attack on his vehicle. He stopped the truck and rolled down his window to see what was the matter.

Buff's father fumed, "Don't put that piece of junk in my garage," he waved his arms in a dismissive manner, "Get that dang thing out of here! It's leaking oil and antifreeze all over the floor and driveway."

"I'm sorry sir — The boy told me — "

"He doesn't own this place! I do — and I don't want that junk on my property! Now get it out of here, before I put some dents in your truck."

The driver, a mild-mannered fellow, looked dismayed, but decided he'd better do as the owner told him.

Distressed by his father's action, Buff ran over to his father's side. "Wait Dad. It's my truck."

Leonard turned to his son. Giving Buff an angry scowl he yelled, "Yeah, and you really made a mess out of it didn't you?"

Buff stepped back. More than once, he had seen his father like this, and he knew not to interfere, lest he get hit, physically.

From the window of the tow truck, the driver interrupted Leonard's heated words saying, "Well, the boy paid for the tow — where should I take it?"

Spinning around quickly for a big man, Leonard sneered at the driver. "I don't give a damn!" he shouted. Then, raising an arm to point down the driveway, he ordered, "Just get it out of here and out of my sight!"

The tow truck driver shrugged, ground gears as he switched from reverse to forward, and eased out the clutch. Gaining speed the whole mess disappeared down the driveway.

Buff watched his truck, with a smashed cab, broken windows, wrinkled body disappear from sight. All that remained of the new truck his father game him was the liquid dripped on the asphalt driveway. As he looked up at his father's scowling face, he pleaded, "Please Dad. . . "

Leonard looked at him and growled, "Just shut up and get your butt inside. You can mop up this mess tomorrow, after school."

Buff was the kind of kid that opposed authority while respecting it. In his mind, the authoritative person made all the rules and obeyed none of them — he knew this to be true — his father had set the example. Striving to be a respected authority in his own right, Buff never seemed to find the right path to gain the respect he craved, and many attempts put him on a collision course with his father. The day's events were no exception.

His father's intimidating look and angry words, blocked Buff's ability to reason or remember. Faced with a punishment of an unknown nature, a wave of fear directed Buff's actions. He immediately turned and headed for the house, leaving the light on and the door open to the ten-car-garage.

Leonard dogged Buff into the house, with an abusive string of swearwords. The drill-Sargent action of Leonard Lanscom continued as he ordered his son to, "Sit down and shut up!" Pointing to a place for Buff to sit, Leonard bent over to intrude on Buff's personal space. "It's about time you took a little responsibility for yourself. I'm tired of you acting like money grows on trees!"

The lecture was interrupted by the phone. Leonard reached for the portable extension on his belt. Straightening his back he answered, "Yeah – Yeah – He did? Well, that's okay, but did you get the check?" There was a pause in the conversation. "Okay, I'm in the living room and I'll call you back from the office upstairs in a minute – " Leonard gave his son another glowering look as he fumbled to reattach the phone to his belt.

Waiting nervously for punishment, Buff fingered the half-inch bolt in his pocket. The young man really wanted a distraction, almost any distraction, to deflect his father's intimidating lecture. Though it was a feeble attempt to change the subject, he removed the bolt from his pocket, offering it to his father.

Interrupted by Buff's childish distraction, he asked, "What's this?" Leonard stared at the silver, half-inch bolt in his son's hand.

"It's magic or somethin'."

"Huh?" Leonard said, wondering if his son was a complete idiot.

"We found it in a bear's nest, today!" Buff offered, in the slight hope it might impress his father enough to forget the pending discipline.

Thinking his son was indeed crazy, he scowled. "Buff – what are you talking about?"

"It changes shape." Buff said, touching the tip of the bolt where he had seen a flat end earlier in the day.

"I don't have time for this!" Leonard slapped the boy's arm, causing the bolt to fall into the trash basket, by the coffee table. "Didn't you hear anything, I just said to you?"

"Yeah but – "

"Don't 'but' me," Leonard scolded, heading for his business office upstairs. As he started up the stairs, he stopped to

289

shake his finger at his son, he adding, "You are grounded! We'll talk more about this later."

Buff sat on the sofa in silence, reflecting on his troubles. He knew things were going to get worse, when his dad found out about the citation the ranger gave him. It was going to be hell at school too. His new status as gang leader had crashed with his new truck. Even worse, the old gang leader, Mako would likely make him subordinate to Wiky and Paul.

Leaning on the arm of the sofa to prop his head up with one hand, Buff pulled the trash container closer with the other. Squinting through his tears, he fished out the bolt. Amazed the silver object was slightly warm and no longer pointed, Buff wiped the tears from his eyes. The initials "BW" glared at him from the head of the fastener. He briefly wondered what they meant.

The sound of a door closing down the central hallway, compelled Buff to look up. He saw the shape of his father's girl friend, Klazzi coming his way. He liked Klazzi very much; she was the first woman to come back into his life, since his mother was forced to leave a decade ago. Buff didn't know much about girls except – he liked them, and felt good around them. Outside of that, he didn't know what to do about it. He had tried numerous times to talk with girls at school, but he always suffered from mind paralysis whenever he tried to say anything nice to any of them. Klazzi was different. Though she was his father's friend, Buff liked the fact she treated him as a person. She made allowance for the fact he was a developing teenage boy, driven by a flood of hormones that both excited and confused him. Guided by beautiful sexy women seen in the movies, Buff often fantasized about making love to Klazzi Korner. Not that he would ever get the chance, or even know what to do, if given the opportunity – still – he flip-flopped between her being his mother and confidante – and her being his secret lover.

Klazzi, a sexy lady in her mid twenties, carried the heavy armload of college books and papers over to the coffee table and let them slide onto the flat surface. "Hi Buff," she said cheerfully as she gave him a big smile.

More than anxious to forget his father's scolding, Buff admired Klazzi's long legs that disappeared mysteriously under her short skirt.

Klazzi noticed Buff's somber mood. "Are you okay honey?"

Warmed by her attention, Buff said nothing; he certainly wasn't happy.

Klazzi struggled out of her tight jacket, dropping it on the end of the sofa. She sat down, next to Buff. "What's wrong honey?" she asked, reaching over to touch his hand.

When she came into Buff's life about a year ago, Klazzi quickly realized he needed a mother figure in his life, even at seventeen. It was her aim to bond with the boy and to provide such support.

"I total'd my truck," he said meekly.

"How?" she said, with shock.

He sat silently for a moment, trying to fix blame on someone or something other than himself. "A bolt got caught under my brake pedal." Buff handed her the half-inch bolt.

She took the object, not knowing what to do with it. "Oh, I'm sorry. Your truck was such a nice present from Len." Klazzi slid closer and put her arms around Buff, drawing him next to her for a big hug. "Maybe it can be fixed."

Buff returned her hug, while trying to hide the fact that her soft breasts pressing against his arm and chest drove him crazy inside. When the hug ended, Buff slowly let his left arm slide down her back, over the curve of her hip, before drawing it back across her lap, at the edge of her very short skirt. Nearly breathless, he wished he was just ten years older. . .

Upstairs, Leonard shuffled through the stack of papers on his desk. After several minutes, he located the document he needed. He reached across the desk and pulled the desk phone closer, punching the numbers to make a call.

"Jess? This is Len."

"Do we have one?" Jess asked.

Leonard waved the paper, as though Jess could see it over the phone. "Yeah, I still have a cheap parcel with a similar description; we can make the substitution."

"Make sure it mentions a view of the lake."

"Is he going to be a problem?"

"I don't think so," Jess said confidently, "The client is an old, retired man and his wife. He keeps babbling on about how they've been planning for forty years and this is going to be their dream retirement home. Makes me want to barf."

"So what's with the lake thing? Anything unusual?"

"Nah. I showed him the parcel next to you. He just keeps saying he wants to sit there and look out on the lake while eating breakfast and dinner."

Leonard tossed the parcel description back on the stack of other parcel documents on his desk. "How is he fixed for assets? Think we can get more?"

"No, I think I squeezed him about as hard as I can, without spookin' him."

"Careful, don't let him get off the hook; we need the cash for our other projects." Leonard heard the familiar footsteps of Klazzi on the stairs. He cut his conversation short. Klazzi wasn't his wife. If some sort of litigation started, she didn't have immunity, and she could be forced to testify in a court of law against him.

Over the phone, Jess replied, "Okay, I'll call him in the morning and get him to sign the papers. Will you be able to make the document change by then?"

"I'll have it by morning."

Leonard put the phone on hook. Looking up, he smiled at the blond woman; ever mindful she was twenty years younger. "How's class?"

She walked to the end of his desk, standing an arm's length away from him. Gently contacting the desk with her leg, her short skirt lifted just a bit as she edged forward. "I think I passed the midterm, but I still have two more tomorrow," she said, while allowing her slender fingers to bend gracefully as the tips probed the smooth surface of the expensive wooden inlay. Klazzi smiled back, briefly, before changing the subject. Raising the pitch of her voice slightly to form the basis of a subtle plead in Buff's behalf, she said, "I was just talking with Buff about his new truck –"

Leonard instantly became angry, "That damn kid! Wish he'd never been born. He's been a rock around my neck, just like his mother was."

Using her best negotiating skills, Klazzi walked behind Leonard and quietly rested the half-inch bolt on a nearby shelf. Slowly, she began to rub his neck and shoulders, "Now Len, you really don't mean that. You know he's just a kid," she spoke softly, barely above a whisper.

Leonard relaxed and moaned from the sensual massage – he'd deal with Buff and his problems later.

She stopped kneading Leonard's shoulders and rolled his chair back from the desk. Walking in front of him, she placed her right knee between his two, to get as close as possible, short of sitting in his lap. She bent down to rub noses. "Can't you cut him a little slack?" she whispered. Smoothly, she retrieved the bolt, where she had temporarily set it on the nearby bookshelf.

Maintaining eye contact, she carefully pulled his hand from her leg and opened it. With a whisper she continued to persuade him, "He says this thing got lodged under his brake pedal on a steep slope."

As the bolt dropped into Leonard's open hand, he felt a brief shock, like walking across a deep carpet on a dry day, before touching a door knob. "Dang!" He exclaimed, tossing the bolt onto the desk, where it came to rest on a stack of papers.

"What's wrong?"

Leonard ran his hand up the inside of her thigh, under her dress. "Must be all that nylon, you're wearing; it's shocking the dickens out of me." He began to tug on her under garments.

"Later Len," she pleaded, raising her voice just below normal volume, "I still have to study for an hour or two tonight."

He continued to pull downward on her clothing.

She stepped backward, "Please Len – Later."

Only the ripping of lacy fabric stopped him. She examined the damage, but didn't object verbally; she still needed his cooperation for Buff's sake. Silently, she turned and headed downstairs to pick up her books and go to her study room.

Leonard stood up, frustrated in more ways than one. He turned around and around two or three times, before remembering what he had started to do, before being aroused. He flipped the power switch on for his computer, then opened his briefcase to get out the removable hard drive, with business records. It was his policy to never leave data on his computer, where anyone, especially the police, could find it as evidence. In fact, he rarely left the removable drive at the house, when he went anywhere.

Distracted, Leonard failed to notice the light breeze blowing across the lake and through the open window fanning the papers on his desk. The paper with the parcel number he just selected, escaped from under the half inch bolt, leaving the one below, in its place. Perhaps, he was still distracted by Klazzi's loving touch; perhaps he was distracted by greed. As Leonard prepared the papers, to switch the parcel numbers on the customer's purchase, he failed to notice the top paper was not the parcel he selected earlier.

* * *

The bell sounded at the local college, followed by a flood of exhausted students exiting the buildings for the day. Outside the door to the sociology building, a well-dressed man in his thirties, tall, dark haired, with a thin mustache waited impatiently for a female friend to appear. A minute later, an expressionless Klazzi navigated the foot traffic toward him. "Hey Klazz!" he bid.

Klazzi pulled up short, to see who paged her. "Oh it's you," she breathed a sigh of disappointment, as she came to a halt in front of the bench where he waited. "What's up Wolf?"

"How about dinner?"

An expression of tolerance formed on her pretty face, "I told you last week, I'm seeing someone."

"Doesn't matter to me, Klazz." He stood up and looked down into her blue eyes. As he spoke, he brushed a wisp of her blond hair from her cheek to behind her ear. "I thought we were still friends."

"We are – " she admitted, with a hint of regret in her voice. Stepping back from his reach she added, "But you always want more friendship than I can give."

"Look – all I'm asking for – is dinner with an old friend." He smiled his best, knowing it had always won her over in the past.

She looked away briefly, trying to think up a good excuse to say "No."

"I'll take you any place you want to go," he bribed her.

Klazzi looked back at her old boyfriend, remembering how she skipped lunch. Wolf, son of a wealthy industrialist, always had money and always went to the best restaurants.

"You need to celebrate passing your midterms," he said, trying to convince her.

She hesitated, while she attempted to read the expression on his face.

Sensing he was winning her over, he added, "I'm just a friend wanting to buy another friend dinner and share a little innocent conversation." He cocked his head before adding, "How about it? Are we really friends or are you just saying that?"

That did it. She was famished and Len wouldn't be home for hours. "Okay! You buy – right?"

"Of course – " He nodded.

Avoiding intimate settings and expensive food, she said, "I want to go to Mac's Steak House."

Without hesitation, he agreed, and they left together. A short time later, they were seated in a secluded corner. That wasn't Klazzi's idea, but she decided there was less chance she'd be recognized, which left less chance she'd have to explain things to Len.

She looked through the entire menu, though she knew what she wanted from her first glance. A young man took their order. He started to flirt with her, but quickly decided against it, when he saw the nasty expression on the face of her male escort.

As the waiter disappeared, Klazzi turned to her companion, "So what's the real reason you have for being so generous today, Wolf?"

The restaurant was noisy, but the level was tolerable back in the corner. Wolf smiled, "Because I think you're pretty."

Klazzi kicked his leg under the table. "Cut the chicanery, Wolf, it's your ex-girlfriend you're talking to, and I know you better. What are you up to?"

"Aaaw, Klazzi." He brought his hands up to his chest in a protective manner. "Give me a break."

"If I had a baseball bat, I'd give you one, right on the head, you — you rat!" she said, leaning over the table at him. Klazzi wasn't truly angry, but she knew she had to keep this predator in his place.

"Please don't call me a rat, and please don't call me Wolf anymore," he begged. He leaned back in his chair, trying to dazzle her with a look of importance. "I've changed. I'm into real estate now." With a serious look, he said, "Call me Mr. Bondano."

Doubting his honesty, she glared at him. "You'll always be Wolf to me," she said, through clenched teeth. "Now what are you up to?"

Bondano looked down at the table between them, breaking eye contact. In his most believable tone, he lied to her again, "Seriously, I missed you and I just wanted to see you and to know how you're doing with that Leno guy."

She felt genuine anger stirring deep within herself. "I'm doing just fine and his name is Leonard, not Leno."

"I know, I know," he replied with a hint of an apology in his voice. Wolf unfolded his napkin and spread it in his lap. "I just wanted to make sure he was taking good care of you. I wouldn't want him going broke and having to throw you out or nothin'."

"Well Mr. Bondano, for your information, Leonard owns a very successful escrow company and at least three construction companies and he's not going broke for your benefit." She looked him straight in the eye, "So — Get used to it. I'm never coming' back."

Wolf held out his arms in a defensive posture, "Whoa! Whoa! Girl, I don't mean anything bad, I just thought you might set up a little meeting with Mr. Lanscom, so we could talk real estate and the like. I'm sure I could learn a lot from him."

"I'm sure you could, but I'm not setting up anything. If you want to see him, you make the arrangements yourself. And — keep me out of it."

He was sure she'd take this attitude, so he shrugged and removed a note pad and pencil. "Uh — let's see." Wolf leafed through the small, but empty pages, pretending to look for a place to make a note. "Okay, where do I find him and what days is he there?"

Klazzi felt a bit confused. Had Wolf really decided to straighten up his act? She had thought so before, but he always had some kind of angle to beat the system. Had it not been for his father's wealth, it was very likely Wolf would be sitting in some cell, doing time with the state. Digging in her purse, she located one of Leonard's business cards with an address and number. Making a mental note to get another one when she returned to the house, she handed the card to her ex-boyfriend. "Here. This should help; just don't tell him I sent you."

Holding up three fingers, Wolf promised, "Scout's honor." Unseen to her, he crossed the fingers on his other hand, under the table.

* * *

From the shadows of the nearby trees, Mr. Bondano watched the Lanscom mansion. He had followed Klazzi home from a distance last evening. She had been right to suspect he was jealous, and even more correct to suspect he'd cause trouble.

In the early morning haze from the lake, Buff plodded slowly down the road toward school, carrying his school books. Minutes later, Klazzi and a grey-haired man (Leonard) exited the house and drove away in a large luxury car. Wolf followed at a distance on his motor bike.

The car stopped at the local college, allowing Klazzi to leave to begin her scholastic day. The car continued on to each of three construction sites, spending a few minutes at each location. The next stop was at a small cottage, in a remote wooded area a mile off the main highway. About nine o'clock in the morning, Len's car finally arrived at Forest Elegante, a local real estate sales office. Wolf smiled to himself, because gossip had it that Leonard actually owned two or more real estate companies in the area, operated by his partner, Mr. Samuels. Bondano used his pen to note the name of this company on the back of the business card Klazzi gave him the night before. It might come in handy. He was comfortable his plan would work, though he hadn't been so sure last night when Klazzi wouldn't let him take her home to Leonard's. Perhaps she suspected he would cause trouble if he knew where she lived, or perhaps, she knew him better than he gauged.

Bondano left, returning a few minutes later in a nice suit, driving a rented car. He parked nearby, waited until Leonard finished his business and drove away. The stalker entered the agency, attempting to look the part of a prospective buyer. He glanced around the office, noting the names and pictures of agents displayed on the wall. He examined the display of pictures on the bulletin board for parcels listed with the agency. Pretending a business interest, he made several notes.

Of course, his presence did not go unnoticed for more than a few seconds. As soon as the middle-aged salesman finished his phone conversation, Wolf was approached, "Good morning sir. Is there anything I can help you with?"

Bondano ignored the request for a few seconds, continuing to look at the pictures. Finally, he drew a breath, "Well, yes." Turning to the salesman, Wolf lied, "I'm Jacob Marson, and I'm looking for a nice piece of property by the lake." Bondano closed his small notebook, stuffing it away in his coat pocket. He then smiled at the salesman.

The salesman feigned excitement, "Oh excellent. Forest Elegante has so many to choose from, " he said, sizing Wolf's monetary caliber. The effect was not unlike a balancing scale with the customer on one side and a pile of gold on the other. Thrusting out a pudgy hand, the realtor bid, "I'm Jess Samuels, Office Manager. Please have a seat." He slipped around the corner of the desk, plopping his plump bottom in the swivel chair. The chair made a grunting sound, as it took on the weight of the salesman's frame. "First let me take down a few details about your needs, and then I'm sure I can help you make a suitable selection."

The interview went pretty much as the real estate business goes: the salesman estimated the size of the customer's wallet, while the client, wary of signing anything, probed for the maximum amount of useful information. At the end, they shook hands and promised to meet again.

Wolf checked the time. It was still midmorning, early enough to get more information. He switched back to his street clothes and motorcycle. A few minutes and a number of miles later, he found his way inside Leonard's home and was in the process of searching for office records. Although he wasn't a polished burglar, he was quite careful when he searched, knowing in advance he might have a need to return later. His first thought was to check the computer. The machine powered-up requesting the removable hard drive, and failed to boot. Wolf cursed. He checked for wall safes, hidden desk compartments. About all he could find, was a small stack of papers on Lanscom's desk. After inspecting the contents, the burglar carefully repositioned the stack, pausing for a moment as he handled the bolt, used as a paperweight. The bolt felt noticeably warm to the touch, even through the latex gloves he was wearing. Seeing nothing unusual, he shrugged and placed the silver paperweight back on the stack of papers, positioning it very close to the exact location where he had found it. He'd have to look elsewhere for information.

Five minutes down the road, Bondano raced his motor bike up the winding road to the cottage where Len had gone in the morning. Finding the cottage empty, except for a nice sofa, covered in a plastic dust-cover, he checked, and found the hard drive underneath. Elated, Wolf shoved it inside his jacket and headed for a friend's house to make a copy. He returned the original to its hiding place about an hour before Len came by to pick it up, in the afternoon.

* * *

Nearly a week later, Jess Samuels pulled Leonard Lanscom into a sales office as soon as he arrived. Closing the door to keep clients from hearing, he asked, "Did you collect payment from the Blemn's?"

Lanscom looked puzzled as he replied, "No. Mr. Blemn said he'd bring it in late this week."

"How about the Wendel's?" Samuels asked, with his voice kept low, but a strong sense of urgency propelling it.

"No," Leonard shook his head.

"Or the Martinz family?"

A scowl set on Leonard's aging face. "Of course not. The papers are all ready, but I haven't received their checks." He noted the dismay on Jess's face. "What's this all about?"

"We got a problem, Len." Jess turned his back to the office window looking out into the room of sales desks. The room was nearly empty with a couple of clients waiting at one of the desks. Keeping his back to them, just in case they could read lips, Jess whispered, "Someone has been picking up our payments."

"What?" Leonard exclaimed with shock. "What are you talking about?"

"The deposits," Jess whispered. "Someone – I don't know who, is picking them up, for your escrow company."

Leonard stood silently with a blank look on his face. Finally he said, "They must be mistaken."

"Nope. Mrs. Waverley, your accountant, just called this morning, looking for you. She said the Johnston's phoned her wondering when escrow would close."

Leonard rubbed his jaw, "Well if they gave the check to someone they'll have to cancel it and reissue my escrow office a new one."

Jess shook his head negatively, "Won't work."

"Why not?"

"The Johnston's told Mrs. Waverley that a – Mr. Lanscom stopped by and took a check. He was an older white-haired man, and he said he was an escrow officer. He even left one of your business cards, when he picked up the check."

Leonard stared at Jess in disbelief. "What?" Locking eyes on Samuels, he questioned him, "How can that be?"

Unsure if his partner was lying, Jess watched Leonard's expression as he told him, "They think you picked up the check!"

"They're nuts!" he said indignantly, "I did no such thing!"

Jess nodded in agreement. "I know that. . . and you know that. . . but the bank and the clients have canceled checks to prove it."

"Checks?" Leonard dropped his briefcase. It hit the floor with a loud bang, causing the couple waiting outside the office to look around. "Gad! How many times has this happened?"

"At least six that I know of – "

Leonard's legs felt weak like soft rubber. He sat down. "The checks have been cashed?"

"All were cashed and three of them went into your personal bank account."

302

"What?"

Jess pulled up a chair to sit closer facing Leonard. "That's right. They were deposited into your personal checking account."

"Into my checking account?" Leonard gasped. "I don't understand. Who would want to do that – and why?"

"I have no idea," Jess said, shaking his head, "but the clients are just getting wind of it. A couple of them called your bank before calling me."

"How did the bank get the checks?"

"Their records show deposits through the ATM."

Leonard leaned forward, putting his face in his hands. His life and his scheme seemed out of control. "How did they know my account number, my bank, my ATM pin number, and how did they know the client's names and addresses?"

"I was hoping you'd know." Jess wrinkled the papers he'd carried with him into the sales room. "Could anyone at your house get that information?"

Len shook his head negatively, "No, I never leave it near the computer where anyone can access it."

The phone rang. Jess picked it up, "Forest Elegante, Jess Samuels speaking. How may I help you?"

The man on the other end was irritated. "I'd like to speak to Mr. Lanscom please. And don't tell me he's not there."

"Just a minute please," Jess replied, putting the line on hold. "I think this is Bert Johnston. You know – the retired guy who wanted to look at the lake while eating breakfast."

Leonard took the phone and pressed the button to connect the line. "Leonard Lanscom speaking?"

"Mr. Lanscom, this is Bert Johnston. I'd like to know what is going on?"

Leonard switched to damage control mode. "Good morning Mr. Johnston. How may I help you today?"

"You can start by returning my down payment on the parcel Mr. Samuels showed me. You picked up the check from me on Wednesday, last week, right after we opened an escrow account with your firm."

"Uh — Mr. Johnston, I believe we need to meet to discuss this matter in person. By the way, did you call me earlier?"

"No — I just got off the phone with your escrow company, and with my bank. Your office said I might reach you here."

"I see." Leonard reached for a pen and paper to make notes.

Johnston raised his voice to deliver the accusation, "You told me you'd take the payment directly to escrow — and escrow would close on Friday or Monday at the latest." Johnston's voice changed, showing more tension in his verbalization. "Well, when I didn't hear from escrow by Tuesday, I called, to see if there was a problem."

"Was there?" Lanscom asked, trying to stall while he came up with a believable explanation.

"Yes! You dang right there was a problem." The volume of Johnston's voice increased, almost to a scream, "Your office claims they never got the check I gave you!"

"I assure you — " Leonard began, but was interrupted by Johnston.

"You are bonded — Are you not, Mr. Lanscom?"

Beads of sweat appeared on Lanscom's forehead, "Yes, of course I am."

"Then, what have you done with my deposit?"

Lanscom steered toward a form of damage control, while trying to sooth the customer. "I assure you Mr. Johnston, if there is a problem, I'll get to the bottom of it."

"What's to get to the bottom of?" Johnston argued, "I gave you the check — and did you, or did you not — take it to escrow?"

304

Len drew in a deep breath. "Mr. Johnston, what did the man who picked up the check look like?"

"Mr. Lanscom, I don't want to play games. You took a lot of money from me and now you don't know anything about it. Is that right?"

"Yes – I mean no." Leonard stuttered. "I – I have reason to believe that man wasn't me."

"You showed me your credentials. You're tall with white hair aren't you?"

"Well yes – but," Leonard stammered.

"I asked about you, when I called escrow. They said you were a tall, white haired man."

"Let me assure you, I didn't take your money Mr. Johnston, but I'll get to the bottom of this, if you'll give me a couple of days."

"To skip the country?"

"No. Of course not, Mr. Johnston. I'm not going anywhere. And – I have no intention of going anywhere."

There was a short pause. "Mr. Lanscom, I'm not interested in playing games with you. The next time I see you, I'll have the sheriff and my lawyer with me."

Leonard held the phone for a few seconds after hearing the disconnect sound on the other end. Slowly, he placed the receiver on hook while staring straight ahead.

"What is it Len?" Samuels asked.

"We've got trouble Jess." Leonard continued to stare blankly. "If we don't stop this thing right away, we'll have a big investigation we can't afford." Without blinking he added, "And with all this attention, things are really going to get nasty if investigators find out about our bait-and-switch."

* * *

In the evening, Leonard paused briefly in his angry exchange with Buff. The young man was close to tears as he tried not to look at his father's face. The sound of the front door opening, brought a temporary form of relief to Buff, as Klazzi returned from her day at college. She entered the room and dropped her backpack at the end of the sofa. She looked at Leonard, then at Buff, then again at Leonard. It was obvious she thought the confrontation dealt with Buff destroying the vehicle his father bought him.

Leonard turned to Klazzi with a furrowed brow, "I don't suppose you know anything about it?"

Klazzi walked over to stand next to Buff. "I know Buff is a little careless, sometimes, but I'm sure it wasn't his fault."

Buff wiped his nose on his sleeve. "It's not about my truck, Klazzi," he said, looking first at her then at his father. "He thinks we sold him out."

"Oh!" Klazzi studied Leonard's face, waiting for an explanation. "What's the problem Len?"

"Someone in this house gave away confidential business information." Leonard took a deep breath, "And – if it wasn't me, and it wasn't Buff, only one person is left."

Klazzi stepped back. She was totally in shock. She had no idea what had happened, or how Len had come to believe she was at fault. Perhaps the worst part is that someone she loved, was accusing her of betrayal. How could it be? "Len -?" she began, but was immediately interrupted.

Leonard raised his arm and pointed to the door. "Out!" he shouted, "I want you out – Now!"

Klazzi grabbed her backpack and stepped backwards toward the door she had just entered. "What about my things?"

"I'll leave them on the doorstep tomorrow. You can pick them up in the afternoon."

* * *

The following day, Leonard and Jess sat in the escrow office, trying to decide what they could do, to get out of their predicament.

Jess poured himself another cup of coffee. Without looking up, he asked, "Refill Len?"

His unhappy face changed little as he answered, "No thanks. I've had so much; my stomach is knotted."

Jess walked back and sat in the chair, across the desk from Leonard. "You know, I'm sure you're right – that Johnston-guy is going to be a real problem." Jess sipped his coffee, made a face and set the cup down on the edge of the desk. "Don't suppose there is any way to buy him off, do you?"

Leonard let out a deep sigh and stared off into space. "I've turned it over and over in my mind, and I just don't see what we can do, to keep him from provoking an investigation into my business practices."

"How much do you think we'll lose fighting them in court?"

"A lot more than I have in liquid assets." Leonard swivelled in his chair, behind his desk, and opened the file cabinet behind him. He pulled out a stapled stack of papers with a list of customers on it. Many of the customers had a red check mark next to their names, indicating the property had been switched. Lanscom counted the names then tossed the stack to Jess. "Looks like about twenty or thirty total."

Jess took the list and examined the names. "Probably have each of them for another five or ten-grand apiece eh?"

"At least. . . "

"What do you have for assets?"

"As I said, not enough – I'll probably have to sell the escrow business and stick with one or two of the construction companies." Leonard turned to Jess, "I suppose you want the real estate business?"

Jess grunted, "Well it is already in my name, though I wouldn't have it, if you hadn't set me up with it."

Leonard left his chair and began to wander around the office. Looking through the glass wall, out into the mostly-empty lobby area, Lanscom watched Mrs. Waverley as she worked on the company business. He mentally counted the six employees; all were busy with their chores. Without looking back at Jess, he said, "You may as well keep it as long as you can." Sorrowfully he added, "You'll probably be sued too." Making a mock stranglehold, he grimaced, "I just wish there was some physical way I could get my hands on whoever set us up."

As Len turned to look back at Jess, he saw a police cruiser pull up in the parking lot, out front.

Nodding toward the car through the window, he told Jess, "I think they're here."

Moments later, the Sheriff, Mr. Johnston and a professional looking man, in a dark suit, entered the building. Mrs. Waverley escorted them directly into Lanscom's office.

The sheriff, a tall, square-jawed man studied Jess and Leonard. Speaking first, the lawman asked, "Which of you is Mr. Lanscom?"

Len nodded, "I am."

"Mr. Lanscom, I have received a complaint from Mr. Johnston, who says you have taken money from him under false pretenses."

Leonard looked at the small man, who was staring at him strangely. Neither Lanscom nor Johnston had seen the other before.

The sheriff turned to Johnston, "Is this the man you gave your deposit to?"

Johnston looked pale. He looked closely at Leonard, especially his white hair. Not sure, he slowly circled Leonard, all the while looking up at the tall man. Finally, he shook his head negatively. "I'm not sure, Sheriff, the height and hair are correct, but the fellow I gave my money to, was thinner and a bit darker complected – and younger." Johnston squinted as he looked at Len's face. "Can't tell eye color, he wore dark sunglasses. . . But the chin is much too square, and this guy is a lot older – more wrinkles."

"Mr. Johnston, if you're not sure -?" the lawman began, "I can't arrest him without a positive identification."

"I know, Sheriff. But I can't have you arrest the wrong man either."

Nodding in agreement, the lawman turned to look out into the lobby and general work area. "Is it possible one of the other employees out here took the payment?"

Johnston turned and looked carefully. Seeing none that resembled his expectation, he sighed. "I don't see anyone that even looks close, sir. Perhaps Mr. Lanscom was correct when he said it was someone else. Could we have a few moments alone with him?"

The Sheriff looked first at Johnston then at Lanscom, he nodded back at Johnston, "I'll be out front by the vehicle." He strode out efficiently, closing the door behind him.

"Mr. Lanscom, I don't know what is going on, and it seems I may have been duped by another man, but on the other hand, this could be some kind of scheme you've concocted. At any rate, I'd like to introduce you to an old classmate of mine. We went to school together back in Berkeley. This is Prosecutor Keys. And in case you don't recognize him; he is now the district prosecutor for this county."

309

The well-dressed man stepped forward. Keeping his arms folded in a defensive posture; there was no attempt to shake hands. The Prosecutor left little doubt why he came. "I've heard many things about you Mr. Lanscom – and you too, Mr. Samuels. Though it lacks solid proof, much of what I have heard has not been good. In fact – if I am to believe only a very small percentage of the complaints, you both could be in a lot of trouble." He paused three or four seconds to stare straight into Lanscom's eyes. "I'll be keeping my eye on you." His piece said, he waited for no reply. He simply turned and followed the sheriff.

Johnston looked one more time at Lanscom, before he turned to follow.

"Wait, Mr. Johnston. I'd like a word with you, if I might."

The little man stopped to listen.

In his most diplomatic voice, Leonard said softly, "I know you think I did something to you, but it's untrue and I'd really like to help you – if you'll let me."

"Are you going to refund my deposit?"

Shaking his head negatively Lanscom replied, "I can't give back what I haven't taken, but I might be able to negotiate the purchase of your property ignoring your missing deposit."

"Go on. . . " Johnston said, with an interest.

"I'm sure you still have the initial contract you signed, the one with the parcel number on it. Go have a look at it again, and drop by my office after you see it. Make sure it's what you want. I have some influence with many of the builders and land suppliers around here and I might be able to work something out."

Johnston smiled lightly. "I'll consider that. Of course, any dealings I have with you from this point on, will involve legal council."

"I understand Mr. Johnston, and I'm sure you'll have no trouble from me."

"I'd better not," he said flatly, then he left.

Leonard watched as they left. He breathed a sigh of relief. "That was a bit too close for comfort," he said, shaking his head. "If Johnston had been dishonest or had poor eyesight, I'd be in cuffs now."

Jess, also shaken, reached with an unsteady hand, to pick up his coffee cup. "You know Len, we aren't out of the woods yet." He sipped his coffee, spilling it slightly, before setting the cup back down. "I'm sure Johnston is one of the guys we switched the parcel number on."

Leonard looked directly at Jess, "Oh no! Was he?"

"I think so! We better figure out what to do when he shows up again."

Reaching for his briefcase, Leonard looked as though he'd been struck by an arrow. "I'm going home to think about this."

Lanscom stopped by Mrs. Waverley's desk to tell her where she could reach him. "Mrs. Waverley, I'm feeling a bit ill and I think I'll go home for the rest of the day."

* * *

A few minutes after Leonard arrived home, he got a call from Jess at the real estate office. "Len, I just wanted to let you know, Johnston and the Sheriff just dropped by to pick up a parcel map."

"That's all right Jess. We couldn't fool him on this one anyway. We'll just have to sell him the parcel shown on the paper, or we'll have a real fight on our hands."

"Okay Len, that property is only worth another ten thousand or so isn't it?"

Lanscom thought for a moment. "Maybe a bit more than that, unless they have structures on them already. Do you remember which ones you showed him?"

"Hold on for a second. I'll check my notes." The sound of file drawers opening and closing lasted for a few seconds before Jess replied, "Here it is. . . We – uh – Oh nuts! It was one of the properties that had lake edge frontage, with a moderate size house on it. In fact, it was the parcel next to you."

"That's too bad!" Len grimaced. "What did we substitute?"

"I don't know?" Jess said helplessly. "You picked it out, don't you remember?"

"No. I really don't remember, except that was about the time I was having problems with Buff after he crashed his truck." Leonard rubbed his forehead as he thought, "It was probably one of the units just over the first ridge in that terraced section. I know it didn't have a view of the lake. Do you have the parcel number there?"

"Yeah, it shows number: AK2378325."

"Are you sure?"

Jess read it a second time. "Yeah that's the number."

"That doesn't sound right, Jess. That number is over here in the section by my house. I think all of those were sold off, except for my – " He was interrupted by the doorbell ringing. "Someone's at the door Jess. I'll look it up and call you back." Leonard hung up the phone and looked out the window. In the yard below him was the Prosecutor and Mr. Johnston.

Leonard started down the stairs to see what they wanted, when it suddenly struck him what had happened. The shock of it nearly knocked him flat. He stumbled the last few steps to the door and opened it. "Mr. Johnston and Mr. Keys – What can I help you with?"

Both Johnston and Keys were surprised to see Leonard at the door. They looked at each other then back at Len. Johnston stopped to check the parcel number one more time, comparing it against the map location. Finally, with a puzzled look, Johnston spoke, "Uh – Mr. Lanscom? Do you live here?"

"Yes, I do." Leonard noted the papers in Johnston's hand and realized his worse fears had come true. Quickly he attempted to correct the situation. "Uh – but, there is an error in the map, if you are looking for your parcel."

"There is?" Johnston looked puzzled.

"Yes. These maps are printed by an outside source and they frequently have errors." Leonard looked away from the map, where he had been pointing and into the steely eyes of the Prosecutor. Lanscom knew his comments weren't going to convince a man who was accustomed to extracting the truth from criminals on a daily basis. "Uh – well, there are minor flaws in the map."

Stepping forward, Keys looked Leonard directly in the face. "Tell me, Mr. Lanscom, since you are so knowledgeable about these numbers and since you work with them in your daily business, what is the parcel number for this property, right here."

Leonard began to sweat. "Right – Right here," he pointed to his feet. "Where we are standing?"

"Yes. For this property. . . Tell me, what is the parcel number?"

Leonard paused. He could think of nothing to say that would thwart the direct question of the Prosecutor. Beads of sweat rolled down his forehead; his palms became clammy; he wished to be anywhere else, except jail – and, jail was a distinct possibility, depending on what he said.

"Perhaps we should question your friend, Jess Samuels, since his name is on the original agreement, along with your signature as the notary public."

Realizing any investigation involving Jess would likely result in a full audit of all business transactions between the real estate company and the escrow company, Leonard decided it would be better to not let it go that far. "Actually," Leonard stammered, trying to find the words to yield to the pressure, "Let me see the number again." He took the paper from Johnston and pretended a healthy interest, though he knew it was the same number as his own parcel. He never suspected the half-inch bolt had allowed the substitution of the numbers. "Ah yes, I'm sorry, I misread the number." Barely able to force the words out through his tightened larynx, Leonard squeaked, "It is the same number as this property."

"You're sure?" Keys asked, not being fooled for a moment.

"I'm sure," Leonard whispered.

Keys looked at Johnston, "Is this the property you agreed to buy?"

Johnston looked light-headed, "Uh no — it isn't the property Mr. Samuels showed me. I think that was next door, but it appears to be the one I signed for."

"Well then Bert, is it acceptable?"

"I — why yes! I'm sure it's more than acceptable."

Johnston looked at Lanscom and asked, "May I come inside and inspect it now that we are all in agreement?"

Leonard wanted to cry, but it wasn't in his nature; he wanted to rage, but he didn't dare. He simply stepped aside and allowed the prospective owner to enter.

"Ah yes!" Bert Johnston smiled, as he entered the breakfast nook and looked out over the lake, "This is more than I dreamed of. . . "

* * *

In the afternoon, Klazzi returned to the Lanscom residence to retrieve her things. Although she had a key, she rang the doorbell and waited.

A few seconds later Buff answered the door. He was both sad and happy to see the young woman, "Klazzi! Come in — " Buff paused in mid-sentence to look her in the eye, "Uh – I'm really sorry about all this – " He stepped aside to allow her space to enter, "Dad hasn't been himself."

Klazzi crossed the threshold. Looking around the entrance hall, filled with her things, she expected to see Buff's father. "Where's Len?"

Buff shrugged. "Don't really know, Klazzi, but I think he's out looking for a house to move into?"

"A house?" Klazzi was shocked, "Why's he looking for another house, Buff?"

Buff shrugged again. "Donno – he said som' thing 'bout havin' to move out."

"That's strange?" Klazzi walked over to pick up things from the first pile along the hallway. "Len told me this was his dream house. I can't imagine why he'd want to move out."

"Don't think he wants to move." Buff looked sadly displaced. His whole world had crashed with his pickup. "Dad said someone stole his bank account or som' thin' and then dressed up like him to get in trouble with the Sheriff an' Persecutor." Hanging his head, he added, "Dad's pretty mad 'bout havin' to sell the business an' house. He says lots of people he sold to – were lookin' to find him and sue."

Klazzi put down her things and went directly to Buff and hugged him. "Now you just wait. Things are going to be fine again – soon." She hoped they would be fine, but inside she felt Buff probably had good reason to fear what the future might bring. She, herself, was uneasy about changes experienced in the last few days.

Buff hugged her back, tightly. He felt her breasts squeezed against his chest, and though she was ten years older, he could easily place his chin over her shoulder as he held her close. It wasn't clear to Buff if he would miss her more as a friend or as his only physical contact with the opposite sex.

315

D.Malisch

Klazzi released Buff, who held her tightly for a few more seconds. Gently she removed his open hand from her derriere as she stepped back. She wished she had more time to help him learn the proper way to interface with women; she knew his father certainly wasn't going to teach him. She smiled and asked, "Help me load these things in the car, will you?"

Buff tugged upward at his pants, which slipped down a bit over his snake-hips during the embrace. "You got a car?"

Klazzi nodded, not proud that she had been forced to move back in with her ex-boyfriend, Wolf. "Yeah, it really belongs to a male-friend of mine." She was careful not to refer to Wolf as her boyfriend, though it is likely she'd be forced to sleep with him until she could find other arrangements.

They quickly loaded the few things she owned into the car, chatting back and forth in small talk until the task was completed. When Klazzi was ready to leave, she approached Buff one more time. She removed the small locket on a gold chain that hung around her neck. Taking his hand, she placed the locket into his hand and gently closed it. She looked into his eyes, (he was just a bit taller than she) and smiled a whimpering type of smile, while fighting back a tear. "Here – I want you to have this, to remember me by." She wiped the corner of her eye with the back of her hand, trying not to smear the mascara. Her voice crackled. "If you – if you ever need my help. . . You know – to talk about girls or whatever – just call me." She slipped her hands over his shoulders and behind his neck. With a gentle pull, she nudged his head forward while she planted a kiss on his lips.

It felt like lightning hit him, but it wasn't. It felt like pillows on his lips, but they weren't. The fragrance of her perfume overwhelmed him. If she hadn't held his head, he would have fallen down. Buff was speechless. He wanted more, but somehow he knew, he'd ruin it if he grabbed her to return the kiss. He simply

closed his eyes and savored the effect for as long as he could. When he finally opened his eyes, he could think of nothing to say. .
.

Klazzi backed away slowly and opened the driver's-door to the car. She paused to wink, as she slid into the seat.

Suddenly, Buff realized, in an instant she'd be gone, maybe forever. She'd likely never see him again, or so he thought. He looked at the locket in his hand, he'd remember her always, but would she remember him? He panicked. "Wait! Wait Klazzi. I got som' thin' for you too." Buff quickly disappeared into the house. Moments later, he returned, gasping for air. "Here!" he said, swallowing quickly, "I want you to have this." His open palm held the half-inch bolt.

Klazzi looked at the object. She really didn't want it, but the way it was offered, how could she refuse?

"Go ahead, take it," he begged. "It's magic or som' thin'. It didn' bring me luck, but maybe it'll work better with you."

Through the driver's window, she looked at Buff. His radiant smile warmed her. "Thank you, Buff," she smiled back, "I hope it does." She took the bolt and placed it on the passenger seat before starting the car. They exchanged hand-waves as she drove away.

* * *

Klazzi arrived at Wolf's apartment in time to hear an argument between Wolf and his father. She had known Wolf and his father had not gotten along for many years. It was one of those cases where the wealthy parent was forced to repeatedly come to the aid of a worthless son. As she approached the door, the heated discussion became louder.

"This is your last chance Everit. I'm not going to pamper you anymore. If you can't make a success out of yourself, you won't get anything more from me." The aging businessman,

317

walked smoothly across the room to pick up his coat from the chair, where he had dropped it shortly after his arrival.

"Yeah. . . Yeah. . . Yeah. . . I've heard all that stuff before, Pop." Wolf stopped to take a breath as he paced the room. "Just give me the stupid check and leave."

Mr. Bondano Sr. opened his coat and searched an inside pocket. He removed a flat leather wallet and dropped it on the coffee table. Having done that, he turned toward the door, where he saw Klazzi. He paused to exchange greetings, "Hello Miss Korner. How are you this evening?"

"Just fine, Mr. Bondano, it's good to see you again."

"Thank you, Miss Korner, it's good to see you too."

"Can you stay for dinner?"

Bondano Sr. shook his head negatively, "No, I'm sorry, but I really just stopped by to speak to Everit about a matter." Delaying his departure, to speak with the attractive young lady, he added, "I didn't know you were still seeing my son?"

"Well," she hesitated, "I had a bit of misfortune the other day and had to ask Everit for a place to stay for a few days, until I can make other arrangements."

"Sorry to hear about that." He placed a hand on her shoulder. "You know there was time I wished he'd been smart enough to marry you, because you're the best woman he ever met," and looking over his shoulder at his son, he jeered, "you're definitely too good for the likes of him."

Klazzi blushed. "Thank you. You're very kind."

"I see you're carrying lots of books. Are you still in school?"

She nodded, "I've got another year."

"That's terrific." He squeezed her shoulder, "Let me know if you need a job, when you get out. I'm sure we can find a good position for a bright young woman like you."

"Thank you, Mr. Bondano. I'll keep that in mind."

As he left the apartment, he ended the exchange with, "You know where to leave your resume."

Klazzi nodded before closing the door. As she turned around, she noticed Wolf was still pacing the room. "It was nice of your father to drop by."

Wolf ignored her.

"Want to talk about it?" she offered.

He ignored her.

She waited for several moments before shrugging. She turned her back and took the load of books to the spare room she had cleaned earlier. She arranged the books beside a small card table where she planned to study. She methodically set the books she needed to read on the table, in the order needed and proceeded to open the first book.

Wolf opened the door to the small room. "Let's go get some supper."

"I'd like to, but I really need to study tonight."

Wolf fumed. "I don't have to let you stay, you know!"

"I know," she answered, "but can we go to dinner tomorrow, instead?"

"You want to stay here?"

"Yes."

"Then you better get your coat and come."

Klazzi let out a long sigh. She closed her book, leaving it on the table, in front of her chair. Silently, she reminded herself this was one of the reasons why the relationship went sour in the first place. She got her coat and glanced at her watch as she quickly ran the comb through her hair. "Let's go," she said, without emotion.

It was obvious Wolf was in a bad mood. He drove the motorbike past six or seven restaurants; each had a problem. There

319

were too many people there; there were too few people there; the food he liked, wasn't served that night; the place was a hangout for losers; there was no parking up-front. At last they stopped at a bar. Once inside, Wolf wasn't interested in eating. He wanted to drink.

Klazzi knew if she had intoxicants, she'd never be able to study later. Yet she knew there were questions she needed to ask Wolf. Maybe if he was drunk, he might answer more freely. She ordered soda on the rocks, then tonic water. She was able to get a hamburger and fries to go with her drink, though it cost extra. The extra cost didn't seem to bother Wolf, for which, she was grateful.

About an hour after they arrived, Wolf was showing signs of serious intoxication. When the band stopped for a break, Klazzi posed her first question. "Wolf. Did you ever call Leonard?"

"Call who?"

"You know – Leonard, the guy I was living with – the guy whose name was on the card I gave you last time that we had dinner together."

"Huh – Oh sure," Wolf gulped his drink and signaled the cocktail waitress for another. "We had a real nice get-together."

His response sounded like another of his usual lies, but she wanted to know the truth, "What did you ask him?"

"Ask him?"

Klazzi persisted, "Yeah, I want to know, what did you guys talk about?"

Wolf leaned over the small, round table toward her. At the same time, he reached under the table and ran his hand under her dress, up the inside of her leg, toward her panties, "Oh we talked about what a good piece you was." Then he laughed.

Klazzi pushed away from the table. She wanted desperately to whack him one, but resisted. Instead, she grabbed his hand and tossed it aside. "No, Wolf. What did you really talk about?"

Bondano sat more upright and waved an arm in circles while tilting his head, left and right. "Oh we just talked and talked about stuff."

"You didn't go see him – did you?"

"Heck no, why should I?"

"Because he knows more about real estate, than you'll ever know!"

He laughed loudly, causing people at neighboring tables to stare. "That candy-bass – why he couldn't find his cucumber if he had both hands on it."

"Did you set him up?"

"Huh?"

"Did you – set him up?"

"Set him up?" he asked, as though too groggy to think straight.

Klazzi raised her voice, "Yeah, did you make trouble for him?"

Wolf threw his head back and laughed obnoxiously. When he finished, he leaned forward and whispered, "Yeah, I fixed the ol' white-haired bastard for messin' with my girl, and I'm not through with him yet."

On the one hand, Klazzi felt warmed that Wolf wanted her badly enough to go through all the trouble, but on the other hand, she had a terrible urge to beat him with her shoe. "What did you do?"

"I did the same thin' my dear old Pop did to me. I screwed him."

Klazzi pried at the opening, knowing his ego would force him to brag. "Tell me about it."

"Oh it'z zimple," his speech became more slurred, "he tol' me if I don' do'ble the check he gave me in a year, I get nothin'."

"Len told you that?"

321

"Huh? Oh heck no – Pop tol' me that." Wolf took a big swig on his drink and set the glass down. "I get no inher- no," he paused to try to say the multi-syllabled word again, "in-hare-it-tanze if I don' double my money by nex' year." Wiping his mouth on the back of his sleeve, he grumbled, "I gotta stay out of jail too."

Suddenly aware of what had been eating Wolf, Klazzi almost felt sorry for him. Still, it wasn't right for him to target Len for knowing her. It was times like this, she had the feeling she'd like to become a nun and go live in a convent. Of course, that was a wild thought, she realized. Her own sexual drives had caused her problems too, and living a life without men wasn't a viable solution. Well, whatever? She still needed to figure out what Wolf had done to Len and find a way to undo it. She knew she wasn't likely to get much more information from her intoxicated escort, but if she was ever to get him to admit to any of this, now was the time to question him. "Wolf, tell me again how you outsmarted Leonard."

"Did I tell you the firs' time?" he laughed.

"Well, not exactly, so tell me everything."

"Wha's to say. I jus' put on a white wig and picked up checks for him."

"You picked up checks for him?"

Signaling for another drink, Bondano looked cross-eyed at Klazzi, "Want a-nudder one?"

"No. Just tell me why you picked up his checks."

"Oh no you don'." He wagged a naughty finger at her. "I ain' tellin' – ask somin' else."

"I don't believe you," she lied, to force him to brag. "How did you know where to pick up these checks?"

Wolf sat across the table from her, smiling from ear to ear. After a few moments of silence, he whispered, "Bee'cauze I got the recordz from your house."

"You were in Len's house?" she said, alarmed.

322

"Oh I was there too, but I got 'em from your house."

"What are you talking about? I don't have a house."

The drink came and Wolf handed Klazzi a wad of bills from his trouser pocket. "Pay up and give a big tip," he commanded.

The waitress took payment and as she walked away with her tray, Wolf watched her. "Your butt is nicer than her'z you know."

"Never mind that, Wolf, what do you mean when you said you got records from my house?"

"You know, the one 'bout a mile off the main highway." After sipping his drink he scolded, "Don' play dumb with me, Kazz. You know – the cot – tage," he said with a belch.

Looking around her to see if anyone was close enough to overhear the conversation, she pressed on. "No! I don't know. Who says it's my house?"

"The recordz show it. You sign'd for it, so don' play dumb."

Klazzi was dumfounded. She thought for a few moments, before remembering signing a few documents for Len. It was shortly after she moved in with him, but she had never read the contract. What was Len's reasoning? Why hadn't he told her? Well, whatever his logic, Len needed her help now to reverse whatever Wolf did to him. "So, Wolf – where did you hide the wig and stuff?"

He laughed again, just a bit quieter than last time. "I ain't tellin' you nothin' bitch. You'd go tell Leno." Wolf reached for her arm, which she withdrew quickly.

The band, returning from its break, struck up a chord and conversation in the room became impossible. Shouting over the noise, Klazzi asked Wolf to take her home. After about the third attempt, he understood the question and took the roll of money from her and pealed off a couple of twenties. He handed the loose bills to Klazzi and stuffed the wad back into his pant's pocket. With his palm turned down, his fingers emulated the bristles on a broom, as he made a sweeping motion with his fingers. He obviously was indicating he was tired of her and wanted her to go away.

On her way out, she stopped to glance back at Wolf. He had grabbed the cocktail waitress and forced her to sit in his lap. Klazzi knew the display was for her benefit. It was Wolf's way of saying he could have any woman he wanted, so she'd better appreciate him while she could.

After taking a cab back to the apartment, Klazzi scoured the rooms for any evidence of the records and white wig. She was unable to find anything. In a fit of desperation, she called the Sheriff's Office and left her number. The Sheriff returned her call a few minutes later.

"So — that's the story as I know it Sheriff. Leonard isn't responsible for the trouble he's in."

The lawman drew a deep breath, "Thank you for calling my office Ms. Korner, but I have to operate on fact, not on hearsay evidence. If you have proof of any of this, I might be able to do something about it. Until then, I'll have to assume Mr. Lanscom took the checks and cashed them, simply because some of them are in his bank account. That fact is backed by his bank records."

"That's crazy, Sheriff. Why would he ruin his reputation by taking checks from clients and put them into his own account?"

"I admit it sounds crazy Ms. Korner, but many times people do things just because they are bold enough to try it. If no one ever points it out to law-enforcement, they'll likely get away with it. The only reason Mr. Lanscom is not locked up right now, is that it is possible another person fed them to the ATM machine."

"But I just explained who actually took the money. Can't you do something?"

"As I said, Ms. Korner, while I appreciate your interest, I don't have enough information to arrest anyone, on this matter, including Mr. Lanscom or Mr. Bondano."

"Suppose I was able to find his white wig or the records belonging to Mr. Lanscom?"

"Well, it would certainly cast doubt that Mr. Lanscom took the money, but it wouldn't be enough to lock up Mr. Bondano, unless you could prove he wore the wig?"

"I understand, Sheriff. Thank you for your help. I'll call you if I find anything." Klazzi hung up the phone.

She walked slowly across the room, trying to think of any place where she hadn't looked. Methodically, she retraced all the places she had looked before. Unable to locate anything, she realized she had never checked the car containing all her things she picked up earlier in the evening. She rummaged through the trunk and felt under the seat – nothing. As she braced her hand on the passenger seat to search the glove compartment, the half-inch bolt rolled down against her fingers. It felt warm. Curious, she picked it up from the seat. In the dark, it seemed to feel sticky. She grimaced. She had visions of sitting in the seat later, only to find some substance attaching itself to her clothing. She decided it would be better to take the bolt up to the apartment and find a cleaner that might work on the seat.

Once inside the apartment, in the better light, she discovered, the bolt wasn't sticky. She examined it closely. It looked normal. Well, this was only one of a list of strange things that had happened to her lately. She shrugged it off, to continue her search. Putting the bolt in her coat pocket, she got the flashlight, preparing to search the closet and bedroom. . . areas previously searched.

D.Malisch

She found nothing in the closet or beneath the mattress. In fact she found nothing on her hands and knees when looking under the bed. Nothing. Just as she was preparing to get up, the bolt fell from her pocket and rolled under the bed. Since it was a gift from Buff, she felt obligated to retrieve it. She looked but couldn't see it. Mumbling under her breath about Murphy's Law, she got the flashlight and turned it on. A reflective glint told her the bolt had somehow bounced and was sticking out of a space connected to the wooden headboard for the bed. It was very hard to reach. Her arms were too short to reach it directly. She laid flat on the floor and slid her shoulder under the bed frame, until she could feel the bolt. Strangely, it was warm, and it seemed to be stuck. She felt around the object and felt a roll of paper and a fuzzy object inside. Thinking it might be a dead rat, it unnerved her, but she suppressed her urge to abandon her attempt at retrieving the half-inch bolt. Instead, she pulled the paper-roll out to better enable access to the bolt. As she got the roll near her head, she heard the bolt drop on the floor and roll next to her. She slid back out, from under the bed, and retrieved the roll of paper and bolt. As she examined the paper, she found it was a computer printout, rolled into the shape of a tube, stuffed with a white wig. The printout appeared to be a listing of customers, purchasing properties from Forest Elegante and using Leonard's escrow company in the process. On the back, in Wolf's handwriting, was Leonard's bank account number, ATM pin number and other important data.

* * *

The following day, after giving the information to the Sheriff and moving out of Wolf's apartment, Klazzi went to see Leonard, hoping to let him know she had never betrayed him. As she drove up to the Lanscom residence, in her rental van, she saw Leonard directing Buff and several hired men to move things from

326

the house. She parked her van out of the way and walked up to Leonard. "Still moving, I see."

Leonard directed his helpers to go pack things from the hall closets before answering. "Thought I'd seen the last of you," he said in a calm voice. He watched the crew grab empty boxes and head back into the house for the hall closets.

"You might have," she admitted. She tugged on his sleeve until he turned and she could see his face. "I wanted you to know it was my old boyfriend that set you up." Leonard started to speak, but she stopped him. "I turned him in to the Sheriff." With a sigh she lamented, "They're holding him for further questioning."

Leonard didn't smile or comment. He stepped forward and put his arms around her, giving her a big hug.

Klazzi continued talking as they embraced, "He told me he burglarized your office upstairs and also the cottage." She pushed back from Leonard gently. "By the way. . . Why is the cottage in my name?"

Lanscom motioned for Klazzi to follow him as he walked a few steps to the gazebo where they could sit and talk. "It's a long story, my dear." He sat in his usual place and she in her's. "I appreciate your help, but it's just like Buff's truck. I crashed my life. At first I couldn't see it, but after seeing my dreams taken from me, I realize the way I was running my business, was doing the same thing to others."

"Oh Len – "

"No wait, there's more," he interrupted. "I'll get along. I'm not destitute, but it'll be tough for a while. I still may face the law, if I can't satisfy the people I cheated." He looked at Klazzi. "Inside, I knew you never did – and never would – do anything to intentionally hurt me or Buff. But my rage was just too strong." Leonard signaled Buff to come over after he pushed the box he was carrying onto the moving van.

D.Malisch

Buff ran as soon as he saw Klazzi. "Hi Klazzi," he said with a big toothy grin. "Have you come back to stay with us again?"

Klazzi stood to give Buff a hug. "No," she admitted, "I just dropped by to share some news."

Buff looked saddened. "I thought – "

"I know, Buff. But I have other plans."

"But Klazzi – "

His father interrupted, "Buff, go bring me the green box on the entry room table."

He hesitated for a moment, not wanting to leave, but did as he was asked by his father.

"I meant to ask you Klazzi, would you like to come back and start where we left off."

Klazzi took his hand, holding it with both of her's. She looked him in the eye, "Len, I still have feelings for you, and probably always will, but I know I really need more in my life than to be your possession."

He put his arm around her, drawing her close, "Yeah, I failed in that too, didn't I?" He held her closely, neither one saying anything.

A minute later, Buff arrived, out of breath, the box in his hand. His father took the box and opened it. He fished out a door key and leaned to one side to remove the key-ring he kept in his pocket. Carefully he attached the loose key to the ring before handing the keys to her. "Here Klazzi, I want you to have this."

"What is it?"

"It's the key to your cottage. I don't see any need to keep you from it, and I'm sure you'll need it as a place to live, while you finish school."

"No Len, you should sell it to – "

He shook his head, "No, it rightfully belongs to you, and Buff and I will survive just fine without it. Right Buff?"

Buff grinned, "Just as long as I can go visit once in a while."

Klazzi took the keys, and hugged both of her men.

* * *

Klazzi had the half inch bolt mounted onto a chain by a friend at school. She wore it from time to time. At Spring break, she decided to visit her Aunt in the San Francisco Bay Area, and she took along her good luck charm.

* * *

Chapter 9   Bank Robbery

Protagonist: Detective Brian Weeder SFPD

Guests:
Klazzi Korner   Brings bolt back to San Francisco.
Karen Metz   Klazzi's aunt
Gerald Jones   Robber — (nickname: Hulk)
Al Jones   Robber — brother to Gerald.
Petey Jensen   Robber — cousin to Darrel
Darrel James   Robber — cousin to Petey

T he chilly weather seemed to pass right through her clothing as Klazzi looked over the rail of the Golden Gate Bridge at San Francisco. Even the wet weather of the Seattle area never seemed to have the same bite to it as this bay area version. She pulled her coat tighter, while squinting, to keep her hair from beating her eyes. The wind behind her seemed to violently shake all remnants of warmth from her slacks, as it flapped any looseness wildly. Klazzi turned to her aunt, "It's beautiful, but I think I'm ready to get back into the car."

Aunt Karen, laughed, "Me too! We've got pictures. Now let's go some place more hospitable to human life." She turned to look back at Klazzi as she headed for the car. Shouting over the roar of the wind, she said, "I know this great little spot to have lunch. . . You are hungry, aren't you?"

Through the thunder of traffic on the bridge and the howl of wind in her ears, Klazzi barely heard her aunt. "Famished! Any place is fine with me, as long as it's indoors."

Back in the car, a short drive in the heavy traffic took the women into the heart of the city of San Francisco. Karen guided the car expertly to a small restaurant on Geary Street. She parked on a slope, turning the wheels so the car would roll into the curb, if the brakes should fail. Carefully, they waded through the traffic to cross the street to the restaurant. They were quickly seated in a quiet corner, surrounded by antique lighting, antique furniture, and striped wallpaper. They ordered the house special and sent the waiter on his way.

Karen gestured toward her own neck as she commented, "That's really a very interesting necklace you have Klazzi. Is that a screw?"

Klazzi laughed, "No — it's a bolt."

"Well, I just wondered; it looks mechanical."

"Actually, it is a real bolt. A special friend gave it to me."

"Your boyfriend was a mechanic, no doubt?"

She shook her head negatively, "No, he was the teenage son of a fellow I had an affair with."

Karen sipped her drink. "Does he make jewelry?"

"No, the bolt he gave me is this part." She carefully unscrewed the bolt from the gold nut fastened to the gold chain. As she placed the bolt on the table, it gradually changed to a silver color.

"Goodness, it's changing color," Karen remarked, "How does it do that?"

"I don't really know. It seems to have some kind of power, but I don't know too much about it. When a friend of mine, at college, tried to mount it for me, he couldn't weld a loop on it, so he welded a loop on this nut. Then the gold chain goes through the loop to fasten it around my neck. He told me to just screw the bolt into the nut to hold it." Klazzi smiled as she recalled events, "But immediately after I picked it up to wear it – it turned this gold color. I had to have the nut gold plated to match."

"How odd?" Karen said, picking up the bolt. It had a slight feel of warmth to it. "Where did it come from?"

"I have no idea, but it does have initials on it."

Karen squinted in the dim lighting. She adjusted her glasses carefully before announcing, "Looks like – 'B' something. Oh yes, 'B' 'W', that's right, isn't it?"

"Yes, that's right. My friend at college tried to buff them out, but after he laid the bolt down, the initials reappeared again. He tried several more times, but it seems the initials belong there."

Karen chuckled. "Does this mean you'll have to find a man with those initials to match?"

"I suppose," Klazzi said thoughtfully, "but none of the men I know, have matching initials."

Karen handed the bolt back to Klazzi, who screwed it back into the nut hung around her neck. Seconds later, the bolt returned to a bright gold finish. "There, see – it's gold again."

"That's absolutely amazing," Karen said, with a slight hint of envy. Glancing at her watch, she remembered a forgotten errand. "Oh, let's finish lunch and go to the bank around the corner. I need to get a little cash for the evening."

* * *

The ATM in front of the bank seemed to be broken, so Klazzi and her aunt went inside. As they stood in line chatting, the door opened and four masked men entered. One stood guard at the entrance. A second one went directly to the bank manager's desk. The remaining two pulled sawed-off shotguns from beneath their coats and began shouting orders to the bank patrons and bank employees.

"I want your attention, everyone! This is a hold up!" Peeking through a green "Incredible Hulk" mask, he aimed at the camera and fired a round, smashing it. The deafening shot caused dust and paint to filter down from the ceiling. "Now if you all do as you're told, this will all be over quickly and no one will be hurt!"

The other man with a shotgun wore a devil's mask. He screamed, "You there! Get back away from that silent alarm, or I'll blow your stupid head off!"

The Hulk looked to the man, wearing a Nixon mask, by the bank manager's desk. "Bring him here, Nixon!" The bank manager was trotted to the center of the bank, in front of the green Hulk. Speaking to Nixon, he ordered, "Find everyone in back and send them out here too!"

Nixon nodded silently, as he quickly headed to the rear of the bank.

The large man, in the green Hulk mask, grabbed the bank manager's suit-coat lapel, shaking it violently. "Now old man, if you know what's good for you and these people around you, you'll give us everything we ask for." He stopped shaking him, to push the manager backwards to the marble floor.

The falling man cartwheeled over the plush velvet ropes set up by the bank to maintain order. The bank official landed on his back, in an uncontrolled and undignified manner.

"Do you understand me?" the Hulk shouted.

"I can't – " the manager started to explain, but was interrupted by the discharge of the Hulk's shotgun.

The echo from the gunshot had barely subsided when the big man screamed, "Don't tell me you can't anything! You can! – and will! – do anything – and everything – I ask! Do you understand?"

The acrid smell of burned gunpowder drifted on the bank's filtered, air-conditioned air, along with a fine powder of damaged sheetrock from impact with the double-ought buckshot. A small child cried, as its mother tried to console and comfort it. The green

D.Malisch

masked man turned and lowered his weapon at the little girl.
"Keep her quiet, if you want to keep her alive." He turned back to
the bank manger who was still sprawled on the floor. "Do we
understand each other?"

The bank manager nodded yes.

"I didn't hear you mister, answer up!"

His voice cracked under the strain, as he answered, "Yes."

The robber nodded to his brother, wearing the devil's
mask, who held the other shotgun.

The devil waved his gun, directing people in the bank.
"Everyone over here! Sit down on the floor! Put all your valuables
in front of you! I want to see all your wallets, purses, rings,
valuable necklaces – on the floor, in front of you." He fired
another shot into the ceiling. "Do it now!"

By this point, Nixon had rounded up the tellers and
remaining bank officials, taking them to the area designated by the
devil.

The Hulk noted the progress made by Nixon. Seeing he
was through with the chore, he shouted, "Nixon! Take this parasite
of a bank manager to the vault. He's going to help you fill bags
with money."

The bandit guarding the door threw a wad of empty bags
across the lobby, toward the sprawled bank manager. The package
unraveled as it traveled, landing like huge noodles on the bank
official, some draped over his head.

"Now get up! Take the bags with you – all of them – and
help Nixon with campaign contributions from your vault." He
laughed hoarsely, "Make that – my vault! – It's mine now." The
Hulk tromped over to the area where the hostages sat. To ensure
no one withheld valuables, he looked for a suitable target to
become an example. Seeing a sweet, little, elderly lady, he shouted,
"Is that all you have old lady?" he grabbed the collar of her coat and

334

hoisted the woman to her feet with one hand. The frail woman tried to speak, but was too frightened to utter a sound. "Where's the money for your grandchildren?" He lowered her to her unsteady feet. Grabbing her chin roughly, he forced her to look up at him. "You want to see your grandchildren grow up?" He looked past her at the other hostages. "Then you'll give us all of your valuables. And – I mean everything?"

The tiny lady trembled. She had already given all she carried with her. What more could she do? This evil, green-faced monster towered over her; even his breath smelled badly.

"What are you hiding in your garter-belt?" he roared. He reached down to the hemline of her dress, and with a massive stroke of his free arm, ripped the long dress she wore. The violent action sent her sprawling across the hard marble floor onto her face.

A younger man, watching this, could no longer stand this uncivilized behavior. He jumped up to attack the Green Hulk. But he was no match for a man of this size. The best he could do was to knock the giant off balance. They wrestled for control of the shotgun, briefly. The Hulk punched him in the face with a massive fist, knocking him to the floor. As he attempted to get up, the big man kicked him in the rib cage, causing him to roll over. Slowly, but steadily, the volunteer attempted to gain his feet for another round. The Hulk would not have it. He laughed as he kicked the man away from the other hostages, then with a sneer, to his voice, he shouted, "Die!" and discharged the shotgun into his face. With little or no regard to the loss of life, the big man ejected the spent cartridge and reloaded his weapon. He never bothered to even look at the bleeding corpse behind him.

Meanwhile, his brother, the devil, collected items offered by the people on the floor. As he came to the row where Klazzi and her aunt sat, he was instantly attracted to the younger woman.

335

He watched Klazzi as he collected items from the people next to her. When it became her turn, he held out the bag. She quietly dropped the wallet containing money and credit cards into the bag. She purposely did not look up to make eye-contact.

"Hey Bitch! What about the necklace?"

Klazzi still did not look up. She quietly stated, "It's not valuable, it's just gold plated."

The devil, a large man, like his brother, grabbed her arm and forced her to stand.

Klazzi looked down.

"Look at me, Bitch, when I talk to you." Before she could react, he pushed back on her forehead, forcing her to look up. "It's the necklace or your life, Bitch. Make up your mind."

"I told you it's not valuable," she pleaded, "It was a gift from a friend."

Without warning, he struck her in the face with his fist, knocking her to the floor. She grabbed the side of her face, where struck, as though covering it would remove the pain. It didn't help.

The devil bent over, his hand gripped the inside of her blouse and bra-strap. He pulled hard, ripping her clothing as he set her on her feet again. "Now do the right thing, Bitch!"

Klazzi stood passively, head bowed. Slowly and carefully, she removed the gold necklace, with the bolt attached and prepared to drop it into the bag.

"Uh! Changed my mind," the devil announced, "Put it around my neck."

Klazzi looked up, his mask showed signs of drool from the mouth. Some of it had already dried, creating a white paste. She carefully and quietly unfastened the clasp, because she was too short to drop it over his head. Just as she finished reattaching the chain and started to back away, he grabbed her, and drew her head to his, where he forced her lips onto the wet, nasty lip area of the mask. When he finished, he pushed her to the floor violently. He continued on to rob the next victim.

The green monster, laughed as the hostages, one-by-one cowered beneath him. The ones who resisted, even the slightest amount, were shown the business end of the shotgun. After the killing, there was no further opposition. Still – with great malevolence, he threatened, taunted, and struck the cooperating hostages. When he finally tired of the sport, he called to the vault, "Come on! Hurry up! We've got to go – "

Seconds later, the thief, wearing the Nixon mask, forced the bank manager to carry a large portion of the loot back into the lobby. The bags were split up among the four robbers and they quickly left the bank with the promise: "If anyone moves or touches a phone during the next five minutes, I'll personally look you up and see that you die quickly."

It was an idle threat, of course, but everyone waited until the robbers were out of sight, before touching the alarms and phones.

* * *

The thieves had planned their exit well. They changed cars several times. Each car was a stolen vehicle, not directly traceable to any of them. Finally, they changed into their van and slowly made their way through the traffic, out across the Golden Gate Bridge on highway 101.

An hour later, they loaded their loot onto a small yacht at a small dock, up the coast. The Green Hulk, better known as Gerald Jones, directed the other members of his gang as they prepared to cast-off. "Get the lines Petey, we gotta make Mexico by tomorrow."

Petey, who had been the guard at the door, obeyed quickly. He really hadn't been in favor of the robbery and had been given a subordinate role, lest he foul up. He rightfully considered the two large men dangerous under most any circumstance. These brothers had a long record of violence and mayhem behind them. It was beyond his understanding how his cousin, Darrel James, had gotten mixed up with them in the first place. Darrel wasn't really a bad guy, but he let others do a lot of the thinking for him. In this case, the thinking certainly wasn't good.

The boat engines raced, tugging against the remaining rope. As Petey released it, the boat nearly dragged him off the dock. He dropped the rope and dived for the lip of the boarding area. The boat, under power had rocked back into its plowing posture and the angle made it difficult to board. Petey's legs dragged on the water. He looked at Al Jones, a true devil, with or without the mask used in the holdup. Petey tried to climb on board, but there was too much drag on his legs by the roiling water, to board. He signaled to Al for help.

Al pulled his nine-millimeter automatic and pointed it at Petey. "Hurry up Petey, or you'll be history!"

"I can't make it by myself. Give me a hand," he gasped, "or stop the boat so I can make it myself." Petey struggled, trying to kick a leg up over the rail, so he could roll onto the deck.

"We don't want no one who can't carry their own weight, Petey," Al threatened. Then carefully, he aimed next to Petey and squeezed off a shot.

The blast nearly deafened him. The bullet whizzed past his head crashing harmlessly into the wave of water behind him. "Dang it Al! Don't screw around. I need help!"

Al laughed with a nasty tone. He did nothing to help Petey.

Below deck, Darrel heard the shot. He dropped the bags of loot he had been stowing and raced topside to see what was the matter. Instantly he knew it was another conflict with Al. This conflict had been going on since he convinced his cousin to join the

338

group. Darrel leaped to his cousin's aid. He grabbed the leg highest on the side of the boat and dragged it over the rail, allowing Petey to fall onto the deck. "You okay Petey?" he asked

"Yeah," Petey replied. With a nasty scowl at Al, he added, "No thanks to him!"

"Well you know how Al is – just stay out of his way."

Al sneered as he turned and climbed the ladder to the bridge. The cold wind off Point Reyes blasted the brothers in the face as the yacht turned south to follow the coast into Mexico. It was their hope that they could safely wait for the Federal and State investigations to cool off before returning. In the meantime, they expected to live like kings with a nice house equipped with servants and beautiful women. "How's the weather look, Ger?"

The older brother nodded, as he glanced at the compass. "The coast is clear, baby brother. We'll make it to Mexico in about thirteen hours." The rumble of the two, big diesel engines forced them to shout to hear each other.

"It's getting dark. Where's the lights?" Al asked.

"Running lights? We got 'em on already."

"No. Where's the headlights?"

Gerald laughed. "Yachts don't have no such thing," he pointed to switches on the instrument console. "We have running lights and docking lights, but nothing else."

Al looked worried. "Well, what if we hit somethin'?"

"What are we going to hit, little brother? This here's the ocean. It's just salty water – a heck of a lot of it."

"No rocks?"

"Oh there are a few rocks out here, they're shown on the charts." Gerald threw the stack of charts toward Al. "I'm heading far enough out that I won't have to worry about them."

Al studied the charts for a few minutes in the flapping wind, before giving up. He couldn't make sense out of them, but

339

would never admit it to anyone, especially his older brother. Al went below to supervise counting of the loot. He and his brother had discussed how the proceeds would be divided, and once inside the Mexican border, it would be split two ways. In the meantime he didn't want any of it skimmed by Petey or Darrel. It would really gall him to sell the boat while in Mexico, only to hear later, that the new owner found loot hidden by one of the two cousins.

Counting money, Darrel, sat on the floor; he never looked up as Al climbed down the ladder into the galley. Petey, sitting at the table, looked at Al briefly, but went back to keeping track of the amounts on paper.

"How'd we do?" Al questioned.

Darrel kept counting until he reached the end of the wad of bills in his hand. "Not bad, but we could have done better."

"What do you mean?"

Pointing to the stacks on the floor where he placed them, Darrel said, "Most of the bills are twenties. That's good, because they are easily passed." He picked up a stack placed above him on the sink. "These are hundreds." With a sigh he added, "There's more money here, but they'll likely be watched closer than the smaller bills."

Al leaned on the support pole going to the bridge above. "Got any idea how much we'll have when it's all counted?"

Looking up, Darrel made a face. "Maybe half a million, more or less."

"Only a million?" Al exclaimed. "All that work and all we get is a measly half million?"

Al slammed his fist into the steel post, making it oscillate. "Hell, the big corporate guys make that in stock options in one year. It ain't fair."

Darrel shrugged and returned to counting.

The drumming of the diesel motors were suppressed inside the galley by layers and layers of sound deadening material, but it still allowed the deep mechanical throbbing to seep through. Al stood there, grumbling beneath the ambient sounds of the engines. It seemed like a lot of money, yet it wasn't nearly enough to satisfy him.

Suddenly and without warning, the yacht lurched. A loud splintering noise like an axe cutting oak startled them.

Al's eyes opened wide, "What the blazes was that?"

"Donno?" Petey answered. "Sounded like it came from the master bedroom, up inside the bow."

Al shouted a string of profanity as he leaped over Darrel, still sitting on the floor. The engines suddenly reduced power, causing Al to miscalculate and ram the wall. "Damn! I hate boats!" he swore. Al opened the cabin door to look into the master bedroom.

In the bow, where the two sides of the hull merged to make the vee, a log, the diameter of a man's head, poked into the cabin above the bed. Water gushed into the chamber at an alarming rate. "We're sinking!" Al screamed, "We're sinking!" He stepped backward, smashing Petey into galley wall. "Get the hell out of the way, you idiot! We gotta do somethin'!" Al ran up the ladder to the bridge.

The remaining diesel engine made a throaty sound and abruptly stopped. The cabin lights dimmed, and all was quiet, save the thumping, tearing sound of the impaling pole trying to open the entrance to the bow with each passing wave trough.

Petey took a deep breath to replace the one knocked out of him by Al's rapid retreat. He pushed the door aside to look into the room. His eyes also widened in disbelief. Al was right; they were sinking. Petey closed the door and locked it, as though it would stop the flow of water into the galley. The water was already

341

beginning to flow under the door into the galley area. "Quick, Darrel, put the money back into the bags and let's get 'em out of here. This boat is going under in about five minutes or less."

Darrel jumped up, stuffing the money already counted, back into the bags. Petey hauled several bags to the boarding deck.

In the opposite direction, Gerald followed his blabbing brother, Al, down into the forward cabin to see the damage for himself. Seconds later, they appeared on the boarding deck with several bags of money and two life jackets.

"Quick! Launch the dingy!" Gerald ordered Petey. The order was superfluous, since Petey was already working on the rope and pulleys to drop the small life boat into the water from the stern.

Al threw his bags of money into the small boat, before helping Petey struggle with the plastic boat, to set it into the water.

Gerald got the medical kit and flare gun.

Darrel struggled up the galley steps with the remaining bags of money. He was soaked with sea water. The bow of the craft had lost buoyancy and was beginning to go stern up. Each degree it pitched, caused the log to rip away more of the bow — which allowed more water to flow inside the boat.

Petey started back down the stairs toward the galley.

"Petey! Where you going?" Darrel asked, with alarm.

Looking over his shoulder, he answered, "To get water and some food. We're going to need it."

"You're crazy! The yacht's sinking! There's no time!"

"I know, but I've got to try." He disappeared beneath the water starting up the galley steps.

"Let him go," Al said in a "who the heck cares" tone.

Al and Gerald climbed aboard the dingy. Darrel held the bow rope, waiting for his cousin, Petey to return.

"Get in," Gerald demanded. "I'm starting the motor, and if he's not back, he's done."

Darrel objected, "I can't just leave him. He's my cousin."

"Well it's now or never," Al growled.

Gerald connected the fuel line and squeezed the priming bulb. He set the choke, and gave two quick pulls on the starting rope. The motor came to life. "Cast off!"

"Cast off now!" Al agreed with his brother.

Darrel reluctantly got into the boat, delaying as much as he dared against the two, mean brothers. With one foot slightly on the yacht, the other in the dingy, Darrel grabbed the lip of the life boat as Gerald gunned the motor. Seconds later they were several hundred feet away from the yacht.

From the sinking craft, Petey's small voice could be heard, encouraging them to come back and pick up the food and water.

"We don't need it," Al growled.

"We might," Gerald countered.

"We will need it," Darrel demanded, "Besides, Petey's still on the boat."

"We're about twelve miles out," Gerald said, with calculation." Wherever we go, we're going to need food and water."

"We'll just take it from whoever crosses our path," Al pleaded with his older brother.

"Not this time, Al. We got to make land first. Even then, we don't want to alert the cops, so they come searching for us." He opened the tool box and handed his brother a roll of bailing wire. "Better tie the money in the boat, so we don't accidentally knock any of it overboard." Searching the dark eastern horizon, for signs of land, he added, "When we get to land, we'll go to the nearest town and buy what we need to move on."

"We're only twelve minutes from land. We don't need the damn water or food," Al grumbled.

"Twelve minutes if we were a car on the freeway," Darrel commented, "But out here with wind and tide — well, we'll be a long time getting in. We don't even have a compass." He looked overhead at the fog beginning to settle on them. "Now, we don't even have stars to navigate by." With a sigh he added, "Even if we knew which way to go, we probably don't have enough fuel to make it to shore. We'd be wise to get the food and water."

Gerald turned the small boat to head back toward the yacht. It was dark now, and the battery-powered lights of the sinking boat would appear and disappear each time they experienced a wave crest and trough. Slowly, they approached the yacht.

Wearing two life vests, Petey, soaked and dripping, was standing on the stern. The rest of the boat was under water. A hissing sound could be heard, as the remaining air bubbles escaped from the engine compartment, past the seals on the propeller shaft.

"Quick! Get in, Petey," Darrel coaxed.

Petey didn't need a second invitation, he knew the yacht would go under, in the next minute or two. He tossed the four small bottles of water into the boat and the small cardboard box of crackers to his cousin, Darrel. That done, he quickly dived into the dingy, lest the nasty brothers take off and leave him behind again.

The two Jones brothers argued and argued over which way to go to reach land. Both were afraid of drifting farther out to sea, but they differed in opinion which direction to go to reach land. In the end, they flipped a coin. Well — since the half-inch bolt was hanging around Al's neck, it was fate who won.

The boat engine ran for about four hours. Gerald tried to keep the craft going as straight as he could. He knew something of the prevailing winds. He knew something of the fog patterns and wave patterns, but there was a storm in the north coast above them. An earlier storm of the same type had flushed the tree down the rivers, into the Delta, and out under the Golden Gate Bridge into their path. Eventually the motor sputtered and stopped. Gerald pulled the start rope again; the motor started and ran a few seconds before dying again. Then it wouldn't start, period.

Darrel looked into the tank. In the pitch black conditions, he saw nothing. He felt around the boat and found a piece of fishing line with a sinker attached. Dropping it into the tank, he retrieved it and smelled the line for gasoline. After he reached the bottom of the sinker, he announced, "It's official, we're out of gas."

Gerald was still the captain, out ranking everyone by age or size. He sat quietly for a few minutes while the others argued. Finally he spoke, "We gotta row to shore, but we don't know which way to go. We'll wait for the sun to come up so we can see which way is east. Then we'll take turns rowin'."

They sat in the darkness, drifting for hours. The constant bobbing of the sea made Al sick. He vomited several times. He opened his bottle of water and slugged it down, only to toss it back up again, a few minutes later. There had been only four bottles of water when they picked up Petey. They had each had a few crackers and opened their bottles of water. Petey and Darrel, both were smaller people and required less water. Gerald, was wise on conservation of resource, but his water needs were greater than the smaller men.

As it has for billions of years, the sun finally appeared in the eastern, morning sky. Unfortunately, the fog filtered all sense of east. Just before noon, the sun slowly chased away the fog. While it brightened their spirits, it did little to show them how far they were from the closest land. It was water, water everywhere.

Squinting at the sun overhead, Gerald gauged which way must be east. He ordered his brother, Al to row the first four hours. After that it would be Petey, then Darrel, then himself.

* * *

D.Malisch

San Francisco Police Detective, Brian Weeder, was dispatched to the bank to investigate the homicide. He talked to the witnesses, one, by one. When he finally came to Karen Metz, she told him all that she knew, including the thief taking her niece's necklace. Brian did his job, routinely taking notes, until Ms. Metz mentioned the necklace was a bolt.

"Tell me again, Ms. Metz, what did you say her necklace looked like?" She had Brian's full attention. He wasn't sure, but he strongly suspected the half-inch bolt had returned.

The petite, dark-haired woman looked into the detective's eyes, wishing she was a few years younger. There were many men in San Francisco, and some, like Brian, would make interesting partners. At least she'd like to find out for herself. "Uh, Detective – what did you say your name was?"

"Brian Weeder, Ma'am."

"Oh yes." Karen made a mental note to remember the name. "My niece had this necklace." She waved her arms as she told her story. "It was made out of a screw or bolt or something. Anyway, one of the big guys – the one wearing a devil's mask – took it from her. She didn't want to give it to him, but he forced her – "

"Excuse me Ma'am, does your niece live here?"

"No, she's visiting me from the Seattle area." Karen pointed to Klazzi, who had just come out of the ladies room. "That's her over there."

"Thank you, Ms. Metz. Please stick around, I'd like to question you a bit more in a few minutes."

Brian zeroed in on Klazzi and wasted no time introducing himself. "Uh, excuse me, I'm Detective Brian Weeder, San Francisco Police. Your Aunt Karen was telling me you are from the Pacific Northwest."

"I am, Detective. I live near the Seattle area."

Brian nodded. "She told me you lost a necklace to one of the bandits. Is that true?"

"It is."

"Would you describe it for me?"

Klazzi smiled, "I'd be glad to. It was a bolt," she made a finger gesture showing the bolt to be about three inches in length, "and it was gold."

"Gold?" Brian's heart skipped a beat.

"Why yes," Klazzi smiled. Then she saw the look of disappointment on Brian's face. "Well actually, it was silver, but when I hung it around my neck, it turned gold." She looked up into Brian's eyes, "Strange isn't it?"

Brian's interest renewed itself. He was certain the bolt was on a mission, but he needed to confirm this "necklace bolt" was his missing half-inch bolt. "Did it do anything else that was strange?"

Klazzi was quick to reply, "Oh yes. It occasionally would feel warm. And the boy who gave it to me said it had been pointed for a while."

Brian could hardly contain himself. "Did — did it have any initials on it?"

A big smile of embarrassment crossed her face. "Yes it did. The friend who mounted it to the chain tried to buff them out, but they kept coming back." She rolled her eyes, "My aunt said I'd have to find a boyfriend with the same initials, to find happiness."

Brian blushed, "And. . . Were — " he coaxed, "were the initials 'BW'?"

Looking shocked, Klazzi stepped back from the detective, "Did Auntie tell you?"

"No," he said, almost feeling giddy, though it definitely set the wrong tone for a homicide investigation. "In case you haven't noticed, those are my initials."

347

Klazzi looked at the detective, a little embarrassed, a little shocked, a little pleased with this encounter. Trying not to be too obvious, she gave Brian "the inspection"; her pulse rate raised a couple of notches as she realized she found him attractive. Suddenly conversation became difficult for Klazzi as her thoughts raced around in circles, tangling themselves in knots. Completely unaware of her words, she asked, "You think this is your bolt?" She meant it as a tease, for the sheer joy of sharing idle conversation with the young man.

"I lost the bolt in the wilderness," Brian said, accepting the tease.

"It couldn't be the same bolt, detective," she said, looking up into his brown eyes.

Brian grinned from ear to ear. "Ms. – Uh, – I'm sorry, I don't have your name?"

Holding out her hand she filled in the blanks by saying, "Klazzi Korner."

"What an interesting name, Ms. Korner. I'm sure your parents must have had an interesting sense of humor."

"They do." Feeling more in control, Klazzi slipped into a more aggressive form of flirtation with Brian. "A lot of men want to take me out of the corner and put me into bed."

Brian completely forgot whatever it was he started to say. He smiled while his mind raced to process the information he just received. He really liked her face, and her voice, and her personality. Casually, he looked down at his shoes, as if to see if they were untied. His eyes went across the floor to her shoes and he scanned her upward. Yes, she was very, very attractive. "Uh – may I call you Klazzi?"

"I'd be unhappy if you didn't," she teased.

This was going too easy. Brian tried to slow it down, but his mind didn't want that. "Do you think I could buy you dinner, tomorrow evening?"

Klazzi had watched him look her over. She knew her pheromones were interfering with his thought processes. She liked what she saw and decided to play just a little hard to get, to watch his reaction. "Actually, my aunt and I were planning to have dinner together," she said, pointing in the general direction of her aunt.

"Oh, well, I wouldn't want to intrude," he lied. "Maybe some other time."

"We could make it a threesome," she teased. "I'm sure she wouldn't mind."

"Uh – well – Yes! We could do that," he conceded with a smile.

"Good, then it's settled." Klazzi helped herself to the pen and pad from Brian's hands and carefully wrote her aunt's phone number. She rolled her eyes upward shyly, "Call me here for directions before you come." She returned the pad and pen, touching his hands lightly, before walking away, toward her aunt. When she had walked far enough away, he could see her full length, she turned and asked, "About seven ish?"

Brian nodded and watched, as she turned again, to display her most seductive saunter for his benefit.

* * *

By late afternoon, the bank robbers were more than weary of their boat ride and wished to see land again. They had slept little during the previous night in the crowded boat, leaving them terribly irritable. The day's rowing left their muscles aching and the palms of their hands with broken blisters. Missing their daily meals made them tired and hungry, not to mention – terribly thirsty. Their lips were sunburned, as were their noses, the backs of their hands. Even their ankles were burned, after they had foolishly pulled off their wet socks. Petey and his cousin, still had three or four ounces of drinking water, but the two larger men exhausted their supply hours ago. Al had finally stopped throwing up, but his mood hadn't improved.

Petey worried, rightfully so, for his and his cousin's safety. They were likely to be sacrificed for a single swallow of water as the day wore on. Their only value was as rowing slaves. The larger men watched the near empty bottles coveting them every few minutes. Petey couldn't decide if it would be wiser to drink the remaining water immediately, or try to use it as a bargaining chip, when the shortage became life threatening. If he drank the water now, in front of the men, they might execute him anyway. Life had become terribly unpleasant.

Silence had been the rule for nearly a day on the dingy. Though they must be near the coast, there had been no sign of ships or even aircraft, just the constant bobbing up and down. Suddenly, something nudged the boat. The movement was gentle at first, then it pushed violently.

"What the heck was that!" Al exclaimed, climbing to his knees to look over the starboard side. He shifted his weight enough to raise the center of gravity just as they entered a wave trough. The next nudge, forced the boat to overturn, casting everyone and everything not tied down, into the water.

Gerald was the first to discover the source of the problem. His arm felt something solid beneath him; it had a sandpaper texture. He kicked away struggling for the surface. As he broke the surface, he screamed, "Shark! It's a damn big shark."

There was panic in the water. The boat was still capsized, so they couldn't climb aboard. Everyone was shouting at once. Everyone was attempting to climb aboard the slippery bottom of the boat. Both of the smaller men had their life jackets on, but neither of the brothers had bothered. Their jackets were now on the way to Japan.

Something had to be done, if they were to survive. Gerald eventually realized this and took command. "We've got to turn the boat over, so we can get back in it."

"How?" Darrel cried.

"Let's all get on the same side, and push up!"

They struggled to line up along the side and pushed upward. It was useless; their best efforts couldn't raise the boat more than a few inches.

Fortunately the shark seemed to have disappeared, at least for the moment. Still, getting the boat turned over was a priority.

Darrel swam to the stern of the boat and climbed up onto the output shaft of the motor. As he did so, his bulk raised the starboard side out of the water slightly, but not enough to right the boat. "Get the bow rope. Swim under the boat and loop it through the first seat. Then bring it to me," he shouted. It took several tries, but eventually the task was completed. "Now," he commanded, "Everyone get over on this side and put your toes on the lip of the port side. I'll hand you the rope and if everyone pulls on the rope, we might get the starboard side high enough to flip." The attempt took several tries, but eventually, they succeeded with the aid of a wave trough. One by one, they climbed on board and breathed a sigh of relief.

"Oars? Where are the stupid oars?" Al cried. He looked around. The oars too — were headed to Japan — as if the Japanese needed American oars.

The situation had changed, for the worse. The cold Pacific water gave them temporary relief for their sunburned skin, though the salt was soon to irritate all exposed skin. Sadly, the few remaining ounces of drinking water and all their clothing, not worn, was floating West.

351

"I tell ya, it was a dang monster shark that flipped us," Gerald exclaimed. "I felt him. I landed on him."

Al reached for the necklace and kissed the bolt, "This is what saved us," he exclaimed, "Good as any rabbit's foot." He looked at the bolt, surprised by its color. "Hey, the ocean's turned this thing black. The chain and nut are still gold though — what gives?" He examined the chain a few minutes more before shrugging. "Well so long as it works. I'll get a new one when we get to Mexico anyway."

"Get to Mexico!" Gerald exploded, "Al, in case you haven't noticed, we lost our boat, our food, all of our water. We don't have gas for the motor and no oars to get back to shore. We're stuck in the great-white triangle off San Francisco, and we aren't going anywhere!"

Suddenly the boat began to move. Each man looked at the other, puzzled. Petey was the first to see it. "Look at the bow rope!" They looked forward to discover some large thing beneath the water had grabbed it and was towing them rapidly across the water.

Gerald strained to see beneath the water. They had mixed feelings. Was it a great-white shark, or was it a submarine? They were glad to be moving, but frightened by the lack of control. Looking at the setting sun, Gerald determined the direction was South, not east. "Turn the motor to steer Petey. We want to go that way," he said, pointing east, away from the sun.

Petey steered, but it did little to change their direction. They tried for a half-hour, but eventually gave up. It had gotten dark again, and the hot sun was replaced by the chilly air resting on the cold Pacific Ocean. Their speed wasn't fast, but still they moved, sometimes slower than other times. Sometimes the direction changed. They tried for an hour or more to free the bow rope, but the large wet knot where it connected had been pulled into a rock-hard knot. After the boat overturned, they had no knives or saws to sever the rope. They resigned themselves to remaining passengers on their way to an unknown destination.

Well after dark, the movement suddenly stopped. The lack of movement startled them.

"What happened?" Al questioned, "Did we break free?"

From the bow, Gerald retrieved the rope. "Guess he got tired," he lamented, pulling the rope onboard.

The boat was nudged. "Oh no! Not again!" someone cried.

Minutes passed, nothing happened. They were nudged again, harder this time.

"Hang on!" Petey shouted.

* * *

Brian called early for his dinner date with Klazzi and her aunt. He was given directions, but once he heard the address, he knew how to find it. As he arrived and climbed the steps to the door of the brick and stucco house built on the hillside, Auntie Karen opened the door for him, on her way out.

"Good evening, Ms. Metz." Brian glanced at her coat and the overnight bag she carried, "Uh – are you going somewhere before dinner?"

Karen gave him a big-sister grin. "I won't be able to join you kids this evening," she said, with a note of excitement. "I'm going to stay with a friend for the evening." Setting her bag on the floor, she waved him inside and closed the door. "Klazzi's upstairs waiting for you, but first – " she paused to push him gently against the wall, so he couldn't retreat, then she slipped her hands behind his head, pulling it forward to plant a sweet kiss on his lips. "There!" she smiled, "I always wanted to kiss a cop." Karen picked up her valise and opened the door to the street. As she backed out the door, she winked. Licking her lips, she said, "Ummm, 'B' 'W'

353

eh! If you had any other initials, you'd be mine, 'cause I saw you first." She blew a kiss, before pulling the door closed behind her.

Brian smiled and wiped the taste of Karen's lipstick from his lips. He climbed the stairs, filled with awe and expectation. At the door, he knocked and waited patiently, for what seemed to be an eternity. Finally, the knob turned and the yellowed door opened to reveal Klazzi in her house coat.

Brian was pleased, but confused as he asked, "Uh! I thought we had dinner plans for three tonight?"

Klazzi said nothing; she took his hand, smoothly pulled him inside and closed the door. Silently, she wrapped her arms around him and kissed him with a lengthy kiss. She looked seriously at him when she finished, as if to see if he was in anyway damaged. "Auntie won't be joining us this evening," she said shyly.

"The two of us can still have dinner," Brian grinned.

"We can, and we will," Klazzi said, coaxing him to the sofa. "Don't go away. I'll be right back." She disappeared into the kitchen area, reappearing with cocktails. "Had to check on the chicken – didn't want it to burn."

Brian took one of the drinks, holding it up for a toast. She responded accordingly. "To the half-inch bolt," he toasted.

"To the half-inch bolt," she replied. They tapped glasses and sipped. She waited for Brian to find a place set his drink on the coffee table, then she dimmed the lamp next to him, and pulled him on top of her.

Dinner was a bit later than planned, but at least it wasn't burned – badly. Certainly, no one in attendance was complaining.

Later with their chicken and other appetites satisfied, they talked and talked about their lives and needs and desires. Finally they were exhausted and simply went to bed for rest.

* * *

For the last three hours, the boat was shoved on the water in an erratic fashion. Sometimes it was raised almost out of the water, before being allowed to splash back to the surface.

Al removed the necklace and fingered the bolt, screwing and unscrewing it, time and time again, hoping his good luck charm would drive it away. "It's hungry," Al shouted, "We got to feed the damn thing to make it leave us alone."

"We got nothin' to feed it," Petey countered.

Al set the necklace down, while he tried to see in the dark. Though no one could see, he pointed a pudgy finger at the tool box. "Petey, get me the flare gun out of the tool box."

Petey hesitated, but decided he'd better do as told. As he handed the gun to his antagonist, Al snapped the safety off, pointing the gun at Petey's outline against the stars.

Sensing Al's violent intentions, "No!" Petey protested, loudly.

The protest went unheeded as Al discharged a blinding flash into Petey's chest, killing him. Petey fell overboard from the impact.

Al pointed the gun toward Darrel, thinking he might object to his cousin's ultimate sacrifice.

Darrel wisely objected silently.

Illuminated by remnants of the burning flare, Petey's body could be seen floating off, slowly, toward Japan, un-menaced by the great-white.

The boat was nudged again. Al fired the remaining flare charge into the water where he expected the shark to be. It missed and the fireball quickly quenched in the water.

Minutes later, the shark bumped them again.

"Stupid-damn shark! I'm goin' to beat the tar out of it, if I can find something to do it with!" Gerald screamed. He went to the stern and attempted to remove the throttle handle on the motor. It wouldn't come off without tools. In his anger, he planted both feet beneath Darrel's seat, and lifted on the seat. Darrel moved immediately. The seat plank broke loose as the lip of the boat splintered. Gerald moved forward and looked over the port side, into the black water. He could see nothing.

The night was devoted to hitting the shark as it toyed with them. Gerald had little luck. The morning promised a slightly brighter day, under high, thin clouds. As the light increased, Gerald watched carefully over the bow for an approach. When the shark neared, he swung the boat seat. The effort missed its mark, causing him to fall overboard. He quickly scrambled back on board to relative safety. With regret, he lost the seat, which headed for you-know-where.

Two miserable, foggy days and freezing, cold nights, in wet clothing, without food, water, or sleep exhausted the bandits. They were willing to go to jail, just for the comfort. Temporarily left alone by the shark, the strain of staying awake was too much in the warm, filtered sunlight. Everyone fell asleep. Gerald stretched out across the bow seat to Al's seat. Al rested beneath his brother's feet across the center of the boat. His own feet hung over the water. Darrel was probably the most comfortable, on the damp floor near the stern. The shark had left them alone for the last hour, allowing them to relax.

In his slumber, Gerald's arm dangled in and out of the water. The large, primitive vertebrate rolled onto its side before clamping onto the dangling appendage. Quickly the shark rolled the large man overboard before he could awake. His next breath was under water. The terrified man pulled and yanked on his hand, clamped in the shark's mouth. The animal rolled over, tugging back. Gerald's head and other arm, broke water. He splashed wildly, in an attempt to reach the boat. He tried to shout, but his lungs were mostly filled with water.

356

The commotion, awakened the others. Al noticed his brother's absence first. "Hey, Ger! Where are you? What happened?" The panic was normal as the two remaining survivors, watched the roiling water beneath the boat turn pink, briefly. . . Then all was calm. "Poor Ger." Al strained to see a sign of his brother through the reflections on the water. "He never had a chance."

Darrel nodded silently.

The voracious appetite of the great-white was appeased for about an hour. With almost no sleep, the two blurry-eyed survivors stood a nervous watch, wondering about their own fate. Dedicated to his reputation, the great white, nudged the boat about every forty minutes or so, to remind them there was more to come.

All through the day, and into the night, the harassment continued. Sometimes the contact with the boat was harder than other times, but each and every contact was terrifying for Al and Darrel.

In the morning, the fog lifted early, allowing them a clear view of lots of water. There were birds coming and going, but no sign of land. Shortly after daybreak, the marine creature discovered a new trick. It came up and crunched a golf-ball-sized hole in the rear corner of the boat. The boat begin to slowly fill with sea water. First they bailed by hand, but when it was apparent they were losing to the sea, Darrel ripped the engine cover loose and used it as a large bailing bucket to stay afloat. Al looked for something to plug the hole. Everything was on its way to Japan.

Ignoring Darrel's protest, Al ripped the shirt from Darrel's back. He wadded it into a ball and stuffed it into the hole. It refused to stay in the hole, causing him to reset it, over and over again.

They continued to take turns bailing, but the boat always had a couple of inches of water inside. The only good news was

357

the shark had finally moved on to more interesting and probably more tasty prey.

Late in the afternoon, they were spotted by a Coast Guard vessel. Within minutes they were aboard. An officer opened one of the numerous bags tied to the sinking boat. Having seen news of the robbery on television several nights ago, he quickly placed the two men under arrest, ending their life on the high seas.

Al and Darrel were given food and water and a place to rest. Coastal Dispatch had given the unit orders to bring the prisoners directly to port for questioning. All of the money was recovered from the sinking dingy.

As the Coast Guard cruiser approached the dock, Al made a sudden charge. He grabbed a loaded sidearm, before knocking over several officers on the vessel, then he jumped ship. The guarding officers discharged their weapons to stop him, but he showed no signs of being hit.

The guard authorities called the San Francisco police. Unable to raise Brian on the police radio channel, his office paged him. He was quick to meet with the Coast Guard officers to discuss Al's escape.

Brian underscored the time of Al's escape on his notepad. "And he is armed?"

"Yes," the officer replied, "He took a nine-millimeter pistol with a full clip from a crewman guarding him, as he jumped ship."

Brian pointed toward the southeast. "And he headed that general direction?"

"That's correct," the naval officer said.

Brian scribbled a note to himself. "I have his clothing color and description. What type of shoes was he wearing?"

Shaking his head the officer corrected the record, "He didn't have shoes when he came aboard, and he left without them, as far as I know."

The detective raised an eyebrow, "No shoes – that should slow him down a bit." Brian squeezed a note into the margin of the tiny page. "Thank you for your cooperation, Captain. If you come up with anything else, you can contact me at this number." Brian handed him his business card.

"Oh, Detective! There is one more thing, I just remembered about his appearance."

"What's that?"

"He was wearing some kind of gold necklace."

Brian stopped to look up. "Did it have a gold bolt attached to it?"

The officer hesitated, "Uh – no."

The news made Brian's heart sink. "Can you describe it?"

The official looked back at his busy crew, as he thought. "You know, I think it was a bolt – but it was black." He looked back at Brian, "Yes, I'm sure that's right, because I remember thinking it looked strange that the nut was gold and the bolt screwed into it looked badly tarnished."

A big smile formed on the detective's face. "Thank you, Captain. You've been a big help."

"What about the other prisoner and the money?"

"Oh yes, I nearly forgot. Guard them carefully and I'll have a unit sent over to take them off your hands." Brian reached for his cell phone to contact headquarters. That done, he climbed into his car and headed off into the general direction of the city where Al had last been seen traveling. Many interviews later, Detective Weeder concluded Al had switched clothing by stealing it from a tourist shop and had stolen shoes from a homeless man. After that, the murderer's trail had simply vanished.

Late in the afternoon, Brian Weeder returned to the precinct. He hoped to interview the remaining prisoner for clues leading to Al's whereabouts. He badged into the interrogation area and crossed the floor, waving to friends at various desks along the way. He stopped to ask the attendant sitting at the beat-up unvarnished wooden desk, "Have they finished questioning Mr. James yet?"

The older police woman, looked up, "Oh – Hi Brian. I hear you have a new girlfriend."

Brian nodded.

Her brassy voice complained, "Come on, you can do better than that. Let's hear some details." The woman laced her fingers before leaning back in her squeaky swivel chair. Officer Shella, had known Brian since he joined the force. She prided herself on keeping up with the social lives of the many officers around her; Brian was no exception. While the comradely and noseyness of Shella seemed natural, it also served as a means to gauge the psychological fitness of the officers in the department. Shella also was secretly on the committee to oversee department morale.

It was obvious to Brian that someone in the department had a big mouth. "She's from Seattle. You wouldn't know her," he said, hoping to discourage Shella.

"Oh. . . that serious?" she paused, looking him in the eye.

Brian looked down at the papers on her desk. He tried to read the assignment sheet for the interrogation rooms upside down. "She's really nice, but I've just met her."

Putting her hand over the page, so Brian couldn't see it, she added, "Well, honey, if you give me her name, I'll be happy to run a background check on her for you."

"No thanks, Shella, I'd rather check her out myself."

Shella waited for him to look up, adding, "From your look, I bet you already have."

Brian blushed.

Shella smiled, knowing she made her point. "Your guy's in room two-ten."

Knowing that Shella would still be watching him, he refused to look back as he walked away. Brian knocked once and slipped quietly through the door.

Inside, two detectives sat quietly watching Darrel James across a four-by-eight foot table. James watched the two lawmen with no particular interest. As Brian approached, one of the men looked up. He picked up his coffee mug and emptied the cold contents of it in two large swallows. Silently the officer pointed to the door, where Weeder had entered. Brian followed him back into the hallway.

"What do you have?" Brian questioned.

The subordinate officer put his hands behind him as he leaned against the wall. "He's confessed."

"Good. Anything else?"

"We got one heck of a frightening story about their boat trip."

"Okay, I'll listen to it later," Detective Weeder leaned against the dismal-green wall, where he had done so, countless times before. "Has he given any info on his buddy's hangouts?"

The other detective pursed his lips, "From what we hear, they ain't friends."

"Oh?"

"That's right. Seems Al Jones shot his cousin."

"What about the other big guy?"

"Shark food."

"Too bad. Couldn't happen to a nicer guy?" Brian made a mental note; the bolt was still administering justice. "How well does James know Jones?"

"Better than he'd like. Says they worked together for a couple of years."

"I'd like to ask him about where he thinks Jones went after he jumped ship today."

361

The subordinate detective pushed away from the wall, nodding toward the door – Weeder followed. The pair entered the interrogation room quietly. The junior officer took his seat again, while Brian walked around the table and pulled up a chair next to the suspect.

Brian turned the chair toward himself, sitting on it backwards, so he could lean forward on its backrest, giving a more casual appearance to the prisoner. "How you feeling?" Weeder asked.

Darrel rubbed the clean, dry jumpsuit he had been given. His unshaven, peeling face tried not to wrinkle, as he spoke. "Glad to be here."

Smiling in return, Weeder, nodded, "I bet! I hear you had quite an ordeal out there."

"Yeah, it weren't much fun."

"I understand you and Al aren't the best of friends?"

With almost a tearful look, he answered, "You could say that – he killed Petey."

"And you'd like to see him caught and punished for that, right?"

Darrel nodded.

"How about giving us a little help to find him?"

Darrel shook his head no. "Not unless I get some help from you, first."

"What is it you want from me?"

"Immunity," Darrel said flatly.

Brian sat silently looking at him. "Sorry, can't do that. Got anything else?"

"Nope," he said, and just sat quietly staring straight ahead at nothing.

Silence filled the room. Except for the breathing of the four men, it was quiet. "Sure we can't do anything else for you, Darrel?" Brian asked.

"Nope."

They sat in silence for a long minute or more.

Weeder got up from his chair. He turned and walked toward the door. As he reached for the knob, he looked back. The prisoner hadn't moved.

Brian spent the next hour in the office of the District Attorney. At last, he got an agreement for a plea-bargain. Returning to the interrogation room, he knocked and entered smoothly. Only one detective remained, otherwise, nothing had changed. Brian returned to the chair, exactly where he had left it. He seated himself in the same manner as before, leaning forward against the backrest. He watched James for a minute or so silently. "Changed your mind?"

"Have you?"

"Can't give you immunity."

"I know."

"Would you go for a lesser charge?"

Darrel sat silently for a few seconds. At last he replied, "What ya got?"

"Since bank witnesses all say you were passive in the robbery, and since it seems highly unlikely you killed your own cousin, we're willing to drop the murder charges and let you spend your full time on bank robbery." Brian drew a breath, "In return, you help us find Al Jones."

"Can you reduce the robbery time?"

Brian shrugged. "You know, Darrel, robbery is robbery, and we can't reduce it more." He looked into the prisoner's eyes, which had moved toward him. "If we can find Al, right away, I'll personally put in a good word for you at the trial, and I'll try to get you a lighter sentence."

Darrel didn't flinch.

"Deal?" Brian asked.

He didn't respond.

Brian got up to leave. He didn't look back when he reached the door. As he opened the door, he heard the prisoner say, "Deal!"

Detective Weeder closed the door and returned to his seat. He spent the next hour discussing possibilities where Al might be located. Darrel gave names of people Al knew, he gave locations of special hangouts, he gave descriptions of cars Al might borrow. He even gave names and descriptions of Al's women friends, and where they might be found. Brian took notes and left to search.

Four hours later, well after dark, Brian got lucky. Myya, one of Al's girlfriends, was more than angry. "He told me we'd be rich and come and go as we like," she said, "then he shows up — lookin' like dog-doo-doo, he's broke, the law's after him and he wants me to pay for everything." She grabbed Al's picture from the table and threw it across the room. "So when I told him to get out, he grabs my car keys and leaves."

Weeder walked across the room and stooped to pick up the picture, with broken glass. "Mind if I take this? It'll help to find him."

Myya leaned forward, resting her forehead in the palms of her hands, her elbows braced against her knees. "I don't care, so long as he never comes 'round again."

Walking back across the carpeted room, decorated with gaudy pictures, rhinestone, flowers, and nicked tables and appliances from the many throwing fits of her past, Brian stopped within speaking distance. "Can you give me a description of your car?"

"It's the yellow one behind him in the picture."

Brian checked the license plate number on the small yellow Ford. "I think this may be enough. Does the car have dents on the side you can't see?"

Myya moved toward Brian to look. He held the picture up for her inspection.

"Uh – No – it don't have no big ones there, except for the time I backed into the damned fire hydrant. You know the city puts those things everywhere – and they're just so short I can't see 'em until – Bang!"

Suppressing a laugh, the detective sympathized, "Yes, I suppose the city has spread them around a bit more than they need to – "

"Yeah, and they give tickets if you park next to 'em. Now I ask ya, where can a person park in this city, if it ain't next to a plug?"

Brian shrugged.

Myya stopped to take a breath. As she caught a whiff of Brian's cologne, she changed the subject, "Say, you seem nice. Are you married or anything?"

"Uh, I don't have much time for a wife. My job keeps me very busy," Brian smiled, retreating toward the door, "I have such long hours, you know."

Looking slightly depressed, Myya admitted, "Yeah, I know, and it's a shame. All the good ones seem to have the same problem."

Brian opened the door and stepped backwards onto the porch, "Thank you for your help, Ma'am. Please call my office, if you think of anything more I should know – Er – I mean, if you recall where I might find Mr. Jones."

"Oh sure – I mean, I will, Detective Weeder." Winking at him she added, "If you have extra time, and your wife don't mind, stop by and see me. I like you."

Brian waved and quickly fled to the safety of his double-parked car.

Grinding his way through the late evening traffic, Brian decided to check out the list of bars, given him by Darrel Jones. Now that he knew the kind of car to watch for, he might be able to zero in a bit quicker.

Three bars later, and twenty-three witnesses later, he decided, it wasn't going to be as easy as he'd hoped.

Though yellow was an easier color to spot against the sea of dark cars, the city's orange street lighting shifted the color spectrum, making it nearly impossible to detect yellow without shining his own headlights on each light colored vehicle. Every white car looked orange. Every orange car looked off-white. Fortunately, yellow wasn't a popular color. The few he did spot, gave him a better idea of how the color had shifted under the street lighting.

Brian pulled his car into the small lot adjacent to the fourth bar on the list. He maneuvered the car into the terribly tight space. As everyone who drives and parks in the city knows, parking is a nightmare. It's a wonder all of the vehicles don't have mangled fenders from the nearly impossible parking conditions. He turned off the ignition and checked off the name on the list of bars to visit.

A quick interview with the parking lot attendant, was non-productive; he hadn't seen any yellow cars all evening, and probably wouldn't admit to it, if he had.

The bar was typically dark, with the strong smell of cigarette smoke. San Francisco has a no-smoking policy, but the patrons usually light up anyway. Perhaps a more effective way of fixing the problem would be to force bar owners to filter the air leaving their establishments and allow smoking only in bars. Brian pondered the thought of the politics involved in such a concept.

The crowded bar had the usual items, thirty-seven inch television for watching games, mirrors behind the bar, next to the TV. A group of regulars sat near the end of the bar, waiting for opportunities. Some waited for friends, some waited for sex, some waited for a free drink, some waited for drugs, some just waited.

Brian looked around the room carefully before sitting down at a small table. He wanted to speak with the cocktail waitress, away from the bartender; he'd question him separately. He ordered a tonic on the rocks (no alcohol) and looked carefully around the room as he waited. When the waitress returned, he held the money as he asked, "I'm a friend of Al Jones. Have you seen him this evening?"

The aging waitress, whose thick makeup appeared to be spread on her face with a putty knife, stepped back to give Brian a closer look under the dim light. She glanced around the room as though she'd left her serving tray on another table and needed it again. Then she leaned forward, toward Brian, allowing him a good look down the front of her blouse. "He was here earlier, but I think he left," she said, putting her foot on the chair next to the detective. Taking one of the clean napkins from the stack in her hand, she spit on it, rubbing the damp paper on her stocking, at the edge of her short skirt, to remove something a customer had spilled on her. As she rubbed, the bottom of her thigh swung back and forth, showing lack of muscle tone, though the leg looked shapely. She wadded the napkin, stuffing it in her pocket for trash. As she reached for the money Weeder gave her for the drink, she told him, "I'll check around, maybe someone knows where he went."

Weeder released the ten, giving her a two-dollar tip from the change. He watched her walk away, tilting her hips left and right as she dodged tables and customer's touches. Savoring his drink, he watched the waitress work her way across the room, near the alcove. Immediately after, the waitress spoke with a short, little guy across the room, Brian watched him leave the table to go into the men's room. The short man returned too soon to have used the facility, making the Detective suspicious. The waitress made a couple more stops and picked up an order at the bar before coming back his way.

At Brian's table she squatted slightly as she spoke into his ear, "His friends say he went over to The Red Tea Garden." She looked into Brian's eyes, questioning, "You know where that is?"

Brian nodded, he'd been there several times before.

She straightened up, tapping him gently on the shoulder, as she went on to deliver drinks.

He sucked the last of the liquid from the melting ice and set the glass back onto the table. He wiped his lips with a clean napkin and stood up to leave. A departing glance over his shoulder, as he went out the door, gave him an uneasiness. The group of guys, at the table with the short fellow, were all watching him leave.

Brian went immediately to his car. He paid the attendant and took the car down the block, where he made a "U-turn" and parked on the other side of the street. He turned off the lights, but left the car running as he waited. About three minutes later, a large man, wearing a plaid jacket over a tourist shirt with a picture of the Golden Gate Bridge on the front, exited. The man went down the block toward an alley servicing another business. Seconds later, a set of lights came on. The lights widened as they came out of the alley. The light-colored car never stopped as it made a turn onto the street going the opposite way the detective's car faced. Brian muttered an obscenity as he turned his car around in the light traffic.

Weeder pressed the accelerator hard as he tried to keep up with the yellow car, weaving through traffic. He grabbed the microphone for the two-way radio and announced the pursuit. Units were on their way, but it would be a few minutes before they could get into position to block the fugitive's forward movements. Brian pushed hard to shorten the lead. Cars honked at him and several blundered into his high speed path. He avoided all of them. The light ahead turned red, and he gritted his teeth. The fugitive made it through okay. Brian slowed nearly to a stop allowing a fast-moving van to clear the intersection. With his fingers clenched on the steering wheel, he gunned the car, burning rubber to get to the relative safety of the other side. The distance between the two vehicles was nearly a block. Brian wanted to hit his siren, but if there was any chance the guy didn't know who he was, he didn't want to lose the edge.

Down one block and up the next, they continued. Brian reported the change each time on the radio to dispatch. Suddenly, a police cruiser crossed the path of the fugitive. If he wasn't going fast enough before, now the driver panicked. The cruiser made a tire-burning turn to pursue. Brian came up behind.

At the next turn, the wheel covers on the yellow car flew off, as he skipped over the trolley-rails. Brian hit his siren and flipped the red light up, so it could be seen by others. The patrol car in front, already had lights and siren going. Dispatch stopped all routine traffic on the channel, while the pursuit continued. The radio came alive with conversations between dispatch and the support units. The yellow car attempted to turn left, but saw the white door and rotating light on the roof of the patrol unit, just in time to avoid going down the street. The fugitive lost some time, but continued straight. Two more attempts were thwarted as the driver in the yellow car avoided being forced into a street blocked by police.

369

The car turned into an older part of the city. Street lights were almost nonexistent, or the ones there had been vandalized badly. The drug dealers, scattered as the yellow car followed by a half dozen police vehicles chased it through the dark street. The small Ford made a mistake. Its driver turned onto a street, blocked by construction. The car attempted to run the barricades and jump the ditch left by a trenching crew during the daylight hours. It didn't work. The car cartwheeled into a pile of gravel, landing upright. The driver's door swung open and the big man fell out. He scrambled to his feet and ran to the other side of the construction area.

Brian decided to reverse direction, if he could. He'd let the officers watch this end of the street, while he circled the block. It was like a salmon swimming upstream, but he got past the flock of cruisers coming in behind him, by driving in reverse, on the sidewalk. Once he was back on the intersecting street he sped down to the corner, killing his lights and siren as he turned right. He spotted the suspect heading through his headlights into a condemned apartment building. Brian threw the car's shift lever into park and killed the ignition. He grabbed his flashlight. Within seconds, he was on foot chasing the large man down the sidewalk toward an old condemned building.

The fugitive ran up the steps, tossing aside the plywood sheets, that forbid entry. Drawing his gun Weeder charged up the steps, just seconds behind him. Inside, Brian looked around the spooky room with his flashlight. In the dim light, the entrance was full of people in various stages of "crack" use. They were scattered around the wooden floor, both male and female, some clothed, some not. Aided by his bright flashlight, Weeder looked for a large man. All had the wrong clothing. Brian pressed on, through the door on the other side. The hallway was nearly pitch black. Pieces of broken wall board jutted out from the wall into the hallway. The remaining wallboard had a multitude of holes where gangs and graffiti artists had abused it. The place reeked of narcotic smoke, feces and vomit.

Brian stopped to listen. He heard foot steps – those of a big man – echoing through the building. The detective chose the next hallway, in the direction of the sound. He raced down the corridor, and up the flight of steps at the end. The stairwell boards were broken, uneven, with nails protruding. They moved as he stepped on them, but they held. At the top, he listened, but heard nothing. Slowly, and quietly, he walked down the hallway, past the long row of rooms. Many of the doorways lacked doors. Brian shined the light down the length of the hallway; several large rats objected by disappearing into rooms along the way.

With his best caution, Brian looked into the rooms, one by one. He knew fate was on his side, but that didn't slow down the adrenaline rush he felt. Nearing the end of the row, he felt an ever-increasing likelihood that the next room would be the one with the suspect. Brian heard a noise behind him. He turned and ran back toward the top of the stairs. His light showed it was only a rat dragging an old shoe. Disappointed, Brian felt the urge to shoot it, but resisted; even rats have to live somewhere, he considered. He turned and walked briskly to the room he had been about to enter. Slowly he approached it. He crouched low to the floor, to reduce his chance of being a good target. A quick pan of the light showed it to be empty. He moved toward the bedroom area of the dilapidated apartment. His light caught a moving figure appearing to have a gun pointed in his direction. At the last instant, he kept from firing at the figure, realizing it was only his own reflection in a fractured mirror. This place was giving him the creeps. Looking around the room, he noted a wall had been knocked out, leading into the next apartment. He approached the opening. His light showed the floor was also missing. Anyone coming this way would fall about six feet into a pile of debris, some of it sporting rusty nails. He examined the wallboard on the pile next to sharp sticks, for signs of blood. He hadn't heard anything big fall, nor had he seen any signs of blood. It wasn't likely Al Jones had come this way.

A rustling sound behind him caused Brian to turn quickly. He suspected another rat, but it turned out to be a much bigger one. Just as Brian's light reflected a glint of gold from the chain around Al's neck, a flame erupted a good two feet toward the detective. The bullet stuck Brian in the shoulder, above his flashlight. The impact drove him backwards over the brink onto the pile of rubble below. Everything seemed in slow motion as he fell, but the sudden stop knocked the breath out of him. He lost the light, but managed to keep the Glock glued to his gun hand. Slowly he slid head first, on his back into a dark void, where he took stock. Yes, he was still alive, and yes he had been wounded, but he had landed on some wallboard instead of the sharp wood. Everything seemed to work except his breathing. He waited agonizing seconds for his breath to return. Just as he was about to black out, he felt his chest move and the damp San Francisco air returning to his lungs. He heard a noise and looked upward. The big man had his flashlight and was looking for him. There was no time or place to hide. The light hit him in the eyes, blinding him. Somewhere in the back of Brian's memory, he remembered hunting frogs with his uncle. He remembered how it paralyzed them as it shined in their eyes. He wasn't a frog, but felt as helpless. He knew he had to act, if he could just remember how – the fall had nearly knocked him senseless.

A gruff voice, that of a big man, came from above. "Now who's got who?" Al said, pleased with himself. The grammar was incorrect, but the murderer didn't care.

Brian moved his gun hand slightly.

"Auught, I wouldn't do that, if I were you, cop," Al growled. "On the other hand, go ahead, let's get this over, since I have other things to do."

Brian didn't like the situation. He felt the hair stand up all along his spine, even though he was lying on his back. His feet pointed up toward the robber, as he lay on the pile. If the bolt was going to help, now would be a good time, he judged.

"You have a radio with you?"

"I left it in the car," Brian said honestly.

"Too bad. Might have given you a few more seconds to live while you called off the dogs."

"You're not going to get away, no matter what happens," Brian promised.

Al laughed, "Don't be so sure. I got a good luck charm."

"The charm doesn't bring you luck, Al," Brian warned, "It brings justice."

"Seems to work pretty well for me so far. I've survived everything."

"That's so the scales of justice can make sure you pay for your deeds. Your best chance is to surrender and take your chance in the courts."

"I don't think so. . . Besides," Al countered, "I've got to go before your buddies arrive." Al aimed carefully at Brian's chest, planning that the bullet would enter under his rib cage and make its way up into his heart, unimpeded by bone.

Brian realized his time had just run out. He decided that to do nothing would also mean his death. If he could wound or possibly kill the suspect, it would mean his life wasn't wasted. Slowly, he began to move the gun into a position to fire a shot before Al could notice, but the light was so bright, he couldn't tell where to shoot. The dust floating in the air didn't help. He gauged Al was right-handed, so his gun would be there. The flashlight would be in his left hand. His head would be somewhere in between and higher. His chest should be about a foot higher and to the left of the light. He felt the light move from his eyes onto his chest; he reasoned this was Al's target. With his own gun out of the spotlight, he tried to move more quickly.

A sudden, brilliant, flash of light exploded above him. It illuminated Al's sunburned face with a blue-white light. The giant man screamed and toppled over the edge onto the mass of sticks and nails that Brian had narrowly missed in his fall.

Weeder rolled to his feet. He scrambled around the pile to get a bead on Al. The fugitive was face down and Brian couldn't budge him to roll him over. He picked up the flashlight, which had fallen onto the pile of old sheetrock, rebar and other debris. He shined the light on the robber, wedged between wooden swords. It took half a minute, but Brian freed him enough to roll him over. Brian looked at the gold chain around Al's neck. From it hung a golden nut, and within the gold nut was fastened a white-hot bolt, still glowing from some kind of electrical discharge. The skin and clothing were badly charred. Al was still alive, barely. Brian leaned forward to listen to the murderer's last words.

"Thing!" he whispered, then died.

Brian tugged on the chain, pulling it around to access the clasp. He unlatched it and removed the chain. The bolt's color had returned to a silver again. Carefully, so he didn't burn himself, he wrapped the warm bolt and chain in an old rag he found on the pile, and put it in his pocket. Just before closing it up, he spoke to the bolt, "I don't know where you came from, or what you are, but thanks for saving my life again."

Brian didn't try to explain what had happened. Since he hadn't fired his gun, he wasn't put on administrative leave while the incident was investigated. Since Al's body was already badly sunburned, some reasoned the deep burns on his chest were somehow a result of the sunburn he received at sea. The coroner, puzzled by the event, listed the death as trauma to the heart during his fall.

* * *

The kiss lingered, followed by heavy breathing. Klazzi disengaged his arm to feel for the switch on the table lamp. The brilliant light, caused Brian to squint painfully, "Oooh, that's bright," he complained.

Klazzi twisted his arm to look at his watch, "I've got to leave now. Auntie Karen will be waiting for me." She unfolded herself from Brian's embrace, pulling her short skirt down into a more presentable position. "You know she's flying back with me to Seattle this evening, don't you?"

Brian pushed himself to a sitting position. "I think you mentioned it three or four times, Honey."

Klazzi stood in front of the full-length mirror adjusting her clothing. "She's going to help me rent out my cottage so I can make a little income to help with school expenses."

His attention raised a notch, "Then you're really going to do it?"

She tugged her panty hose down, then up, then left and right, doing a little dance until it felt right. Smiling at Brian in the mirror, she teased, "You do want me down here to be with you, don't you?"

His clothing still disheveled from their petting session, the part-time lover glided across the carpet of his living room, in his stocking-feet. Gently he wrapped his arms around her from behind. "You bet I do."

She giggled, "Now that's what I like — a man that can say 'I do'."

He kissed her neck. Looking over her shoulder into the mirror, he proceeded to button the blouse that he'd opened minutes earlier.

Klazzi tried to not impede him as she reached for the comb in her purse. "I never did get it straight, Mister," she glanced into the mirror, to make eye contact, "Am I moving in here or am I living with Auntie?"

"Your Aunt Karen would get really tired of me being over at her house all the time, don't you think?"

"Yeah – so?"

"And you'd get really tired of sleeping by yourself, wouldn't you?"

"Yes I would," she confessed, slipping into her street shoes. "So. . . ?"

"So, where do you want to stay?" he teased.

"Ask me. . ." she whispered.

"I just did," he said, nuzzling her neck, while enjoying the light fragrance of her cologne. She flinched slightly, when he planted a passionate kiss that sent tingles up and down her spine.

"No." She complained, "You didn't ask me to stay with you." Turning to look him in the eye, she buttoned his shirt, smoothing it as though the wrinkles would go away. Her voice almost had a lisp as she teased him again, "I just want to hear you say it."

He looked at her in silence; his brown eyes wandering back and forth across her pretty face. Seconds passed and the silence was replaced by more kissing.

Klazzi pushed him back. "I've really got to go," she pleaded. "Help me take my bags to the car?"

Brian nodded, picking up the valise, and makeup kit.

At the car, they hastily placed the items inside the trunk. Klazzi unlocked the driver's door, swinging it open to climb inside.

As she began to slide in, Brian pulled her back. He pulled her close, her eyes reflecting the amber street lights on for the evening. He whispered, "Please. . . come live with me."

Klazzi took a deep, passionate breath, her breasts rose upward as her arms grabbed Brian's head. She kissed him with a lengthy, french-kiss. At last, she released him with a promise, "I'll be down at the end of the quarter. I just have to transfer to a school nearby."

"Promise?"

"I promise," she winked, sliding behind the steering wheel. "Make sure you don't fill up my side of the bed with anyone."

Brian winked back, "Promise." Brian stepped away from the car, lest a tire run over his stocking-feet.

She started the car and shifted into drive. "You have the bolt?"

"I do."

"I love it when you say that," she grinned. Without further delay, she drove away, waving and watching him in the rear-view mirror.

* * *

Chapter 10

The Cult

P urging his apartment of space-robbing junk, Brian Weeder, sorted through gag-gifts, and old letters, trying to discard what he didn't want to keep. An envelope, obviously addressed by a young author, halted his progress. For a lengthy moment, he studied the bold, imperfectly printed letters forming the envelope's address: "To Uncle BRian." The detective was quite certain of the source, though he hadn't seen the yellowed envelope for nearly a decade. Removing the card and opening it, he read the contents of the handmade, Father's Day card from his goddaughter, Tiffany Lau.

Dear Uncle **BRian**,

HAPPY fatHers day. Cinse you do not have Kids of your own. . . pLease Let you have ME. . .

LOVE and KISSES

Tiff.

Below the writing was a hand-drawn picture of two rigid figures, standing side by side. The tall, thin man with dark hair, was obviously meant to represent Brian. The much shorter, black-haired girl, holding his hand, wore a dress covered with tiny red hearts. The name, "Tiff" was written at the edge of the page, and an arrow pointed to the girl.

Today, nearly a decade later, Brian could still feel the warmth of the personal greeting card; he bit his lower lip as he remembered the little five-year-old smiling and presenting him with the card. Carefully he returned the card to the envelope and gently placed it in the stack of things to keep.

* * *

At the office, the next day, Brian went into the file room to pick up a folder for a case he was reviewing. At the sign-out window, his long-time-friend, Jerry Lau, seemed to be having some kind of confrontation with the clerk.

"No! I need it now," Jerry complained. "If I wanted it tomorrow, I'd have asked for it tomorrow. Why can't you understand?"

The young female clerk was upset, but stuck up for herself, "I told you, Officer Lau, the file has not returned to the drawer, and I can't get it until it does."

Jerry rubbed his forehead, "But I told you, I returned it this morning by mistake, so you already have it."

"That may be true, but it has to be logged in — before I can log it back out!"

"But, I need it now!" he demanded, pounding his fist on the counter.

The clerk turned and pointed to the large stack of files on her desk. "It's in there somewhere, and I can't get it for you until I get down to it."

Jerry looked red in the face. He turned and walked away.

Brian dropped his note on the clerk's desk. "If you can get this file for me, I'd appreciate it." Glancing in Jerry's direction, he told the clerk, "I'll be back to pick it up in a few minutes."

Brian Weeder ran down the hallway after Jerry. He approached the Vice Detective at the water cooler. Brian knew from the way his friend's hand shook handling the small paper cup with water, a lot more than not having a file available to him was bothering him. Slowing his pace as he approached Detective Lau, Brian walked up to the water dispenser with a nice, smooth, nonchalant step. "Hi Jer, how's it goin'?"

Jerry turned to look, but didn't answer.

Brian bent down to take a paper cup from the dispenser. He filled it slowly while renewing his effort to get Jerry to speak. "Haven't seen you for a while. How's the wife and kids?"

Without answering, the Vice Detective slugged the water down and waited impatiently for another turn at the cooler.

When Brian stepped aside, Jerry stepped closer to the cooler to refill his cup for a second time. Lau's hand continued to shake as the water slowly filled his cup.

Brian studied Jerry's composure, realizing he wasn't likely to get small talk from his longtime friend. The parent of his godchild refused to make eye contact, and had the look of a man teetering on the edge of a tall building, ready to jump. The second cup of water lasted slightly longer than the first, but not long enough to be social.

"Want to talk about it Jer?"

There was no reply, just a blank stare into his empty paper cup.

"Come on Jer – we're friends. I'm a godparent to your kids – remember me?" Brian paused, then said softly, "Please. . . I really want to help."

Jerry wadded his cup into a ball and threw it hard into the trash bin. He backed up to the wall, tilted his head back and closed his eyes. With a grimace, he stood there shaking.

Brian finished his own water and discarded the cup. "Come on Jer, let's go where we can talk." He touched Jerry's elbow lightly, in a pleading, yet authoritative manner. Jerry followed him silently. Brian went down the hall to the conference room. Seeing it was empty, he opened the door, and flipped the "DO NOT ENTER" sign to active. He and Jerry went inside, closing the door behind them.

There was a deafening silence between the two men. Finally, Brian spoke softly, "Is it medical? Is something wrong with Liz?"

Jerry shook his head negatively, "No — nobody's sick, I'm just — " he paused, "I just — don't know what to do."

Brian sat patiently, listening.

"I'm having problems with Tiff."

A look of surprise appeared on Brian's face as he heard his godchild was the source of her father's distress. "Is she in trouble?"

Shaking his head no, Jerry resumed, "I can't seem to reason with her. She's running wild."

"Bad crowd?"

"Yeah, that — and more. . . A lot more."

"Drugs?"

"Just the light stuff so far." Heavy signs of distress formed on Lau's face as he spoke. "We had her in therapy, but she wouldn't stay."

"I see. . . " Brian made a grimacing face, "She's about fifteen now, isn't she?"

"Yeah, fifteen going on thirty."

"What have you tried?"

"I've tried everything. Nothing seems to get through her thick skin."

"She won't talk?"

"No. She just complains that we don't understand her."

"Do you?"

Lau looked down at the top of the conference table. Shaking his head he said, "I guess I don't." After a short pause, he added, "If I did, we wouldn't be having this conversation."

Brian nodded. "So what's she doing, besides refusing to talk it out?"

Jerry sighed, as he shook his head in frustration. "I grounded her a couple of times for coming home late and smelling like pot. She responded by climbing out the bedroom window late at night."

Brian rested an elbow on the table, "Want me to talk to her?"

Jerry looked up at Weeder. He paused then said, "She's not the sweet little girl she was the last time you saw her."

"Doesn't matter. She'll always be my goddaughter," Brian said, with conviction.

Jerry pulled a handkerchief from a coat pocket. Wiping his nose on the cloth; he breathed deeper. "It's your call Brian. I can't reach her – maybe you can."

Brian sat quietly for a moment, recalling his experiences with Tiffany. "Why don't I take her out to dinner tomorrow night. We haven't done that for a while."

"I don't think she'll go," Jerry said, with a shrug, "Her values have changed."

Brian gave Jerry a reassuring pat on the shoulder as he said, "I'll send her a personal invitation."

Later that same afternoon, Brian dropped by the school. He chatted with the student counselor regarding the problem, and gave him a hand written invitation, asking him to deliver it to Tiffany's classroom. Following that, Brian went to the florist and ordered two-dozen red roses. He attached a short reminder, asking her to have dinner with him tomorrow evening at seven. He called her house at bedtime, and asked her personally again. She consented.

The next afternoon, Brian cleaned up after work. Putting on his best suit, he dressed as he would for a date with an older woman, including a dab of aftershave. On his way to pick up

Tiffany, he stopped by a candy store and bought a fresh box of chocolates, as he always had, for their little dinner-dates.

At her home, Tiffany was ready to go, but instead of a pretty dress and a flower in her hair, she presented herself in freshly washed blue-jeans and a black sweatshirt. Her shoulder-length hair was combed, but was cut uneven — almost hacked in places. She gave Brian a quick peck on the cheek, instead of a more formal hug and kiss. As they left the house, Tiffany never bothered to wave a good-bye to her parents, leaving that task to her escort. The short ride to the restaurant was quiet, causing Brian to believe a lot was on this child's mind too.

Brian paid the waiter for seating them in a quiet area, where conversation was easier to hear. "So Tiff, it's been a while since we did this, eh?"

She nodded, but failed to make eye contact with her escort.

"How are things at school?" Brian asked, looking for an opening to get her to converse.

"Okay," she said, chewing her gum rapidly, but still refusing eye-contact.

Brian took a deep breath, "How are things at home?"

Tiffany played with her silverware as she looked around the room. "Fine," she lied.

"Do you have any plans for the summer?"

"Some."

"What kind of things are you going to do?"

"Uh. . . this and that."

The conversation went quiet for a period. Brian recognized the symptoms of a child trying to find her own identity. He knew the short answers were a method of isolating herself from friends and family, but he didn't like the signs. "Say Tiff, how'd you like to go to the beach with me this weekend. We might do a little fishing."

In the past, fishing was one of Tiffany's favorite activities. She looked at Brian with an excited look, then her eyes glazed over as she answered, "Uh, thanks, Brian, but I got stuff I gotta do."

The dinner was served and they ate quietly. Later, after they returned to the car, Brian started to take Tiffany for a drive up to Twin Peaks to look out over the city lights. In the past, this was another favorite activity following their dinner. As Brian turned onto the street to go up the hill, he sensed tension in his passenger. "Something wrong, Tiff?"

She rolled her eyes left and right as though she was afraid someone she knew might see her with the detective. "Yeah, I don't want to go up here."

Brian pulled to the curb and stopped. "I don't understand. Is there a problem?"

Tiffany raised her voice, "Yeah! I don't want to go up the stupid hill. Is that alright?"

He thought for moment, feeling some of the frustration Jerry showed yesterday. From her level of reluctance, he knew Tiffany was likely to jump out of the car, if he continued. "Okay, we won't go up the hill." Brian turned the car around, "Is there somewhere else you'd like to go?"

She started to answer "Home," but caught herself just in time. "You could let me out here, if you like."

Brian shook his head negatively. "Can't do that princess, you're priceless cargo and somebody'd steal you."

"It's alright; I'm grown up now."

Brian glanced at the clock on the car's radio. "What time is it?"

Reluctantly, Tiff looked at the same clock, "'Bout nine," she answered.

Making a face, by jutting his jaw outward, Brian fired a salvo, "That means you'll be an adult in about three more years, young lady."

A cheeky reply nearly came out, but she held it back.

Brian drove the car to the beach and parked it where they could watch the ghostly-white breakers roll to shore under the waning moon. "Tiff, Honey – I know things aren't the best for you right now, but believe me, they'll get better, if you just hang in there."

She sat silently.

Something told Brian, she had all the markings of a runaway child, and he didn't like it. Being aware and powerless to stop it, made the situation even worse. He talked to her for some time, trying to persuade her to cooperate with her parents, her teachers and the people who loved her. All of it was met with silence.

At last, he reached into his coat pocket and pulled out the necklace with the half-inch bolt. He turned on the car's courtesy light to show her. "I have something for you, Tiff. I don't know where you are going, or what fate has in store for you, but I want you to wear this to protect you." The bolt, was silver, the nut and chain were gold in color.

She looked at it with great suspicion, as though it was a bribe to dissuade her from her path.

"Think of it as an amulet," Brian encouraged. "You believe in astrology, and a bit of magic, don't you?"

Finally, it seemed he had her attention. "What is it?" she asked.

"It's something very special – just like you." he began, "If you wear this, I believe it will protect – and hopefully guide you through your trouble."

"It looks a little strange. . . " she said, with a trace of doubt.

"Yes it does, and I'm sure there is nothing else like it in the whole universe." He looked at her pretty face, in the dim car lighting, "Can I get you to wear it?"

Somehow, it appealed to her, but she held back. "What does it do?"

Brian unscrewed the bolt from the nut. He held the fastener near the light, to show the silver color. "If you are good and pure, it will change to a gold color. But if you are evil or bad, it won't be either silver or gold. Do you understand?"

She nodded. "But do I have to wear it or can I just carry it?"

Fearing she'd leave it behind, he coaxed, "Wear it every minute you can." Carefully screwing the bolt back into the nut, he added, "If you promise to wear it, for me, every time you leave the house, for the next year, I'll – Well, I'll think up something nice as a reward."

"That's too long Uncle Brian. I can't – "

"Well then, wear it for at least two months. It would make me feel a whole lot better. After that, you can return it to me, and I promise not to object."

Tiffany leaned forward, as Brian motioned her to do so. He slipped the chain over her jet-black hair and centered the bolt where she could look down on it. "Oh look. It's changing to gold." With the first hint of glee all evening, she chirped, "That's really neat!"

Brian breathed a sigh of relief. "Wear it every day, wherever you go, whenever you leave your house, do you understand?"

"Sure. I'll try."

"Don't forget – and never, never take it off away from home."

She squeezed Brian's arm briefly in response.

* * *

Jerry came to Brian's desk the next day. He handed Brian a cup of coffee. "I owe you one."

Looking up, Brian smiled, "What'd she say?"

"Said she had a great time."

"Think she was telling the truth?"

"Donno, but she seemed happier than I've seen her for months." Jerry sipped his own coffee, "But what's the deal with the amulet?"

"It's just that," Brian said, sipping his coffee.

Jerry pushed his eyebrows together, "Just what?"

"It's a magic amulet to protect her against dragons and ghouls."

The lowering of one eyebrow, showed Jerry wasn't buying into his story. "Well, whatever – it seemed to help," he admitted.

"She's got a long way to go Jer. But, keep a close eye on her for the next couple of months. And – whatever you do, make sure she wears that amulet anytime she leaves home, for any reason."

Jerry resumed his course toward his own desk, but stopped just long enough to mess up Weeder's hair, saying, "Sure. Sure. Whatever you say, Master Merlin. . . "

* * *

Tiffany sat on the bed in her room, counting the money from her Christmas savings. She felt badly about using it to buy drugs for Goyle, but Christmas was all about sacrifice, wasn't it? She knew she loved Goyle, and knew he loved her. His very touch sent tingles down her spine, and he could be so gentle. She hadn't been with him for several days, but he had promised her they'd be together again when she brought the heroin.

Carefully, she wrapped the bills and coins in a scarf, tying the ends together in a knot. She picked up her shoes and quietly tiptoed across the floor, avoiding the squeaky board under the carpet. She shoved the money into her pants-pocket and unlatched the window, silently. Several seconds later, she was out the window, running through the deep shadows of the yards along the street. When she was nearly a block away, she paused to slip into her shoes and place an old baseball cap over her head. She pushed the shoulder-length, jet-black hair up inside the cap, hiding the fact she was female. Tiffany adjusted Brian's necklace, positioning the bolt between her small breasts. As it touched her hand, it felt slightly warm to the touch in the damp, foggy San Francisco air. Perhaps it was still warm from being in the house, and her bulky winter coat retained the heat? She couldn't stop to think about it now; it was nearly time for the transit bus to arrive at the corner. She hurried.

Twenty minutes later, the bus dropped her at Union Square. Wasting no time, she made her way to the park above the underground parking garage. A chilly breeze, blowing from under the fog, compelled her to grab her hat, before it could become airborne.

Tiffany looked around the park; her drug contact was late. An old, grey-haired man sat on a bench nearby, huddled against the cold, as he nursed his bottle of red wine. To the south, a young couple, oblivious to everyone, cuddled on a bench, necking. Two young people, about her age, sitting on separate benches did their best to protect themselves from the heat-stealing, foggy breeze; they were runaways, no doubt. She thought about it for an instant, perhaps that would be her soon. She discarded the thought. Goyle would never allow her to become that desperate. She would join his gang and become his woman. Together, they would travel and live from day to day off the fat of the land.

Finding an empty bench, she sat facing the direction that her contact would come. As she sat down, the cold, damp bench sucked heat from her legs and bottom, making her tense even more. Quickly she unzipped her coat and tried to secure it over her knees as she pressed them up against her chest. It was no use; the coat wasn't large enough. She arranged the gold chain and bolt again, before re-zipping her coat.

She wished Goyle was there. Remembering the two times they made love, she slipped her hands in her coat pockets and rubbed her tummy. His tattoo was so cool. Perhaps she'd get a tattoo; maybe it would have an evil face like the gargoyle on Goyle's chest. Actually, his tattoo started on his chest and the handle went all the way down into his underwear. She knew, because she had seen it for herself.

"Ah, there's my contact – the Foonie," she thought. "Now, I can get the drugs and meet Goyle at the camp, in Golden Gate Park, within the hour." Tiffany hurried over to the Foonie. Her teeth chattered as she spoke, "Have any 'Mexican Brown' with you tonight?"

The young man, dressed in black, from head to toe, turned to see who spoke. "Ah, my child, I see you're back. I feared we had missed each other, this eve."

Tiffany came closer, looking up into his clean-shaven face. His combed, short hair fluttered loosely in the icy breeze. She clutched the collar on her own coat against the wind, "Did you bring anything tonight?"

"Ah my child, you should have given me more notice."

"More notice?" Tiffany stiffened, partly against the wind and partly because of his response, "I thought you told me you always had supplies close at hand, Subee."

"Oh I do, my child, but almost never on my person."

Her heart sank. Her nose was numb with cold, and her ears had begun to ache; what more could go wrong?

The Foonie unfolded the collar of his overcoat, positioning it as a wind break, for his own comfort. "If you desire it tonight, we can get it." He looked around the area suspiciously, before asking, "Did you bring payment?"

Tiffany removed a hand from her coat pocket and thrust it into the pocket of her tight jeans, where she had put the money.

"Oh no, dear child," he waved, and shook his head, "Not here, we must go to the 'haven' across town."

"I can't do that," Tiffany protested, "I have to meet a Goyle in a few minutes."

He gently put a hand on her shoulder, "No matter. I shall have you back within the blink of an eye."

"You have a car?" she asked, with an amazement that a disciple of the cult would possess such a worldly object.

"Of course my dear," glancing around a second time, he added, "Shall we go?"

She felt uneasy about this man. He had strange manners. His speech was peculiar; even the way that he dressed was weird. Perhaps he felt the same about her? Her gut feeling was to reverse direction and go home, but it wasn't the first time she had bought junk from Subee. In the beginning, he had given her marijuana. On other nights, he had offered her a place to spend the night off the chilly, damp streets. Goyle didn't like him, but Goyle disliked nearly everyone.

Against her better judgment, Tiffany followed the Foonie into the parking garage below. From behind, she watched his long, black overcoat fall against his black leather boots with each step. It was silly to think of him as Count Dracula, but something about him made her feel painfully uncomfortable.

The drive through town was uneventful, the heater in the modest, small car, felt good against her nearly frozen legs. She

D.Malisch

relaxed a bit, but remained quiet. No conversation passed between the young delinquent and the Foonie driver.

At last, the car turned into a small, narrow, dark driveway and tilted downward into an underground garage, large enough for a single, small car. They exited the car into the nearly pitch-black darkness. The driver produced a small penlight and lighted the path for Tiffany to stumble her way up a flight of old wooden steps, into an unlighted room above the garage. Once inside, the Foonie, turned on the room lights, showing a plain, older-style dining area, complete with yellowed walls and heavily worn linoleum flooring. Except for a very old refrigerator and old dilapidated wooden table, the kitchen and dining areas were bare. Tiffany followed the man into the next room, their footsteps echoing against the bare walls as they traveled.

The second room was darkened, but a light under the door on the far side of the room gave hope they had finally arrived and Tiffany could, at last, finish the transaction.

Her guide opened the door, waiting until she entered before joining her. Inside, a small man, clean shaven, with a similar hair cut as her guide, sat at a table, counting money. He glanced up as they entered, but continued his count until he exhausted the coins held in his hand. "What have we here?" he questioned.

"We have a disciple in need," Subee replied.

Suddenly it occurred to Tiffany she was in a strange place with two strange men she didn't know nor like – and there was no clear path of escape. She heard the door latch behind her. She turned to look at her guide, who blocked exit through the door behind him. Feeling very uneasy, Tiffany looked back at the person counting the money. "I just came here to get a bag of 'Mexican Brown'," she said, almost apologetically. She heard the sound of a key being pulled from the locked door behind her.

Subee tried to appease her by saying, "The Master Far-Wind will see to all of your true needs now."

A terrible sense of error, filled her. Her only immediate need was to get out – and away – far away from there. "Uh – I changed my mind, Subee." Backing toward the locked door, she motioned for him to unlock it, "I'll get it another time," she said, trying to smile.

"My child," in slow, soothing tones, the Master implored, "No need to be frightened. We are all friends here."

She wasn't convinced, even by the slightest amount.

The Master stood up from his table of money and walked around it toward her. "Please," he said, reaching toward her.

Tiffany shied away.

"Is it drugs you want, my child?"

No response.

"You look tired. Perhaps something to relax you?" On que, Subee handed Far-Wind a soft drink, from a small refrigerator, kept beside the money table. As he handed the bottle to Tiffany, he twisted the cap, removing it. There was no sound of escaping carbon dioxide gas. Had the drink been altered? "Here, my daughter, drink this, it will make you feel better."

Her mouth had become dry, but drinking anything was not her first priority; she resisted.

"Go on, child; take it."

She looked at him, the terror showing in her eyes.

"You think I have tainted your drink?" he apologized, using slow, placid speech.

Gently, she nodded yes.

The Master Far-Wind handed the bottle to Subee, who tilted it up and pretended to drink, but never swallowed.

Subee handed the bottle back to the Master.

Far-Wind set the bottle on the edge of the table and reached for a small wooden box near the wall. Opening it, he pulled out a plastic packet of brown powder, a shade lighter than the color of brown sugar. He handed the packet to Tiffany, "Here you are, my dear. This is what you came for, wasn't it?"

Tiffany stared first at the bag, then at the Master. She made no move to take it.

"Go on, my dear," he urged, "I won't even charge you this time."

Seconds passed, as she looked first at the bag – then at the Master. Slowly, she reached for the bag held in the unwavering hand of the Master. She took the packet and put it in her coat pocket. As Tiffany turned toward the door, she looked toward Subee for the key.

Subee handed the key to Far-Wind.

Tiffany looked back at the Master.

"My child, must you leave so soon?" His voice was smooth, nearly tranquilizing. "Let us toast our friendship." On que, Subee handed him another soft drink, taking one for himself. The caps hissed as they were twisted and removed from the bottles. The Master reached for Tiffany's bottle, sitting on the table. When she wouldn't accept it, he offered her his own. She took it.

The Master drank deeply from the bottle Tiffany refused. Subee drank from his bottle. Tiffany sipped her drink, cautiously at first – then faster in an effort to leave as soon as possible.

This was her night for mistakes. By the time her bottle was half empty, she realized she had been drugged. They knew somehow; she would choose the Master's bottle, which was unsafe. The drug began to overrun her consciousness, everything became confusing and unimportant – she fell to the floor.

Far-Wind nodded and returned the key to Subee, who unlocked the door and disappeared down a dark hallway for a moment. He returned a minute later with two female members of the cult. They looked at the Master after entering the room. Without pointing, he stated authoritatively, "You have a new sister. Prepare her."

"Yes Master!" they said in unison. They knelt and began to remove Tiffany's clothing. They stripped her bare and removed all valuables from her pockets, while the Master watched. As one sister held her, the other hacked off her shoulder-length hair. Everything, except clothing and hair, was placed in a small cardboard box and set on a chair. A third sister arrived with a plain green smock, made by the cult. Tiffany, barely conscious, was quickly dressed and taken down the hallway to a programming room.

The third matron, picked up the clothing for future use, and as she turned to leave, she heard the Master say, "Bring her to me when she's prepared. I wish to plant my seed in her." The young woman did not look at him; she simply nodded and left the room quickly.

Aided by two women, Tiffany stepped into the darkened room, still groggy from her experience. Suddenly, her guides shoved her forward, toward the floor, and retreated. The door slammed loudly behind her. The bare floor was dirty, as though it hadn't been mopped or swept for weeks. She pushed herself upward to get to her feet. The near total darkness hampered her ability to gain her balance. Back on her feet, she wobbled badly as she tried to walk, partly because of the drugs and partly because of the strange and foreign surroundings. Slowly, she felt her way around the limits of the room, past the boarded-up-window, searching for the door. When she found it, there was no doorknob on her side. She searched in vain, again, for a light switch. After several minutes, she decided there might be a lamp hanging from the ceiling that she could turn on. Carefully, and methodically, she crisscrossed the room, feeling for furniture, lest she trip over it. There was no furniture and no indication of any lighting. After several hours of exploration, she found herself getting tired and wanted something – anything to sit on, to rest. There was nothing except the dirty, bare floor in the room.

* * *

An evil looking man, dressed totally in black, offered Brian a spoon heaping with white powder. When Brian didn't open his mouth, the man insisted. Brian struggled to push the man's arm away, but realized his arms were tied to the chair where he was sitting. He clenched his mouth shut, but the man continued to try to force it open. Brian resisted. The man reached for a pair of electrical wires. He tied one around Brian's neck, and just as he touched the other to the detective's nose, a bell sounded.

Brian bolted upright from his bed, gasping for breath. In the blackness, of his bedroom, he realized it was only a dream. The bell sounded again. Brian breathed a sigh of relief and picked up the telephone.

"Weeder here," he said, glancing at the illuminated clock. The hour was shortly after six in the morning.

"Brian, this is Jerry."

"Morning Jer. What's up?" Brian yawned softly.

"She's gone again."

"Tiff?" Brian asked in disbelief.

"Yeah. Liz found her bed empty this morning."

Brian sighed. "How long's she been gone?"

Jerry sounded upset, "We don't know yet."

Brian realized this problem was too close for Jerry to act rationally; he'd have to guide Jerry through the procedures. "Any clothing or money missing?"

"Just her coat so far. Haven't had time to check everything."

Crossing his fingers, Brian asked, "Did she leave the amulet behind?"

"How should I know!" Jerry exploded, "I called you for help. I've got a daughter that's missing, why should I care if some trinket is gone?"

"I know, Jer, but it's important."

"How can it be more important than Tiff?"

"It isn't Jer, but – "

"Some godparent you are – "

Before Jerry could finish, his wife, Liz took the phone. "Hello Brian, it's Liz."

Weeder gave a sigh of relief, "Liz, this is important. I want to know if Tiff has that necklace I gave her when we had dinner?"

Liz, also distraught, seemed a bit more composed as she fought her loss. "I don't know, Brian. Let me look." The phone went silent for a moment while she searched. When she came back on the line, she said, "It's not on her jewelry-stand, where I saw it last evening. Why? What's it matter? Was it valuable?"

"I can't explain now, Liz, but I know it will protect her. Let me speak with Jer again?"

The line was quiet for several seconds before Jerry's voice appeared on the other end. "What are we going to do, Brian?"

Weeder glanced at his watch, "Get ready to go and I'll pick you up in fifteen minutes." Struggling to dress himself with one hand and hold the phone in the other, Brian tried to comfort his friend, "Don't worry Jer, we'll find her."

There was a muffled grunt of anguish at the other end, before the phone went dead.

Weeder arrived twenty minutes later, and was quickly invited inside. Liz and Tiffany's younger brother, Herman, were still wearing their bed-clothing, as they showed Brian into Tiffany's room. In another part of the house, Jerry was busy strapping on his service weapon.

Brian questioned Liz as he waited. "When Tiffany ran away in the past, do you know where she went?"

"We could never get her to say, Brian."

Weeder flinched; he'd need more clues than that, to began any effective search. "Do you know any of her friends?"

"A couple, but not many of her friends have come over lately."

"Uncle Brian, I think they hang out at the park down by Lincoln Street?"

Liz turned to look at her son, "How do you know that?"

Sensing his mother might think he'd been hanging around there too; he hesitated briefly. "I won't get in trouble if I tell you will I?"

Liz bent down to look him in the eye. "No! Herm, this is very important, we have to know the truth." She touched him on the shoulder, "But don't make up anything. Your sister's life could depend on you telling the truth."

Herman, five years younger than his sister, concentrated on his mother's face as he spoke, "I heard her on the phone, talking with some guy a bunch of times last week." He made a serious face as he thought hard, "I think the guy's name was 'Girl' or somthin' like that. Anyway, he called lots of times."

Brian interrupted, "Did you listen in from another phone or did you just hear her talking?"

"You kiddin'? She closed her door and turned up the radio. I couldn' hear nothin' 'cept from dad's phone, in the room where he works."

Brian glanced around the bedroom, taking mental notes. Tiffany's space was unusually neat for a teenager. Her things were all placed in an orderly fashion, right down to the drawings hanging on her bulletin board. Seeming out of place, in an otherwise benign cluster of drawings, a drawing of a double-bladed axe snagged Brian's attention. Its head had the usual cutting blade on one side, and a gargoyle's head on the opposing side. Neatly stenciled, at the bottom of drawing, the name "GOYLE" stood, in an old-English font. Brian reasoned, the name "girl" didn't seem plausible, but the abbreviated form of gargoyle or "Goyle" might have been what Herman heard. "Think carefully, Herman, could the boy's name have been 'Goyle', instead?"

The boy's face lit up, "Yeah! That's it. Kinda like the way Rick says 'girl'."

Weeder looked puzzled, "Who's Rick?"

"Oh he's my best friend."

"Your best friend?"

"Yeah. And he's from New Yoke or somethin'."

"Oh, you mean he's from New York, back East?"

"Yeah that's right."

Brian breathed a sigh of relief, "Do you think this Goyle was her boyfriend?"

"Donno," he said, tilting his head to look up at the detective, "It's kinda hard to tell sometimes." Wiping his nose on the back of his pajama sleeve, he added, "She don't want me to know who she likes."

"Do you remember exactly what you heard her say?"

Shaking his head, Herman admitted, "No. All's I remember was he wanted her to buy some stuff and bring it to him. She said she'd get it from Subee."

Jerry came back into the room just in time to hear his son's last comment. "Herman! Why didn't you tell us this before?"

Herman cringed, "Am I in trouble?"

Afraid Jerry's harsh words would alienate Herman and his cooperation, Brian gave Jerry a look of disapproval.

Jerry caught the facial expression. Temporarily putting aside his strong concern for Tiffany, Jerry squatted down to look Herman in the eye. "No son, you aren't in trouble, but we are going to have little talk, just you and I — after school tonight, do you understand?"

"Sounds like I'm in trouble again," he lamented.

Jerry stood up again. Suddenly appreciating his remaining child more, he ruffled the uncombed hair on the boy's head.

Nodding toward the door, as a sign to Brian, Jerry indicated he was ready to leave.

A tug on Brian's coat pulled him up short. He turned to see Liz holding onto it. She waited until her husband was out the front door before saying, "Look out for him, will you? He's pretty upset with all this."

Weeder nodded and gave her a wink before rushing to catch up with Jerry.

Their first stop was at the Golden Gate Park, where Lincoln touches it. Except for a few homeless looking through the trash cans, or sleeping near the sheltering bushes, the part-time soccer field was empty. The morning sun glinted on something shiny, in the grass. Brian bent to pick it up. He paused and ripped a page from his notebook to drop over the object before touching it.

"What do you have?"

"Looks like a syringe." Brian held it up to see light through it. A film inside the syringe told him it was used. "Probably dropped by Florence Nightingale," Brian said, sourly.

"I'll bet!" Jerry agreed, catching the sad humor. As thought of his missing daughter returned, he feared for her safety, and a look of sadness fell on his face.

"Relax Jerry; it's early yet." Seeing a discarded, plastic drink bottle with a re-closable lid, Brian dropped the used needle inside the bottle, sealed it and dropped it in the closest trash barrel.

Weeder made his way over to a middle-aged lady who was looking through the other trash-barrels, for aluminum cans. She looked cold, but was bundled up in an old coat, its insulation erupting in random places. Blotches of dirt highlighted her wrinkled face as though the black makeup had found a place to hide from soap. He watched her extend the full length of her arm into the barrel for a treasure, which seemed to be just beyond her reach. The heavy trash barrel righted itself with a thump as she stood upright without the aluminum can. Brian pulled the barrel forward and using his longer arm, pulled the sticky item free from the bottom.

"That's my can, Mister!" the toothless woman said defensively.

The detective handed her the can. She took it suspiciously, stowing it in her bag. She moved to the next barrel and began to unload items on the ground for better access to the bottom. Finding more riches, she struggled again to reach the two cans on the bottom. Without prompting, Brian stepped forward, and retrieved them for her. The straggle-haired woman took them, giving him a big toothless grin for receipt. "Say Ma'am," Brian struggled with words, attempting to get the woman to identify with him, "Do you have any children?"

Her smile dissolved, leaving a look of distrust.

Weeder pointed to Jerry, who partly in skepticism and partly in disgust for her body odor, stood some twenty feet away. "That man lost his daughter last night. We think she may have come here to meet someone."

The woman took the two cans from Brian and dropped them in her bag. She shook the bag to make room for more aluminum. Twisting the top of the sack, she rested it on a bench while tying a rope around the opening. Cautiously, she glanced upward at Jerry. "He the father?"

"Yes, Ma'am."

"Need take better care," she growled.

"Pardon?"

"He needs to take better care of his family, so they don' need run away," her hoarse voice rose in volume.

"Did you see her?"

"Donno – " she said, looking up at Brian, "Mebe." She studied Weeder for a moment, "Who you?"

"Me?"

"Yeah?"

"I'm Detec – er – I'm his friend." Nodding toward Lau, Weeder said, "He's really a good father."

"Yeah?" she said skeptically.

"Yeah," he emphasized.

She looked back at Jerry. "Then why he no ask?"

"He's hurt too badly to ask."

"Heart hurts?" she asked, while continuing to work with her bag of cans.

"Yeah, that's right."

The woman dropped her bag of cans back on the park bench. Taking a deep breath, she leaned backward as she poked her skirt, which more closely resembled an old shower curtain, back into the belt she had underneath. When she finished, she turned and flopped down on the bench beside her bag. "What her name?"

"Her name is Tiffany."

"Don' see."

"You haven't seen her?"

"No," she said, removing her left shoe and turning it upside down to allow a piece of gravel to fall out.

"She's about this tall," Brian described, "she has black hair and may have a gold necklace with a gold bolt hanging around her neck."

Without looking up, the old lady said with a rejective tone, "No see."

Brian took out his wallet. Opening it, he removed ten dollars. He handed the bill folded between his first and second fingers.

The woman looked up. Startled by what she saw, she hesitated. She flashed another toothless grin at Brian, and took the bill. Looking first left, then right, to see who might be watching, she rammed the paper down between her breasts, adjusting it so it would be there when she needed it and wouldn't poke her in the meantime. As though movement pained her, she forced herself from the park bench to her feet, she shouldered her bag and hefted the protective walking stick she had been carrying. Turning to walk to the next barrel on her daily route, she paused. "Some," she said, pointing with her stick toward a dense thicket across the clearing, "Kids. They's here a lot. Use drugs. I no like drugs. I stay away. . . they mean. Real mean. They stay over there two, three hundred paces. Sleep there all times." She turned toward Brian to see if he was listening. "Ask 'em?"

"I will," Brian promised, "Thank you."

The bag-lady turned and moved down the path with a distinctive, but unique shuffle.

Ten minutes later, after fighting their way through thick brush until they found a path, Brian and Jerry stopped to catch their breath. Brian picked cobwebs and pieces of foliage from his pants and sports-coat. "Wish we'd found this path about twenty minutes ago."

403

Jerry nodded, brushing debris from his own clothing. "Wouldn't hurt my feelings if the ground's keepers cut everything high enough so you could walk under it."

A twig snapped nearby, causing the detectives to cease conversation. They listened for a moment, hearing nothing more. Brian whispered, "Their camp must be just down this path. Let's go in quietly and get a good look instead of spooking them."

Jerry nodded agreement.

Fifty feet down the path, they encountered a small clearing with six or seven youths sleeping at random angles. Most were covered with blankets or thick cardboard. Without moving closer, they tried to see faces, hoping Tiffany would be among the sleepers.

Whispering as he pointed, Brian asked, "Don't see her anyplace Jer. Do you?"

Disappointed, Jerry sighed quietly, "No, I don't."

"Let's go in quietly." Brian moved carefully around the group for a better look.

"Cops!" a male voice from the bushes yelled. The sound of thrashing brush and snapping twigs pursued his disappearance. Except for a couple of heavy sleepers, the group came alive and scrambled to escape in every direction.

Brian and Jerry each grabbed one of the males for questioning. Of the two females in the group, one fled, the second remained asleep on the ground with her male companion.

The captured young men fought hard, but the detectives had experience on their side as they worked to maintain control.

"Settle down," Brian demanded. "We just want to ask you a few questions."

The youth continued to resist Brian's best attempts to restrain him. Together, they struggled until their legs became entangled. Realizing he was about to lose control, Brian toppled the scratching, cursing combatant in such a way as to use him for a cushion. As the young man fell backwards, the detective's impact knocked the wind from him. Resistance ceased, temporarily.

Jerry pushed his captive into the sharp thorns of a pyracantha bush, and held him there. The unyielding, long, sharp thorns forced the youth to hold still.

Resting on top of the unshaven, grubby captive he'd forced down, Weeder repeated his previous claim, "We're just looking for someone, and if you'll help us, we'll let you go."

The uncooperative youth, under the detective, gasped for air to fill his lungs. To maintain a better control, Weeder pulled the struggling youth's body forward while shoving a loose arm under the two of them. The detective pinned the offending arm by shifting his own body weight on the angry youth. The young man's other arm was under Brian's tight grip. Several deep breaths later, the delinquent answered by spitting on Brian's face.

Weeder was upset, but expected it; after all, it wasn't anything he hadn't already experienced in his career with the force. Grabbing a blanket nearby, he covered the captive's mouth, preventing a second spitting experience. "You may as well take it easy and answer some questions, or we'll take you to the station, and you can answer the questions there. It's up to you."

The captive huffed and puffed, struggling with all of his might to free himself from Brian's control. Once he realized he was wasting his time, he calmed slightly.

Brian looked around the camp; he and Jerry each had a captive. The remaining male and female were in a stupor or asleep nearby. Looking back at the belligerent youngster under him, he asked again, "We want some information from you. If you give it to us, we'll let you go. If you don't – we'll take you to the station and get it there. Do you want to talk here?"

The captive grunted.

"I'll take that as a 'yes'," Brian smiled lightly. Moving the blanket from the uncooperative man's face he asked, "Do you know Tiffany Lau?"

"Never heard of her," he said defiantly.

"You're not helping," Brian's voice trailed off. "And if you don't help, we'll have to get nasty."

"You're breakin' my arm," he complained.

"Well, the sooner you answer our questions, the sooner I can let you go."

The aging-teenager wiggled unsuccessfully to free himself, then realized again, that escape was not likely to happen. "She's one of Goyle's bitches," the youth grunted.

Brian looked up at Jerry, who was inflamed by the statement. "Cool it Jer!" Turning his attention back on the man beneath him, Weeder pressed him, "When was the last time you saw her?"

No answer.

"When was the last time you saw her?"

Still, no reply.

Brian shifted his weight, applying more pressure onto the body beneath him.

The young man grunted loudly, struggling to breathe for several seconds, "About three days ago," he wheezed, "She was with Goyle."

"And — where can I find Goyle?"

The aging-youth tilted his head forward, nodding toward the sleeping couple next to them. "That's him sleeping there, with his bitch."

"I see," Brian said, relaxing just a bit. "Well, I definitely want to ask him some questions, but I'm not sure you've answered everything I want to know, so — " The detective reached for his handcuffs and snapped one on the arm he was holding. "I'm going to let you up now, but just so you hang around until I get the answers I'm looking for, you're going to relax next to this tree." Brian pulled him to his feet and pushed his back against a small tree. He cuffed the young man to the trunk for security.

Together, Brian and Jerry questioned the second captive, who was more cooperative, but was new to the group and knew little.

"Do you know Tiffany Lau?"

"No, I don't officer. I just arrived in the city yesterday, from L.A.," he paused to glance around the thicket enclosed area. "I don't know any of these guys very well."

"What are you doing with them?"

"They needed someone as a lookout while they did something."

"What were they doing?" Jerry asked.

"They wouldn't tell me, 'cause I'm new. They just offered me some 'speed' and place to crash."

"Are you sure?" Jerry questioned. He shoved the youth back into the thorny bush to make his point.

The boy drew a sharp breath, "Please don't!" he pleaded. "I'm telling you the truth."

Jerry relaxed, allowing the youth freedom to move. "Stick around until we say you can go."

The young man nodded and breathed a sigh of relief not to be in such a thorny situation.

Brian and Jerry approached the couple on the ground. Jerry peeled the blanket from them. The girl, looked to be about Tiffany's age. Her arms showed signs of drug abuse, but she appeared to be breathing normally. Brian lifted an eyelid. She brought her hand up in protest, but didn't respond quickly.

Next to the couple, were the telltale signs of white powder, a spoon, syringe, candle and restricting cord.

"Looks like they both took a hit recently," Brian sighed.

Nodding, Jerry agreed, "Won't be much good for questioning for several more hours."

The youth handcuffed to the tree struggled to free himself, causing Brian to look up temporarily. Seeing the handcuffs were restraining the youth, the detective looked back at the male, sleeping before him. There were gang symbols tattooed on the knuckles of his hand. Weeder checked the female. She too, had similar gang markings. Brian looked up at the youth just released from the pyracantha; there were no markings. Curious, Weeder got up and walked behind the tree, inspecting the hands of his captive. He too had similar gang markings between his fingers. The young male continued to struggle as Brian looked him over closely. The dark, stringy hair partly covered his face. Brian pushed the long-greasy strands back to look at the captive's forehead. There were other symbols beneath. The man leaned sideways, objecting to Brian's touch. His shirttail lifted showing a patch of skin. On the skin, Brian got a brief glimpse of an axe handle. Quickly, he caught the edge of the shirt and lifted it. On the stomach, extending down into his underwear, was a tattoo he had seen before. The head of the axe had a blade on the left side and the head of a gargoyle on the right side. It was the same as the drawing in Tiffany's room. Brian grabbed him by the throat; he pressed him against the tree. "You're Goyle!" he yelled.

"No! He's Goyle," the young man protested, moving the eyes of his pinned head toward the sleeping figure.

"No chance, buddy," Brian gritted his teeth. "Now, what have you done with Tiff?"

Jerry rushed to them, grabbing the man's throat over the top of Brian's hands, "Where is she?" he screamed!

No answer.

Weeder pushed away and dragged Jerry back. "We've got to do this with more finesse," he whispered to Lau, "play along with me." Brian turned to the visiting teenager, standing by the pyracantha bush. "You can go now; we're through questioning you. But don't come back here. Do you understand?"

The grateful youth nodded and left quickly.

Brian drew his Glock 44. He pointed the barrel in the air and cocked it, loading a shell in the chamber. Slowly he lowered it. "I'd like an answer, please," he said menacingly.

"Go to hell!" the handcuffed man spit.

Slowly, the detective lowered the gun until it pointed at Goyle's chest. "In case you hadn't noticed, this is a real gun, and it may just be the last thing you ever see."

He stood silently.

Brian continued to lower the gun, pointing it between the man's knees, which were spread wide as he was tethered to the tree. The Glock spit out a bullet which tore into the tree, splintering the bark and shaking the trunk. The sharp retort, stung the ears, the spent shell bounced on the ground, still hot.

Goyle shouted, an obscenity of surprise. .

Brian stood silently, listening to the heavy breathing coming from Jerry on his left. Raising the gun upward slightly, he aimed at the crotch of the baggy pants. He artificially induced a slight shaking motion as he took bead, knowing Goyle would really take notice. "On the count of three – " Brian warned.

Goyle pulled desperately against his handcuffs. "You bastards are crazy."

"You better answer," Jerry advised, "He's getting shaky!"

"One!"

"He'll nail your butt, Goyle. I've seen him do it before," Jerry lied.

"Two!" Weeder, said loudly.

"Wait! Wait! Don't shoot," Goyle begged, "I'll tell you what I know."

Brian lowered his automatic and stepped closer. "Where is she?" he demanded.

"I don't know."

With a sigh of discouragement, Brian stepped back and raised his Glock again.

Goyle pleaded, "No, wait! It's the truth. I really don't know where she is." He threw his head back against the tree as he talked. "She was supposed to bring me some 'Mexican Brown' last night, but she didn't show up."

Brian lowered his weapon again and stepped closer. "Who was she buying it from?"

"A guy named, Subee. He sells over near the Union Street garage."

"What's he look like?"

"He's a stupid Foonie. I hate them creeps!"

"So you send an innocent child over there to buy your daily fix."

"Look man!" Goyle pleaded, "It's part of the initiation. All bitches have to do it. 'Sides, I don't have no cash."

Brian popped the clip from his Glock and ejected the live round from the chamber. He picked up the live cartridge putting it back in the clip. In his pocket, he located an extra cartridge to replace the one spent and snapped the clip back into the handle.

Weeder glanced around the area, strewn with trash from fast food places. A clutter of expensive electronic toys, "boom-boxes", CD-players and other junk, dotted the sleeping area. "Tell me Goyle, if you don't have cash, how do you get money for all your food and toys?"

The gang leader swung his head from side to side in protest, "Look man! I can't tell you everything."

"Why not Goyle? You afraid of us?" Brian baited him.

"Hell no!" he ejected, "We'd tear you apart." His eyes looked as though they were about to pop out of his head, "We do worse every night." Realizing his loose bragging had opened him for more questioning, he fell silent.

"Go on Goyle, tell us about it."

He remained silent.

Brian reached in his pocket for the key to the handcuffs. Dangling in front of the defiant man, he coaxed, "You want to be free? Then you better tell us now."

More silence followed.

Brian put his weapon away. He turned and pulled lightly on Jerry's elbow, indicating it was time to leave.

"Hey! Wait! What about me?"

"What about you, big man?" Brian responded, not looking back. "You're a big boy now. Your gang members will find you some time today." Turning to look back, the detective added, "They're not afraid of us, they'll be back soon – won't they?" With a shrug he turned, pretending to leave again. Over his shoulder he said, "Well, if not today, maybe they'll be back in a couple of days, won't they?"

His mouth dry, Goyle worried, "Wait! You win. I'll tell you what you want to know."

The detectives exchanged glances and turned back toward their prisoner.

"Okay Goyle, what kind of mischief have you been up to these nights?"

"It ain't much, we just hold up some 'johns', take their cash and sometimes borrow their cars for joy rides."

"Now tell me Goyle, since you are so ugly, how would you get a 'john' to let you in his car?"

"I send one of the young bitches down to hook him."

411

D.Malisch

"Explain?"

Speaking softly; with his gaze centered on the ground in front of him; Goyle elaborated. "The 'johns' like 'em young and innocent, so I send a couple of the young-bitches down around the clubs to offer sex to these guys as they pass by. Once they are in the car, she tells 'em to drive up to Twin Peaks, where they can get it on. We watch for our bitch to come up the hill, and zero in on the car. When she sees us, she opens the door for us and we jump in, take his keys and money." Goyle looked up, "The johns' usually are so worried we'll tell the cops they were with a minor, that they never report it. We just tell the johns' we'll drop the car off at the base of the hill when we finish drivin' it around."

Suddenly, the light went on in Brian's head. He remembered Tiffany refusing to go up the hill after they had dinner. She was protecting her godfather from attack by the gang. Then it hit him, if Tiff had been involved in a crime against someone and she touched the bolt, she'd likely be punished in some way. If anyone was killed, her punishment could be severe. "You guys ever seriously hurt anyone?"

"Na. Na, we just rough 'em up a bit, have a little fun, you know – "

Brian breathed a sigh of relief. Walking around behind Goyle, he used the handcuff key and released him.

The man rubbed his wrists, trying to erase the red marks incurred during his struggle to free himself.

Jerry, reflecting what he'd just heard, came closer now that Goyle could defend himself. "Did you ever give her drugs?"

Feeling haughty again, Goyle looked Jerry up and down. Feeling he had bragging rights he smiled, "Hell yes, man. She's my bitch. She does what I tell her – and if she don't – " he said, making a back handed motion as if to indicate he hit her, "She don't get no candy."

412

The response was instant and predictable. Jerry planted his fist square onto Goyle's nose, sending him sprawling backwards. It took Goyle several seconds to realize what happened. Then he dragged himself to his feet, holding his bleeding nose delicately.

"You broke my nose, you bastard, you!" He raised the pitch of his voice, repeating himself, "You broke my nose! That's police brutality!" Pointing at Jerry he threatened, "You're going to pay for that. I'll have you up on charges! I'm going to sue."

Brian stepped between them, lest Jerry get into more trouble. "Better forget it Goyle. In fact, you may want to get out of the country. Tiffany is a minor and I'm willing to bet you're over the legal age. If anything has happened to her, you'll be an accessory to murder. I don't think you'd be wise to try to push her father around using the legal system." Brian turned to nudge Jerry back onto the path. Brian looked back over his shoulder, "As it stands, Goyle, we could take you in for statutory rape, contributing to the delinquency of a minor and possession of a controlled substance. Consider this your lucky day and get lost!"

Minutes later, Brian and Jerry looked around the Union Street Garage. The place had become a hangout for people you don't want your children to meet. Weeder remembered coming there as a kid, it was a different place back then. The thought irritated him and he made a mental note to see if the bolt could help correct the problem at a later date. The park area, topside, was full of winos, and addicts, but no sign of any Foonies. Selecting one of the sleeping drunks, Brian kicked his feet to wake him. "Hey, mac! Wake up." When the response was slow, Brian shook him gently several more times until the man moved. The wino was sluggish to react, but did eventually awake enough to answer questions.

"You here often?" Detective Jerry Lau asked.

413

Squinting into the morning sun to see Jerry's silhouette, he replied, "Sometimes – Yeah, guess so."

"You ever see a little black haired Asian-girl 'bout this high?"

The unshaven man worked his tongue as though it was glued to the back of his throat. "Guess so. I've seen several. What about her?"

"Did you see one last night? She'd probably be wearing a gold chain with a bolt and nut attached."

Thinking for several seconds, the man finally answered, "Well. . . Yes, I think I seen one, 'bout couple hours after midnight." He scratched under his left armpit, "Yeah, it musta been after two 'cause most all the yuppies left in their s'pensive cars when the bars closed. You'd think with all the money they got; they'd be able to give an ol' man like me a few bucks to buy a bottle or two."

Jerry's face showed the first signs of enlightenment. "Did you see her with anyone?"

"Yeah, I think she's with that Foonie, fella." He looked and pointed to the area where they had stood, "That Foonie – He's always tryin' to get the young kids to follow him home." The sober man looked back at Jerry, "He turns 'em into slaves, ya know." The drunk licked his thin lips, "Never see 'em again, 'round here, after that."

Jerry winced.

"Is the Foonie here now?" Brian asked, encouraging the wino to point him out.

"Shucks no, mister. He don't show up 'till 'bout midnight, when all the homeless kids are here in the park." Running his gnarled fingers through his long, graying hair, he added, "He gives 'em drugs and a place to sleep. After a while, he just takes 'em and makes 'em slaves."

414

Jerry and Brian looked at each other.

"Isn't much more we can do, except question some of her classmates. She might have mentioned something to one of them."

Brian nodded agreement. "Let's go."

"Ya might look for her over by the Mosconi, next month." The wino looked back at Jerry, squinting to see his face better, "They'll probably have her beggin' money over there. Seen lots of new ones there, back when I hung out there," the old man remarked.

"Uh, thanks, mister," Jerry said, patting him on the shoulder.

The alcoholic watched as the detectives started to walk away, "Glad to help out," he chortled. "Say! You fellas wouldn't happen to have a couple of bucks to help an old man like me, would ya?"

The lawmen stopped slowly. They exchanged glances. Jerry took out his wallet; he removed a five and walked back to hand it to the gray-haired, old man, before leaving.

* * *

The room felt cold — it was then she realized, her clothing was gone — only the smock remained. The feeling of abandonment began to take its toll, causing her to cry gently at first, then loudly for several minutes then back to a docile whimpering.

During the next few hours, as the drug wore off, her senses gradually became more aware of her surroundings, though all, except her sense of smell, were blunted by the lack of input. The room smelled of urine and feces. As her reasoning became more rational. She became terrified of her situation. She strained her ears for sounds, but could hear little except the occasional, distant din of a horn honking on the street. Just when she thought things couldn't get any worse, she needed a bathroom. She located the door and pounded on it. She screamed at the top of her lungs,

415

hoping someone – anyone would hear her. No one came. She tried again and again, for hours, begging for anyone to come let her out. Eventually, she selected a corner, the one with the worst smell and relieved herself.

In an attempt to keep her sanity in the pitch black room, she whistled, listening for the echo. She located a corner and paced the twelve steps to the other side; she called it the "X" axis. Returning to the same corner, she paced the eight steps of the "Y" axis. The sensory depravation, disoriented her. To fight it, she searched for textures in the darkened room just to assure herself she hadn't died. Hunger and a terrible thirst constantly reminded her of better times. She swore at the monsters who put her there, then cried because, they didn't return to visit. When she became so weary sleep overwhelmed her, she crawled to a corner and curled up in a fetal position.

Tiffany had no idea how long she had been asleep, when a noise awoke her. She listened. Someone was at the door. She felt her way to the door, but it hadn't opened. She begged and pounded on the smooth hard surface, to no effect. Just as she turned to go back to her corner, her foot spilled something. She felt cool liquid surround her bare feet; she knelt and touched the fluid. It was a bowl of water, but most of the liquid had spilled to the floor. She lifted the bowl to her lips, savoring the few remaining drops. She dropped to her knees, feeling around for more water or food; there was nothing more. Carefully, she probed around the base of the door, finding a small recess. It was blocked now, but they must have pushed the bowl through the opening, closing it afterwards.

Tiffany returned to her corner, where she sat and thought in the darkness. Her stomach growled continuously, distracting her. Her parched throat, was running out of saliva to wet it. She tried reciting nursery rhymes or singing to occupy her time. Both dried her throat more, forcing her to quit. The hard floor pained her, causing her to get up and stretch. After repeating a short pacing routine, she returned to her corner and slept. Several sleep periods later, the noise at the door returned. She was more careful this time, lest she spill the water. Crawling carefully to the door, she discovered a bowl of water and a few crackers. They were plain saltines, but were delicious. The bowl of water had an acrid smell, but felt wonderful as it wet her throat. She sipped it slowly until it was completely gone. The water – then food – ritual repeated itself during the next few sleep periods. Time began to distort; she was unsure how long she had been there. Repeatedly her mind resisted the thought she had always been there. Her major fear was quickly becoming that she was never going to get out.

* * *

The questioning of Tiffany's classmates proved unsuccessful. A couple friends knew she was seeing Goyle; one of the girls talked about Tiff's infatuation with the tattooed man. Apparently, his likeness to some of the personalities in the music culture attracted her.

As the hour drew close to midnight, Jerry and Brian stood a silent vigil a distance from Union Park, waiting for the Foonie to make his nightly appearance. By two in the morning, the detectives had checked in with the old man they had spoke with earlier. He too was puzzled that the Foonie had not come to the park. The detectives waited two more hours, taking turns attempting to sleep in the uncomfortable seats of their surveillance car. Finally they gave up, leaving the phone number where they could be reached if the old man saw the Foonie again. Brian promised him a ten-dollar reward for his cooperation.

Reporting in the morning, for their regular shift, the two blurry-eyed detectives discussed the situation over scalding-hot coffee. "Caliente!" Brian hissed, burning his lip a second time. He set the cup down carefully on the edge of Jerry Lau's desk, trying not spill it. "Did you call Liz?" he asked Jerry.

Swallowing quickly, then wishing he hadn't, Jerry drew air in across his own scalded tongue, "Dang that's hot!" He reached for the artificial creamer and poured enough into the black liquid to ruin the coffee-taste. "Yeah I did, – there's no word yet."

"How's she holding up?"

"It's draining," Jerry said with a hint of pain in his voice.

Weeder licked his burned lip several seconds. "Sometimes I think it's harder on the women than the men when this sort of thing happens."

"Liz waited by the phone all day, yesterday. I know this is really eating at her."

The same was true for Jerry, but Brian didn't comment. He knew it would be better to keep him busy trying to solve the problem and not dwell on grief issues. Brian thought to himself for a few seconds before suggesting, "Maybe what we need is a Foonie expert to talk with."

"Who'd that be?"

"I don't know, but there must be someone around that knows how to de-program people who have been taken."

Jerry thought for a moment, "It's a little out of my field, but maybe some of the folks in the juvenile division have had some contact with de-programmers." Testing his coffee again, he found it was still too hot to drink. "Don't you have an old girl friend over there?"

Memories flowed back into Brian's recall. "Whom are you talking about? Debbie?"

"Yeah, the little dark-haired one; the one with the big smile."

"She probably won't speak to me," Brian considered. "We didn't part on the best of terms."

418

"She's still a single woman, isn't she?"

"Heck, Jer, how would I know? I haven't talked to her for a couple of years. A lot could happen in that time."

"You could just turn on your charm and – "

"And what?" Brian interrupted. "I'm seeing someone now."

"You are?" Jerry looked surprised, "Why haven't you brought her over?"

With a tone of exasperation, Brian explained, "I haven't brought her over yet, because she's not down here yet!"

"Well," Jerry paused, "When are you planning to bring her over?"

"We'll do that. I just don't know when."

"Sounds to me like you're making this up, because you're afraid of talking to Debbie."

Brian nearly spewed his hot coffee across the table. "Look Jer, I'm not afraid of talking to Debbie, I just don't want to get involved with two women at the same time."

"Then you are afraid to speak with her?"

"No! I'm not," Brian protested. "Look – Let's go over there and see if Debbie knows anything that could help us."

"Thought you'd never ask," Jerry said, getting up from the table.

"I didn't ask. It was a suggestion," Weeder said looking at Lau for expression.

"Well then, I suggest we go," Lau said, abandoning the offending coffee until later when he would have a good excuse to throw it out.

The detectives found their way past the entrance desk of the juvenile division. After several quick inquiries, they located Officer Debora Holtz's desk. She was busy filling out forms and didn't look up until Jerry elbowed Brian in the ribs, urging him to speak. "Uh – hi Debbie," he bid.

The voice caught her by surprise. It is amazing how years can pass and the tones of someone you knew well – can suddenly catch your attention – you know who it is immediately. Debbie looked up, peering over her reading glasses. "Brian?"

"Uh yeah," he smiled quickly, returning his face to a blank look. He too, had missed her. Quickly he recalled her reluctance to continue the relationship without a better commitment from him. A sense of guilt poked at him as he struggled to begin the dialogue, "We uh – "

Debbie put down her pen and removed her glasses. "How are you?" The pitch of her voice indicated a genuine interest in the conversation.

Brian relaxed a bit, but still remained tense. "I'm okay. And you?"

"I'm fine. You married?" she asked smoothly.

Somehow he knew she'd ask, "No – How 'bout you?"

She fingered the picture on her desk, turning it around so the detectives could see. "This is Jimmie, my little boy." She looked at Brian specifically as if to say, "If you had been more agreeable, this could be your son." With a warm, motherly smile, she boasted, "He's my little love."

Brian leaned over the desk and examined the picture closely. Noting it was a cute little toddler, with eyes and hair the same color as Debbie's, he offered, "Looks just like his mother."

"Yes he does," she sighed.

Looking around her work area for other pictures, Brian asked the obvious, "Where's the picture of his father?"

Debbie set the picture back on her desk, her tone changed, "Oh – well – we aren't together anymore." She looked back at Brian.

"Sorry to hear that," Brian said, unsure if he really meant it. He looked away to break eye contact.

"Why don't you come over some time for dinner, and I'll introduce you to Jimmie. I'm sure you'd like him."

"Well I'm — " Brian broke off. He was about to say he was seeing Klazzi, but felt he'd likely get better cooperation, if she didn't feel rejection by his comment. He continued by changing the subject, "Er — we're here to ask you a business question."

"Oh?" She searched Detective Lau's facial expression, for the first time.

"Yes," Brian continued, "do you know anyone who has dealt with Foonies?"

Debbie sat quietly, looking back and forth at the men across the desk from her. "Yeah, I know a couple," she replied, storing her personal feelings for a better time. "What is it you want to know?"

Brian's throat felt dry. While he felt better discussing business with Debbie, he still felt uncomfortable in her presence. Brian tried not to alienate her saying, "Jerry and I are looking for their compound. You know, the place where they usually program their new captives."

Debbie's mood turned serious, her voice scolding, "Who's been taken?"

Moving his glance to Jerry, Brian tried to avoid a direct answer, "Uh — we aren't at liberty to say, until we know for sure." He looked back at Debbie, "We're still in the process of investigation."

"Look. If this involves a juvenile — "

"I know. I know," Brian agreed, raising his hands in protest. "When we are sure, we'll talk, and you'll be the first to know."

Debbie cast a dubious glance at the two detectives. Weighing the situation for several seconds, she opened her desk and removed a small book at the back of the drawer. She thumbed through the pages, stopping suddenly and pressing the book flat, to see it better. She quickly scribbled a name and phone number on a sticky tag. Offering the information to Brian, she held fast to the edge of the note as she gave warning, "Now if you discover a juvenile is involved in this, I want you to contact me first." She paused to ensure eye contact, first with Brian, then with Jerry. Looking back at Brian, she emphasized, "Contact me before you do anything!" She gave Brian a final stern look, "Do you understand?"

Brian nodded agreement, though he knew he wouldn't hesitate to remove Tiffany, once he found her.

* * *

The number Debbie gave to Brian led to the group leader of a de-programming group. The group consisted of parents who had all suffered the loss of their children to the Foonies. In the past, their recovery rate had been between forty and seventy percent, depending on circumstances. The usual process involved kidnapping the child by the parents, and sending him or her to a remote location in Utah or Idaho where a team of experts worked with the parents to reverse the "brain-washing" experience.

The recovery group hadn't worked a recovery for several months, and was a bit uncertain their information was current. The Foonies, moved their compound frequently to avoid problems with orphaned parents and with law enforcement. They gave Brian and Jerry the last known address.

Driving down a less-than-prosperous street in the city, Brian searched for building numbers. Soon he began to recognize descriptions of the area given him by the recovery organization. "There it is," Brian pointed. "They said it would be a boarded up building – probably that one, over there."

Jerry parked the unmarked car, trying to avoid attention. The two detectives, dressed in baseball caps, flannel shirts, and jeans, left the car quickly and silently. They had rehearsed the plan several times with the help of an expert in the recovery organization. Wearing hidden two-way radios, Brian took one side of the building, while Jerry went down the other side.

In addition to their weapons, and radios, crowbars and flashlights, each carried a battery-powered, electric drill and a handful of patio-deck screws. Brian stopped at the entrance to fasten the door shut using three or four long screws; Jerry climbed the flight of stairs and repeated the process on the rear door. Finished with the task, Jerry reported by radio, "Got mine, Brian. I'll be in place in about ten seconds."

"Ten-four," Brian replied, "I'm in place now."

"On my mark, Brian. Five. . . four. . . three. . . two. . . one. . . hit it!"

Both doors, on opposite sides of the building were yanked open and entered. The place was pitch-black inside. Their flashlights showed only trash strewn around the entry rooms.

"Got anything Jerry?"

"Looks empty, Brian."

"Check out your rooms and I'll do the same. Meet me back in the center, upstairs."

"Ten-four."

They searched in vain; the entire place was empty. The detectives met as promised upstairs. Both looked saddened by the turn of events. It seemed to Brian the bolt was working against him, but he wasn't ready to give up yet.

"Think I found the office up front, Jer."

Lau's face showed a look of hope as he said, "Let's go check it out."

After several minutes of searching, the best they could find was half a sack of walnuts and a discarded bottle of foul smelling wine. Jerry shined the light around the room, looking for a light switch. He found it, but flipping it accomplished nothing. Brian looked overhead. Every light bulb and several fixtures were gone. He put on his plastic gloves and wiped a finger on the old wooden desk left behind. A very thin trail of dust covered it.

"Think they must have gone about a week or more. What do ya think, Jer?"

"Maybe longer," he agreed. "Let's go find some neighbors."

"Good idea. Get your tools and I'll meet you back at the car."

Minutes later, tools stowed, they set out to find neighbors. Weeder knocked on the door of an older home that showed signs of aging and slipping maintenance. He waited a minute or so, and knocked again, when the first attempt was ignored. Finally an elderly lady came to the door, followed by a man about the same age, using a walker to stabilize his movement.

Brian and Jerry displayed their badges, which seemed out of place on their plaid shirts. "Excuse me ma'am, we're with the San Francisco Police department and we'd like to ask you a few questions, if we might."

Her voice had a waver, but her spirit seemed strong. "Of course, come right in." She stood to one side allowing the officers to enter. She looked out front, in both directions, then closed the door behind them. She circled the policemen and stopped in front of Brian. Looking up she asked, "What can we do for you?"

"Well ma'am, this is officer Lau and I'm officer Weeder. We were interested in knowing where we might find the neighbors over on this side of you?" Brian pointed toward the old Foonie compound.

"Oh, they left, 'bout a week ago."

"Do you have any idea where we might find them?"

She adjusted her eye glasses to better see Brian as she spoke, "No, we got up one morning and it was as if they just vanished." She looked at Jerry, "Strange group, you know. They weren't very friendly – kinda kept to themselves. They'd come and go at all hours of the night." She pointed to the window on that side of the house. "We kept our blinds closed all the time, because they'd look in here at night. Liked to scared the heck out me several times. They'd come and go all hours of the night, you know."

"Did they ever contact you or say anything?"

"Well, right after they moved in, a couple of kids came to the front door. They wanted to do work on our house, for pay." She pointed to the old man, "Homer don't get around as well as he use to. . . and we need some things fixed. But I took one look at them and decided they gave me the creeps. I told 'em we didn't need any work done. But they'd still knock on the door every week or so, wantin' me to reconsider."

"Was it always the same individuals you saw?"

"Hard to tell, they kinda dressed alike, black mostly, but they had all kinds of teenage kids with them at different times. Some had purple marks on their arms." She looked back at Brian, "I didn't like that neither, 'cause I was afraid they'd steal from us to support their habit. We had to keep everythin' locked up tight. You know what I mean?"

"Yes ma'am. Thank you for your help." Brian gestured with a waving motion, "Do you know any of your other neighbors?"

The lady looked thoughtful for a moment, "Well, we still know a couple. Most have died, or sold out through the years. The neighborhood isn't the way it used to be, you know." She walked to the window to point. "There's the Blackman's over there, nice couple. Kids are all raised, and then two houses over that way — there's the Washington's. They're black you know, but they're nice folks, and we also know the young couple next to the Washington's, but I can't remember their name just now. I have problems remembering from time to time."

Brian handed her a business card. "Thank you for your assistance. If you think of anything else we should know, please give our office a call."

The lawmen checked the other neighbors. The story was much the same. The Foonies came and went at all hours. They frequently had other young kids with them. The cult members bugged them about doing work for cash. The kids that did work, weren't particularly good workers, but they expected pay anyway. Then without notice, they simply disappeared.

The signs of frustration and lack of sleep were showing badly on Jerry. He was quiet most of the time, despondent, and when he wasn't quiet, he was argumentative. The searching had also gotten to Brian, but he knew something Jerry didn't and decided it might help Jerry feel a little better if he knew.

"Jer, we've been good friends for a long time now, haven't we?"

"Yeah, I guess." Jerry sat looking out the passenger window, watching the houses, cars, street lamps and people pass by their moving vehicle.

"Have you ever known me to say anything or act weird?"

"Heaven's yes — Brian." He said, looking at the driver, "You're the weirdest guy I know."

"No — Seriously, Jer. Have I ever seemed to go off the deep end on any kind of strange notion?"

Jerry thought for a moment, "No. You've always seemed pretty straight forward and rational. . . almost to the point of being a pain-in-the-butt."

"Thank you. . . I think?" Brian scowled. "Well Jerry I've got an ace up my sleeve." He paused to switch lanes and get around a slow driver ahead of them. "You know that necklace, I gave Tiff?"

"Yeah."

"Well, it's not really a necklace."

"I knew that."

Brian felt a trace of relief, "You did? Oh great! But how did you know?"

"Any fool could see it was a piece of hardware, not jewelry."

"No! It's not hardware," Brian protested, "Well, yes it is. But it isn't." His explanation was not getting very far. "Let's try it this way. . . Do you believe in angels?"

"Not in a lot of years," Jerry hesitated. "Just what is it you are trying to say?"

Weeder stopped for a red light. "Well Jer, this thing I gave Tiff is more like an amulet or charm than anything I have ever seen. It's like some guardian of justice is guiding it. It's like magic. Every time someone bad touches it, justice does to them, an equal amount of harm."

"You're nuts Brian."

"No. Seriously Jer," Brian protested.

"Brian, this thing with Tiff has pushed you over the edge."

"Jer, I'm giving it to you straight. You've seen my success ratio lately haven't you?"

"Well – yes," Jerry admitted, pausing, mentally to review the long list of successfully solved crimes attached to Brian's name. "But you seem to be striking out on this one."

427

"I know it looks bad Jer, but the bolt is working for us. I don't have the foggiest idea how or what it's going to do, but we are going to get Tiff back, and anybody who tries to harm her will receive a suitable punishment."

Lau looked at him and shook his head, "You're nuts Brian."

The light turned green and Brian continued through the intersection. Brian stopped trying to convince Jerry, choosing to drive instead. Every few minutes, Jerry would repeat himself, "You're nuts Brian." If the situation hadn't been so serious, it would have been laughable.

Two days passed without progress. Under a doctor's care, Jerry and his wife, Liz managed to get a bit more sleep, but the waking hours were still horrible. They had played all the mind games of "What if" until they were nearly delirious.

* * *

At the Foonie compound, the Master, Far-Wind, finished counting the week's money. All of the nickels and dimes, quarters and dollars brought in by begging or by selling drugs was counted and was ready for his conversion to diamonds for easy storage. It had been a profitable week for him, including acquisition of a new sister. He contemplated the pleasure it had brought him to see her naked body, as she was prepared for programming. It warmed him to think he would have complete control over her, when the process was complete. In another two weeks, she would think of him a god, obeying his every whim. Perhaps he would keep her or perhaps he would sell her for a very large sum of money after taking his pleasure with her. He'd think about it. His eye settled on the cardboard box, sitting on the chair, with her personal effects. He strolled to the chair and peered inside. Removing the handkerchief, he untied the knot. A smile crossed his face as he saw the money. Carefully, he set it on the corner of the table for the next collection. Looking back into the box, he sorted through the lipstick, eye-shadow, feminine hygiene products, throwing them into the metal trash can already half full of papers.

Digging deeper into the box, he saw the gold necklace. He lifted it by the chain, admiring the craftsmanship. It would fetch a nice price from a jewelry dealer he knew, especially if the object was actually gold. He bounced the chain on his finger, trying to determine the gold content. In an attempt to further satisfy his curiosity, he reached out to turn the bolt, to see if it might unscrew. At the last moment, he saw the package of heroin given the female when she arrived, causing him to change his mind, about touching the bolt. Still holding the necklace in his left hand, and not wanting to misplace the valuable drug, he took the Mexican Brown in his other hand, intending to return it to the small wooden box on the table next to the wall. As he stepped toward the wooden box, he shifted the packet into the hand holding the necklace. His attention toggled back to the content of gold in the half-inch bolt. Greed drove him to, once again, consider separating the bolt and chain, to better estimate their value.

Alone in the quiet room, Far-Wind was totally unprepared for the horrendous, blue arc that leaped from the bolt to his fingers, charring them black – instantly. The recoil was so strong and so powerful that he threw the bolt and heroin in his hand across the room. Blasted in the opposite direction, Far-Wind bounced off the wall, hitting his head on the corner of the table. He shook violently on the floor, for a minute or two, rolling in agony. When he finally pulled himself to his feet, his charred fingers were blackened and throbbed as though they'd been held in a fire for nearly a minute. Fresh blood trickled down his face from a gash dealt him by the glancing blow with the table edge.

Far-Wind was totally unsure what exactly had happened and totally unaware the heroin packet had fallen into his unzippered, personal travel bag. He staggered around the room dazed for minutes. Slowly, he recalled the events prior to the electrical shock. It took him several minutes to locate the necklace in the metal trash can, on top of discarded papers. The bolt had turned moldy-green, and its corroded appearance made it totally undesirable to touch. At this point, Far-Wind determined it was a thing of the devil (as if he wasn't) and wanted nothing more to do with it. He'd leave it right where it fell.

The Master gathered a wad of bills from the cash he had counted, stuffing them into his personal travel bag. He'd pay cash for medical treatment, so there would be no trace. He painfully put on his black trench coat and left with his travel bag for treatment at a nearby emergency room. In his haste to leave, he failed to close the doors to the compound behind him.

A suitable time after the Master left, the bolt changed to a cherry red color, catching the papers in the bottom of the metal trash can on fire. The room filled with smoke before passing through the open doors of the compound, until it made its way to the kitchen. An open window provided the only place for the smoke to exit. The fire continued to burn, until a neighbor spotted it and called the fire department.

Tiffany was fortunate. Locked in her room, the Foonies had sealed the door to prevent light from entering, lest it ruin their programming techniques. Her only source of fresh air came through a pipe into the dark attic. She smelled no smoke.

The sirens awoke her. Tiffany stood up. She heard several more sirens as the emergency vehicles arrived. Her heightened awareness allowed her to hear footsteps within the compound, as the firemen raced to the source of the smoke. She began to pound on the door and scream for help. Several minutes passed while the noises on the other side of the door became the loudest she had heard for days. She kicked and pounded on the door, begging to be released. Just when she thought no one could hear her and it had all been an illusion, the door unlatched and opened. The smoke-filtered light was blinding, but she loved it. She couldn't see, it was so intense, but she was no longer alone.

Tiffany ran toward the fireman. He sprang back, thinking she was a crazed lunatic. She grabbed his arm and hung on for dear life. Her tears flowed freely and when her sobbing slowed, she began a dialogue.

Brian was at the Lau residence when Jerry got the call informing him his daughter had been found. The war whoop was jubilant. The scene was unbelievable as the adults danced and screamed their relief. Seconds later, Brian and Jerry were on their way to the compound with lights and siren going.

Two fire trucks and five or six patrol cars cluttered the area when Brian and Jerry arrived. They left the lights flashing and abandoned the car in the street. A huddle of firemen, policemen, Emergency Trauma personnel and civilians drew Weeder and Lau as they raced toward the building. They flashed their badges to cross beyond the uniformed officers assigned to keep spectators out of the area.

"Who's the incident commander?" Brian asked the cluster of people. A woman wearing fire fighting equipment answered, "I'm Hartman, are you Detective Lau?"

Brian pushed Jerry forward.

"I'm Detective Lau. Are you the one that called?" Before she could answer, Lau looked around for Tiffany. "Where is she? Where's my daughter?"

Hartman pointed to the back of an ambulance where Tiffany sat, wrapped in a blanket. "She's over there. Technicians say she'll be fine."

Jerry's heart leaped. He rushed to the ambulance, stumbling over the fire hoses cluttering the sidewalk. Brian followed.

Tiffany sprang from the back of the ambulance to her father's arms, while tears of joy washed her dirty face. "Daddy!" she screamed.

Father, Jerry Lau, found himself speechless as he held his teenage daughter tight, comforting her.

Brian came up and hugged both father and daughter briefly, before returning to the incident commander.

Detective Weeder caught the commander's attention, "Uh, Hartman, I need to talk for a minute." He motioned for her to follow him to a place away from the circle of professionals.

Brian showed her his badge, and introduced himself.

"What can I do for you Weeder?" she asked, while listening to the traffic on her busy radio.

"Did you find other people in the building?"

"Yeah, two men and three women, all in their early twenties. They claimed to be staff to the guy running the place."

"Did you find their leader?"

"Nope. We think he set the fire and left in a hurry."

"Why would he do that?" Weeder asked.

The commander shrugged, "Donno' maybe he did it to cover up his sins."

"I'd like to go in and see for myself."

"Better wait, we still have people checking the place out."

"Foonies don't build bombs," Brian countered.

"I know that and you know that, but it's department policy."

Brian backed down. She was right. Changing the subject he asked, "Where are the five people removed from the building?"

She nodded toward the two patrol cars, on the other side of the fire truck. "Thanks," Brian said, as he stepped over the hoses and rounded the corner of the noisy fire truck, its big diesel engines clattering away constantly. Brian opened the door of the first police car. Three women inside. He closed the door and went to the second car. Looking inside, the two men looked dazed. "Subee?" he asked. There was no response. "Where is Subee?" Still no response. Brian thought for a moment. Perhaps he had asked the question incorrectly. "Is your brother Subee safe?"

"We do not know," one of them answered.

"Did he leave with the Master?"

"We do not know," the same one answered.

Weeder left the car to return to the circle of professionals. He came up behind Hartman again, who had rejoined the group. "Who found the people inside?"

Hartman looked past Weeder, "He's uh – right there – " she said, pointing to a fireman rolling up a hose.

Brian hurried over to speak with the fireman. "I'm Detective Weeder," he announced to the fireman. "Are you the one who found the people inside?"

The fireman set his hose on the ground between his black rubber boots. Standing upright, he arched his back to reduce the pain of bending over for the last few minutes. "Yeah, that's me."

"Did you see anyone else except for the people in the patrol cars over there?"

"Yeah, I found the little girl in the locked room," he said, pointing toward Tiffany and her father.

"Anyone else?"

"Naw!"

"No one in black?"

Surprised by Weeder's question, the firemen replied, "Except for the little girl, they're all dressed in black, officer."

433

Brian realized the fireman was correct. "Yeah, I guess you're right. Thanks!"

"Anytime." The fireman returned to his job of rolling up hose.

The ambulance was preparing to take Tiffany to the hospital for medical examination. Jerry intended to ride along with her. Brian caught the door before the technician could close it.

"Jer?"

"I'm going in with Tiff."

"I understand."

"Does Tiff know where the guys are, who run the compound?"

Jerry shook his head no. "She was locked inside a dark room for days, hasn't seen anyone 'till now."

"I was afraid of that," Weeder said, making a face. He looked at Lau, "Where's your radio?"

Jerry reached for his belt where he normally kept his radio, "Left it in the car, I think."

Brian handed Jerry the hand-held, two-way radio from his own belt. "See if you can get a description from Tiff, and we can put out an A.P.B. for them."

Lau nodded, as he took the radio.

Brian saw Tiffany looking his way. He gave her a wink. She smiled in return. Convinced he wasn't needed in the ambulance, he returned to his own vehicle.

Weeder slid behind the wheel of his unmarked vehicle and stowed the flashing light. He proceeded to cruise the neighborhood, watching for anyone dressed totally in black. Evening was fast approaching and it would be difficult to see them in another few minutes.

When he could find nothing in the immediate neighborhood, Brian began to check the bus and train stations. He asked the ticket agents to phone the police, if anyone, dressed totally in black, approached them to buy a ticket. His next stop was the airport. The evening commute had begun, making traffic a bear. Brian put his emergency light back on the roof and turned it on. He drove down the shoulder of the stalled freeway to hasten his trip to the airport. By the time he arrived to talk with airport security, Jerry had gotten physical descriptions from Tiffany.

* * *

Master Far-Wind, finished with his trip to the emergency room, returned to his compound. He found it overrun with police and firemen. He desperately wanted to reach his cache of diamonds and available cash, but that would be impossible. Assuming he was a wanted man, he chose to find the nearest pawn shop and cash in some personal jewelry for money to buy a plane ticket out of the country.

"How much will you give me for these?" Far-Wind asked the agent in the pawn shop.

The man took the diamond-studded ring and emerald bracelet. He peered through the jeweler's loupe at the stones, checking for flaws and damage. While he was checking the silver mountings for signs of origin, the television interrupted its programming to show a composite picture of Far-Wind and Subee. It went on to ask the public for cooperation in capturing these two fugitives.

Far-Wind suddenly became very nervous. He looked at the agent checking his jewelry, hoping he hadn't noticed the announcement. The agent showed no sign that he had.

After taking his time to check all of the stones and mountings and quality of silver, the agent went into the back room and returned with a pouch containing money.

The cult leader smiled lightly, assuming he would be paid handsomely for his fine regalia.

The agent began counting out the twenties. "The quality is quite good, my friend," the man smiled as he looked up briefly. "I'd estimate them to be worth several thousand dollars, wholesale."

"I'm pleased you like them. It pains me to part with them."

"I'm sure it does." The agent dropped ten twenties on the counter, before folding his pouch and stuffing in his rear pocket.

"What's this?" Far-Wind asked, with a startled expression.

"This — my friend is what I am willing to pay."

"That's robbery!"

"I'm sure it is. . . " he smiled.

"Bring me back my stones. I'll take my business elsewhere."

"Perhaps I should call the police for you, if you think I'm cheating you."

Far-Wind seethed, but was powerless to do anything. He gathered up the bills, "Why pay me anything?"

"I considered that, but it might be best for you to go purchase a bus ticket, and for neither of us, to ever see the other again." The agent gave him an icy stare.

Stifling his rage, the fleeced man realized the agent was a much stouter man and was undoubtedly armed. He'd be wise not to press his luck. Instead, he left with the two-hundred dollars.

Making his way to the nearest thrift store, Far-Wind purchased a change of used clothing; nothing was black. In front of the store, he intercepted one of his cult members preparing to return to the compound. Taking the five dollars he had collected that day, the Master dismissed him.

From his days before starting the cult, Far-Wind remembered a small shop several blocks away, where could buy stolen credit cards. He'd need a credit card to buy a plane ticket, because the Federal Government watches closely for anyone paying cash for air fares. He certainly did not want to be detained. The balance of his two-hundred dollars was spent on a newly stolen credit card and forged passport under the name of Julian Hayes.

The coins clanked as alias Julian Hayes dropped the quarters and dimes into the phone, ordering a ticket out of the country. The closest one was to Mexico, but he wanted to put more distance between himself and the U. S. border. He scheduled a flight to Istanbul four hours later in the evening. It took him several more hours to find a buyer for his ruby earrings, but they helped him purchase a shuttle ride to the airport.

Detective Brian Weeder sat at the monitoring station in airport security, watching people standing in the check-in lines for the various airlines. During the last six hours, he had not seen any sign of anyone matching the description of the fugitives.

The phone rang. The security officer sitting beside Weeder picked it up.

"Officer Smith?" he answered. "Yeah, he's here. Hold on." Handing the handset to Brian, the security officer remarked, "It's for you Detective Weeder."

"Thanks." Brian adjusted the phone, pulling a bit of extra cord, so he could continue watching the monitors as he talked.

"This is Weeder."

"Brian, this is Jer."

"Oh, hi, Jer. How's the family?"

"We're all just happy as if it were Christmas. Even Herm is getting along just fine with Tiff."

"Glad to hear it Jer. What's up?"

"We found Subee."

"Did huh?"

"Yeah, but he can't tell us where to find his boss."

"Why not?"

"Well – he's quite dead. Been that way, for a couple of days."

"Dead?"

"Yeah."

"How'd he die?"

"Looks like he must have been caught giving away drugs in someone's territory. Anyway, he was found over in Marin county, tied to a tree."

"Tied to tree?"

"Yeah, so he couldn't fall over while they beat him to a pulp, I suppose."

Brian whistled, "Well, he must have deserved it."

"According to the Sheriff, his mouth was stuffed with the same kinds of dope-packages found in his pockets."

"He'd have gotten a lot better treatment if he'd come to us."

"Yeah he would have. Say, how's it going?"

Detective Weeder, pushed back in his chair. He repositioned his feet again, trying to find a more comfortable way to sit. "Tell you what Jer. It's been a whole lot of nothing out here. I think he hitched a ride out of town."

"How much longer you going to be there?"

Brian looked at his watch, "I was thinking I'd leave in about a half hour. I think the guys here can do this job better than I can."

"Okay buddy, why don't you drop by and visit for a few minutes before you go home."

"I'll do that Jer. I could use a little hug from Tiff, if she's up to it."

"See ya."

"Soon. . . bye." Brian said, handing the phone back to Officer Smith. The monitor changed to the next airline. A man in a black trench coat walked up to the end of the line, with no sign of luggage.

Brian hit the stop button to freeze the scan. "This might be our guy, Smith. Have someone detain him and let's go."

Weeder threw open the door to the security room. He slid into the passenger seat of the electric cart. Officer Smith took the drivers seat. Brian flipped the switch for the rotating beacon and away they went. Speeding along at about fifteen miles per hour, Officer Smith beeped at every intersection and at all the slow pedestrians who either didn't see him or didn't respond fast enough to hurry out of the way. The cart stopped about a hundred feet away from the airline counter, just around the corner where the suspect couldn't see it. Both officers hurried toward the line before the suspect could escape.

A tall, thinly built man hurrying in the opposite direction collided in a glancing blow with Brian. His passport and credit card went flying. Barely missing a step, Brian scooped them up and turned to toss them back to Julian Hayes, allowing him to make his flight to Istanbul on time.

Obviously, the man standing in line wearing the dark trench coat turned out to be someone else. He was questioned and allowed to continue his wait in line.

* * *

Two days later, the U. S. State Department was notified by the authorities in Turkey, that an American citizen by the name of Julian Hayes, from San Francisco, had been arrested trying to enter the country with a small packet of brown heroin in his possession. They further advised, this individual was now serving a life sentence in their prison, with no possibility of parole.

They could find no legitimate record of any person by said name or description that matched the person in question. Even, the returned passport proved to be a forgery. Eventually, the State

Department assumed, the person probably was not an American citizen, and they left his fate to the Turkish officials.

* * *

Firemen, investigating the cause of the fire in the Foonie compound, discovered a gold necklace of, no metal value, in the trash can where the fire had started. A fireman carried it back with him to the station, as a souvenir of the Foonie fire.

* * *

Justice is a Half-Inch Bolt

www.ingramcontent.com/pod-product-compliance
Lightning Source LLC
Chambersburg PA
CBHW070613260626
47161CB00007B/2421